RAMBLING STAR RANCH

DIANE J. REED

Bandits Ranch Books

Cover design by Najla Qamber at Najla Qamber Designs, www. najlaqamberdesigns.com

"**G**ood morning, it's Tempest time!" announced Tempest Wright into her radio microphone. "I'm your last-chance psychotherapist for troubles of the heart. Have you been bouncing from buddies to bartenders for advice, feeling tangled into hopeless knots? Tired of getting your butt kicked by so-called love? Well this is your lucky day, because the buck stops here. Yes radio listeners, I've been through it all, and I tell it like it is so your friends don't have to! That's why they call me The Terminator. So let's hear from our first caller this morning—Darnelle from Dry Creek, you're on the air."

Tempest looped a strand of toffee-brown hair behind her ear and fiddled with the dials of the console on her office desk that streamed her show to the local radio station. Despite her brassy persona, her heart began to skitter. This was the part where she had to nail the perfect wisdom for her listeners who depended on her for daily guidance. Sure, the ranchers and cowboys who phoned in from the mountain town of Bandits Hollow, Colorado often wanted as much advice for finding their lost cattle as they did for solving their latest love triangles. But deep inside, Tempest adored the rural residents who looked at life a lot like she did—in black and white terms, with no time for lollygagging or lame excuses. For them, problems were best diced up into clear solutions, which just happened to be Tempest Wright's specialty.

"Oh my gosh, hello!" squealed Darnelle on the other end of the line. "Thank you so much for taking my call! I've been a *huge* fan of yours ever since you started this radio show six months ago. You're like a celebrity in Bandits Hollow—I can't wait for your help!"

"Why, thank you," Tempest replied, flattered. "What can I assist you with today, Darnelle?"

Tempest heard a light sob—along with a woeful sniffle that was common during her broadcasts. She stole a glance at her young intern Ivy, who was sitting on a couch on the other side of their therapy office that stood downtown at the corner of Main Street and Colt Avenue. Ivy had a worried look on her face.

They both had a hunch this call might be a doozy.

"Well, first of all, I read your new book, *Shock Value: How to Stop Whining and Get on With Your Life*," Darnelle confessed. "I felt as if it were written just for me! I was married to a philandering jerk like you. Except he didn't die in another woman's bed. But boy, I sure wish he had!"

A clench tightened Tempest's stomach, and she darted her eyes from Ivy's empathetic stare. It had only been a year since her shark-lawyer husband had passed away of a heart attack in the arms of another woman, and she was still kicking herself for staying in their dried-up marriage way too long. But between her hectic job at a mental health center in Denver and raising her eight-year-old son virtually by herself because of her husband's workaholic ways, she'd been too exhausted to pull out a magnifying glass and examine his red flags.

Oh, what a price she'd paid! Not only had she met half a dozen pretty women at his funeral who weren't exactly "cousins", she'd also discovered that he'd gutted their bank account and canceled insurance policies to keep up his romantic liaisons. In one fell swoop, she'd lost her husband, her savings, and her house in a swanky suburb, since there was no way she could maintain the mortgage on her county therapist's salary. Her life had hit rock bottom, so when the job came up at the mental health office in Bandits Hollow, she leaped at the chance for a new start in a small town that offered plenty of outdoor opportunities for her growing boy. But more than anything, Tempest vowed to use her career to empower others, so that no one else's heart or funds would ever get fleeced again.

"You're my hero, you know!" Darnelle continued to gush. "I can't imagine what it was like to get a call from that tramp after your husband kicked the bucket in her bed. The way you picked yourself up and self-published that bestselling book is amazing! But my problem is I've tried to throw my lousy ex out of my house a hundred times. He just won't leave!"

Ivy's eyes grew wide with concern. As if on cue, she jumped from the couch and grabbed the local phone book from a shelf, then plopped it onto Tempest's desk. She'd heard

Tempest deal with stalker issues on the radio before, and she understood how dangerous these situations could be.

Tempest gave her a grateful nod and flipped the pages to the number of the Bandits Hollow police. "Can you clarify what you mean by *won't leave?*" she asked Darnelle pointedly. "If you feel in danger, remember you can always call the police station or 911."

"Well, it's not that I feel in danger, exactly," Darnelle admitted.

"Then what *do* you feel?" Tempest probed further. "There's never any judgement here on my show, so you're free to express your truth. But I warn you, Darnelle, if you take that loser back after he boldly cheated on you, I *will* look up your address and smack you. You'll need the restraining order for *me*, not your ex. They don't call me The Terminator for nothing. Ending dysfunctional situations is what I do."

Darnelle erupted into a chuckle. Tempest's brash radio humor had won her legions of fans in Bandits Hollow, and served to lighten the mood so her callers could relax enough to truly face their issues. But a part of Tempest really meant it— if she could spare even one woman from wasting the number of years she'd lost over a lying, two-timing, black hole of a spouse, it was worth it.

"What I feel is…well, I guess I feel torn," Darnelle said. "Don't worry, I'm good with a shotgun. And I have no problem racking it when Larry comes over to my porch, all moondoggie in the middle of the night, begging me to give him another chance. But the hard part is that his new girlfriend does, too."

"Does what?" Tempest asked.

"Begs me to take her in!"

"You mean, Larry's new girlfriend wants a…threesome?"

"No!" spouted Darnelle. Another light sob trembled through the line. "Sh-She wants me to hurry up and shoot Larry so she can get rid of his ass! She's hoping I'll let her stay at my house till Larry's gone."

Ivy's eyes stretched even larger this time as her mouth flung open. Tempest bit her lip, attempting to maintain her composure.

"So, the new girlfriend wants you to…*murder*…Larry?"

"Hell no—just fill his butt with enough buckshot to drive him far away." Darnelle issued a hefty sigh. "She claims she's got this *mad* crush on me."

The moment Darnelle uttered those words, Ivy's lashes fluttered as tears summoned in her eyes. At only 21, she was an incurable romantic, and the very thought of anyone finding true love sent her into a spiral of sentimentality. With her frizzy dark hair, heavily-rimmed glasses, and oversized cardigan in a rosy hue, Ivy was the valentine poster girl of every nerd's dreams. Tempest had chastised her about not getting too emotionally wrought by the broken heartstrings of others, but it was no use. Ivy wanted to wrap her arms around the whole world to make everyone feel better, and "clinical detachment" wasn't in her vocabulary. She scurried over to the extra chair next to the desk and clasped Tempest's arm, sinking her fingers into her skin a little too deep.

"Ouch," Tempest whispered, yanking her arm away.

"Don't ruin the possibility of a love match!" Ivy said in the lowest tone she could muster, given her excitement. "Maybe Darnelle doesn't know it yet, but she needs to come out."

Tempest raised a brow, considering the possibility.

"Darnelle," Tempest qualified carefully, "since you never mentioned aiming the shotgun at the girlfriend, and you sounded like you were crying earlier in this broadcast, are you torn because there's a side of you that would like to... entertain...the girlfriend's proposition? Not the shooting of your ex part. But taking her in and getting to know her better?"

"Good Lord, no—old cowgirls like me ain't gay!" Darnelle protested.

"And what rule book did you read that in?" Tempest said. "Last time I checked, cattle cutting and barrel racing don't require certain relationship approaches."

"Well, it's just that it doesn't conform to my notions of western tradition."

"Oh honey," Tempest huffed, "nobody's followed tradition better than me, sticking around in a stale marriage until the man became a cold corpse in someone's else's arms. If you want to lead an empowered life, then you need to be brutally honest with yourself. Is this a situation you want to try out?"

"I'm not sure—I don't think I'm wired that way," Darnelle said in a soft voice. "It's just that I've been so lonely since I kicked out Larry. Yet at the same time, I feel like I deserve a break from men. What I'd really like is....a good friend."

Tempest reached over to Ivy's hand and gave it a squeeze.

"Complex emotions aren't a crime," Tempest said kindly. "And getting over a break up is no picnic, so give yourself some space. In the meantime, can you mention something to Larry's girlfriend—what's her name?"

"Jane," Darnelle replied.

"Can you please tell Jane the truth? That you're not ready for a new relationship—with a man *or* a woman—and you're not even sure you play on her side of the fence. But you'd appreciate her friendship?"

"How do I know if she'd go for that?"

"You don't," Tempest said flatly. "She could turn on her heels and run the other way. That's the thing about life—sometimes you have to just buck up and go forward with the best choice you've got. However, entertaining Larry and Jane on your porch with a shotgun night after night isn't going to cut it. Aren't you getting tired of losing so much sleep?"

"I am!" Darnelle burst. "I think that's why I've been so teary lately—the whole thing has me exhausted."

"Of course it does! So either shoo both of those people off your porch for good, or let Jane know she can try out a neutral friendship with you on a trial basis. But don't you dare let her move in. It's time for *you* to call the shots in your life—gun or no gun. Not Jane, no matter how pushy she is."

"Um…okay," Darnelle agreed, sounding relieved that she now had a plan. "Oh my gosh, you got to the heart of my problems right away and pointed me to solutions in a jiffy. You're a wonder, Tempest!"

"We'll see about that," Tempest said. "Give me a call back at the end of the month and tell me how things are going. Meanwhile, you're going to be healthy and socialize in lots of other ways, right? After all, Jane is the ex of your ex, which could get weird pretty quick."

"But how do I find other people to make friends with?" Darnelle asked. "Seems like everyone I know is married with a bunch of kids and is super busy ranching or mining."

"Well, it just so happens that the county fair starts in Bandits Hollow next week," Tempest offered. "There'll be outdoor music, dancing, and lots of folks milling around in the food and beer tents. Everybody attends, so meeting people should be like shooting fish in a barrel! But don't bring your shotgun this time—it's a bit of a buzzkill for friendship. By the way, yours truly will have a therapy booth set up each morning at the fair. I'll be offering fifteen minutes of therapy for a buck for anyone who stops by between nine and ten AM. Plus, I'll be the proudest mom there, because my son has entered his Angus yearling in his very first show class."

"You mean, you're not only a popular radio therapist, you're a 4-H mom too?" Darnelle gasped. "Is there anything you can't do? Thanks so much for all of your advice. Hopefully, I'll bump into you at the fair."

"My pleasure," Tempest replied before Darnelle hung up. She swiped a glance at the digital clock on her computer. "Well folks, looks like we've run out of time already, but I encourage you to stop by my booth at the fair for more guidance from your Queen of Tough Love. Until then, have a tippity-top, triumphant day!"

As the radio station concluded the show with the usual legal disclaimers that it was only for entertainment, Tempest slid the controls on her console to the off position. Then she unzipped her tan vest and drew a breath, filling her lungs with satisfaction. Regardless of how bold she sounded on the radio, she always whispered a prayer fifteen minutes before each broadcast to find the right words. Closing her eyes, she offered up a moment of gratitude that her time with Darnelle had gone well. When she opened them, she turned to where her intern had been sitting so she could thank her for her support.

But Ivy wasn't there.

Tempest swiveled in her chair, spotting her intern back on the couch. Only this time, Ivy appeared slayed, stretched into a reclining position with her legs across the sofa cushions, her pink Mary Janes dangling over the arm rest. A tissue was in Ivy's hand, and she was dabbing the corners of her eyes.

"Wasn't that beautiful!" Ivy exclaimed between heartfelt sniffles. "The way Darnelle and Jane met through the tragedy of Darnelle's break up was like pure magic!"

"Oh Ivy," Tempest scolded, "Darnelle and Jane aren't even lovers. They're simply exploring the possibility of friendship, and you're already in a puddle." Heaving a sigh, Tempest unraveled the dark-blue bandana from her neck that she wore to appear less citified in Bandits Hollow and scooted her chair beside Ivy. Tenderly, she used the bandana to wipe the tears that had slid down Ivy's cheeks.

"I know, I know—they've barely met," acquiesced Ivy. She sat up and clutched her elbows to try and hold herself together. "But the way they found each other is downright kismet, don't you think? They took a bad situation and made it better. Out of the ashes of broken love with Larry, Darnelle can now forge new possibilities with Jane!"

"Didn't you hear the part where a shotgun was involved?" Tempest replied in a testy tone. "And Darnelle mentioned she's *not gay?* Listen, Ivy, you need to temper your rosy views about everything or a therapy career will constantly disappoint you. Our job isn't to hand people happily every afters. Our job is to get them to take a hard look at their lives and make quality choices. Here—"

Tempest handed the bandana to Ivy and got up to open a drawer at her desk. Pulling out a sheet of marked paper, she returned to the sofa and sat down next to her intern. "See these large ink blots?" Tempest pointed to the broad patches of black that stained the page. "This is called a Rorschach test, and the way people interpret the images reveals a lot about what subconsciously drives them. It's time to get to the bottom of your fixation on love. Be honest—what do you see here?"

Ivy dried her moist face with the bandana and squinted. "Ooh, I see two butterflies. I think they're kissing!"

"Oh my God, you really *are* a hopeless romantic." Tempest shook her head. "Do you realize that ninety percent of people view this image as two gladiators clashed in mortal combat?" Tempest set the sheet on her lap. "Leave it to my intern to only perceive rainbows and unicorns."

"Come to think of it, I *do* see a unicorn!" Ivy flapped her hands excitedly. "It's at the bottom of the page. See?" She tapped a section of ink blot that looked to Tempest like a black cloud ready to spit out lightning. "And there's another unicorn right next to it. Wow, they look like *they're* in love, too!"

Tempest hung her head. It was moments like this that made her pray a true sociopath never walked through Ivy's clinical door, because surely she'd be a lamb to the slaughter. Ivy was completely genuine, albeit with her head in the clouds —preferably pink cotton candy ones with colorful sprinkles.

To Tempest's surprise, Ivy's eyes narrowed at her. "You know what I think the *real* issue might be?" she pointed out, tilting her head as though she'd just she'd stumbled upon an epiphany. "Hard knocks in life have made you cynical and paranoid. I read all about this last week in my psychology class!"

Aglow with her revelation, Ivy reached over to grab a copy of the DSM psychology manual that sat on a nearby stand. Flipping through the pages, she paused at a description in the book. "They talk about it right here. Diagnostic code 300.39: Intense, unreasonable fear that interferes with social functioning. In this case, your anxiety and distrust over true love."

Ivy clapped the book closed and studied Tempest's eyes. "You're afraid to lend your heart out again because you've been hurt, so you refuse to see the beginnings of genuine love for anybody. Remember that show where the guy called who was totally gah-gah over his hot neighbor chick? You told him it was all projection. Haven't you *ever* heard of love at first sight?"

Tempest had to hide her smirk at her intern's amateur effort to make a clinical analysis, as if falling in love could cure everything in the universe. She stood to her feet and patiently folded her arms. "Hasn't it occurred to you that what *you* call paranoid, I might call healthy discretion? Believe it or not, by the time you hit the age of thirty-eight like me, you can't just wax prosaic about romance all day. On top of my radio broadcasts, I have a busy counseling career and a young son to raise."

"A-And that means you have to rule out true love?" Ivy asked, her voice tremulous with sincerity. She stood up and surveyed Tempest's shoulder-length, warm-brown hair with loose curls and her practical outfit of a tan vest and a green shirt with khakis over hiking boots, chosen to blend in with Bandits Hollow's mountain residents. "Maybe wearing a little pink might actually do you good—brighten up your look. I discovered a psychological study that said color is *very* important for attraction, so I'm creating an app in my spare time to help people find perfect partners. It's called *Rainbow of Love!* Here, try on my heart charm bracelet, just for fun. It has lots of great colors."

"You're relentless," Tempest conceded, knowing it was easier to humor Ivy when she was in one of her pushy moods about romance, because her intern enjoyed nothing more than prescribing love matches for friends, family—even strangers. Tempest took the bracelet from Ivy's hand and slipped it on her wrist. She had to admit it was pretty, with delicate heart charms of every hue. Holding out her arm to admire the jewelry, she happened to notice a shimmering ruby heart that caught the light from the office window, making its facets sparkle.

"Hey, your eyes were immediately drawn to the bright red one!" Ivy piped up. "That means you need a fiery kind of man who knows exactly what he wants and isn't afraid to take it. Quick, twirl around. It's my turn to do an inventory of *your* subconscious attitudes, the same way you performed the Rorschach test on me."

To Tempest's astonishment, Ivy gripped her by the shoulders and swirled her in the office until she'd completed a circle. "There's no greater Rorschach test than what you chose to wear to face the world this morning," Ivy remarked with a gleam in her eye. "Subconsciously, it reveals the kind of love you think you deserve. Along with colors, I made sure to include fashion analysis in my new app. I'm going to launch it next week!"

Tempest bit her cheeks to fight back a laugh. Despite the fact that Ivy was a walking Hallmark card wired for sound, her frumpy sweater made her look about as sexy as a pink garbage bag. Yet she actually believed she could offer style advice and help people find romance? How was this sweet, gullible girl ever going to land a real job?

"I'm not sure focusing on fashion in one's clinical practice will fly at most mental health centers," Tempest offered gently. "You might come across as a bit of a kook—"

"Not if I solve people's love problems!" Ivy insisted. She headed over to her floppy pink purse hanging from a nearby coat rack and pulled out a large hand mirror. Then she held it up to Tempest. "Take a look. I hate to say it, but you've covered up most of your body with beige and brown, which indicates you're trying to throw a muddy blanket all over your emotions. But you're in luck—"

"Luck?" Tempest gazed into the mirror, thoroughly confused.

Ivy tapped the green fabric of Tempest's shirt directly over her heart. "Right here, this green color that matches your hazel eyes means you're perfectly ripe for true love. And your dark-blue bandana says you're gonna fall hard for a man of deep and honest character, in spite of the brown wall you've put around yourself that shows you're afraid of losing control again. Don't worry, a simple shopping trip for more colors can take care of it."

Before Tempest could argue with her, Ivy whipped off Tempest's tan vest and tossed it onto the couch. "There," she said, "that will help you loosen up. Relax so your potential for true love can come true."

Tempest gazed at herself when Ivy held up the hand mirror again, and it forced her to take a step back. She couldn't help noticing that removing the vest *did* make her feel lighter, like she'd lost her trusty shield.

Ivy's eyes twinkled, and Tempest swore that even the fleeting thought of openness to romance could make her intern as giddy as huffing paint. Matchmaking was Ivy's motivational fuel and drug of choice all rolled into one.

"You know, Darnelle's not the only one who might meet a new person at the fair," Ivy pointed out in a chirpy tone. "The place will be loaded with cowboys, and they might swing by your booth for advice! No harm in letting them buy you funnel cakes and whirl you onto the dance floor when the bands break out, right?"

Tempest clenched her hands, attempting to ward off such flirty images from her mind. "I-I told you," she reiterated, "I've got a son to raise. Aside from work, he takes up all my time and energy."

"But not your whole heart." Ivy set her hand sympathetically on Tempest's shoulder. "That green color you always wear shows your heart is big enough to love all kinds of people. Including a few good-looking cowboys."

"Where on earth do you get all these ideas?" Tempest countered. "Ivy, don't you realize that love *doesn't* conquer all, and sometimes it's best to let relationships take a rest?"

"How would you know?" Ivy asked softly.

She paused for a moment, making an effort to be gentle.

"You told me earlier this summer you weren't sure you ever

really loved your late husband," Ivy reminded her. "You got pregnant and thought you were doing the right thing by marrying him, like a lot of women do. Would it really hurt to explore the possibility of genuine romance? From the look of that green shirt you always wear, you've got a decent chance."

Tempest swallowed hard, speechless. She shifted her gaze from her intern to the hiking boots on her feet.

Somehow, Ivy had probed to the hidden corners of Tempest's heart in her weird, roundabout way and uncovered Tempest's deepest fear—that maybe real love wasn't *ever* going to be in the cards for her. All under the guise of analyzing her color choices.

Damn, Tempest thought, maybe there *is* something to Ivy's odd methods after all. Despite Tempest's effort to maintain her professional demeanor, she suddenly felt exposed, as well as the one thing that scared her most: *vulnerable.*

"Well," Tempest said, "I haven't noticed *your* love life blossoming lately as a result of all this color talk. Aren't you still single?"

"That's because my first priority is to help others with my app," Ivy said brightly. "I figure once I get it going, with all the pink I wear, love will come after me like a bullet! I just hope the guy has red hair. Ooh," she sighed happily, "how I do *love* red hair."

"Oh Ivy," Tempest shook her head, "this kind of approach isn't considered professional therapy. It's more like…meddling. If this is the route you really want to take with your career, maybe you'd be better off as a dating coach?"

"What's the difference?" Ivy's lips slipped into a grin. "Don't you spend all *your* time on the radio untangling peoples' love lives? As long as everyone comes out ahead, what's the harm in it?"

"But I'm not running a matchmaking service!" Tempest defended. "There's a world of difference between clinical therapy and your focus on romance—"

"Not according to that green you wear," Ivy observed with a wry tone.

Before Tempest could fend off Ivy's next wave of skewed logic, her cell phone clanged loudly in her pocket. Plucking it from her khakis, she recognized the number from the local 4-H leader and clicked to answer.

"Tempest? This is Annie," the woman immediately broke in. "I'm sorry to bother you at work—you need to come to the fairgrounds right away. Your son Owen was knocked down at showing practice by his yearling Dumpling."

"*Again?* Oh my God, is he hurt?"

"I don't think so. Right now, he's wiping the mud from all over his face and backside. Dumpling plowed into him in the arena and bowled him over." She let out a weary sigh. "But you know Owen. He's got a grin as wide as Texas."

"That boy," Tempest said. "The dirtier he gets, the happier he is. I'll be right there with a change of clothes to help him clean up. Then I'm going to have a talk with that wretched animal. I've never met a more passive-aggressive creature in my whole life."

"Dumpling's cantankerous, that's for sure," Annie replied in a tone that sounded rather fed-up. "If you ask me, it's high time he got some straight shooting from Tempest The Terminator."

2

T empest hopped out of her compact car in the dusty fairgrounds parking lot and sucked in a breath, bracing herself to head to the arena to face Owen and his willful yearling Dumpling. Clenching her fists, she began to march with quick strides, fantasizing about walloping that animal upside the head for toppling her son again. Okay, so it was a terrible idea, and she'd only get accusations of animal abuse from the 4-H community she'd tried so hard to fit into. But could anyone blame her? It boggled her mind how Dumpling seemed to exist to arouse her ire—and Owen *loved* him for it. Dumpling was like the little furry brother he never had, and the two of them always ended up rassling in the dirt. No real harm ever came of it—but what if it soon did? Especially as the yearling grew bigger? Dumpling had been a trial ever since they'd brought him home from a ranch nearby to the house with a corral she'd rented six months ago, just in time for Owen to start 4-H. One minute the animal was sweet, the very picture of a chubby red Angus yearling who knew exactly when to bat his eyes and look adorable. The next minute, he was hell on hooves, charging at her son without warning and relishing the game of trading mud and manure. Only the unruly tuft of red hair on top of Dumpling's forehead hinted at his mischievous personality, and Owen wouldn't have him any other way.

Is it possible to return livestock for a refund? Tempest wondered as she kept on marching. Surely this hunk of beef has a personality disorder and no amount of show training will make him toe the line. When she reached the door to the fairgrounds arena and swung it open, the corridor that lead to the indoor arena was dark. Like usual, she had to wait for her eyes to adjust, and then she'd head down to find Owen in the ring, probably grinning at her with only the whites of his eyes visible beneath caked mud. But instead of waiting, Tempest got impatient, and as she took a hurried step into the darkness, she slammed into something hard and formidable.

Startled, Tempest swiftly held out her hands. She patted them onto a smooth, firm surface that was oddly warm and inviting—unexpected for a stiff pillar or some other form of building support. Soon, she realized she was sliding her palms up a contoured male chest with outrageously rippled muscle. The tactile stimulation of the stranger's sculpted skin was nothing short of heavenly for a woman who hadn't touched a man in a year. Despite her better sense, Tempest allowed her fingers to linger. A soft chuckle brought her to her wits.

"Can I help you?" asked the stranger in a husky voice

laced with amusement. Tempest noticed he hardly backed away from her touch, seeming to enjoy the moment as well.

Nevertheless, her breath hitched in embarrassment and she yanked back her hands. When she glanced up, her gaze had begun to adjust to the darkness, and she was able to distinguish his features.

Damn!

He was the handsomest devil she'd ever seen, with a shock of light brown hair flecked with gold and high cheekbones, a square jaw, and the kind of midnight-blue eyes that were designed to torment women. His tall height and wide shoulders accentuated his narrow hips, and his plaid shirt was unbuttoned to reveal deliciously toned abs—along with the biggest, shiniest rodeo belt buckle she'd ever seen.

At a loss for words, Tempest's intimidation was compounded by the man's winning smile, which rivaled the swashbuckling grin of Errol Flynn. Part mischievous and part…at least in Tempest's estimation…*dangerous*.

Tempest noticed he had a firm grip on the side of Dumpling's halter. When the animal began to wriggle fiercely, he wrapped his arm around the yearling's neck in a secure hold, his large bicep bulging to keep the rebellious animal in place. Unwittingly, Tempest felt a rush of heat, wishing she could run her fingers along his tempting bicep. He was so good-looking that she imagined her touch against his skin just might sizzle—

Shocked by such a heady sensation, Tempest shook her head, attempting to come back to her senses. The man still had a hold on the animal's neck that was getting tighter by the second, and she had to admit that she'd wanted to throttle Dumpling a few times herself.

"E-Excuse me," she stammered, trying to take her eyes off the man's delectable chest, "is that kind of grip on a yearling sanctioned by 4-H?"

Dumpling tossed his head and bucked in place, but the man easily maintained his hold with his drool-worthy, thick bicep. His grin stretched even broader.

Combined with the midnight-blue eyes that she swore reflected hues of indigo, just like her deep-blue bandana, he was downright dazzling.

God almighty, Tempest groaned to herself, whoever this guy is, he hardly needs to throw me into a neck lock to get my knees to buckle. One flash of that smile will do the trick.

"I have no idea if it's sanctioned," the man replied with a gleam in his eye, as though fully aware of the effect he had on women. "I'm just trying to keep him from mowing you down. This animal is quite the character and will head butt anybody within a hundred yards. Since he's in such an ornery mood, Annie asked me to walk him to the paddock while she took the 4-H kids to the conference room to watch a video about showmanship."

"Including Owen?" Tempest said, surprised. "She just called me five minutes ago and said he was all coated in mud." Tempest held up the fresh t-shirt and jeans she'd brought for her son, which she always kept in the trunk of her car for this purpose. "I assured her I'd bring him clean, dry clothes right away."

"Aw, no worries about the clothes—dirty is the way boys like 'em. I told Annie to go ahead and let him watch the movie with the rest of the kids. He won't need to clean up till it's bedtime, anyway."

"And how would *you* know what my son needs?" Tempest retorted, irked at the man's arrogance. "Who are you, anyway, one of the 4-H dads?"

"No, ma'am. Simply a steer wrestler who's been using the arena to practice today for the competitions. But I *am* on the Fair Board as the Safety Commissioner, and that makes me responsible for keeping everyone protected around here." Dumpling crow-hopped with a vengeance, easily subdued by the man. "Which is why Annie asked me to keep this yearling under control so he wouldn't crash into Owen again—or any of the other children." The man gazed at Tempest with an arched brow. "Even though your son seems to love it. My guess is that things are a bit too clean and tidy at home, so he needs this outlet to be a real boy."

"What are you implying?" Tempest burst at his audacity. "That I'm not a good parent?"

"No," he countered without missing a beat. "I'm saying you're probably a fussy parent. And the kid needs a break."

"How dare you insinuate I don't know what's good for my son!"

For a moment, the man glanced Tempest over, his gaze lingering on the gentle curves that nicely filled out her khaki pants and vest. Then his appreciative regard settled on her pretty face and remarkable hazel green eyes framed by loose curls of toffee-brown hair. He gave her a wry smile.

"Well, for starters, you sure don't look like the typical 4-H mom."

"W-Why's that?" Tempest's voice faltered as she self-consciously hugged her vest tighter. She'd bought outdoorsy clothing on purpose in the hopes of blending in with the 4-H crowd. But at this point, she was glad she'd worn mostly brown, since Ivy claimed the color was a kind of muddy emotional armor. Anything to keep this handsome stranger at a distance.

The man leaned in to peer at the brand label sewed onto Tempest's tan vest. "REI, huh? What the hell's that—some newfangled company in New York? Most ranch moms around here wear Carhartt or Wrangler. Plus," he brazenly gazed her up and down again, sizing up her soft curves with a particularly male nod of approval, "you're quite the looker."

As Tempest's cheeks flared into a blush, he studied her hands, with her perfectly manicured fingernails painted a tan color that matched her vest. His lips slipped into another self-satisfied smile. "Besides, something tells me you ain't handled a whole lot of cattle before."

"That's not true!" Tempest protested. "When we bought Dumpling from the nearby ranch, we walked him right home to the small corral on our rental property and we've taken care of him ever since. He even has his own stall—we filled it with fresh straw so he'd be cozy. Here, give me that animal. I'll show you I know my way around an Angus yearling, mister, um—"

"Ramsey. Dixon Ramsey." His eyes lit up at the prospect of seeing Tempest attempt to manage the yearling. Then he swung open the door for her, letting a shock of sunlight inside. Guiding Dumpling forward a few steps onto the dirt parking lot, he handed Tempest the lead line.

"Be my guest," Dixon said.

Tempest threw her chin proudly into the air and wound the lead a few times around her hand to get a good hold. "C'mon, Dumpling," she jerked the animal forward in a huff. "Let's go to the paddock and get you some hay while Owen finishes watching the showmanship video. No need to listen to some nasty cowboy who doesn't even know us."

At that moment, the funnel cake truck roared past them, steering toward a gravel lane where all the deep-fried candy bars, fruit pies, and butter-dipped roasted corn would be sold. The loud rumble the truck made over the rutted, dusty avenue spooked the dickens out of Dumpling, and before Tempest knew it, he leaped into the air like he'd been shot from a pistol.

"Dumpling, stop!" Tempest cried, dropping Owen's fresh clothes as the yearling hit the ground running. Tipping the scale at nearly a thousand pounds, it was easy for the yearling to drag lightweight Tempest through the fairgrounds like a rag doll. They toppled over barrels, construction pylons, a kettle corn stand, and even a snow cone booth that had already been set up for the opening festivities the next morning. A plastic tub of raspberry syrup spiraled in the air and landed on Tempest's head, cracking open and drenching her in red goo. Yet the rope that was wound around her hand only tightened with Dumpling's every stride, burning her skin like a hot iron. Desperately, she tried to uncoil the rope to free herself while Dumpling zig-zagged past carnival games and shooting galleries, but it was no use. Through the clouds of dirt they stirred up, Tempest could barely see until a break in the dust enabled her to spot a blockade near the end of the lane. It was her Dollar Therapy booth, alongside the stand for Viola's Crocheted Dog Collars. Tempest knew the booth was built like a brick—she'd designed it herself out of two-by-fours and three-quarter-inch plywood. All she could do was squeeze her eyes shut and brace her body for a world of hurt.

All at once, she heard a brief scuffle and a weight came crashing down on top of her as her movement halted. To her surprise, when she blinked opened her eyes, she was nose to nose with none other than Dixon Ramsey.

And his lips were threateningly close—

Tempest coughed at the dust clouds that had engulfed her face. What is this, she panicked, the Hallmark movie from hell?

Dixon didn't say a word.

He simply smiled that evil grin of charisma that got under Tempest's skin like a new-found drug. He had one arm tightly wound around her, with the full weight of his chest on top, while one of his knees and his boot had firmly pinned Dumpling's rope to the ground so the spitfire yearling couldn't jerk her hand any further. At that moment, he searched her face as though he had half a mind to kiss her—and the way he'd engulfed her body, there wasn't a dang thing she could do about it.

But instead of a kiss, Dixon searched her lovely hazel green eyes for a second. Then he wriggled his arm out from beneath her and brought his finger to her check. He slowly scooped off some raspberry syrup and took a lick, savoring the flavor.

"Well, hot damn," he began to laugh, his chest jiggling on top of hers. "I've wrestled a hell of a lot of cattle in my day, but never one dragging such a beautiful woman. Covered in raspberry syrup to boot! You've got some honest to goodness grit, girl."

Tempest blinked hard, still in shock. It was then she put two and two together and realized that Dixon must have raced to catch up with them and toppled the yearling to the ground, then protected her with his body before Dumpling could hop to his feet and ram her. In spite of the fact that Dumpling still tried to yank against his lead line, Dixon refused to let up on his anchored knee and boot to keep Tempest's hand from further injury. The yearling sunk his head and let out a defeated moo.

Dixon swiftly unraveled Tempest's hand loose from the rope, grabbing the end before Dumpling could get away. Then he stood to his feet and walked over to a nearby truck to tie the animal to the tail gate. When he returned, Dixon gallantly held out his palm to give Tempest a hand up.

"Ain't you a sight," he chuckled as she scrambled to her feet. His gaze traced her body that was thoroughly caked with dirt and small pieces of straw and popcorn that had stuck to the red goo like glue. "Welcome to my world, darlin'. Now you know what kind of fun Owen's been having rassling with Dumpling. I bet Owen will make a great steer wrestler someday with a momma who can hang on like you."

All at once, Dixon's face clouded over and grew serious. He glared at her with his intense, deepwater-blue eyes. "But can I give you a pointer?"

Tempest hadn't stopped clutching her chest to calm her racing heart from the moment she'd stood up. She sucked in her bottom lip, still traumatized by the whole ordeal. Gently, Dixon grasped her sore hand and carefully unfolded her fingers to check the damage. The whole time, Tempest bit the insides of her cheeks, trying with all her might not to let on how much her skin smarted.

"Don't you *ever* wrap a lead line around your hand like that again," Dixon said in a grave voice. "Or next time, you might lose a finger or your whole damn hand. Always make a figure-eight loop out of the extra rope and grip the entire thing inside your fist so you can let go in an instant whenever you want to." His former smile had faded entirely, and as he released her hand, Tempest was startled by how hardened his eyes had become when he meant business. "Bet your hand hurts like hell right now, don't it? That's a good thing," he told her, "'cause you won't never make that mistake twice. And you'll keep your hand."

Tempest nodded and leaned her elbow in exhaustion against her therapy booth, which to her relief had been spared from destruction during the accident.

"It's-it's okay," she lied nonchalantly, worried she wouldn't seem like a rugged 4-H mom if she dared to acknowledge the pain. In her mind, the bottle of Motrin she knew was in her car's glove compartment kept calling to her like heaven's sweetest angel. Drawing a hesitant breath, she slowly curled her fingers, clenching her teeth to keep from showing the ache. Then she opened and closed her hand a few more times, noting that nothing seemed broken. As long as she could bend and straighten her fingers, she figured she'd be okay.

"Mom!" Owen hailed from a distance. Tempest turned and saw her son running like gangbusters toward her, barely recognizable with all of the dried mud on his face and clothes.

"Mom! You okay?" In his panic, Owen rammed into her

full throttle, nearly as hard as Dumpling was famous for, and he wrapped his small arms tightly around her waist. "Are you all right? Dumpling sure pulls hard, don't he?"

Tempest squeezed Owen tenderly with her good arm, hiding her rope-burned hand behind her back so he wouldn't worry. "I'm fine, sweetie," she fibbed. Then she used her good hand to lightly tousle his wheat-blonde hair with a smile. "Guess you and I are quite the match, aren't we? Filthy as all get out."

Owen stepped back and gazed into his mother's eyes with all of the sparkling gratitude of an eight-year-old who was relieved his mother seemed okay. But then he covered his mouth with both hands and began to giggle.

Owen's little belly shook with laughter, and he shot a glance at Dixon. Together, they broke into outright guffaws.

"Mommy," Owen said between fits of giggles, "you've got...um...you know—"

"Raspberry syrup all over you," Dixon finished his sentence.

Tempest closed her eyes, wishing she could disappear into the center of the earth.

She'd been too dazed to completely internalize that she was covered in syrup when Dixon had pointed out that fact and taken a lick. Mortified, she dashed over to the truck where Dumpling was tied and snuck a peek into the side mirror. Lord have mercy—she looked just like Carrie from that blood bath prom scene in the classic horror movie with streams of bright red dripping down her face and hair.

Tempest swiveled toward Dumpling, furious.

"I swear to God, you are *this close* to becoming tonight's

burger, do you hear that?" she cried, holding out her thumb and forefinger nearly together. "You passive-aggressive beast from hell! I have half a mind to zap you with a cattle prod and call it electric-shock therapy to drive the devil out of you!"

"No, Mommy!" Owen cried. He ran over to his yearling and hugged him around the neck. The two of them stared up at Tempest with big eyes, looking perfectly innocent and adorable. Owen squeezed his cheek beside Dumpling's to further accentuate their charm.

Crap, Tempest thought. This kid's a master.

Tempest threw her head back in frustration, struggling to keep from letting out a primal scream.

"You been licked ma'am, and you know it," Dixon smiled, enjoying the irony of those words. He walked over and ruffled Dumpling's tuft of red hair on his forehead. "You ain't got the heart to butcher this bundle of red Angus cuteness."

"At least he didn't knock over your booth, Mom," Owen reminded her, his voice hopeful.

"Wait, *your* booth?" Dixon broke in, stunned. He squinted at the words Tempest had carefully painted onto the plywood in big black letters:

Dollar Therapy: 15 Minutes for $1 by Tempest Wright

"*You're* Tempest the Terminator? The freaking radio host?" Dixon said, flabbergasted. He began to laugh harder than before. "My God, everybody in the county listens to your show while they're moving cattle and bucking hay. You wouldn't believe all the jokes folks make about how much you hate men."

Dixon tilted his chin and held out a finger to slide a syrupy lock of hair out of Tempest's eyes. "Funny, you don't look like you're having a 'tippity-top, triumphant day.'"

"Aaaaagh!" Tempest finally howled in that primal scream she'd been holding in all this time, her hands squeezed into balls. "This is the worst day EVER!"

"It's okay, darlin', you can wallop me," Dixon offered with a chuckle. "I'm sure that's in one of your therapy books somewhere. Might do you some good. Just pretend I'm a punching bag—I won't even charge you."

And there was his confounded smile again, the one that sent electricity through Tempest's body at precisely the wrong moment. Despite the dirt all over his face, a brief flash of his ivories made Tempest tremble against her will. As much as she wanted to take Dixon up on his offer and slug him, she stiffened and wrapped her arms around her waist to pull herself together.

"Excuse me," she said, spitting fury, "I deeply appreciate the fact that you stopped Dumpling's run before we could crash into my booth. But there's no reason for you to claim I hate men if I'm *forced* to advise callers to get rid of jerks. Nor will I allow you to ridicule me for helping people sort out their lives each day on the radio. For *free*, I might add, even if I do happen to be covered in raspberry syrup. Now if you'll please pardon us, we need to get Dumpling back to his paddock."

"I'm afraid that won't be possible," an authoritative woman's voice cut in.

Tempest whipped around and saw the 4-H leader Annie, a thick woman in tan, Carhartt overalls who was nearly forty like Tempest and Dixon. Her brows were furrowed and her hands were perched on her hips. "There's no way I can keep allowing

Dumpling to be around the 4-H kids with his out-of-control behavior. I'm sorry Tempest and Owen, but that yearling is clearly a danger to himself and others, and he has no business competing at the county fair."

"What? I've worked so hard!" Owen yelped. "Tell her, Mommy!"

Annie raised her hand to halt Tempest before she even began.

"I know you have, son," Annie replied to Owen. "But you saw for yourself what Dumpling just did to your mother. He's extremely headstrong."

"What if I spend extra time training him? We could work really hard night and day. This is my big dream!"

Annie shook her head. "The kind of training he needs requires a cattle expert to make any progress at all. Certainly more than an inexperienced eight-year-old can provide."

Owen began to sob into his palms.

Speechless, Tempest's heart broke, and she felt guilty to her core—

This was exactly the kind of painful regret that had been plaguing her ever since her husband had died. That somehow *she* wasn't enough, and she could never lend the type of rugged man's influence to Owen that he would need while growing up. Never mind that most men in Denver didn't have a clue how to train cattle either, and there were probably plenty of women around Bandits Hollow who could do the job. Tempest understood her fear wasn't rational, yet she still couldn't shake the feeling that Owen lacked a positive male influence in his life. She stepped over to Owen and gave him another hug, devastated by the turn of events. When she glanced up, her gaze met Dixon's.

And his dark-blue eyes were filled with a seething anger that threw her.

No longer were they cold, like when he'd chastised her about the way she'd held the rope. They had turned into burning blue flames—the kind that had seen injustice before, and were damned if he didn't do something about it.

"I'll help him," Dixon vowed to Annie with a resolve that shook Tempest, as though he would refuse to take no for an answer.

Annie heaved a sigh and rolled her eyes, looping her thumbs into her overalls. "Oh Dixon, you're the king of rescuing lost causes around here and you know it. Every wayward child that needs a hand in this county can count on you to be the first in line. But in case you haven't noticed, this isn't a situation where your dad was too drunk to help you as a kid. That animal is honestly a hazard."

The faint whisper of a wince crossed Dixon's eyes. He glared at Annie, furious that she'd let out that information.

"Don't get all huffy on me," Annie warned him. "Everybody knows your dad neglected you when you were around Owen's age, but that doesn't change the fact that Dumpling is a lawsuit waiting to happen. He doesn't need more training—he needs to go to the butcher."

"No!" cried Owen. "Please, Mom," he begged Tempest, "tell her no!"

Tempest recoiled in more guilt. When she'd threatened Dumpling a few minutes ago, it was in a fit of emotion. She hadn't been serious—she would never in a million years send her child's pet to the slaughterhouse.

"I don't agree, Annie," Dixon growled, defying her as he folded his thick arms, his muscles bulging against the fabric of his plaid shirt. He trained his arresting blue eyes on Annie, and as tough as she was, even she appeared to shrink from the force of his gaze. "You and I have known each other since kindergarten," he said. "What's more, I'm not only the Safety Commissioner around here, I've won more steer wrestling championships than anyone else in the state. And if *I* think all this animal needs is some extra training, there are very few cowboys in Colorado who would have the guts to defy me. So this is how it's gonna be—I'll help Owen each evening, starting on Sunday, till it's time for his Angus show class in two weeks. We'll work at my place, the Rambling Star Ranch, so he and his yearling will stay separate from the other kids and cattle until show day. In return, you'll let Owen and Dumpling compete for the 4-H club this year, with no promises for next year until you see how it goes."

Dixon's words weren't merely a proposition—they were stated as an established fact.

Annie shook her head. "Look, Dixon, you can't cure a lifetime of disappointment in your dad by taking on the spawn of Satan with Dumpling."

"Dumpling is *not* the spawn of Satan, and this has nothing to do with my dad," Dixon replied adamantly. "He's just a very energetic red Angus who needs a firm hand from a man who knows what he's doing. All I ask is that you let me work with these two and allow them to enter the Angus show class. I promise the yearling won't embarrass you or hurt anybody.

After the fair, if you still feel Dumpling's too rowdy, then you can ban him from 4-H for life and he can be put out to pasture. But not now, not after this boy has been working so hard. I refuse to let his dreams be ground to dust."

"Please, Miss Annie!" Owen begged. "We'll practice really hard. I promise!"

Annie folded her arms and tilted back on her boot heels. "So you're saying you'll give this boy *advanced* lessons in showmanship? And you'll take it upon yourself to make sure Dumpling's *absolutely safe* around the other kids and calves on show day? Or your ass is the one I'll come after?"

"Roger," Dixon replied. "I'll take full responsibility—as the Safety Commissioner."

Tempest's mouth dropped, her mind reeling. Was this an answer to prayer, or her worst nightmare? To meet in the evenings with the handsomest, most arrogant and infuriating cowboy she'd ever seen? Despite her racing thoughts, she couldn't think of any other way to rescue Owen's 4-H ambitions.

"Dixon, if you didn't have so damn many belt buckles the size of platters, I'd never go for this," Annie asserted. "But I guess, given your track record with competitions…" She released a sigh as her voice trailed off.

"It's a deal, right?" piped up Owen. He gave Annie a big hug and implored her with his eyes. "We'll make the Bandits Hollow 4-H club proud—honest!"

"All right," Annie relented. She shot a glance at Tempest. "Are you okay with this as his mother? Because I warn you, you'd better have a voodoo rattle along with all of your therapy techniques, because taming Dumpling is going to take some mad skills." She turned to Owen and gave him a reluctant smile.

Tempest nodded her agreement, in spite of all her trepidations.

"Then I'll see you at the fair, Owen," Annie said before turning on her heels and heading to the show arena. She lifted up a hand and waved as she left without glancing back, walking away with the kind of deliberate strides that indicated no one should mess with her.

Dixon faced Tempest. "So, I'm expecting you to meet me with Owen and Dumpling right here on the second night of the fair, starting at seven o'clock—not one minute later. Then we'll lead Dumpling to the Rambling Star Ranch for lessons. My ranch is right next door to this fairgrounds, and I've got all the equipment the boy needs. In return," Dixon thought about it for a moment, "Owen can take care of my champion quarter horse Bullet. That means brushing him, picking his hooves, and cleaning his tack."

"You're on!" cried Owen, jumping up and down. He stepped up to Dixon and gave him a high five.

Tempest was left sucking air. All of a sudden she wasn't in control anymore—*Dixon was.* And though this appeared to be the opportunity of a lifetime for her son, she couldn't help feeling like her life and her relationship to Owen were careening out of her hands.

"But-but—" she stuttered.

As if reading her mind, Dixon leaned beside Tempest's ear.

"Isn't this better than making burger out of your kid's pet? Give the boy a break. I promise Owen will *never* get dragged the way you were today. And his dreams *will* come true."

Tempest slowly rubbed her injured hand, feeling like her cheeks had just matched the redness of her rope-burned skin. How on earth could she refuse?

"Why are you doing this?" she pressed. "We hardly know you."

Dixon leaned in again to Tempest's red-syrup stained ear. "You heard Annie—when I was close to Owen's age there wasn't a goddamned person in my life I could count on to steer me in the right direction. I don't want to see that happen to another boy. So for God's sake Tempest, don't lecture me with any of your therapy talk, or I guarantee I'll take my offer right back."

Tempest swallowed a breath, his vehement words ringing in her ear. Of course, to her way of thinking, this deal had psychological transference written all over it. Dixon had never resolved his own issues with his father, so he was trying to do so now. But it would also mean allowing a man into her son's life to help him out with an outdoor activity—the kind of pursuit she knew nothing about.

"Okay," she committed, "we'll see you at seven on Sunday night."

"Before you come," Dixon instructed, "rub some Bag Balm on that hand of yours. It's a medicinal ointment that will heal you right up."

Tempest glanced down. Her hand was as red as a hot poker, and her skin sure looked like it could use a soothing salve. She made a mental note to look for Bag Balm at the Bandits Hollow Mercantile in town.

Just then an owl called from the trees in the distance, making her startle. Its long, lonely echo traveled over the fairgrounds with a haunting insistence that seemed foreboding. Tempest happened to glance at her other hand and noticed she was still wearing Ivy's heart charm bracelet on her wrist. She'd completely forgotten to give it back when she'd rushed off to take care of Owen. The silver jewelry was so dusty it looked dull, with a few pieces of hay stuck into the round links.

And the ruby heart charm was gone.

3

"Oh Ivy, I'm so sorry!" Tempest confessed as they were setting up the portable radio console at her booth. It was nearly nine o'clock in the morning, and Ivy had met Tempest at the fairgrounds back gate where workers arrived early for the first day of the fair. "Owen's crazy yearling dragged me headlong through the concessions aisle yesterday. The ruby heart charm must have broken off the bracelet and gotten buried in the dust. Owen and I looked all afternoon—we couldn't find it anywhere. Please, let me buy you another one, okay?"

Ivy glanced down at her charm bracelet, now back on her wrist and shiny as a newly-minted coin after Tempest had cleaned it. She watched the myriad-colored charms dance in the morning light and nodded with a slight shrug. "It was my favorite," she muttered in a barely audible whisper.

But Tempest had heard her.

Boy, had she ever heard her—and her heart sank.

"Ivy," Tempest said, feeling horrible, "I promise I'll work harder. I'll take a rake and scour this whole area, all right? As soon as I'm done with my broadcast. I won't stop till I find that charm."

Ivy offered Tempest a weak smile. Her intern was such a good soul, despite her quirky ideas, never one to hold a grudge against anybody. Nevertheless, Tempest wanted to crawl into one of the deep potholes in the nearby dusty lane and die. Just then, a booming voice pummeled through her thoughts.

"Attention, fair staff and booth attendants!" the man in the announcer's tower called out. "We are now opening the front gates to let ticket-holders through for this year's county fair. Please have your cash boxes and big smiles ready. Let's make this the best fair ever for Bandits Hollow!"

Tempest drew a deep breath, glad Owen's 4-H club had cattle grooming inspections each morning with Annie so she could focus on business. She turned to Ivy. "Don't worry, right after the show, I'm determined to find that charm. Or I swear I'll buy you another one just like it—with a real ruby."

Tempest took a step back and double-checked the sturdiness of her wooden booth with *Dollar Therapy: 15 Minutes for $1 by Tempest Wright* written in big black letters. As early fair goers began to trickle by on their way to snag cinnamon rolls and coffee from *Hedda's Happy Homebaked* food truck, Tempest set a stack of her bestselling books on her booth and turned to the radio console. She gave Ivy a quick nod before flicking on the operating switch.

"Good morning, Bandits Hollow!" Tempest crooned into

her wireless microphone. "It's Tempest time, and I'm broadcasting today from the county fair. It's beautiful and sunny here in the mountains at 9,000 feet with a perfectly blue mid-summer sky. If you come down to the fairgrounds right now, you can not only catch the alpaca show in the outdoor arena, you can also stop by my booth for fifteen minutes of therapy for a buck! And I'm happy to autograph my new title *Shock Value: How to Stop Whining And Get on With Your Life* for anyone who makes a book purchase. So let's get started. Who'd like to fork up a dollar to solve their problems this morning—"

"Me!" cried a disheveled woman in a t-shirt and jeans before Tempest could finish her sentence. Though only in her twenties, the poor creature appeared beleaguered as she trotted up to the booth. She looped a strand of stringy blonde hair behind her ear and waited for Ivy to hand her a wireless microphone. "My name's Abby," she explained, "and I've completely lost my…"

The woman hesitated for a moment, her cheeks flashing pink. She gazed into Ivy's sympathetic eyes for courage.

Tempest held her breath, expecting Abby to say she'd lost her marbles—particularly given her harried face and frayed clothes with stains that made them look like they hadn't been laundered in a month.

But then Abby rubbed her eyebrows and cautiously announced, "Sex drive."

"Oh," Tempest responded, a bit surprised at her honesty at such an early hour. "Well," she said in a kind tone, "that's awfully brave of you to admit in public. I've often found in my practice that this can happen not because of a lack of desire but due to exhaustion from an overly hectic schedule. Can you fill me in on how busy your life is?"

"It's been crazy!" Abby heaved a fatigued breath. "I've been working at three different jobs for as long as I can remember."

Tempest's eyes narrowed. "And why is that—is your rent high? Do you have big debts?"

"No," Abby admitted. "My boyfriend lost his job, and I'm the only one paying the bills right now."

"Really? How long ago was that?"

Abby shuffled her feet. "Three years."

Tempest gasped. "You're telling me your boyfriend hasn't worked in *three years?* Abby, you don't need a bigger sex drive—you need a nap! Tell that man to get off his duff and do something about contributing to your household or you'll change the locks."

"But—"

"But what?" Tempest pushed, crossing her arms.

Abby gazed down at her worn, threadbare sneakers and cringed.

"He…he says he loves me," she mentioned shyly.

"Of course he does—you're doing all the heavy lifting!" Tempest replied. "Abby, like I always say on the radio, history is destiny. Users constantly say they love their women, while real men *show it*. If this guy has a track record of not getting off the couch while you do all the work, nothing's ever going to change. Don't tell me, let me guess—he's very good looking and has great excuses."

"How'd you know?" Abby replied. "You must be psychic!

He always tells me he has terrible allergies that make him sluggish and give him headaches."

"Believe me, I'm *not* gifted with psychic powers," Tempest sighed. "It's called approaching forty and having been around the block a few times. Listen, Abby, repeat after me: The first sign of a sociopath is the sob story."

Abby cleared her throat. "Okay, the first sign of a sociopath is the sob story," she echoed softly.

"And most handsome men are takers because everything comes easily to them."

Abby nodded with a wince. "Oh yeah," she recalled, "you've said that a bunch of times on the radio, huh?"

"Yes, ma'am," Tempest replied. She turned to her intern. "Ivy, show Abby where to drop her buck for her therapy session and then please give her a free copy of my book *Shock Value*."

Tempest's lips set into a firm line while Ivy pointed to an old Ball jar on a corner of the booth for Abby's dollar and handed her the book.

"Now Abby, listen up," Tempest said. "This is no longer a book. Do you understand? It's a weapon."

"It is?"

"Indeed. Next time your boyfriend dares to come over to your place for sex, a free meal, or anything else you have to offer, I want you to whack him over the head with this book and tell him to get a job. Are we clear?"

Abby began to giggle. "How do I know he'll ever come back?"

"Hopefully, he won't—unless he's got a paycheck! And if he doesn't, then you can brag to everybody on social media about how you lost a hundred and fifty pounds. Besides," Tempest gave Ivy a wink, "my intern tells me there should be plenty of men hanging around the fair today. Nothing revs up a sex drive like finding a hard-working cowboy who knows how to treat a lady right."

"Ooh," Abby swooned, glancing over at a booth across the lane that was selling pies, "like that hunky cowboy over there?"

Tempest slid her gaze to the pie booth, her eyes widening as she caught the flash of Dixon's ever-charming grin while he was about to dive into a steaming piece of pie for breakfast. Despite gritting her teeth, Tempest's heart yanked at the sight of the sun glinting off Dixon's tousled, golden-brown hair and tan, rugged cheekbones. The manly contours of his broad shoulders and rodeo-toned biceps unexpectedly made an electric current snap and crackle through her system, and she couldn't help but flinch.

"Why does Dixon Ramsey have to look so damn hot at the break of day—does he exist to torture women?" Tempest wondered.

Aloud.

On the radio—

Tempest sucked a horrified lungful of air as Ivy slapped her palm over her lips to hide her giggles.

"Oh my God, please tell me I didn't say that out loud," Tempest whispered to Ivy. She buried her face in her palms and let out an embarrassed squeak.

Ivy grabbed Tempest's microphone for a quick save. "Well, folks, that's it for our broadcast today!" she trilled. "Please tune in tomorrow for more advice from your Queen of Tough Love. Until then, have a tippity-top, triumphant day!"

Ivy reached over to the radio console to turn it off. Then she gave Abby a wave as the woman began to head over to Hedda's food truck for hot breakfast treats. As soon as Abby was out of earshot, Ivy swiveled to face Tempest with a smug look.

"Yes, as matter of fact, you *did* say that out loud for the whole world to hear," Ivy chided, setting the microphone on its stand. "You actually admitted your attraction to a man on the radio! Quite the Freudian slip, don't you think? Luckily," she stole a glance back at Dixon Ramsey, "he's gorgeous!"

Tempest shook her head, her cheeks the color of cherries. "Isn't there a rule somewhere that I can fire you for impertinence?" she mentioned, her voice laced with chagrin.

"You can't!" Ivy chuckled. "I'm an intern—I work free for college credit, remember? Besides, you *are* wearing yellow today."

"What's that supposed to mean?" Tempest glanced down at her yellow shirt tucked into her khaki pants.

"Well, the color yellow is a clear indication that you're *very* receptive to opening up your heart like a sunflower to the golden rays of love!" Ivy informed her.

Tempest plunked her face into her hands again. "Oh Ivy," she mumbled through her fingers, "just because a guy is good looking doesn't mean I need his nonsense in my life. Didn't you hear what I said earlier about handsome men usually turning out to be takers?"

Before Ivy could respond, Tempest heard a hard clink on her booth. When she peered through her fingers, to her astonishment, there was a large, great horned owl perched on top of the wood.

And in the bird's talon was Ivy's ruby heart charm.

Tempest gasped as the owl alighted into the air, flailing her hands to try and grab the charm before the bird got far away. Yet the owl escaped her grasp, and with silent beats of its wings, headed over to the pie booth across the lane next to Dixon, who was still digging into his slice. An old woman in a black velvet dress stood at the booth with a wry look in her eye. She held up a black-gloved hand and the owl landed at her wrist. The woman gazed into the owl's big yellow eyes as if she were listening to it speak.

Tempest slipped out of the booth in an effort to dash after the bird, when Ivy grabbed her by the collar, yanking her to a stop.

"Hold on!" Ivy yelped. She squinted at the pie booth. "That spooky woman over there is wearing *all black*. In broad daylight. In July."

"Who the hell cares?" Tempest said, trying to wriggle free. "Maybe she went to a funeral. The owl on her arm has your heart charm!"

Ivy maintained a firm grip on Tempest's collar. For the first time ever, Tempest spied a sharp determination in her eyes. "When it comes to love, black is the sign of protection *and* destiny," she confided. "And her owl has the same charm *you* were drawn to. Kind of a strange coincidence, considering she's looking straight at you."

It was true—the beautiful woman with long, flowing gray hair in the black velvet dress had her eyes locked on Tempest. She nodded with a knowing smile as though she were listening to the owl's whispers.

A chill ran down Tempest's back. She shook her head, trying to dispel the sight like it was an apparition.

"Ivy, are you sure you don't have synesthesia?" she said. "You know, that neurological disorder where your senses get all tangled up, and you project way too much meaning onto random colors or numbers, even though they're irrelevant?"

"There's nothing irrelevant about the way that woman's fixated on you," Ivy replied. "It's like, I dunno, she's met you before or something—"

"Or pegged you as her next target," winked a stout, middle-aged woman. She had on a floral, appliqued sweatshirt with a heaping plate of curly fries in her hand. Leaning an elbow onto Tempest's booth, she dipped a few fries into ketchup and stuffed them into her mouth. "That's Granny Tinker. Of the Trinity."

"The Trinity?" Tempest said.

"Yessiree," the woman replied confidently between chews. "There's a reason the line to her pie booth is so long." She lowered her voice. "Everyone in Bandits Hollow knows Granny Tinker and her two cohorts, Pearl and Jubilee, like to cast spells on people each spring. Sure, those old ladies may wear frontier dresses and act like they're selling pies to fundraise for the Historical Society. But in reality," she arched a brow, "they're picking their next victims."

"Victims? Of what?" asked Tempest.

"Why, *love* darlin'! It's how they get their jollies, by matching folks up."

"Hmm, sounds like somebody else I know." Tempest glared at Ivy.

"On top of that, Granny Tinker's also known for making

eerie comments that seem like riddles at first, but then always come true."

"Wait a minute—come to think of it, I happened to run into her earlier," Tempest admitted. "She passed by me on the way to setting up her booth this morning and let out a long cackle for no reason. Then she looked up at the sky and said something really odd."

"Whoa, she *talked* to you?" the middle-aged woman replied, dropping her handful of fries back onto her plate.

"It's not like she bothered to say good morning or anything." Tempest shrugged. "When she walked by, out of the blue she stopped and gazed up at the morning star. Then she blurted that I was just like it—a rambling star who needs to find rest."

The woman gasped, her plate falling from her fingers to the dirt. "Holy moley! I've heard Granny Tinker only talks to people she's about to put a spell on." She looked around to make sure other people didn't hear. "And her pies are rumored to be spiked with *magic*."

Ivy glanced toward the pie booth and tapped her lip. "Wow, the people leaving that booth are grinning like fools. And Dixon Ramsey just bought his second helping."

"That's because folks don't get to see Granny Tinker in daylight very often—only when she comes out in spring to cast her charms. There's even a legend she was once a member of Bandits Hollow gang a century ago." She dropped her voice to a low whisper. "And she time traveled to the present day."

The woman pointed to an old wanted poster on the nearby announcer's tower bearing the likenesses of the Bandits Hollow Gang—commemorative of the namesake of the town.

In the sepia-toned image were three men and a beautiful woman dressed in black who looked like Granny Tinker might have in her youth.

"Nowadays she comes to town each June to find the fairy slipper flower and other aphrodisiacs so she and her friends can meddle in people's business. It's their favorite hobby. Some old ladies knit, others play bingo, and the Trinity rearrange people's lives. Kind of like playing chess."

"You mean, they sort out people's hearts?" said Ivy with an impish smirk. "Just like Tempest?"

Tempest's mouth dropped, aghast—

"Did you know research shows that *arranged* marriages have a much better chance of survival than regular ones?" Ivy pointed out before Tempest could protest. "I learned that in my Relationship Psychology class. Hmm, maybe *I* could use the Trinity's help..."

Tempest rolled her eyes. "You can't leave that kind of thing to chance! Or to some type of backwoods hocus pocus."

"What's the matter, are *you* afraid of surprises?" Ivy countered. "You know, love isn't supposed to be a diagnosis you can peg with a therapist's ICD code. And not every handsome man is necessarily a sociopath—"

At that moment, while Tempest and Ivy were faced off in debate, they hadn't realized that Dixon had stepped up to their booth until he arrogantly ducked inside and wedged himself between them. He held up a piece of pie on a paper plate with two fresh forks jabbed into the top.

"Good morning, ladies! Thought I'd bring you some thimbleberry pie," he boasted with a devilish twinkle in his eye.

"Best in the whole county. After that radio broadcast, you must be starving."

He handed the plate to Tempest first. "Bet this defies your idea that all handsome men are *takers*, huh? You did say on the radio you thought I was *hot*, right?"

Tempest pinned her gaze to her hiking boots, so embarrassed that her throat clasped shut. For once in her life, she couldn't muster a word. Where's that secret trap door to China when you need one? she moaned to herself, her heart lugging with awkward beats.

Dixon appeared to relish the crimson that suffused her cheeks, and he leaned his elbow against her booth to face her. His long legs and tightly-muscled frame made him look as lithe —and as lethal—as a mountain lion as he trained his dark-blue eyes onto her.

"How's the hand?" he asked Tempest with challenge in his tone. "If guys like me are users, wonder why I would have bothered stopping that yearling from dragging you to kingdom come?"

"W-Well," Tempest managed to stammer, angry at herself for stumbling over her words, "you *did* mention you're the Safety Commissioner around here. Heaven knows, if you hadn't stopped Dumpling, he could have charged into somebody else."

Dixon startled Tempest by gently taking her hand and examining the burn mark that had already begun to fade after she'd applied Bag Balm on it last night. He ran his fingers tenderly over the pinkish wound, the careful sensitivity of his warm stroke sending tingles up her arm.

And into a few other places.

Tempest winced—

Not from pain.

But to get rid of those confounded tingles that swirled through her body, which she hadn't felt for a man in a very long time. Much less, one *this* good looking.

"Tell me something," Dixon leaned forward and whispered provocatively in Tempest's ear, "if I'm such a taker, why on earth would I have offered to give your son showmanship lessons?"

Far too many rubber bands snapped inside Tempest's belly for comfort.

Along with those flighty tingles that kept surging, only getting stronger.

Damn, he's even *more* handsome close up, Tempest thought, trying to keep her gaze diverted from his chiseled face. And he smells deliciously like fresh field grass and alpine air—

Tempest closed her eyes for a second to regain control.

Naturally, she understood that Dixon didn't want to see Owen's showing chances ruined due to Dumpling's bad behavior, because he identified with the plight of the boy.

But Dixon was also being generous to her and her son, and Tempest knew it.

The question was—why?

As if he'd read her thoughts, Dixon's lips rose into a half-smile.

"Charity isn't a sin, you know," he said, his voice tinged with a bold confidence that indicated he knew he was getting to her. "Has it ever crossed your mind that I actually *care* about this fair, and the people who show their livestock here?"

Tempest's stomach twisted into tiny knots.

Generosity, altruism, charity—why am I so cynical that I no longer believe such kindness exists, she thought, especially from a *man?* Oh yeah, because the last time I trusted a handsome guy, I got burned beyond belief.

Tempest shot a nervous glance at Ivy, whose brow was raised with a self-satisfied look on her face from Dixon's words, like she'd won a bet.

All at once, the owl at the Trinity's pie booth hooted, making Tempest nearly jump out of her skin. When she glanced in the direction of Granny Tinker and her friends, the three silver-haired women were smiling as if they shared a secret.

"No need to worry about that ruby heart charm," Ivy assured Tempest, wiggling her fingers in a brief wave as she headed out and began to walk toward the pie booth. "I'll let those ladies know they can hang onto it till the end of the fair, as long as they promise to give it back. Heaven only knows what kind of *fun* they're going to have."

"Wait!" Tempest replied, setting Dixon's pie plate down. "At least let me talk to them about when they'll return it—"

Tempest impulsively bounded after Ivy, when she happened to run smack dab into a large, black blockade that moved directly in front of her.

A particularly furry blockade, and it knocked her back on her butt.

Tempest shook her head. When she glanced up, she recoiled at the sudden awareness that she was now nose to nose with a *bear.*

Heart pumping fast, she felt Dixon's strong arms circle

beneath her shoulders and pull her several steps back, then lift her to her feet. It was then she noticed that the bear appeared quite old with a frosted gray nose and a raggedy coat, and his brief yawn demonstrated he was nearly toothless. An old, barrel-chested man in overalls held a lead line attached to a collar around the bear's neck.

"Tempest Wright," Dixon sighed after helping to dust off her back side, "meet my dad, Bear Ramsey." He pointed to the bear. "And his best friend, Bonner."

"Best friend?" Tempest replied, brushing the dirt off her elbows as well. "A wild animal?"

"Well," Dixon explained, "when a bear saves a man from a mountain lion attack ten years ago, that makes him a pretty damn good friend. Unfortunately, Bonner fell off a boulder in the process and broke his back, so my dad took him to a vet for emergency surgery and nursed him back to health. They've been inseparable ever since." Dixon shuffled his boots for a moment in the dirt. "Bonner's like his favorite son."

"Pleased to meet you, ma'am," Bear Ramsey said, extending out his hand to shake Tempest's. Despite his age, his blue eyes glinted with the same bright charisma of Dixon's. "Sorry my Bonner tripped you up. He gets real excited when he spots a pretty woman and just about yanked my arm off to reach you. He may be old, but he's as strong as an ox—and he knows a looker when he sees one."

Tempest shook her head, hardly surprised that lady-killer charm ran in the Ramsey family.

"So what brings you over here, Dad?" Dixon sighed, as though the combination of his father's and the bear's antics were hardly unusual. "Besides your over-eager furry friend."

"Well, I came by to tell you there's an emergency meeting of the Fair Board going on right now. We need you to come to the fairgrounds office lickety split."

"What's wrong, is there trouble with the livestock? Carnival rides working okay? The fair's barely started, and there's already an emergency?"

"Something like that," Bear Ramsey replied with a gleam in his eye. "Reckon you'll see soon enough."

4

"This is madness!" Dixon roared in disbelief.

He stood in front of the small group of ranchers and farmers on the Fair Board who were seated in the fairgrounds office and shifted his gaze to Bonner. The disheveled black bear plunked down on his rump beside his father's folding chair with a "boof" while Dixon tried to ignore the surge of chuckles that filled the room. At least the old bear was too busy chomping down a honey bun to have an opinion.

Dixon held up the sticky slip of paper with his name on it at eye level and squinted as if it were the root of all evil. "Why would any sane group of people pick *me* to be the eligible guy in the Cowboy Roundup?" he asked. "Everybody in the county knows my dating track record is a train wreck. What makes the Fair Board think I could be suitable?"

"Because," Tripp Conway insisted, slipping his thumbs into his faded green overalls and leaning back in his folding chair, "back in the day, folks flocked to our fair from miles around just to see the ladies compete for dinner with the best-looking fella in the county. Last night, we put the names of every man with single status we could think of into a big milk pail. Then we shook it, drizzled it with honey, and the first name Bonner pulled out with his paw was…you!"

To Dixon's annoyance, Bonner echoed Tripp's words between chews of his honey bun with an emphatic "boof."

Dixon tilted his head back in frustration, hardly believing his ears. He drew a breath and glared at old Tripp Conway, who'd been Fair Board President nearly forever.

"I already walked around the fairgrounds this morning," Dixon defended in a measured a tone, thinly disguising his frustration. "Even bought a few pieces of pie. There were plenty of folks purchasing tickets."

"Those are the die hards. The kinds of folks who are always the first ones at yard sales and flea markets," pointed out the Fair Treasurer Faye Simmons, who was almost as old as Tripp with a mind like a steel trap. Her beady eyes narrowed as she held up an official-looking spreadsheet. "Our online ticket pre-sales have plummeted to *half* of what they were last year for opening day," she informed the group. "We need to be more competitive about our attractions. Even Jared Button's donkey, the one he taught to jump from a diving board into a portable pool, only sold an extra fifty tickets last summer. And the contest we held to watch your dad and his bear compete at beer drinking merely sold another hundred. We couldn't do that again even if we wanted to, because your dad told us he quit the booze six months ago."

Dixon sniffed as if he had doubts about his father. "What

about our TV and radio advertising budget?" he persisted. "I thought we were spending twice as much this year."

"We are," confirmed Faye, settling her clasped hands into the lap of her yellow square dancing skirt. "And we doubled our ads. We even brought in Tempest the Terminator from the radio and encouraged her to get a booth. There was an initial spike, but now ticket sales have fallen flat again. Dixon," she warned, "this is an emergency. If we want this county fair to continue, we have to do something drastic."

"Whether you like it or not, we've got to hold the Cowboy Roundup—and you're the star," Tripp insisted. "Faye and I checked the old records, and we found that attendance at the county fair was *triple* what it is today when the Cowboy Roundup first started in 1915, even though there were far less folks living in the area. The event fell out of favor a few decades back because the board got a high-falutin' idea that people prefer slick, new carnival rides to our time-honored dating competition. Unfortunately, that turned out not to be true. According to our recent poll, folks in this county like vintage rides the best. And everybody *loves* the Cowboy Roundup for one basic reason: good old-fashioned sex appeal."

Dixon rolled his eyes at the notion, especially since he'd been bucking hay and cleaning horse stalls earlier that morning. He glanced down at his typically soiled jeans and boots. "How can anybody romanticize cowboys when half the time we smell like a barn?"

"Get over yourself, Dixon—it'll be a hoot!" Faye reprimanded like a seasoned grandma. "All you gotta do is sit back while three ladies take turns at fair games to win a date with you. Then fair goers write their favorite contestant for each day on the backs of their ticket stubs and put them in ballot boxes. The grand prize winner will be announced on the last day of the fair at the Wranglers Waltz and get to ride in a horse-drawn carriage with you to the Golden Wagon Restaurant. What could possibly go wrong?"

She stood in a huff from her folding chair and marched over to a wall, her square dancing skirt bouncing over her thick support hose. Then she pointed to a faded black and white photo that depicted three cowgirls on separate horses in an arena, about to gallop through a hoop lit up with flames. "Of course, we'll make it a little easier on the women compared to 1915—no fire this time around," she chuckled. "And we'll broadcast the front runner every night during the fair on the county's rural TV channel." She shot a glance at Tripp. "In our estimation, tickets should sell like wildfire!"

Dixon shook his head. "Have you forgotten the town gossip about me lately? According to the quilting guild, the bingo league, and every other rumor circle around, there's a reason I'm still single—I'm a dating disaster. Just for kicks, let's review."

He held up a finger.

"My last date took a selfie during the surprise picnic I planned for her and stumbled back and bumped her head, then tumbled down a hill. After I rescued her, she claimed to no longer remember my name. Funny, the doctor said her brain was fine—it's just that her memory had become extremely selective. In other words, I got erased on the spot."

He held up a second finger.

"Another date never told me about her sticky finger habit

until the pawnshop called to ask if I really wanted to sell my six championship saddles. She'd thrown them into the back of her truck, not noticing that my name is tooled into the leather of each one. Later she got arrested, but only after she'd already tried to fence my stuff."

He held up a third finger.

"Then there's the gal who said she had a multiple personality disorder as her excuse for cheating on me during our very first date. After I took her out to dinner and headed to the arena for the steer wrestling competition because she said she wanted to watch, I discovered her behind some hay bales sucking face with a rodeo clown. She told me it's all okay because no one can be held responsible for what their 'alter' did. And besides, at least he made her laugh."

Dixon folded his arms. "Getting the picture? I can tell you half a dozen more——"

"That's why you need fair ticket holders to pick out better women for you!" exclaimed Faye. "Obviously you're attracted to crazy. I hate to say it, Dixon, but the common denominator with all of these hot messes is…you."

Before Dixon could object, his father stood up. "Do I have to remind you, son, that the Fair Board helped us rebuild our barn last August after it got struck by lightning and burned down? That's the way folks do things in Bandits Hollow—they pitch in for the common good. Is it really so hard to go on *one* date to save the fair?"

Dixon surveyed the rugged faces in the small group, each one weathered and etched with the trials and responsibilities of being ranchers and farmers. Deep in his gut, he knew they were the best neighbors anyone could ask for. He heaved a long breath—he owed them one, and he knew it.

"Well," Dixon said resolutely, "I should at least get a couple of rib eyes from Brady's Butcher Shop for agreeing to do this—with a few dinner rolls for Bonner thrown in. If I have to embarrass myself in public, I might as well eat high on the hog. Since Brady is a fair sponsor, I imagine he'll be able to write it off—"

As if in agreement, Bonner tilted his nose in the air and bellowed "boof".

"Deal!" Tripp said, walking up to Dixon and shaking his hand too hard. "Now don't you go skipping the county or anything. We're relying on you to keep your word."

"No worries," Dixon shrugged. "When it comes to dating, I'm nothing if not a glutton for punishment."

Out of the corner of Dixon's eye, he happened to spy through a window that Tempest was outside wrangling with Dumpling's halter to keep him under control. Owen stood next to her, appearing damp and scruffy beside Dumpling as if he'd spent all morning washing and grooming him. Yet this time, Dixon noticed that Tempest held the lead line far more safely, the way he'd taught her, and she even grabbed the yearling around the neck like a WWE champion to make him behave. When the animal settled down, she wagged a finger fiercely in his face if she were giving him a lecture, the way she did to her clients on the radio. Dixon couldn't help but smirk.

Well Tempest, he said to himself, I can't decide which one is the bigger handful, you or that Angus. Thank God you're not part of this dating scheme. Because with your hot temper, you'd probably set the fairgrounds on fire.

Deep within a forest grove that evening, Granny Tinker of the infamous Trinity stepped softly between the towering ponderosas, careful not to allow her crimson lace-up boots to crush any of the tender shoots along the overgrown trail. Under a thin band of moonlight filtering through the trees, she spied what she was looking for.

The mountain wild rose.

The blush-pink flowers on the plant shivered, as though familiar with this night wanderer and expecting her gaze. Just like she did with the fairy slipper when she returned to Bandits Hollow every June, Granny Tinker smiled at the plant with its deep green, oblong leaves and then bowed her head for a moment to ask for its blessing.

When she finished, she pulled a small vial from the pocket of her long, black velvet dress and dipped to her knees. She ran her hand beneath the delicate head of one of the flowers, cautious to avoid the plant's bristles and slender thorns, and plucked the wild rose. As she did so, a breeze began to pick up, whistling through the ponderosas like a faint song, its light melody caressing the long, swaying branches. As if in harmony, crickets started to rub their wings, chirping in a steady rhythm to the gentle wind. Several birds released nighttime chirrups as well, until it seemed to Granny Tinker that the entire grove had begun to tremble with anticipation. Granny gazed at the pretty rose in her hand and stroked its petals, soft as velvet, before plucking them one by one and dropping them into her vial.

The moment she sealed the vial with a small cork, like the disturbance of an invisible portal, an owl began to call through the forest, its voice ominous and commanding. Granny Tinker tucked the vial back into the pocket of her dress like a secret and waited. She closed her eyes as if in prayer.

Before long, a great horned owl alighted on a branch nearby with the ruby heart charm in its talon, glinting in the moonlight that shimmered through the trees. Granny opened her eyes and held out her hand to welcome the heart charm from the bird.

"Good evening, ol' friend," she whispered to the owl. "I do believe that young lady you had your eye on this morning could use our help. She's gonna be a tough one, though, if what folks say about her temper is true." Granny narrowed her eyes and gazed at the charm that still remained in the owl's talon, sparkling in the moonlight. "But I suspect you've gotten a glimpse into her heart, the way you always do."

As the owl descended to the forest floor, in front of her a tall, Native American man appeared, dressed in a long, black coat with shiny brass buttons and deerskin pants along with moccasins. His face was rugged and handsome, with a jagged scar over his angular cheek, and he had long black hair sifted with strands of gray. On his head was a flat-rimmed hat with two owl feathers in the band. He stepped forward and handed Granny Tinker the ruby heart from his palm and folded his large arms. He stared at her with an unflinching gaze.

"The man who was with her this morning. He's like your Virgil," he said. "Outlaw at heart. That road is rough for all who take it. I heard him vow yesterday to help her child. His heart is big for children. The lost, the lonely, the fatherless."

"Children," Granny Tinker nodded, her lips slipping into a smile.

She should have known Iron Feather would say that—and it would be the reason Dixon Ramsey had become his mark. The entire existence of this Native American outlaw had been about helping children. She gazed at her partner in crime from over a century ago, back in 1895 when they used to rob wagons and trains filled with Colorado gold. It was to fund Iron Feather's missions, rescuing children under cover of darkness from government-run boarding schools to bring them back to their Ute and Apache families. Though Iron Feather was a renowned medicine man, far more powerful than anyone Granny Tinker had ever met, she too was known for her gift of sight, having come from Irish Traveller ancestors with a book as thick as a brick that contained her people's every omen, spell, and charm.

Iron Feather had brokered a deal with her back then—if she used her gift to help him find the children and their families, in return he would help her transcend time to come back to the present day, where she was actually from. Then she could continue her work of ferreting out people's secrets and healing hearts. It was Granny Tinker's passion and calling, until she'd gotten tangled up with the love of her life, the notorious outlaw and best friend of Iron Feather, Virgil Hollow. He was the only man who could have ever tempted her to stay in the nineteenth century. But he was a true highwayman who needed to roam this world like he needed to breathe, and Evangeline was a fortune teller who was tethered to her wagon, collecting her magic herbs and stitching broken souls back together.

Neither one could change.

Nor could Iron Feather, who believed in a love that gives and gives and can never be separated by time. Both soft and hard, his heart was as wide as an owl's wings, yet his word was law. And his word was always directed at taking care of children. For Granny Tinker's continued help, to this day he promised to reunite her and Virgil Hollow once a year, with a love that knew no time, each December under the Cold Moon. The portal was Iron Feather's to open and seal—and Granny Tinker took his offer.

"Pearl and Jubilee will help you," he promised. "They're headed here right now—because the magic tracks you."

Tracks...

Granny Tinker trembled a little.

She knew all too well the power of those words—and that she was as marked as anyone Iron Feather had ever targeted with his famous tracking skills.

Did she have regrets? Over discovering the love of her life who'd lived his outlaw days more than a century before her?

Granny Tinker hugged her waist for a moment and closed her eyes.

Never.

As long as Iron Feather brought them back together again every Cold Moon.

Iron Feather studied her face, rimmed by the moonlight that glinted over her long gray hair and extraordinary features—the intense wolfish eyes, regal cheekbones, and full lips that transfixed everyone who saw her. Yes, Evangeline was old now, but just as stunningly beautiful as the day he'd first met her, when she was young and looking for her magic plants. She thought she'd cast a spell in those days to go back in time to find a rare herb, not knowing that it was really Iron Feather who'd summoned her there, enabling her to discover a rare soul in Virgil Hollow. For the woman who prided herself on knitting hearts together, hers had been torn wide open by Virgil's love. Only Iron Feather possessed the power to reunite his best friend each year with the magical woman who'd stolen his heart.

"I must go now," Iron Feather said. His obsidian eyes were as large and stern as always, yet Evangeline spied a slight lift at the corners that hinted at the genuine warmth behind his goodbye.

"You're all he ever wanted," Iron Feather lowered his tone as a kind of benediction. "As it should be."

With that, Iron Feather tipped his hat to Evangeline and turned. As he walked toward the deep shadows of the tall pines, his form began to grow hazy and disappear. At last, she saw the silhouette of an owl that vanished into the darkness.

The ruby heart charm he'd left with her felt warm in her

hand, making her fingers tingle. Then she heard the echo of an owl hooting through the woods, reminding her of her task.

"There you are!" burst a loud voice from behind her.

Granny Tinker turned and saw the portly figure of her old friend Jubilee with her curly gray hair pulled into a bun, flanked by the willowy frame of Pearl. The two women trotted up to her to give her a hug.

"Are you collecting flowers and herbs under the moonlight again?" Jubilee said. "Ain't you got enough magic plants in that old wagon of yours to last a few centuries? We'd best go inside before we catch a chill."

Jubilee glanced back at her old ranch home a mere half mile away, its outline limned by the light from her front porch. "I got some warm coffee and cookies waitin' for us."

Granny Tinker smiled at the two women, revealing her gold front tooth. "I reckon it's better to go to my wagon, ladies. We can have cookies and coffee afterwards."

"Oh my, did you get a witness, Evangeline?" Pearl grabbed her by the shoulders with her small hands. "Some kind of sign in the stars about that radio woman we saw this morning? She's very pretty, even if she does seem rather…obstinate."

"I got more than a witness," Granny replied. She held up the ruby heart. "Iron Feather came tonight with this charm again, like he did this morning at the fair, just to emphasize his point. I mean, he came…in flesh and blood."

Her two friends' faces went pale.

"Really? He did?" Jubilee gasped. "The same man that's in all those old wanted posters of the Bandits Hollow gang?"

Granny nodded slowly. "That's because this match is extra

special to him. This time, it involves helping a child. You know how Iron Feather is—that's all he ever lived for."

Jubilee and Pearl exchanged nervous glances at each other. "No, we don't—folks like us can't ever see that medicine man, except as an owl. Is he as handsome as that old wanted picture?"

Granny Tinker gave them a wry smile.

"Handsomer."

"Ooh Lordy," Pearl grinned. "Evangeline, I swear to the Almighty, between Virgil Hollow and Iron Feather, you certainly have a knack for attracting the best-looking men who ever trod this earth. Even if they are...shall we say...out of time."

"Love is always out of time," Granny replied. "That's why it's embroidered to the eternal. Now come on, ladies. We got ourselves some work to do."

Granny Tinker linked her arms through the elbows of her two friends and steered them toward a large shepherd wagon that sat in a remote section of the forest. It had been built by pioneers who'd once lived in Jubilee's family, and she'd offered it to her friend Evangeline years ago to occupy. Now, the tall, wood-domed wagon on spoked wheels was filled with jars and vials of all sorts of herbs, concoctions, and mysterious potions.

"Tempest and Dixon," Granny sighed. "From what I can tell, there's already enough tension between those two to blow a damn twister through this town." Her lips curled into a faint smile as she gingerly led her friends toward the glow of a lantern hanging by the door of the wagon. "Time to uncork my vial of wild rose petals and get busy, ladies. We'll crack open my spell book and have a nip of whiskey for good measure, then help those two along a little."

She hugged her two friends' elbows tighter to herself and gave them a squeeze. "You know how it is—every time I link a genuine love match, I get to spend just a little bit longer with my Virgil under the Cold Moon."

Pausing for a moment, Evangeline stared up at the nearly full moon and the stars, tilting her head and closing her eyes as though she could hear their far-away songs. Then she heaved a deep breath and opened her eyes.

"But I promise you," she said solemnly, "we've got our work cut out for us. Because that Tempest is one stubborn, rambling star who ain't accustomed to finding much rest in this world."

❧ 6 ❧

The next morning, Tempest was beyond relieved when an old man walked up to her at the fair and slapped a dollar down onto her booth. At least now she could prove to listeners that she *didn't* hate men, and she was just as willing to help them deal with their troubles as anyone else.

"You Tempest the Terminator?" growled the old man in jeans and a faded denim shirt with a threadbare bandana around his neck. The stray pieces of straw stuck to his beard made him look like he'd just finished stacking hay in a barn.

Tempest shifted a glance to Ivy, prepared for this man's issues to be rather thorny. "Yes, I am," she smiled, hoping to warm up his attitude. She made sure to speak directly into her mike, since they were broadcasting her morning radio show. Ivy dutifully held up a microphone to the old man so that listeners could hear him.

"Good," he groused. "Because my wife just hit me again."

"Oh no!" Tempest blurted, slightly confused since his face didn't show any bruises. Yet she knew there were many sneaky ways to abuse the elderly. "If you don't have anyone to help you, I'll be happy to close my booth right now and take you to the emergency room. Mister...um, what is your name?"

"Bill," the old man replied. "And I ain't angling to go to no hospital. What I mean is, my wife hit me up again for more money to play bingo. It's the sixth time this month! Lately, she's been logging in to an online bingo site on some island off South America and blowing every dollar we got."

"I see," Tempest nodded. "Well, Bill, your wife has what we professionals call a gambling addiction. You don't have to go to Las Vegas to lose your life savings these days. And I suspect the gambling site she's been visiting isn't legal in the US, so there's no telling how much money she can run through. But may I offer you a little advice?"

"Sure, shoot," replied Bill. "That's why I'm here."

"Stop giving her money. Then hide your family jewels, silver, and any other valuables you might have and insist that she enroll in therapy to face her addiction."

Bill began to wring his hands. Despite his weathered, jug-jawed face and rugged rancher's clothing, he dipped his head for a moment and clenched his hands tighter to stop them from trembling.

"She says if I don't give her more money," Bill mentioned softly, "she'll leave me."

Tempest saw Ivy's mouth drop at the cruel pressure put on Bill. She crossed her arms as her lips straightened into a firm line.

"Hold on," Tempest said, her tone drenched in suspicion, "how *long* have you actually been married to this woman?"

"Six months," Bill replied. "We courted after my Emily passed on. We met at the local bingo hall—it all seemed rather quick."

"It was more than quick," Tempest insisted, gently setting her hand on top of his. She could feel Bill's knuckles shake inside her palm. "It was downright predatory. Any woman who starts blowing through piles of your money within six months as a newlywed wasn't trying to marry you. She was after your bank account."

Bill glanced up at Tempest, his eyes resembling a nervous rabbit's and rimmed at the corners with tears. Tempest's heart broke for him, and she clutched his hands even harder.

"Listen Bill, I want you to freeze all of your accounts from any access to her. And then, this is the big one—are you ready?"

Bill sucked a breath and nodded.

"Kick her out. Now. You go home, tell her to pack her things, and arrange for her own ride to her next living circumstances. Then I highly suggest you talk to a therapist *and* a lawyer to inquire about filing for divorce."

Bill's mouth trembled slightly as he stared down at Tempest's hand wrapped over his. His lips attempted to form words, impaired by his own grief while a few tears escaped his eyes.

Tempest kept her grip firm on his hands. She snuck a peek at Ivy who, predictably, had tears slipping down her face as well. Her intern was so caught up in feeling sorry for Bill that she was unprepared for the bomb that Tempest was about to drop. But Tempest had been a therapist for too long not to notice the psychological signs.

"Your wife *did* hit you, didn't she Bill?" Tempest challenged. "Somewhere clever that wouldn't show in public. When you were reluctant to give her more money. Am I right?"

Bill's face swelled with a red hue, and he nodded, ashamed.

Tempest withdrew her hand from his and laid down her microphone, then stepped out of her booth. She walked around to face Bill and hugged him, allowing him to crumple into her arms. "That's a criminal offense, Bill," she told him, "and my intern Ivy will call Officer Barrett Iron Feather right now to take care of this situation—"

"No need for that," a voice contended from behind her.

Tempest released Bill and swiveled to see Dixon Ramsey holding up his cell phone.

"I already called Officer Iron Feather as soon as you mentioned the word predatory on the radio. This man is one of my dearest friends and neighbors, and I'm ashamed I didn't realize what was going on. I told Officer Iron Feather I'd give Bill a lift to the station so they can get the whole story. Bill doesn't have any family left, and it's my honor to support him." Dixon gazed at the old man, his midnight-blue eyes filled with a caring softness Tempest had never seen before. "I'm truly sorry I didn't notice the signs myself, Bill."

Bill nodded at Dixon, his gaze appearing relieved that a friend had volunteered to stand by him.

To Tempest's amazement, Dixon boldly grabbed her broadcasting microphone from the booth. "Thanks for listening today, folks," he said, in as cheerful a voice as he could muster. "Sometimes happy endings take a little longer than we expect." He gave Bill a warm smile. "But with the right kind of friends, they'll come around in the end. Until tomorrow, have a tippity-top, triumphant day."

With that, Dixon set the microphone back onto the booth and slung his arm around Bill's shoulders, hugging him tight as if to hold the old man up. Then he proceeded to lead him toward the parking lot, aiming for a vintage green truck. After they took several strides, Dixon paused and turned his head, mouthing the words *thank you* back at Tempest. Tempest nodded as Dixon and Bill continued their beeline for the pickup, with the old man firmly under Dixon's wing.

Now it was Tempest's turn to cry.

She folded her arms against her waist and bowed her head, stoically attempting to hide the emotion that seeped from her eyes. Before she knew it, Ivy had wrapped her arms around her.

"I *knew* you were a softie!" Ivy exclaimed. She released Tempest and gazed into her eyes. "You may talk tough, but your heart feels as deeply as mine does. No wonder everybody loves your show—you get to the heart of things and genuinely help people." Then she caught something unusual behind Tempest from the corner of her eye.

It moved slowly and steadily, like a large shadow, before pausing beside a milk pail that was perched onto an oak barrel.

"Hey, look at those three ladies over there," Ivy squinted, her tone laced with curiosity. "In dark period clothing, like they just stepped of a historical reenactment. Isn't that the

Trinity? Why are they hovering over a milk pail instead of at
their pie booth?"

Tempest looked over her shoulder at Granny, Jubilee and
Pearl in their typical pioneer dresses, circled around a metal,
double-handled milk pail that looked like it had come from an
old-fashioned dairy. The milk pail had a lid with a slot cut into
it, and the three old women glanced around before they
dropped handfuls of rose petals into the opening.

Ivy and Tempest blinked as a spiral of sparkles began to
rise from the milk pail. It glistened like a swirl of wandering
stars that soon dissipated under the bright, early morning sun.

"D-Did you see that?" Ivy muttered. She noticed
Tempest's eyes had grown as large as plates.

"Oh, those ladies are probably just finishing something for
the arts and crafts competitions," Tempest dismissed. "You
know, like some kind of glittery, milk pail potpourri? That
woman at our booth yesterday said they're weird."

"No, she didn't—she said they're matchmakers!" Ivy
giggled. "And they dabble in magic. Otherwise, how could that
glitter rise in the air? Isn't that against the law of physics or
something?" Ivy clutched Tempest's arm. "You don't think
they've cast a spell, do you?"

At that moment, the three women of the Trinity turned to
gaze in the direction of Tempest as if a spotlight had focused
on her. Granny Tinker smiled broadly, the sun glinting off her
gold front tooth.

"What's really exciting," Ivy continued in a low tone, "is
that I heard people gossiping yesterday that the Trinity can't
make anyone fall in love who doesn't really want to. That
means it's for *real!*"

"Count me out," Tempest retorted. "Because with everything going on in my busy life, I'm definitely off the market."

"What if they know your heart better than you do?" Ivy countered. "The same way you see inside your clients' denials? Besides, you're wearing a charcoal shirt today, the same hue as a pewter chalice. That means you're receptive to a grand and chivalrous kind of love!"

"Oh Ivy, you say that about *every* color!" Tempest replied. "It was dark when I put on my shirt this morning. I didn't even pay attention to what I was doing."

"All the better!" Ivy confirmed. "Then it came straight from your subconscious will."

Tempest was about to ramp up her arguments with her intern, when she happened to notice that the three old women appeared to nod in agreement before they started to amble away, heading back to their pie booth. Tempest issued a breath of relief that their spookiness seemed done for the day. A few seconds later, however, she spotted the fair announcer walking up to the milk pail on the oak barrel. He picked it up and gave the pail a few hard shakes. Then he used a key to unlock a padlock on the lid and reached inside, holding up a ticket while a young man came up to him with a video recorder on his shoulder. The two men conversed for a moment, when they suddenly turned toward Tempest and brazenly pointed their fingers. Without warning, they began to dash toward her. The cameraman thrust his recorder into her face.

"Good morning, everyone!" the announcer cried. "We have some big news at the fair today. Tempest Wright is our very first female contestant for the Cowboy Roundup!"

At that moment, Tempest vaguely recalled being asked to write her name on her entrance ticket that morning by the admission man at the gate before he ripped it and gave her back the stub. He must have put it into the milk pail for whatever kind of lottery this is, she thought.

"Can you believe it?" the announcer said. "None other than Tempest the Terminator has been chosen to compete with two other women in special fair events for the handsomest cowboy in our county!"

"What the hell?" Tempest muttered, looking like a deer in the headlights for the camera that nearly touched her nose. The pushy cameraman who had *Bandits Hollow Rural TV* printed across his t-shirt grinned.

"Not hell—heaven!" The announcer laughed at Tempest's response, which was simultaneously being broadcasted for everyone to see in a live video on the large scoreboard above the outdoor arena. "You now have the chance to win the grand prize of a free dinner at the Golden Wagon Restaurant with the best-looking cowboy we could find. We're even going to throw in a ride to the restaurant in the famous, horse-drawn golden wagon. You'll feel like a princess!"

"What if I don't want to—"

Ivy abruptly stomped on Tempest's boot.

"Shh," she said in a vehement whisper. "This is your big chance to prove yourself to the 4-H moms, like you're always claiming you want to do. By showing you can be a team player for the sake of the fair. They're probably doing all of this for publicity."

Tempest bit her lip, then forced a fake grin for the camera, despite how much her foot hurt. God almighty, Ivy was right—

she *did* want to be accepted in the 4-H crowd, especially since her son Owen was so dedicated to the upcoming competition. Reluctantly, she threw back her shoulders and decided to bite the bullet.

"Wow, dinner at the best restaurant in town?" Tempest managed to say to the camera. "Oh my gosh, that's wonderful. So who's the lucky fella I'm supposed to compete for to get a date?"

In a flash, the image of Dixon Ramsey lit up the digital scoreboard that towered over the outdoor arena with his name in bright letters. The camera swooped toward the scoreboard to capture his ridiculously handsome image in a well-worn cowboy hat.

Tempest's face fell in shock.

"Whoa!" crooned the announcer. "You'd better put that pretty smile back on pronto, Tempest, if you wanna win the grand prize! Because you've gotta contend with two other lovely women who are about to be chosen for the Cowboy Roundup. And the first round of competitions starts *tomorrow!*"

7

"Okay, honey," Tempest directed Owen, "finish putting those books into boxes so we can wrap up everything here. The fair's going to shut down in a few minutes for the evening."

As the sun began to cast long shadows over the fairgrounds, Owen did as he was told, and helped his mother to stack the book boxes into a corner of her booth. Tempest pulled down the large plywood planks she'd attached to hinges at the top so she could lock up her radio equipment along with her book boxes till the following day. When she finished securing her booth, she turned to Owen and tousled his cottony, blonde hair.

"Thanks for being my helper, sweetie," she said, grateful to have his assistance since Ivy left each evening at five. Tempest checked her cell phone. It was seven o'clock already, making her gut tighten into knots.

Dixon wasn't there.

And he *promised* he would be.

Two days ago, Dixon had told Owen that he'd start giving him lessons this evening on advanced cattle showmanship. He even warned him to be on time.

Tempest wanted stop wringing her hands, but she couldn't keep from gnarling her fingers together. There was so much at stake, and all of her doubts crowded into her chest until she felt like her heart had become a lead weight.

What if Dixon flaked out?

What if he broke his promise and disappointed Owen, just like her late husband had done a million times?

And more importantly, why on earth had she *trusted* him?

Sure, Tempest thought, Dixon was kind to Owen when Annie wanted to kick his yearling out of 4-H. And he was very generous to escort Bill to the police station. But two nice deeds didn't necessarily make for strong character, right? Heaven knows, the last thing Owen needed was another male figure who violated his ability to trust again.

And if she was going to be perfectly honest, that's the last thing *she* needed, too.

Tempest snuck a glance at her son, who'd sat down on the ground with his elbows perched on his knees. He slumped his chin into his palms.

Her heart dropped.

Owen had the *same* distant look in his eyes and stoic demeanor that he'd always worn when his dad hadn't shown up for a soccer game, or a class play, or whatever else Owen had been involved in. Poor Owen had learned long ago not to bother crying or throwing tantrums, because such behavior didn't do him a lick of good.

Tempest swallowed at the lump in the back of her throat. She wanted to offer to get Owen ice cream, or maybe a new basketball, but she knew by this point in his life that those perks were just another clear signal to him that he'd been abandoned again. Instead, she forced in a breath and decided to spill the truth, just like she always did for her therapy clients.

"Well, Owen, looks like we'd better go home. Because there sure isn't anything to look forward to here."

"Hold on, little dogie!" hollered a deep voice from behind them. "You've gotta be the most contrary critter this county's ever seen!"

Tempest and Owen whipped around, spying Dixon Ramsey with Dumpling in a head lock again. In spite of Dixon's strong hold, the yearling attempted to buck and rear against him with little success. But that didn't stop Dumpling from trying.

"Holy cow! Or bull, in this case," Dixon exclaimed with his wide, swashbuckling grin as if he were enjoying every second of the challenge. "We sure have our work cut out for us with this wild thing, don't we Owen?"

Dixon dug his boot heels into the dirt as he approached Tempest and Owen to force the animal to an abrupt stop. Even he panted from the exertion. "We'd better rassle Dumpling over to my place right now to get some training in before it gets dark."

Owen beamed like the sun rose and set over Dixon Ramsey, his sweet little mouth breaking into the biggest smile Tempest had ever seen.

"Why are you late?" Tempest asked, still struggling to decompress from the letdown she thought for certain was going to happen. She hated herself for allowing her mood to be triggered so easily, but she couldn't help it—years of neglect from her late husband had created well-worn paths inside her mind to expect dejection.

Dixon jerked Dumpling's head to make him finally behave and stop wriggling. He stared at Tempest with a solemn look in his blue eyes that surprised her.

"You remember Bill, your last booth client? Let's just say I helped his so-called wife pack up and move out of his ranch house this afternoon. Then I went to town to hire a locksmith to get the locks changed, so Bill won't have to worry about her anymore."

Tempest's breath hitched.

That was the *third* deeply caring thing Dixon had done since the moment she'd met him, maybe even the *fourth*—if she counted the way he'd stopped Dumpling before he could destroy her and her booth two days ago. Tempest's cheeks suffused with pink.

"Why, Tempest the Terminator," Dixon gloated, "is that an actual blush I see on your face? You didn't think I was gonna ditch you two, just because I was a few minutes late, did you? As Safety Commissioner of the fair, it's my job to make sure *all* children are protected while they show their livestock— including Owen with this feisty Angus. So come on, follow me to my ranch next door and we'll start putting Dumpling through his paces."

Dixon smiled and hoisted Owen on top of Dumpling to get a ride while they walked over to his ranch.

"What are you doing? That animal's dangerous!" Tempest reached out her hands for her son before Dixon stopped her.

"I'm training both the yearling and your son," Dixon stated firmly, staring at her with that stern gaze again. It was the kind of look that said *You don't know what the hell you're doing lady, so back off.*

Tempest was so unnerved by the gravity of Dixon's expression that it made her freeze.

"Notice anything?" Dixon asked, a warm glint returning to his eyes.

Aside from that fact that Owen was glowing with happiness—more than she'd seen in the entire year since his father died—Tempest wasn't quite sure what Dixon meant.

"He ain't bucking!" Dixon erupted into a big grin as he began to lead the yearling with Owen on his back, heading toward a gate at the far west end of the fairgrounds. "I tested Dumpling out in his paddock before I brought him over here. It's funny, some livestock calm down the minute you get on them, because they feel more peaceful when you demonstrate that you're the alpha. Then all they have to do is follow your lead. Herd animals like horses and cattle look forward to the guidance of an alpha leader—and it turns out Dumpling is no exception."

"What if he starts bucking or charges off?"

"Like he did with you? You survived, didn't you?" Dixon reminded her. "No worries—first of all, we're going to make sure your son is safe." Dixon led Dumpling over to a fencepost beside the outdoor arena's bucking chute that had a spare helmet hanging from it. He set it on Owen's head and carefully adjusted the straps to make it fit. "And second of all," he continued, "the more Owen lets Dumpling know who's boss, the less this animal is going to terrorize him or anybody else. Riding a horse or a cow is all about showing them you're the leader."

Regardless of Dixon's assuring words, Tempest walked on the other side of Dumpling so she could catch Owen in an instant, should he begin to fall. As they covered more ground, Tempest began to realize that the animal really *was* relaxing, seeming more like a fuzzy, red teddy bear rather than his usual, tyrannical self. Although Tempest's heart rate had finally slowed down with Dumpling's new-found calmness, she wasn't fooled—this could be another one of his passive-aggressive maneuvers to get people to lower their guard.

Fortunately, by the time the three of them reached the west fairgrounds gate and Dixon pulled out his staff key to unlock it and lead Owen and Dumpling through, Tempest had become more confident and at ease with the whole idea. As they walked into a fresh, green meadow on the other side of the gate, she heaved a breath, allowing herself to settle a little.

"Are you sure this isn't your newfangled way to get a date?" Tempest ribbed Dixon, listening to the way their feet swished against the lush grass adjacent to the fairgrounds. "You know, I heard you got roped into the Cowboy Roundup as the eligible guy. What kind of man needs the Fair Board to set him up with women?" She arched a brow to tease him. "Maybe you could use some of my relationship advice after all?"

Dixon grew oddly quiet. He led Dumpling forward with purposeful strides past a thick grove of ponderosas until a large ranch house came into view. His silence made Tempest uneasy, and she was glad when he finally cleared his throat.

"Haven't you caught any of the town gossip lately?" Dixon replied. He stared for a moment at the thick meadow grass, speckled with alpine flowers. Then he gazed at the cattle that dotted a hill in the distance before releasing a huff. "Don't tell me you're the last person in the county to know about my dating track record. Let's just say I'm the man considered the least likely to."

Tempest had no idea what he was talking about.

"Least likely to what?" she asked.

Dixon shook his head and kept plodding forward. "Least likely to be…successful. In a long term relationship, I mean. All the women I've dated have been train wrecks."

Tempest felt the prickles rise up the back of her neck that she could potentially join that company.

"Really? Because…*I'm* about to be one of them."

Dixon stopped in his tracks, holding up a hand to steady Owen on top of Dumpling.

"What are you talking about?"

Tempest tossed her hands in the air with a sheepish grin. "Didn't you get the memo? I was picked as the first contestant to compete for you in the Cowboy Roundup."

Dixon sucked air. Then he bent over laughing.

"Tempest the Terminator? The Queen of Tough Love? If that don't sound like some kooky kind of karma, I don't know what does. Near as I can tell from the rumor mill in this town, we *both* have a reputation for being the least likely to. You for slicing and dicing every man a woman gripes about, and me for having a really bad habit of picking…crazy."

"Unless," Tempest defended herself, "you believe all that stuff they say about Granny Tinker. Ivy and I saw her and her cohorts this morning sprinkling something into the milk pails they used to pull out the tickets with contestants' names."

"Those old gals?" Dixon rolled his eyes. He began to take long, swinging strides, leading Dumpling and Owen forward again. "Don't worry, just because they're best friends and Granny Tinker sells wares from her wagon doesn't mean they run riot with magic. From what everyone says, she can't make folks do a damn thing they don't want to. She and her pals just have a knack for…nudging them forward. And I, for one, am taking a break from relationships. I'm only going along with this to help publicize the fair."

"Good," Tempest replied way too fast. She exhaled a breath, embarrassed that her relief showed all over her face. "Besides, the Fair Board chose two other contestants this afternoon from the ticket lottery—a gal in her twenties named Blossom Barnhart and the woman who runs the *Happy Homebaked* food truck."

"Hedda Grimson?" Dixon began to chuckle again. "Honey, you'd better watch out. Hedda was Miss Outlaw Days Rodeo Queen in the 1960s, which means she's one hell of a competitor. Back then, it wasn't enough to be beautiful—you had to be able to shoot a bull's-eye and trick ride on horses."

"Oh," Tempest replied. "They aren't going to make us do things like that, are they?"

"Sure hope so," he grinned. "Because I'd love to see what Tempest the Terminator can do with a pistol. Just don't aim it my way, okay?"

"Then don't give me a reason to," she quipped, trying her best to appear nonchalant, even though the thought of handling a weapon made her uneasy. Luckily, Dixon changed the subject by pointing to a dirt road up ahead that led to a massive gate.

The gate featured random black stars over its wrought-iron bars, and above it were the words *Rambling Star Ranch* burnt into a giant wood beam that hovered over the entrance to the road. Beside the gate was an official-looking sign that said *Winner of the Remuda Award & Home of the World's Greatest Performance Horses*.

"There it is—my ranch." Dixon nodded, surveying the sprawling estate that included several barns and corrals, along with green, rolling hills as far as the eye could see. He turned to Owen and patted him on the back. "You ready to get down to business?"

"Sure am!" Owen replied excitedly. "What's a rem…" He stumbled to try and pronounce the word on the sign. "A remu—"

"A remuda?" Dixon finished for him. "That's Spanish for *remuda de caballos*, or change of horses. In cowboy lingo, that means a herd of horses for sale that are both well-bred *and* well behaved. Let's head over to my training corral to make sure Dumpling earns the same reputation."

Dixon halted Dumpling and lifted Owen from the waist to help him down from the animal. Then he looped the yearling's lead line in a figure eight to make sure Owen knew how to hold it in a safe manner inside his hand.

Despite Dixon's careful attention to detail, all Tempest could do was inhale deeply and close her eyes for a second to say a quiet prayer.

"Please God," she whispered under her breath, "surround my boy with your heavenly angels while he works with Dumpling. Because that yearling sure can be a devil."

8

"All right, Owen," Dixon instructed the boy in his outdoor training corral, "repeat the terms for Dumpling's anatomy that we went over and point to where each part is. It's not enough to just parade your yearling around in the show arena. You need to know all the parts of the animal and what will be judged the most, so you can try to accentuate those features with good grooming."

Dixon threw a cautionary glance at Tempest, who'd been banished to sitting on the corral fence to watch her son. He'd already ordered her *not* to call out the answers to Owen, nor was she to mouth the correct words from a distance, because clearly both would be cheating. Given that she was prone to "hover", as Dixon called it, he warned her that she could either head to the fence willingly, or he'd pick her up and carry her there.

Tempest had grumbled, but when Dixon arched a brow like he was about to hoist her in his arms against her will, she huffed and turned on her heels to head to the fence on her own two feet.

Owen snuck a glance at his mother, then studied Dumpling with a determined look on his face. He aimed a finger at the slight dome on the yearling's head between his ears. "Poll?" he guessed, checking Dixon for validation. Dixon gave him a nod, and Owen nervously gulped another breath. "Loin?" he said, gesturing at the center of Dumpling's back. Dixon encouraged him to keep going by tapping his palm on the animal's hindquarters. "Rump," Owen added, smiling when Dixon gave him an additional nod. With more confidence now, he ran through as many parts as he could recall, until Dixon slid his hand from the edge of Dumpling's jaw to an area of loose skin that ended at his shoulder.

"What's this part?" Dixon asked Owen.

Owen scratched his head, studying the animal's chest. "Brisket?"

"Close!" Dixon replied. "Give it another try."

Owen chewed his lip, his gaze tracing down the yearling's neck, appearing stymied.

"Dewlap," Dixon informed him. "That's the fold of skin along cattle's necks that's bigger on the Simmental breed than Angus, and can help you tell them apart." He patted the boy's shoulder with a smile. "Do you realize you got twenty-five out of thirty parts of the cow correct?" He gave him a high five. "That's great! I can tell you've really done your homework with Annie's 4-H club. Now what other facts can you tell me about your yearling?"

"Can I come down now?" Tempest protested from the fence.

Dixon turned and glared at her with a cold, stop-helicoptering gaze that made her recoil. It wasn't like she knew the answers anyway—she just couldn't help wanting to keep Owen protected from Dumpling's notoriously unpredictable moods.

"Go on," Dixon urged Owen to ignore his mother and focus. "What else should you be able to tell me about Dumpling's physique?"

Owen scanned Dumpling's stature, examining him for any strengths and weaknesses. "Miss Annie told me he's got good bone even though he's kind of leggy. But his body is pretty square, like beef cattle are supposed to be."

"How about his legs?" Dixon asked. "Are they straight, or angling in or out? What ranchers call bow-legged or cow-hocked."

Owen stepped a yard in front of Dumpling to study the way the yearling stood. He squinted and knelt down to get a good look at his legs. "Um, his hooves point straight ahead, like Miss Annie said they should. And his knees and hocks don't twist one way or the other." Owen paused. "I think that means he's good."

"He is!" confirmed Dixon, giving Dumpling an affectionate stroke on the back. "He's a little tall for an Angus, which is probably why he can run so fast. And it's odd that there are nubs between his ears where you can tell his horns were cut off, most likely when he was three months old. Most Angus are bred to be polled, meaning they don't have horns. Hopefully, you won't get too many points taken off for his conformation. But overall, he has a fine, beefy stature."

Owen grinned proudly and straightened his body to a

standing position. He was about to step forward and grab the yearling's halter when Dumpling ducked his head.

And proceeded to ram him.

"Owen!" Tempest yelped, leaping down from the fence. She dashed over to her toppled son, who was lying in the dirt, faster than she knew she was able. Immediately, she dug her hands beneath him to lift him to his feet.

That is, until Dixon tore her son away.

"What are you doing?" Tempest accused in fury, reaching out her arms. "Give me my son!"

"Nothin' doin'," Dixon replied, planting his hand on her chest to keep her away. He dipped his head and glared like he was about to charge her the same way Dumpling did to Owen. Even so, Tempest refused to retreat, flailing her arms toward her son. To her surprise, Dixon grabbed her by the shoulder and dug in his fingers, indicating he meant business.

"You either get back on that fence," he ordered, "or I'll tell Annie your son has quit the fair and 4-H club altogether. You got that? Because you won't be in the ring come show time, and Owen has to learn how to stand up to this animal on his own without *any* help. If you don't let him do that, I refuse to put my stamp of approval on the safety of this yearling. So what's it gonna be, Tempest? Are you going back to that fence right now, or should I return you both with Dumpling to the fairgrounds and call this Owen's loss?"

"Mom!" Owen wailed with piercing urgency. "Let me try again! I can do it!"

A lump spiked in Tempest's throat. How on earth could she let him? How could she possibly stop trying to protect her son, even though he was pleading for her to back off? She stiffened, feeling paralyzed.

Dixon released her shoulder. "Look, I'm sorry about grabbing you so hard," he admitted, shaking his head. "It was just a reflex. But I mean it about Owen. You can't fight this battle. It's for Owen to conquer."

Tempest sank, feeling as if Dixon had knocked the wind out of her. Yet every time she looked into Owen's sweet eyes, what she didn't see was fear or pain. But rather...

Desperation.

He really *wanted* this. To show his very own yearling—by himself.

"Okay," she relented with a crack in her voice, trying to hide the fact that her nerves were still popping from the adrenaline of dashing to Owen. "I'll go back to the fence and let him take charge." She glanced at Dixon with a pleading look, a look that said, *For the love of God, please don't let any harm come to my son.*

Dixon's deep-blue eyes poured into Tempest's with a strength that took her aback. His gaze didn't promise he'd make things perfect for Owen, nor that he'd let him quit if he got head-butted again. His eyes simply reflected a steel will that said, *I'm going to be there for your son, no matter what happens.*

Tempest backed up her steps slowly, finding it nearly impossible not to collect Owen in her arms. She inhaled a deep breath, drawing in the courage she needed to turn and walk back to that fence.

Alone.

Once there, she climbed up the rails and sat on her hands on top of the fence, just to remind herself to stay put.

"I *will* let Owen do this," she mumbled softly as her mantra. "I *will* let him do this."

"Owen," Dixon instructed loudly so Tempest could hear, "it's time for you to dominate this yearling and be in control, not the other way around." He handed him the lead line with the figure eight of the slack in his palm like he'd taught him. "Hold on firm to this lead and don't back down or take any guff."

As Owen proceeded to walk forward a few strides, tugging on the yearling to follow, Dumpling quickly trotted to catch up. Then the animal swung his shoulder hard and knocked Owen back onto the ground. Only this time, Owen didn't pop up with his usual smile.

Tempest saw red.

Damn Dixon's orders all to hell! she thought. She instantly tore toward her son, screaming like a banshee.

Without missing a beat, Dixon slid between her and her son for a body block, but he got more than he bargained for. Tempest slammed right into him as hard as Dumpling had done to Owen.

"Jesus, you got some force, woman!" Dixon blurted.

"That's nothing—get out of my way!" Tempest demanded. "I'll show that yearling who's boss—"

"No, you won't!"

Dixon picked Tempest up like he'd threatened, one arm around her back and the other anchored beneath her legs. He began to march with angry strides across the corral to the fence.

"Put me down! My son's been hurt!" she cried.

"Not until you promise to listen to me," Dixon replied coldly.

"How do you know he's even conscious? We need to call an ambulance!"

"Because he whispered he was okay before you reached him."

"Kids don't know when they're okay!" Tempest railed. "Put me down!"

Dixon shoved his face into hers.

"Yes, they do, Tempest. I saw what happened—and Owen didn't hit his head. Besides, the dirt's soft. He simply got shoved aside by the animal and it startled him. Once a kid can talk, we know they're all right, as long as there was no head injury."

"But—" Tempest wriggled fiercely to free herself.

"I'll only put you down if you promise to sit on the fence and stop interfering. Do I have to tie you with ropes to those rails?"

Tempest slumped in his arms.

"Yes," she said defiantly.

Dixon began to chuckle at her stubbornness, yet his arms held firm.

"No," she finally conceded in a more truthful tone.

Dixon set her gently onto the top fence rail. Then he placed his large hands on her shoulders. The tender way he looked into her eyes made a shiver course through her.

"You've got to let Owen win this one," he urged. "Or that yearling will never respect him. And Owen will never respect himself unless you start getting out of the way."

Tempest folded into her chest like she'd been punched in the gut.

"But he's only eight!" she glanced up and reminded him.

"Yeah, close to the same age I was when I used to have to slap my dad's cheeks when he got drunk after my mom died. To wake him up and run the ranch so we wouldn't lose it. There comes a time when you have to stand, Tempest—even if life hasn't been fair to you. Owen *wants* to compete in 4-H. It's his big dream— you heard him say so yourself. So let him rise to the challenge. It's called courage. Self-respect. Confidence, and all the life skills he's going to need to get along in this world. I mean, without...a dad."

Dixon paused for a moment as if wrestling with his own dark memories. Tempest saw his jaw clench and twist.

"Let me tell you," Dixon continued, "I know all about what it's like to navigate life without help from a true father figure. Owen wants this like crazy, Tempest, so let him do it."

"Do you promise he won't get hurt?" she begged, her voice faltering a little.

"No. I promise I'll stick with him and help every way I can. That's all. This is Owen's responsibility, *his* mountain to climb. So the bigger question is, do you believe in him or not?"

Once again, it felt to Tempest like he'd taken another swing to her stomach.

"Well, do you?" Dixon persisted. "Because you've *got* to, if you ever want him to become strong."

Tears rimmed the corners of Tempest's eyes. Dixon brushed a curly lock of wayward light brown hair from her forehead. He studied her face.

"As strong as *you*, Tempest," he whispered.

At that moment, she gritted her teeth and tried with all her might not to let any more tears well up. To distract herself, she fixed her gaze on her dusty boots. It was true—she *had* been strong. For as long as she could remember. But it had never occurred to her that in momma-bear mode, she wasn't allowing Owen to develop his own willpower and perseverance. And she had to admit Dixon was right about her hovering tendencies. After all, she'd nixed skateboarding this year because it was too dangerous. And certainly BMX bike races—those kids crash all the time. And of course, learning to snowboard had been a definite no.

Now here they were with Owen, who wanted more than anything to wrestle with a creature over ten times his weight. She snuck a peek back at her son, only to see him standing and petting Dumpling with that familiar grin stretching from ear to ear.

Like usual, he was loving every minute of it.

This is karma, isn't it? she thought. My son has dived headlong into the most dangerous thing he could find. Or that I would allow, anyway.

Tempest hauled in a weary breath.

Dixon saw the look of comprehension in her eyes. For a moment, he shrouded her with his broad shoulders and tall height.

"If you'll let me," Dixon said, "I'll teach Owen some bulldogging tricks so this is unlikely to happen again. Unless he wants it to, of course. Owen sure does seem to like rolling in the dirt with Dumpling."

Dixon tweaked Tempest's chin.

"Come on, laugh a little. That was a joke! You know, you're awfully pretty when you're upset."

Tempest bunched into a ball with her fists tight like she was ready to aim a punch at him. But then her face crinkled into a laugh.

"That was a good one," she admitted. "You knew that sexist comment would get me riled, didn't you?"

Dixon bit back a smirk, his eyes twinkling. "You're not that hard to read, Tempest. It's easy to get you going."

At that moment, his midnight-blue eyes locked on hers, as though he really *could* see her strength. Her challenges, her pain.

Her soul…

Tempest winced.

Is this just another one of his lady-killer maneuvers to make women feel vulnerable? she wondered. One minute he's arrogant as hell, the next he's so damn…insightful. Quite the routine to get women to drop their guard. Tempest attempted to steel her face, hoping to not be an easy target.

"I know I talk a good line," Dixon remarked as if he'd detected her thoughts, "and I poke fun sometimes. But I do admire you, Tempest. You're trying to do the best for your son. I never had a parent like that. But for now, your best means backing off. Stop being Tempest the Terminator, and let Owen figure out some things for himself."

Tempest hung her head.

Why does he have to be *right* all of a sudden? she thought, grimacing. It's so much easier to deal with Dixon when he's a jerk.

"Stepping back is really…hard…for me," she confessed.

"I know it is. It's written all over your face." Dixon slowly scanned her features as his lips slipped into his typical cocky smile. "And such a *lovely* face."

Tempest gathered a breath to object, only to catch herself and let out an amused sigh.

"You knew that would get to me, too, huh?" she replied, finally ready to give in. "Okay, I'll let Owen keep trying. But you might have to tie me to this fence with rope after all to keep me from protecting my son."

"Hmm, that could be fun." Dixon rubbed his chin. "Restraining a beautiful woman so she's at my mercy."

Tempest rolled her eyes. "When do you ever quit?"

"Never." Dixon flashed one of his charming smiles. He gently grasped her shoulder and gave it a jiggle. "You're a good mom," he assured her. "Don't forget that."

Dixon then released her shoulder and turned to face her son.

"Hey Owen!" he cried out confidently as he jogged toward the boy. "How about if I teach you some bulldogging tactics to deal with Dumpling?" When he reached the boy, he patted him on the back.

"Okay!" Owen replied, his eyes lighting up.

Tempest exhaled a tired breath. As much as she hated it, this training session was clearly what her son wanted.

"The key for you is to establish with Dumpling that you're the boss," Dixon told Owen, reaching for the yearling's lead line and handing it to him.

Dumpling threw his head and pawed the ground, appearing to enjoy the prospect of another battle with the boy.

"There he is, acting aggressive again," Dixon observed. "So what are you going to do?"

Owen got a mischievous look on his face. He darted around to Dumpling's rump and grabbed his tail, giving it a hard yank.

"Don't pull his tail!" Dixon scolded, tearing him away. "No wonder you two are always rassling." He threw Dumpling a fierce look that made the animal think twice about ramming Owen. "First of all, he could kick you. And given that he's about a thousand pounds, his kicks pack a powerful wallop. Second of all, to Dumpling, grabbing his tail only means to him that you want to play. And by that I mean misbehave together. So what I'm going to teach you is to wrap an arm around his neck like I do and give his head a twist. That way he'll knock off the reckless behavior and know you're the alpha here. Don't worry, it won't harm him."

"But he doesn't have any horns," Owen said.

"Don't need 'em! The important part here is knocking him off his balance, not grabbing horns, so you're in the dominant position. The trick is to go after his body with your hip."

"My hip?"

"You're the top bull, Owen. And you're gonna prove that to him by driving your hip straight into his shoulder to make him submit. Contrary to popular belief, steer wrestlers know that it ain't the arms that dominate the animal, it's your whole body. When you shove your hip into him, it pushes him off course and derails his plan. Then you circle your arm around his neck and give him a yank till he gives in. Okay? Let's practice."

Dixon stepped away so Owen was fully in charge. "I want

you to walk Dumpling forward, keeping a tight hold on his lead. If he dips his head like he wants to pummel you, immediately throw your hip into him. If he tries it again, push your hip into him another time and grab him around the neck and give his head a turn so he'll back off."

Owen gave it a shot, leading Dumpling with determined strides, ready for whatever might come his way. Sure enough, Dumpling got a devilish look in his eyes and began to resist Owen's lead, dancing in place and dipping his head as if he intended to tumble him. This time, however, Owen bumped the yearling aside with his hip. Startled, Dumpling kept walking forward, but then his tail straightened like he was up to no good and he dipped his head again, ready to throw Owen to the ground. Before he could ram the boy, Owen knocked the yearling off his balance with his hip and gave his neck a twist to make him succumb. Dumpling stumbled with such surprise that he dropped to the ground like a sack of potatoes, his expression wall-eyed. He let out a mournful moo.

"You did it!" Dixon hollered, running over to Owen. He grabbed Dumpling's lead before he could scamper away. "I didn't expect you to knock him over, but I'll be damned—you did it! You're a bonafide bulldogger!"

Dixon gave Owen a bear hug, hooting with glee, while Tempest remained planted on the fence, dumbfounded.

She'd never seen her son like this before.

All at once, Owen appeared taller, with his chest puffed out as big as he could muster. Like a little...man.

He seemed so proud he could burst, and equally self-possessed at the same time, which was even more surprising to Tempest than wrangling a yearling. She hadn't realized before how much Owen's *needing* her had built her self-worth, given her purpose during their darkest of days. But now, this glimpse of Owen's burgeoning independence and maturity made her suddenly aware that being a good parent included allowing him to grow up. This was Owen's victory moment to relish with another man he admired, a *real* cowboy who'd taught him the ropes.

What would her alter ego, Tempest the Terminator, say to her now?

Buck up, honey, if you want to prove you're a good mom.

Dixon met Tempest's gaze, staring at her as though he'd understood her enormous restraint in that instant. He waved for her to come over.

Tempest crawled down from the fence and headed toward them with slow strides, cautious not to disturb the unique man-space the two of them had just formed. She gave her son a reticent wave and smiled.

When she reached them alongside the yearling, Dixon leaned into her ear.

"You're brave," he said. "I saw how much it took for you to stay on that fence. You helped Owen grow by leaps and bounds today."

"Without *me*," she whispered back, trying to maintain a smile despite the sting. "Guess letting go is part of… parenting…huh?"

Just then, an owl called from the nearby trees, its voice cutting through the dusky evening light like a herald that darkness would fall soon. Though initially unsettling, the echo of the sound felt strangely comforting to Tempest, somehow giving her the feeling that she'd done the right thing. And that

Owen would be okay—perhaps even watched over. She couldn't explain her strange reaction, but as she shifted her gaze to her son, she was struck by the loyal affection Owen had for his yearling, petting him in all the right places while Dumpling bent into his touch for better rubs. What's more, when she happened to glance up at Dixon, she saw a proud look in his eyes.

For *Owen*—

A look not even his own father had ever bothered to show.

The owl hooted from the trees once more, its voice sharp and authoritative, as if wanting to make certain Tempest paid heed. This time, the piercing sound made her breath catch.

"You seem a little…jumpy," Dixon observed, chalking it up to the waning light. He took that as his cue to start escorting her back toward the gate by the fairgrounds. "Come on, Owen," he waved for the boy to follow. "I trust you to lead Dumpling with good control this time. We have to get to the fairgrounds to put him away for the night. You can work on grooming my horse Bullet tomorrow. Till then, be sure to get enough sleep so you can keep practicing for the fair."

As they headed toward the gate, Dixon turned to Tempest. "It wouldn't hurt you to get a good rest tonight, too," he teased, "since the Cowboy Roundup starts tomorrow. Gotta be at your best for the competition, right?"

"No worries! I don't have the remotest chance of winning," Tempest replied. "Because unlike your *other* women," she swiped a glance at him with a twinkle in her eyes, "I'm *not* crazy."

"Sure about that?" A curl rose at the side of Dixon's lip, enjoying the way she sparred back at him. "With the way you tore after Dumpling this evening like you were gonna skin him alive, I'd say that's all a matter of perspective."

Tempest stopped, setting her hands on her hips. "Wait a second, I shouldn't be blamed for momma-bear behavior to protect my son," she volleyed back. "Any mother would do that, even if I do seem over the top sometimes."

"Say what you will, Tempest," Dixon replied, giving her a wink. "Just remember, crazy is as crazy does."

9

Tempest squinted at the sunlight that glistened off her radio console before making her announcement to start the day's broadcast from the fair. She didn't have to wonder who might show up with a therapy problem to talk about that morning, because there was already a tall woman with gray, bobbed hair in a yellow gingham blouse and matching pants in front of her. The woman drummed her fingers impatiently on the booth.

With a pig at her side.

A large, black pig with a band of white across its shoulders and front legs. Though it must have weighed over 300 pounds, fortunately the animal had on a thick harness that was attached to the woman's leash. Along with a yellow gingham ruffle around the pig's neck to coordinate with the woman's outfit.

"You ready yet?" the woman said in a testy tone before Tempest could get a word in. "Because my name is June, and I got an awful problem on my hands that needs solving real quick."

Tempest shot a glance at Ivy while taking a large swig from her coffee cup. In her clinical practice, the most demanding clients were usually in the greatest denial, and she figured this conversation might go south in a hurry.

"What's your pig's name?" Ivy asked cheerfully, since Tempest had encouraged her to participate more in the broadcasts to get experience. She quickly placed a microphone on a stand beside the woman to pick up her voice.

"Oh, this is my pride and joy, Marigold." The woman beamed. "In fact, she's the reason why I'm here this morning. She used to be a star in the Hampshire breed gilt competitions. But now, as you can see, all she wants to do is lie around in the dirt instead of strutting her stuff. I've had her checked out by the vet, and she says there's nothing wrong with Marigold except for a bad case of stubbornness. If you ask me," June huffed, aiming a finger at the stack of Tempest's books on the booth, "this little piggy could use some of your *Shock Value*."

"Are you saying you want to apply my principles of tough love to Marigold's training regimen?" Tempest guessed. She and Ivy peered over the edge of the booth, observing that the pig had squeezed its eyes shut in order to take a nap. "By the way," Tempest asked, "what's a gilt competition?"

June poised her hands on her hips. "My goodness, everyone at the fair knows a gilt is a young female that ain't had any piglets yet. Boy, you sure are from the city, ain't ya?" she chided. "To answer your question, I do believe Marigold could use a stronger hand to get her to perform in the arena like she used to. She's been sitting down and refusing to walk before the judges every time! Digs her hooves in the dirt and refuses to budge. Lately, I've been dangling my elderberry muffins right in front of her, the same ones I entered into the fair's baking competition this year, but she turns her nose up at them."

Tempest nodded sympathetically. "You've come to the right place, June. Because it just so happens I've been dealing with obstinate livestock myself lately. Have you tried showing Marigold who's boss?" Tempest urged, recalling Dixon's instructions to Owen. "Like giving her a firm nudge to keep her on her feet every time she tries to lie down?"

"Yes, ma'am!" June replied. She held up a thin, white stick that had been in her other hand. "I even tap her with my show cane—hard, if I have to. Don't make a bit of difference."

"All right," Tempest said, full of confidence now after observing how well Dixon's assertiveness training had worked with Owen. "Then my friend Ivy and I are going to get serious with using the principles of *Shock Value*, like you requested. Come on, Ivy," she waved at her intern to follow. They walked out of the booth and stood behind the snoozing pig, who'd begun to snore. "June, you wake up Marigold and give her the cue to walk forward, and we'll do the rest."

Ivy glanced wide-eyed at Tempest, having no idea what was expected of her.

"Git along, Marigold!" June commanded, tugging on the harness leash until she roused the pig, then tapping her with the cane.

As June pulled, Tempest gestured for Ivy to accompany her by placing her hands onto the rear end of the pig. "At the count of three, we're going to give Marigold a hefty push so she obeys you," Tempest promised June. "Keep on pulling, and Marigold will get the picture that her refusal to move won't be tolerated anymore. Ready? One, two, three—go!"

Tempest and Ivy shoved Marigold's rump with all their might, while June dangled an elderberry muffin in front of her snout that she'd retrieved from her purse. The pig leaned her neck forward and took a sniff of the muffin, giving Tempest hope that her idea had worked. But then Marigold crinkled her nose and rolled over on her side with a thump, creating a cloud of dust.

"Marigold!" scolded June, tugging harder and repeatedly tapping her with the cane. Finally, she threw her cane onto the ground in a fit and folded her arms. "See what I mean? Even three people can't get this swine to budge!"

At that moment, a shadow cast across the pig, seeping like dark ink over its body. Tempest's breath halted when she looked up and saw none other than...Granny Tinker.

Granny smiled, her gold front tooth flashing in the morning sun. God as her witness, Tempest thought for sure she caught a glimpse of her own reflection in the sheen. Her expression appeared to be one of downright...dismay.

"You know, I've always reckoned strangers make the best mirrors," Granny commented mysteriously. She stole a glance at Dixon's face on a nearby poster advertising the Cowboy Roundup, and she gave Tempest another sly smile. "Along with the best lovers."

Tempest gulped a breath. Not only because Granny made no sense at all and was quite possibly the most beautiful woman she'd ever seen, but also because something about her presence always made Tempest feel like wild and uncontrollable things might be afoot. Like a storm packed with lightning, a flash flood, a meteor crashing to earth, or—dare she think it—love at first sight.

"Excuse me, have we been officially introduced?" Tempest said in a brisk attempt to take charge. She stood and lifted Ivy's elbow to help her to her feet as well. Then she boldly grabbed Granny's hand and shook it, unsettled by the fact that it was surprisingly warm and comforting. "I'm Tempest Wright, a therapist at the local mental health center. Which is different, I suppose, than—"

"Somebody who stitches together hearts from an old wagon?" Granny appraised Tempest with a cocked brow. "Seems you and I have more in common than most might think. But neither one of us can get credit for being as smart as that pig," she mentioned cryptically, glancing down at Marigold. "'Tis the reason she's still alive, you know."

Tempest, June, and Ivy fell silent, checking each other's baffled expressions before dropping their gazes to the pig, who appeared content to remain in the dirt.

"What the hell is this strange woman talking about?" Tempest whispered to Ivy, confounded over how Granny's words had anything to do with Marigold.

Granny slid a glance at Tempest's two radio microphones, which had been poised on the booth to pick up their conversation, as if the devices were suspicious. Nevertheless, she leaned over to June and plucked the elderberry muffin from her grip, then tossed it into a nearby trash can.

"I'm confident you're a mighty fine cook with all the awards you've won for baking over the years," Granny complimented June. "But the problem is you're offering the pig the wrong treat. You," she pointed to Ivy, "go get my basket of rose petal scones at my booth over yonder."

June's mouth dropped as Ivy followed Granny's instructions. "Are you insinuating my muffins ain't good enough?" she retorted, clearly offended.

Granny shook her head. When Ivy returned with the basket, which quickly sent a heavenly scent of rose petals and fresh vanilla wafting beneath their noses, Granny grasped one of the scones and bent down in front of the pig. Marigold's eyes instantly blinked open, and she nibbled at the scone right away, soon swiping it from Granny's hand and swallowing it whole. Within seconds, Marigold was on her feet, prancing in place and bouncing up and down to beg for another scone, as if she'd consumed some kind of magic.

Tempest felt her stomach flip flop at the spookiness of the moment. What on earth type of spell had this odd woman cast this time?

"T'ain't nothing unusual," Granny assured Tempest before she could pose the question. She met Tempest's gaze with her peculiar, timberwolf-gray eyes as she straightened her knees to stand. Her eyes shifted to June. "But it sure helps if you offer your livestock food that ain't had a history of being poison."

June's jaw dropped again, unable to speak.

"Them elderberries make swine sick, honey," Granny informed her. "Don't worry, we know you'd never hurt your sweet Marigold on purpose. She probably got into an elderberry bush once and ate too much of the raw berries and leaves, and now she won't go near 'em. Can't hardly blame her. Elderberries ain't safe for nobody till they're fully cooked. But if I were you, I'd start making a list of what's dangerous out there in nature to pigs and people. You never know who might want to try and use such things against you."

At that moment, Granny threw Tempest an icy look, sending shivers down her spine. "Be careful not to let that little boy of yours go near suspicious plants. Or people, for that matter," she warned. "Not everything that looks sweet and ripe is safe."

With that, Granny Tinker slid her gaze toward a rather hefty farm girl with long, red hair and overalls standing a few yards away next to an older woman in tight, western clothing. The woman reached over and pinched the girl's stomach with a frown on her face, then began to lecture her. Tempest recognized the girl as one of the contestants who'd been chosen for the Cowboy Roundup—Blossom Barnhart. She was struck by the sad way Blossom crumpled into herself and stared at the ground while the woman scolded, like she was used to it. When Tempest turned back to face Granny, she was gone.

Ivy seized one of the radio microphones. "That's all for today, listeners in radio land!" she chirped in a quick effort to keep the broadcast from lagging with dead airtime. "It's always a treat to learn new things on this show, including baking and livestock tips! Until tomorrow, have a tippity-top, triumphant day!"

Tempest reached her arm around Ivy's waist after she turned off the radio console to give her a hug. "Thank you!" she exhaled in relief. "I got so mesmerized by Granny Tinker that I lost track of time. You rescued the show."

"And thank you two, as well!" June gushed to Ivy and Tempest. She shook both their hands. "I had no idea the problem was elderberries all along till I came to your booth. I'll be sure to use raspberries in my muffins from here on out." She checked her watch. "Shoot! I gotta get Marigold ready for the next gilt class." Then she pointed at the large scoreboard above the nearby arena and jabbed her elbow into Tempest's ribs. "But I'm rooting for you to win the Cowboy Roundup. 'Cause that Dixon Ramsey sure is easy on the eyes!"

As June headed off, she held out an extra one of Granny's rose petal scones that had been left on the booth to keep Marigold moving. Tempest gave her a wave and happened to glance up at the scoreboard.

Her face froze.

Before her very eyes, the handsome, digital image of Dixon Ramsey that had loomed over the arena had evaporated. It was replaced by an image of *herself*—with all of her vital statistics! Not just the usual intrusive facts, like her age and approximate height and weight, but also her lack of rodeo experience as well as her chances of winning the Cowboy Roundup.

Which at this point, listed as a 100-to-1 long shot, clearly made Tempest Wright a terrible bet.

10

"This is the single most *sexist* thing I've ever seen!"
Tempest burst.

Two fairgoers with plates of strawberry crepes
in their hands halted in their tracks, startled by the loud,
abrasive noise.

"Can you believe this?" Tempest howled furiously to
anyone who might listen, jabbing her finger at the scoreboard.
"I am an educated woman and a licensed therapist!"
Tempest's hands balled into fists. "How dare the Fair Board
treat me like some pathetic greyhound people can
gamble on?"

At that moment, the digits displaying her chances of
winning on the scoreboard swiftly scaled down.

Ivy spied the dreadful numbers. She dug into her pocket,
pulling out a piece of paper and holding it up to Tempest.
"Didn't you see the flyer they were handing out this morning

at the entrance gate? I think they're using whatever they can to stir interest."

Tempest ripped the flyer away from her. Scanning the page, she saw pictures of herself, Blossom Barnhart, and Hedda Grimson with their supposed stats listed beside each photo.

Along with directions to the betting booth where fairgoers could place their wagers on the contestants for the Cowboy Roundup. The women's chances for winning would be updated every day on the scoreboard and the rural TV channel, and feature novelty betting categories as well.

"Why, oh why, does the public need to know that I'm five foot six, a hundred and thirty pounds and thirty-eight flipping years old?" she exclaimed. "With a snowball's chance in hell of winning this thing?"

Ivy clasped her fingers together with a clinical air of tolerance. "Because," she reminded Tempest in her best therapist tone, "they're desperate for ticket sales so they can keep things like the 4-H show going. For kids that include *your* son, I should add."

Tempest slumped a little, issuing a dispirited breath at the fact that Ivy was right. She closed her eyes for a second to keep from screaming at the top of her lungs again. When she blinked open her eyes, she felt Ivy's hands clutch her shoulders.

"Tempest the Terminator *always* reminds listeners not to be a victim and to take control of the narrative. Which means this is *your* moment to remove the sting from the way you've been portrayed and use it as your badge of empowerment. Like female wrestlers! Sure, they may wear skimpy outfits—like you're gonna do—but they use it as an opportunity to celebrate strong, powerful women."

"Wait," Tempest stared at Ivy, "did you say...*skimpy outfits?*"

"Yes!" Ivy replied, having no clue she'd just thrown Tempest a curveball. She tapped her finger on the crumpled flyer in Tempest's hand. "It says on the back that you're going to be in a swimsuit competition. You look great, by the way—I'm sure it will bring lots of people to the fair!"

Tempest turned over the flyer, which featured a listing of Cowboy Roundup events that included roping, mounted shooting, and what they called the "Dash and Splash"—a hokey game where women in swimsuits walked a plank over a cattle pond, endeavoring not to fall.

Tempest threw the flyer down and buried her head in her hands. "What have I done to deserve the worst karma on earth?" she wailed. "This is my nightmare!"

Ivy slowly peeled Tempest's fingers from her face and stared her dead in the eye.

"Listen, you're a great mom," she said with a gravity Tempest didn't know she possessed. "Who'll do anything for her son. And from what I've heard, this fair is on the brink of going belly up if the Cowboy Roundup doesn't raise revenue. So what you're gonna do is hold your head high and rock this thing for the sake of Owen. Understand? Because he wants to show his animal in 4-H more than anything."

Tempest's eyes glistened, and she quickly blinked back her emotions. "That's funny," she said with a thin laugh, "you sound just like me on the radio."

"Where do you think I learned it from?" Ivy smiled. "Whether you like it or not, you've been an example to me this summer of courage and becoming a self starter. Which is what gave me the confidence to launch my *Rainbow of Love* app for color therapy."

"I'm really proud of you," Tempest nodded. She scanned Ivy's frizzy, dark hair and schleppy pink cardigan that she wore nearly every day, noticing that the twinkle in her eyes defied her frumpiness. "You had the guts to be creative, and then act on your ideas, and that's amazing. I hope your app takes off like crazy." Then Tempest risked another glance at the scoreboard to see what they might be flashing this time. She burst out laughing.

"What? What is it?" Ivy asked.

Tempest swiveled her to face the scoreboard.

Not only was Dixon's face up there again, looming as large as the size of the funnel cake booth, but beneath his image was his lousy dating track record to boot. Tempest couldn't resist reading aloud the scoreboard's dire forecast.

"Chances of Dixon keeping a woman's attention: 1/100. Chances of Dixon surviving the mounted shooting event: 1/50. Chances of Dixon not screwing up his only chance at true love: 1/100. Holy smokes," she fought to contain her laughter, "you gotta hand it to the Fair Board for their sense of humor!" Tempest turned to Ivy. "Okay, so maybe they *aren't* totally sexist around here, if they're humiliating Dixon worse than the contestants."

"Just remember," Ivy replied with a smirk, "if they ask you questions when you're in your swimsuit, instead of world peace, you should say you want breakthroughs in, um… fertilizers or livestock vaccinations. And don't forget to smile, because I've heard the winner gets a tiara!" She stepped back and narrowed her eyes at Tempest's face. "I think you'd look great in a crown—"

"Oh my God, there she is!" Tempest and Ivy heard a shrill voice interrupt their conversation. "It's really *her!*"

Tempest swallowed a breath, readying herself for another round of radio listeners who'd come by to meet her and purchase her book. Ever since she'd set up her booth at the fair, she'd been signing autographs and selling *Shock Value* like hot cakes. Protectively, she tugged on Ivy's arm to join her inside the booth to keep their feet from getting trampled by fans.

Three young women dashed up to the booth and eagerly held out their cell phones. "Smile," Tempest whispered in a teasing tone to Ivy, "it's selfie time."

"Me first!" insisted one of the girls, pushing the others out of the way. She spun around and, to Tempest's surprise, leaned her cheek against Ivy's. She held her phone out at arm's length and clicked. "I can't believe we've found the *real* Ivy Hughes," she exclaimed, pushing another button on her phone, "and I'm the first to post about her on Instagram!"

The two other young women shoved their faces into the frame and began clicking their cell cameras as fast as they could. "This is awesome!" one of the girls cried, thrilled with her picture. She turned to Ivy. "Do you realize your color therapy app has five-thousand reviews already? Everybody *loves* the way you address dating hurdles!"

"Dating hurdles?" Tempest asked, still reeling from Ivy's instant notoriety. She glanced down at the young woman's cell phone—there was a picture of Ivy with a big smile next to her

Rainbow of Love app description. When the girl clicked on it, up came color advice for being "vampired."

The girl grinned at Tempest, pointing at the color of her sexy, purple crop top and doing a little spin to show it off. "I had this guy totally vampire me recently," she confessed. "Only texting me to see him at night and never posting pictures of us together on social media. Once I followed the *Rainbow of Love's* color advice and wore bright purple to highlight my, well, assets," she thrust up her chest, giggling, "he suddenly booked a vacay for us and changed his status to *in a relationship!*"

Ivy clapped with glee. "You dumped him, right?" She gazed at the girl expectantly.

"In a heart beat!" the girl replied. "He ain't gonna get these goods after treating me like a booty call, just because he threw money my way. I did what your app suggested and used my purple outfits to move on to a better dating pool!"

The three young women huddled together and linked arms. "Bye bye, vampire boy! Go suck somebody else's blood," they cooed in a chorus, pleased with themselves.

"Hey, is this a kissing booth, too?" one of the girls asked, squinting at Tempest's sign. "We came here to find real cowboys, since they're hot and supposed to be a hell of a lot more loyal. Mind if we bring them back here for a little action?"

Tempest's breath hesitated at their boldness. Then her face erupted into a grin, and she shrugged at Ivy before turning to the girl. "Sure!" she replied. "Why not—we serve all kinds of therapy requests here. Right Ivy?"

"Absolutely!" Ivy chimed, folding her arms in satisfaction.

"But only if you charge them ten bucks a pop for a kiss, and give my friend Tempest fifty-percent, since it's her booth."

"No problem!" the girl trilled. "Hey, look at those cute guys hanging around the chutes by the arena. They've got on cowboy hats—come on, let's go!"

As the young women trotted off to catch up with the cowboys who were slated for the next bronc riding event, Ivy turned to Tempest and gave her a high five. "Congratulations! Between the two of us, we've managed to serve *all* age groups."

"And you've become quite the business woman lately," Tempest observed, "getting them to agree to give me partial proceeds. But after all your help this summer," she said, "you don't need to offer me a cut for a kissing booth—"

"Did I hear somebody say *kissing booth?*"

Tempest whirled around and saw Dixon Ramsey. She rolled her eyes. *Of course* he was here—he had a near-psychic knack for showing up at the most perfect moments to dig at her pride.

"Too bad you don't have that raspberry syrup on your lips today," he said in a cocky tone, "you might get more takers. What's this?" He glanced down and spied one of the rose petal scones that Granny Tinker had left on the booth. Grabbing the treat, he was about to take a bite when Tempest attempted to yank it away.

"No!" she said as Dixon stretched his arm and held the scone out of her reach.

"What's wrong?" He took a hearty bite just to defy her and began chewing. "Tastes like a dream to me."

"That was made by Granny Tinker," she gasped. "I'm not
sure if it's m-m…"

Tempest couldn't quite spit out the word "magic" for fear
that she might somehow get infected by the mere term. After
all, she'd seen the peculiar effect Granny's scone had on
Marigold. "Well, everybody knows Granny's rumored to have
a gift for…uh—"

"Making weird things happen, like bringing couples
together?" Dixon said with a raised brow.

"That's right!" Ivy broke in. "And you're the first guy to
actually *eat* that scone and look at Tempest."

"Are you saying it might influence me?" he pressed. "At a
kissing booth? Hell, I could sure use the boost for the Cowboy
Roundup."

With that, Dixon dropped the scone on the booth and
grasped Tempest's cheeks, pulling her in for a kiss. Instantly,
her mouth was riddled with sparks before she could even think.
Dixon's lips were surprisingly warm and tender, and with the
taste of the rose petal scone still in his mouth, he had the
infernal audacity to swirl his tongue around hers. Tempest
stiffened like a board, indignant and raising her fists to give
him a hard shove. Yet her body kept demanding more as she
found her neck dipping into his lips and her arms slowly
drifting back to her sides.

I shouldn't be doing this, she thought.

I *can't* be doing this—

I refuse to melt in front of this man.

Yet despite how much she scolded herself, Tempest
couldn't will herself to hammer at his chest. She knew if she

did, she'd only feel his warm, cowboy-hardened muscles, which were probably as addictive as crack.

Even so, her protests raged within her. There's no way I'm becoming one of his loony-tune statistics, she swore to herself, like apparently every crazy broad does within a fifty-mile radius. But dammit, she thought, Dixon sure has a way with his lips and tongue.

Pull away. Pull away now! Tempest's rational mind ordered.

Too bad those words didn't trickle down to her loosening spine. Tempest felt like her bones had dissolved into her blood stream, coursing through her in a rush of warm liquid. When she finally managed to brace herself, it took all her willpower to shore up her muscles and yank free from his lips, struggling to open her eyes.

Dixon took a step back, smiling broadly like he knew he'd gotten the best of her. More importantly, like he'd made a connection that Tempest wasn't likely to soon forget. Eyes glinting, he dug a ten-dollar bill from his pocket and slapped it onto the booth next to the scone.

"Damn, that's the best deal in three counties," he bragged, his cocky grin pulling from ear to ear. "I might have to buy another kiss before the day's through." He turned to catch a glance at the Trinity women in their booth before he met Tempest's gaze, swiping another bite of the scone. "By God, if those little old ladies are selling magic desserts that can whip up kisses like that," he said as he began to walk away, "their Historical Society is gonna reel in a fortune."

Dixon lifted a wave at Tempest. "See you later at the

competition," he called out. Then he pointed to the image of her giant face that lit up the scoreboard. Her numbers were climbing by the second, as if all of Bandits Hollow had somehow seen him steal that kiss. Dixon's face crinkled into a self-satisfied smirk.

"My, oh my," he gloated. "Better get used to it, Tempest. 'Cause it sure looks like you're the frontrunner now in the Cowboy Roundup."

11

Tempest was left with her face in flames. "What's going on?" she fumed, running her hands frantically all around the top and bottom beams of her booth. "Do they have a hidden camera here somewhere? How could my chances for winning the Cowboy Roundup rise unless somebody's been spying on me?"

Ivy cringed, like the answer should be obvious. "Well, it's not hard to video your booth from the announcer's tower," she pointed out, tilting her head at the two men in the top window. They were gazing at a cell phone and slapping each other's backs, laughing. "Word gets around fast in a small town. But look at the bright side, you two *are* pretty cute together."

"No, we're not!" Tempest retorted. "Women like me are just another notch in the belt for guys like Dixon Ramsey, with all their charm and cocky wit. Which is why I wore a super-boring pale gray shirt, since I was hoping it would make me dull and invisible." She glanced down at her shirt and glared at

Ivy. "This color is nowhere near as dark as charcoal. But it didn't exactly fend him off, I might add."

Ivy shook her head and punched her finger into her cell phone. She held up the instructions from her *Rainbow of Love* app. "Well, if you'd bothered to look up my explanation, you'd know that light dove gray attracts men who are secretly the commitment type. It works like a mirror, where suddenly a man can see himself in your heart and imagine your future together. Like Granny Tinker said."

"What the hell is *that* supposed to mean?"

"When she mentioned strangers can make the best mirrors. You know, like the kind of guy who's good for you, but that you haven't figured out is good for you—"

"Oh my God, that's total nonsense! Ivy, you're talking in crazy riddles like Granny Tinker."

"If you say so," Ivy smirked. "But *you're* the one who pointed out that denial is often a hidden form of confession. In fact, it's in chapter six of your book."

Ivy picked up a copy of *Shock Value* from the booth and flipped through the pages to the correct passage. She held it up for Tempest with a smug gleam in her eye.

"E-Excuse me, is your booth still open?" broke in a young woman's timid voice.

Tempest sealed her eyes for a second, trying to compose herself. If this chick was another one of Ivy's eager fans who only wanted to discuss color therapy, she had half a mind to march off to get a funnel cake right now. Counting backwards from ten, she blinked open her eyes.

There was Blossom Barnhart standing in front of her, her lovely long red hair glistening over the shoulder straps of her faded overalls. She glanced left and right as though she feared she might get into trouble for being at the booth. "Your microphones are off, right?" she asked nervously. "I don't want this to be on the radio."

"Well, those men up in the announcer's tower can see you," Tempest replied bitterly. "Meaning they might shoot videos with their cell phones for the county TV channel. Those guys will do anything to advertise the fair."

Blossom steered a glance at the announcers, her eyes widening. "Oh dear, guess I'd better go, then," she muttered.

"No! Let us fix it," Ivy offered. She stepped out of the booth and shoved at a corner with all her might to turn the wooden structure to the side. Now all the men could see was the back of the booth and its wide swath of plywood.

"There!" Ivy said proudly, dusting off her hands. "No worries, you're as confidential as can be." She held up her cell phone to show what was on the rural TV app. "See? Nobody's live recording this booth now."

Blossom nodded in gratitude. She gazed earnestly into Tempest's eyes as if she were her only hope. "It's my mom," she whispered. "She, um, acts like the Cowboy Roundup is her big chance to marry me off. In between constantly criticizing my looks, that is." Blossom stared down at her lumpy overalls that hardly flattered her figure and sighed. "I don't know if you're aware of this," she continued, "but Dixon's performance horse business is one of the best in the country. Folks say he's a millionaire, and my mom views this as an opportunity for me to, well…"

"Make bank?" Tempest said, appalled. Her brows knit together. "Honey, I hate to be harsh, but pushing your daughter into a union with a guy who's, what—twenty years older than you?—so you can be hitched to rich is completely inappropriate. You're over eighteen, right? Or you wouldn't be eligible for the Cowboy Roundup."

"I'm twenty-one," Blossom nodded.

"Then it sounds to me like it's time for a parentectomy."

Blossom searched Tempest's face, puzzled.

"You need to break away from your controlling mother," she explained. "You're old enough to live on your own, Blossom. I bet your mom clips your wings a lot with her judgmental comments, so you doubt your ability to be independent. Correct?"

Blossom flinched. "Yeah," she admitted slowly, mulling over Tempest's observation. "From the time I get up until the time I go to bed, I hear a non-stop stream about what's wrong with me. I think it's her weird way of trying to help. She's just as hard on herself to be perfect."

"And you love her anyway, don't you?" Tempest added perceptively. She gave Blossom a sympathetic gaze. "Listen, growing up is *not* a betrayal of your mother—it's what everyone is supposed to do. Your mother probably wants you to marry a man of means so you'll be well taken care of. Us moms can't help trying to protect our kids. But the truth is, *good* mothers know how to let go," she added, feeling a twinge of guilt for needing to learn that lesson herself lately. "So you'll have to put your foot down with your mom, in order to forge your own identity."

"Oh God," Blossom whimpered, clutching at the booth. "I've never done that before." She puffed a worried breath and darted her gaze to a petite woman in clingy western clothes who was heading toward them. "Help!" Blossom begged. "Here she comes now. She looks like she's on a mission."

"Good!" Tempest said. "Then you'll have the chance to practice right in front of me. Whenever she tries to coerce you into something, I want you to repeat after me: No."

"No? That's it?" Blossom asked, surprised. "I don't think I've ever said that word to her. Of course with my mom, it's hard to get a word in edgewise."

"Then you need to start now," Tempest said.

"Blossom baby!" cried the woman, waving cheerfully at her daughter. She held a basket with a flower arrangement in her arms and began hastening toward the booth, the petals jiggling. "You won't believe it," she called out. "I made it to the top round of the flower arrangement competition! That means I'm eligible for Grand Champion!"

"Brace yourselves," Blossom cautioned in a low tone. "You're about to hear way too much chatter about flowers."

When the woman reached the booth, she plopped her basket down and stroked her daughter's long red hair. The tips of the flowers tickled Tempest's and Ivy's noses, making them inch back and sneeze.

"Hi, I'm Betty!" Blossom's mother chirped. "These beautiful blooms are Indian Paintbrush, Colorado Columbine, Silvery Lupine, and Candy Mountain Foxglove—all grown in my very own backyard. But they're nowhere near as pretty as my daughter," she cooed proudly at Blossom. "By the way," she spread aside the foliage with her fingers to peer at Tempest, "it's such an honor to meet you! You're a star in Bandits Hollow with your bestselling book and radio show."

Betty bit her lip and stared down at the booth for a

moment before meeting Tempest's eyes again. "I'm so sorry you weren't able to keep your man, either. I-I know what it's like to lose a husband who ran around on you. To end up a struggling, single mother. It's pure hell, isn't it?"

Betty's eyes glistened and she blinked several times, sliding her glance over to Tempest's stack of books. "That's why I treasured *Shock Value* so much. It was the only thing that helped me move on with my life."

Tempest's breath stifled for a second. From Blossom's discussion, she'd pegged Betty for a garden-variety meddling mother, but now she realized the woman was probably acting out of fear. As Tempest knew too well, trauma could make people do controlling things, losing sight of the forest for the trees. She looked Betty up and down, noticing her bleached hair, skinny frame, and far too much Botox that gave her face a mask-like appearance, making her resemble a middle-aged Cowgirl Barbie. This poor woman had endured a similar tragedy to her own, and Tempest figured she must be knocking herself out to look more attractive—*and* trying to ensure Blossom didn't go through the same thing. In her own way, Betty was as hovering as Tempest, which warranted a certain degree of clinical sympathy. But that didn't change the fact that Blossom *deserved* to make her own choices.

"Well, I hate to take off so soon, but I have to refresh my plants for the flower society's photo shoot. They must look *totally perfect* to have a chance in the competition. Not unlike us gals, huh? It was so nice to meet you, Tempest! C'mon, Blossom," she tugged at her daughter's baggy overalls. "We're supposed to stand beside our arrangements for the photo, so I can show you all about personal presentation! At least it will distract you from food. You don't want to gain anymore pounds after the twenty I helped you lose, right?"

Blossom's cheeks grew pinker than Betty's foxgloves at the mention of her weight, as if the diet had been entirely her mother's decision, not her own. She studied the grain of wood on Tempest's booth for a moment. Then her chest began to rise and fall quickly as if she were about to hyperventilate. Tempest handed her one of the paper bags she'd been using to pack customers' books. Blossom gulped a few breaths, inflating the paper in and out like a balloon. She snuck a glance at Tempest for assurance.

"No," she muttered to her mother, setting the paper bag down.

"What?" Betty replied, startled. "Honey, the first Cowboy Roundup event is *today*. You need my tips on how to display yourself to your best advantage! Starting with the nicer clothes I loaded for you in the car. People are going to *vote* on you to win that date, you know—"

"No," Blossom repeated.

She checked Tempest's eyes once more and turned to face her mother. "I'm going to help the kids with their 4-H animals this afternoon, like Annie asked me to. Since I work at the feed store, I'm teaching them tips about animal nutrition for their questions in the show ring."

Betty's eyes stretched wide, her mouth falling.

Then she drew a breath and tilted her head slightly, scanning her daughter as her eyes began to twinkle. "Oh sweetie, that's brilliant!" she enthused, grasping Blossom's arm and giving her a squeeze. "You constantly amaze me. Then

Dixon will see what a team player you are and what a great ranch wife you could be."

She stepped back and appraised her daughter's outfit. "Come to think of it, maybe you *should* keep on those overalls, since your body's rather round anyway, to complete the look. But please remember not to eat anymore curly fries—we can't afford for your figure to get any bigger!"

Betty smiled and pinched her daughter on the cheek before she turned to face the Arts and Crafts building. She gripped her basket of flowers tighter and inhaled a deep breath of pride. "See you in the winners circle, dearie!" she called out to Blossom as she marched away from Tempest's booth.

"For the love of psychotherapy," Tempest pleaded with Ivy as soon as Betty was out of earshot, "if I ever become *that* much of a velcro-mom, you'll slap me and call it a reality check, right?" She turned to Blossom. "Honestly, I've seen overbearing mothers before who think they're being helpful," she shook her head, "but your mother takes the prize. Don't tell me—she always tries to be the best in everything, right?"

"Now you see what I'm dealing with," Blossom said. "I've been saving money ever since I got the assistant manager job at the feed store a couple of months ago, but it takes a while to earn enough for a deposit on an apartment." Her shoulders sagged a little. "After my step-dad left, my mom's whole focus has been on *me*. I think she's really lonely and this is her way of handling things."

"Oh, her last husband was your...step-father?" Tempest clarified.

"Yeah. Well, I've actually had a few so-called step dads, but they didn't stick around very long. I guess my mom is...

relationship challenged. After my dad passed away when I was little, she got married too fast a couple of times, and the guys always fooled around on her and left. She had to tough out being a single mom all on her own. When she finally got hitched to Harry six months ago, he seemed nice enough at first. But then he took off, and it left her pretty shattered. That's when she started using Botox and obsessing about weight." Blossom cringed and glanced down at her boots. "Rumor had it Harry left her for another woman, too."

"I understand." Tempest nodded, trying to swallow back the jagged stone in her throat. She knew first hand the hit to a woman's self-esteem that a cheating husband could make, and she winced that she'd been tempted to try Botox and diets once, too. Sometimes these crazy "self-improvements" were the only control you felt you had. She reached into her pocket and handed Blossom her business card.

"Listen, any time you want to talk, you call me, okay?" she offered kindly. "In the meantime, it's probably best to ignore your mother and give her some slack. She'll get over this phase eventually, but until then you'll have to set some boundaries. Consider any phone calls to me free of charge."

Blossom studied the card information. She nodded and whispered her thanks to Tempest just as an old man with a well-worn cowboy hat approached the booth. Tempest recognized him as the Fair Steward, Horton Brown.

"Time to get ready for the first event of the Cowboy Roundup!" He grinned brightly at Tempest and Blossom. "You two ready to rope Dixon Ramsey?" He held up the two lariats that were in his hand. "When you circle him with your rope, remember to pull hard till he falls down. Then you can hogtie his legs for extra points, depending on how you like your men!"

"I prefer mine standing, thanks," Tempest said. "Points or no points."

"Suit yourself!" he replied. He handed Tempest and Blossom their lariats. "But the sooner you get to the indoor arena, the more time you have to practice."

"Any extra points for roping Dixon around the neck?" Tempest couldn't help muttering. "And yanking it tight, like a noose?"

"As a matter of fact, there are! What's the problem, you still miffed at that kiss he stole? Let me tell you, our rural TV ratings went through the roof! You're in the lead right now for the competition!"

"Oh joy," Tempest replied. Her mouth slipped into a thin smile for Horton's sake, knowing full well that if Dixon hadn't been so kind to her son last night, she probably would have murdered him by now. She stepped out of her booth and held up her lariat, studying it carefully. "What a perfect noose this would make," she mused, turning to hand the rope to Ivy. "Can you please hang onto this for safekeeping till right before the event?"

"Sure. But why?" Ivy asked.

"Because I don't trust myself not to add hanging Dixon Ramsey to my list of therapy techniques." She released a frustrated breath, bracing to face the indoor arena and its eager audience for the Cowboy Roundup event. "At least then he might stop acting so cocky."

12

Hedda Grimson glared at Tempest and Blossom as if her beady eyes could shoot nails. Dixon wasn't kidding when he warned she was a fierce competitor. Dressed in a pink, vintage cowgirl outfit with artfully-placed fringe that had probably come from her rodeo queen days, she swung her lariat over her head like a seasoned pro.

To Tempest's and Blossom's surprise, Hedda roped them together faster than they could blink, making the audience in the arena erupt into laughter. She yanked on her rope until they were squished and released a whiskey-throated laugh. Despite her slim frame, Hedda's sinewy strength rivaled any cowboy's, and she held up her pink felt cowgirl hat to the stands in victory.

The crowd went wild with cheers.

"Can we just quit now?" Tempest whispered to Blossom.

"Concede the competition to Hedda and be done already? There's no way in hell we can beat her."

"She's a firecracker," Blossom agreed. "There's practically a shrine to her cowgirl achievements in the fairgrounds office. I hear folks have been coming from all around to see the famous Miss Hedda compete in the Cowboy Roundup. At least it might help keep 4-H going."

Tempest nodded at Blossom's words, knowing the cause was more than worth it. She ceased wriggling against the rope and leaned against Blossom, wishing she could close her eyes and make this all go away. But when she shot a glance at the stands, she spied Owen sitting beside Ivy, glowing like he was the proudest kid at the fair.

"Hang in there, Mom!" Owen hollered, clapping his hands and pumping his fist to cheer her on.

Tempest had no choice but to throw him a sweet smile.

"Okay, folks!" called out the announcer from a booth in the arena. "We've seen what Hedda Grimson can do! And we're moments away from witnessing the roping skills of Tempest Wright and Blossom Barnhart. So don't forget to write down on your ticket stub who you think should be in the lead for the Cowboy Roundup after today's competition. Then drop your stubs into the ballot milk pails stationed around the fairgrounds for voting. Hedda, please release these two ladies so they have the chance to swing their ropes!"

Hedda refused to budge, maintaining her flinty gaze at Tempest and Blossom.

"Hedda!" The announcer persisted. "Boy, you haven't changed a bit since you dusted the competition back in 1965! Come on, loosen up and give these newcomers a chance."

The Fair Steward Horton Brown shook his head and trotted over to the captive two women. He loosened Hedda's rope so they could step free, making the crowd hoot with anticipation.

At that moment, Dixon burst onto the scene, bolting from a bull-riding chute on none other than...Dumpling! The audience stood to their feet and roared. Though the yearling merely trotted to the center of the arena, Dixon embraced the moment like a full-fledged rodeo champion, whipping off his cowboy hat and waving it as he flashed his kilowatt smile. Dumpling proudly hoisted up his head for the crowd as if they'd assembled just to see him.

Tempest snuck another glance at her son, who appeared elated, cheering for Dumpling and Dixon like his life depended on it. On the other side of him in the stands sat Dixon's father along with his pet bear Bonner. The old bear flapped his paws together as Dixon's dad fed him a honey bun, causing a cascade of crumbs to dribble from his mouth. No one in the stands paid them any mind.

Reluctantly, Tempest stared at the lariat in her hand.

"Twirl it over your head," Blossom advised, demonstrating with her own rope how to swing it high with the wrist action just right. "When you're ready, aim at Dixon and let her rip."

"All right ladies, Dixon Ramsey is in the arena, so have at him! First one to capture this eligible cowboy wins the day."

All at once, the crowds that filled the stands to capacity started to call out their favorite contestants' names like they were world wrestling superstars. Tempest froze when a photographer darted up and snapped her picture with a searing flash, moving along to Blossom and then Hedda.

Before she could even raise her lariat in the air, Hedda had already charged toward Dixon, her rope flying in circles over her head.

Yet as soon as Hedda got within roping shot of him, she happened to stumble over a rock in the arena that sent her flying into the dirt.

"Hedda!" Tempest gasped. She ran over to the woman and helped her to sit up, gently dusting off her wrinkled face. As she began to brush the dirt from her bright pink rodeo shirt, Blossom seized her moment to snag Dixon. She dashed up to him, spinning her rope, and then threw it, easily circling his waist. When Hedda glanced up, she squinted her eyes, registering Blossom's success.

"Yank him off!" Hedda ordered. Before Tempest knew it, Hedda had scrambled to her feet. She rushed over to Blossom and stood at her side to help her by grabbing onto the rope. The two of them leaned back and pulled for all they were worth, until Dixon tumbled off Dumpling and landed on the ground.

The audience gasped. Before the announcer could make a comment, Dixon had wriggled out of the rope and ripped it from the women's grip. Then he straightaway hopped onto Dumpling again, grabbing the lead to his halter. He gave the animal a hard kick and headed toward the women in a full-blown charge.

Dumpling was only too happy to aim for more victims.

"Rope him!" Hedda turned and ordered Tempest, who was the only one left with a lariat in her hand.

Tempest couldn't believe her eyes.

Would that devil Dixon *really* ram those two women?

The audience had become so quiet she could hear a pin drop as she tore after him to prevent impending disaster, swirling her rope over her head. She got as close as she could, given Dumpling's gallop, and tossed her rope over Dixon, pulling to cinch it tight. Within seconds, she lost her footing, and he and Dumpling were dragging her across the arena.

"Don't let go!" Hedda barked fiercely. "I'll get him for ya!"

"Not again!" Tempest howled as dirt funneled into her face. Nevertheless, she hung onto the rope as Hedda had ordered, wincing at the post-traumatic, cow-dragging flashbacks that burst before her eyes. Ducking her head, she prayed for godspeed to be with Hedda to end her misery.

True to her word, Hedda made a beeline toward Dixon and seized the rope from around his waist. She wrenched at it with her pink, gloved hands till he dropped to the ground, bringing Tempest to a full stop. Sputtering dirt from her lips, Tempest slowly unfolded her aching fingers from the rope and sat up. Then she spotted Hedda using the end of the lariat to swiftly tie up Dixon's arms and legs. Hedda vaulted her arms in the air like a veteran calf roper, signaling success.

Tempest climbed to her feet as applause rose from the crowd, shaking her arms and legs to make sure nothing was injured. She had no clue at this point who might be considered the "winner" of this round. All she knew was that Dixon remained with his hands and feet bound, laughing at her like she was the funniest sight on earth.

It was then Tempest realized she was covered from head to toe in slightly moist arena soil, making her appear like she'd just been dipped into a dirt bath. She had half a mind to walk up to Dixon while he was still vulnerable and give him a kick.

But instead, an evil smirk rose on her face and she marched over to grab one of the spare lariats left on the ground. Quickly, she tied one end to Dixon's feet and the other around Dumpling's neck, then gave the yearling's rump a hard slap. Dumpling galloped forward, dragging Dixon across the arena until Horton Brown dashed to the animal and seized his halter to make him stop.

Once Horton untied him, Dixon stood to his feet with his charming smile firmly in place. Gallantly, he removed his hat and stretched out his arms, bowing before Hedda as if she were a queen. As the crowd began to chant her name, Dixon's eyes twinkled at the old woman with a distinct look of...

Admiration.

His warm gaze sent Tempest into a whirl of confusion.

She studied Dixon's broad shoulders and tall, toughened frame, with muscles so jacked on his chest and arms that they could practically pop his shirt. Then she glanced back at the wiry Hedda.

Considering Dixon's obvious body strength, she realized that there was no way Hedda could have managed to pull him off Dumpling and then hogtied him.

Unless...

He'd *let* her.

Tempest scanned Dixon's face that was now every bit as filthy as hers, with a smile as wide as the rafters.

When his eyes caught hers, they crinkled up at the corners as if she'd discovered his secret. He quickly glanced away and walked up to Hedda, grasping her by the hand to give her a congratulatory handshake.

Tempest did a double take.

She couldn't imagine her late husband ever letting her or Owen—or *anyone* for that matter—succeed over him in anything. Whether it was as simple as playing a child's board game or as ferocious as law firm politics, everything had to be about *him*.

And about winning.

Yet the casual way Dixon threw an arm around Hedda's shoulder and gave her a hug made it clear he couldn't care less. Then he grasped Dumpling's lead line and waved at her son in the stands, motioning for him to leave Ivy's side and come down.

For Dixon, it really *was* all about keeping the fair going—

For kids like her son.

When Owen trotted into the arena, Dixon led Dumpling over to him and handed him the lead line. He turned to address the audience.

"If you want to see this charming young Angus show off again in the arena," he called out in a booming voice, "be sure to catch the yearling class next week. Dumpling and Owen Wright are destined to be stars!"

Tempest nearly melted in place at the smile that enveloped her son's face.

In that moment, Owen was on his own in the arena, in front of nearly the whole county, without her attempting to engineer every second of his safety or success. This is exactly what he wanted, what she wanted *for* him. So why was it so difficult for her to watch Owen becoming his own person?

Tempest swallowed at the grains of gritty dirt that lingered in her throat.

Because just like Betty Barnhart, it left her without

someone to lecture as her form of love. To control or *fix*, like she did every day on the radio. And as she'd learned last night from Dixon, she needed to just let Owen *be*—

And let him shine.

"All right, let's review!" the announcer called out, jolting Tempest from her thoughts. "All three women succeeded in roping Dixon Ramsey today. But only Hedda Grimson went on to hogtie his hands and feet. If you ask me, that puts her in the lead for the Cowboy Roundup. But it's up to you folks to write down who you feel is the winner on your ticket stubs and turn them in, pronto!"

Tempest sealed her eyes and tilted back her head, thankful it was finally over. Now if only she could grab a hot shower—

"Don't forget, you *owe* me," she heard an emphatic warning in her ear.

When she fluttered her eyes open, she realized she was face to face with Dixon.

"Excuse me?" Tempest glared at his dirt-caked forehead and cheeks. "I had every right to make Dumpling drag your ass," she replied. "After the way you made the same thing happen to me! That's the *second time* I've been hauled around at this cursed fair."

"For crying out loud," Dixon noted, "both times you could have just let go of the rope."

"And lose my son's cow that day? Or disappoint Hedda when she was counting on me?"

Dixon's lips pulled into a smirk. "So, in spite of all the snark you dish out, you're really quite loyal, aren't you?" His eyes gleamed as if he'd just uncovered her true nature. "Something tells me you don't let go of very many things. But that's not what I'm talking about. Owen promised to take care of my horse Bullet in return for training the rascal out of Dumpling. Since we have another session tonight, you need to come over a bit earlier so we can finish before nightfall."

Tempest wiped the dirt from her cheeks, staring at her palms in defeat. "Do we even have a choice?" she muttered. "Annie was adamant that if we don't go, Dumpling will get kicked out of—"

"No!" answered Owen. "We *have* to go!" He bounded up to his mother with Dumpling lagging behind on the lead line. Then he tightened his lips, trying to hold back a giggle at the dirt that covered her body. Yanking a grooming brush from his back pocket, Owen proceeded to dust off his mother, using the deep strokes Annie had taught him.

Tempest slung a glance at Dixon. "I bet in these parts they call this a cowboy bath, huh?"

"No, ma'am," Dixon replied. "We got plenty of horse troughs around the fairgrounds for that. I'd be happy to give you a lift and carry you over—"

"Don't you dare!" Tempest warned. She stepped back from Dixon and began dusting off her arms and legs. "I can get used to dirt," she swiftly backpedaled. "Seriously, I can totally get used to dirt."

"Don't worry, Mom," Owen assured her, still brushing hard. "If I can get Dumpling clean enough for 4-H, you'll be spiffed up in no time. Wait till you see me groom Bullet! He'll be shiny as a silver dollar."

"Right—shiny!" Tempest scanned her dusty body again in disbelief. Then she shrugged and broke into a chuckle, gesturing at Ivy in the stands to join them. "Aw heck, guess I'll fit in perfect today with the hogs! Ivy and I promised Annie we'd help her keep the scores of the pigs she's inspecting for grooming this afternoon. No time like the present to blend in!"

"Didn't anybody ever tell you," Dixon remarked in a husky tone, catching her eye, "that wild hair and dirt only make you *prettier* in cowboy country? By that measure, you're the best looking woman in the county right now."

Despite his teasing, goosebumps danced over Tempest's skin as Dixon boldly reached out and ran his fingers through a soiled knot in her hair, trying to release the snarl that wouldn't budge. "Which I'm sure will give you an edge over the Cowboy Roundup competition," he added, studying the twisted strands between his fingers. He lifted his gaze, and Tempest spied a gleam in his eyes. "'Cause Lord knows, dirt or no dirt, ain't nothin' can untangle a force of nature like Tempest the Terminator."

Tempest shook her head and stared at the wide outdoor arena at Dixon's Rambling Star Ranch. *Who is Dixon going to be this time?* she wondered, observing the way he led Owen's yearling around to demonstrate more tips for keeping the animal calm. *Will he be helpful and sensitive again, like yesterday evening? Or Mr. Cocky, who plants dangerous kisses on a woman when she least expects it—that are as hot as hell?*

A flight of tingles darted through her, and she had to admit she was still recovering from the sensual storm he'd left lingering on her lips earlier that day at her booth. Not to mention the sultry way he'd run his fingers through her dusty hair after the roping event. *No wonder this man attracts unstable women,* she thought, *with all of his erratic behavior. It's a miracle he hasn't become the bi-polar poster boy.*

Tempest watched as Dixon modeled for Owen a few more showmanship techniques, like using a long show stick to gently tap Dumpling's legs into place and make him stand square. Then all four hooves were planted directly beneath the yearling's shoulders and haunches, displaying good conformation. Afterwards, he had Owen tie Dumpling beside his horse Bullet at the arena fence for additional grooming tips that they didn't always teach in 4-H. Dixon's weapon of attack was a large bottle of ShowSheen, a hair polish intended to make an animal's coat look extra sleek. He showed Owen how to use the spray on Bullet and rub it along the direction of his hair with his hand to create an impressive glow. Then he sprayed Dumpling and carefully teased up his fur in strategic places with a special comb to make him appear extra beefy. As soon as Owen got the hang of the spray bottle and tools, Dixon set him loose to work on his own for a while. He strolled over to join Tempest at her place by the fence, giving her son some autonomy.

"Dumpling sure has made big strides," Tempest mentioned as Dixon folded his arms and leaned back against the rail. "I'm sure Annie will be totally amazed when she sees how obedient he's become in the ring. But…"

Tempest worked her fingers together, searching for the right words to broach the subject.

"But what?" Dixon said, tilting his head at her son. "Owen's doing really great."

"That's not the issue," she replied. "Look, it's really wonderful how far you've brought Owen with Dumpling already, even if that beast did drag me around in the dirt again today." She brushed at the remaining soil on her arms, releasing a small cloud of dust. "But…I don't appreciate the way you kissed me at the fair without my permission—in public, in front of everybody. They even streamed it on the rural TV channel! That's my *professional* therapy booth, you know. "

"You seemed to like it, as I recall." Dixon cocked a brow, turning to face her. "You could have pushed me away any time. Besides, a friend told me it made your radio ratings skyrocket."

"I don't care!" she protested, curling her fingers tight. "Next time you try that, I swear I'm going to knock you senseless, if that's what it takes to get through to you."

Dixon laughed, his eyes glinting.

"With your reputation, I believe you. But why are you getting all huffy? It's just theater. Haven't you figured that out yet?"

"What?" Tempest's mouth fell. "What did you say?"

"I did it to help publicize the fair." Dixon's face appeared puzzled, as if that should have been clear by now. "You saw how your stats climbed on the scoreboard. We became the talk of the town. Ticket sales tripled today."

Tempest was flabbergasted.

"That was *planned?*" she said. Her eyes darted back and forth. "What does that mean—you'll be stealing kisses from Hedda Grimson next?"

"Maybe," Dixon replied with a sly smile, slinging his thumbs into the pockets of his jeans.

"Oh my God." She reached out her hands and began to pat his flannel shirt and jeans, then pried open his pockets to peer inside. "Are you *recording* this right now? You're making me totally paranoid—"

"Honey, you started out paranoid. When do you ever relax, Tempest?"

"When I'm safe!" she replied. "From people who don't have ulterior motives."

"Isn't that what chemistry is all about?" He gave her an easy grin. "When you never know what somebody's gonna say or do, and you can't wait to see what happens?"

Tempest blinked at him several times, stunned. "Wow, no wonder you attract loony tune chicks. You actually find that exciting? At nearly forty?"

"Sure beats the way you try to keep everything under control. Like life's supposed to be saran-wrapped with no surprises. That's gotta create boring relationships."

"Not if it means stability!" she spit out, instantly wishing she hadn't betrayed how good he was at piquing her temper.

"To be honest," Dixon countered, staring her straight in the eye, "I didn't mind looking under the rug for once with that kiss to see who you are when you're not focused on the radio. The minute you aren't being bossy and telling everybody how to run their lives, you can sometimes come across as downright… accessible. Instead of the Queen of Tough Love. I don't know how you manage to fit both personalities in one body."

Tempest's face flushed. She gnawed the inside of her cheeks, realizing that in her mind she'd just been accusing Dixon of the same thing—having a split personality.

Dixon moved in closer, as if sensing her vulnerability. "So what does *stability* mean to you, anyway? Not to Tempest the Terminator, but to the more…approachable…woman who's here now?"

Tempest's cheeks sent up another flare of heat, embarrassed that he'd read her so easily when she hadn't even observed that duality in herself. *Some therapist I am,* she thought. Drawing a breath, she waffled for a moment, then decided to answer Dixon truthfully, since he'd enjoy pouncing on any evasion like a cat on a mouse.

"Um, well…instead of renegade kisses in front of the whole county," she explained cautiously, "stability in relationships to me means things more like…chatting to get to know each other…and maybe cuddling by a fireplace." She folded her arms, thinking it over. "Sharing your hopes and dreams under a cozy blanket, with the understanding that the person will be back tomorrow—"

"Now you're talking." His eyes lit up. "With wine?"

"Sure," she shrugged. "Perhaps some tasty appetizers and chocolate. The whole point is that everything's gentle and happy for once. And…safe."

"So you really *do* have a tender side," he remarked with an arched brow.

"You do, too!" she turned the tables on him. "Or you wouldn't be helping Owen." Then Tempest studied the ground, tracing her hiking boot in circles in the dirt. She flinched and glanced up at Dixon. "Which, to be frank, I'm really ashamed that I haven't thanked you for enough yet. It means the world to him."

"I know," Dixon said.

Tempest's breath snagged in her throat.

Dixon *did* know. He was doing for Owen what had never been done for him. An adult male taking the time to truly

coach a young boy. To care enough to steer him in the right
direction.

"I don't get you, Dixon," Tempest finally said, feeling at
the end of her rope. "Being around you is like riding a
constant roller coaster that ranges between cocky and kind. I
never know who I'm gonna meet next."

"And that's a bad thing?"

"It is! I mean, if you've been through…a lot…lately."

Dixon dropped his focus to his cowboy boots. His jaw
clenched for a period before he lifted his gaze to meet hers. He
searched her hazel-green eyes, his expression taking in the
impact of what she'd just said.

"I, um…," he paused for a second, "I didn't mean to—"

"It's all right," she lied, waving her hand dismissively.
"This last year has just been…a rough time. Dealing with so
many changes and all."

"And you're more…fragile…than you act."

Tempest bit down on her molars.

She wanted to throw that term back at him, to claim he
was being sexist again. How dare he call *her* fragile? She was as
tough as they come—everybody knew that. Tempest averted
his gaze, knowing as a licensed therapist that she was being
ridiculous. People are always complex, strong and vulnerable
and everything in between at the same time. But she didn't
relish the fact that she'd admitted to him that she still felt
emotionally raw, and sometimes didn't have all the answers.
She was as full of flaws and contradictions, and as…human…
as everybody else.

"It's okay," Dixon said softly, setting a gentle hand on her
shoulder. "I understand more than I let on, Tempest. And with

you alway pretending you're such a brick, that make us quite the pair."

"I swear to God," she glared at him, trying not to smirk, "if you are recording this for the sake of the fair right now, I will fricking kill you."

Dixon laughed. "I told you, I'm not!" He held up his flat palm in oath. "Promise. This evening really *is* about Owen. So come on, Queen of Tough Love who happens to have a soft underbelly." He gave her a warm gaze. "Let's go check on your son."

"Only if you do one thing," she said.

"What's that?"

"Be honest with me for once." Tempest pulled in a breath. "Leave Mr. Cocky in the rodeo arena, and I'll keep Tempest the Terminator for the radio. But from now on, when you're helping Owen in the evenings, can you be who you really are?"

Dixon gazed at her son across the arena, who had his back to them while he was still working hard on making Dumpling and Bullet appear glossy. He turned to look Tempest in the eye.

"Sounds like you play for high stakes." Dixon's dark-blue eyes narrowed. "That means *you* have to stay above board, too. Which gives me full license to dish out tough love whenever you're full of shit, right?"

Tempest bit back a smile. "Yeah, I guess so."

Without warning, Dixon stepped forward and wrapped his large arm around Tempest's shoulder, seizing her for a kiss. His palm gently clutched her cheek, and in spite of the total abruptness, she felt cocooned in the warmth of his embrace. This anchored, secure feeling was so foreign to her that her body began to tremble, becoming softer and more pliable by the second. As Dixon's lips tenderly molded over hers, he gripped her tight, sealing her body to fit perfectly against his. Suddenly, all Tempest wanted was to dissolve into this man's hold like a warm pool. A safe harbor that offered her what she hadn't even known she'd been wanting…

Sanctuary.

Dixon's draw on Tempest was so strong that she couldn't manage to break free. Despite a flood of racing thoughts, the notion of separating from him was trumped by her body's demands—

And her body's wisdom told her to just feel.

Just breathe.

Just *be*—

Dixon slowly ran a finger down her throat to her cleavage, a low moan escaping his lips. He pulled away like he was afraid he might not be able to restrain himself. Then he shot a glance at Owen to make sure the boy still had his back to them.

Dixon's burning blue eyes met Tempest's.

"I did that because I *wanted* to," he stated, his voice so low it was nearly a growl. "Not for publicity. So don't you dare tell me you didn't like it this time. Or I'll call you a liar."

Speechless, Tempest stepped back, every nerve in her body still ablaze.

"F-Fair enough," she stammered, her thoughts a swirl. She clenched her teeth for a moment to keep from stuttering more. "But wasn't that kiss, like, breaking the rules or something? Fraternizing with a Cowboy Roundup contestant?"

"Damn straight. And it's *my* ranch, so I can do whatever

the hell I want." He smiled arrogantly. "In case you're wondering, that's the *real* Dixon Ramsey."

Tempest sucked the insides of her cheeks, attempting to calm down her rocket-fired nerves. Damn, she thought, I think I'm starting to like this version of Dixon. He may take what he wants—but he sure makes it feel divine to be wanted.

Hold on to yourself, girl! Tempest chastised herself, warning her soul to take things slow. Don't forget, this cowboy's track record is full of high-speed collisions.

"Mom!" Owen cried, piercing through Tempest's thoughts. "Come here and see what I did! Dumpling and Bullet look perfect!"

Tempest rotated to face her son, grateful for the distraction. She noticed that the horse's gray coat shimmered in the late afternoon light, revealing every toned muscle on its athletic frame. And Dumpling had a smug look on his face like a newly-coiffed poodle.

"They look fantastic, honey!" she called out to Owen. "You did an awesome job."

"And so did *you*," Dixon whispered to her, "letting Owen work on his own to finish the task. Maybe we should celebrate this non-hovering milestone of yours some time by firelight? To promote *stability*, I mean."

Tempest's breath caught, followed by a soft giggle. "That would be... really nice," she answered honestly. Nevertheless, her gut squeezed a little, making her feel more vulnerable than she had in years.

"Don't worry," Dixon replied, detecting her insecurity, "real cowboys watch over those they care about. And make sure they're safe." He gazed out over his massive ranch with land as far as the eye could see. "In case you forgot, I'm a *real* cowboy."

At that moment, Owen untied Dumpling and began to lead his animal toward them, when Tempest saw a bear wriggle awkwardly through the fence rails. It was old Bonner, and he bounded slowly toward the center of the arena with a lumbering gait. In response, Dumpling bolted free from Owen's grip on the lead line. Tempest thought for certain the yearling must be running away in terror, but to her astonishment, Dumpling dipped his head and began to charge toward the bear. Within seconds, the bear met the yearling head on and toppled him into the dirt, then began cuffing at Dumpling like a naughty cub. The yearling scrambled to his feet and swapped more head butts with Bonner, until the two animals succeeded in taking turns knocking each other down. If Tempest didn't know better, she'd swear they were rassling like old pals.

"Looks like Dumpling finally met his match," Dixon chuckled. He shielded his eyes with his palm and spotted another truck in the parking lot. "Well, if Bonner's here," he turned to Tempest, "that means my dad's back home." He quickly gauged the position of the sun in the sky. "Time to get to work and squeeze in a few runs of bulldogging practice before it gets dark."

14

"Can we watch, Mom?" Owen begged, tugging hard on her shirt as Dixon led his horse to the barn to saddle up. "I've never seen live steer wrestling before!" He studied the ground to come up with more arguments in his favor, then implored her with his big eyes. "Just think," Owen persisted, "I'll get to see Mister Dixon's bulldogging skills up close!"

"Not *too* close," Tempest countered. "If we watch Dixon practice, we're going to sit a distance away." She checked her cell phone for the time—they still had about an hour left of light before they had to get back to the fairgrounds, so she couldn't think of an excuse. "All right, you have to promise you'll stick next to me on the fence," she insisted. "I don't want you getting between the steer and the horses—both can trample you."

"Promise!" Owen nodded vigorously, happy at the prospect of seeing the action. He'd already walked Dumpling to a nearby corral and locked him inside until they needed to leave. And after hearing a dinner bell, Bonner had wandered slowly over to the ranch house porch to fetch his evening meal. With the animals taken care of, Owen followed his mother and climbed the arena fence to sit beside her as one of Dixon's ranch hands herded a steer into a bright yellow chute.

Dixon's father was on a horse on the opposite side of the chute, while Dixon was astride Bullet in the bay next to the steer with his horse standing behind a rope. Dixon had told them earlier that his dad is the "hazer"—a crucial wingman whose job is to keep the steer running in a straight line once he's been released. That way, Dixon could ride up alongside the steer without the animal zig zagging too much and then tackle him to the ground. But if Dixon charged forward before the steer was given a brief head start that loosened the breakaway rope, he'd get ten penalty points—enough to keep him from winning any competition. Timing is everything, Dixon said, and he'd assigned another one of his ranch hands to manage the stopwatch, who wouldn't halt the time until the steer had landed on his side with all four hooves pointing in the same direction.

Fortunately, ever since his dad had given up drinking recently, Dixon said his hazer skills were among the best in the county—and he could only hope his sobriety would last. Now, with both men on their horses, they stared into the arena like two warriors ready for attack. Their horses stood to attention with their ears erect, every muscle in their bodies rippling and ready to spring, waiting for the slightest nudge from their riders.

The chute gate swung open with a loud clang, and out

bolted the steer at approximately thirty miles an hour. He was soon followed by the two horses, who exploded from their positions and shadowed him like guided missiles. Within a few strides, Dixon had leaned entirely out of his saddle and did precisely as he'd taught Owen—he threw his hip into the steer's body at the exact same moment that he'd grabbed the animal's horns and planted his boots into the dirt. Then he allowed his heels to slide as he gave the steer a twist that made him fall flat with his hooves in the air, surrounded by dust.

Owen clapped wildly, cheering at Dixon's success—all within a matter of less than five seconds. Tempest lost her breath at the sight, astonished at Dixon's raw athleticism and ability to wrestle an animal over twice his weight. Then there was the sprinting power of his performance horse Bullet, who possessed such swiftness that Dixon accomplished his task far faster than she could ever imagine.

No wonder he sells his horses for a pot full of money! Tempest thought. They're trained to release so much power they rival drag race cars.

As Dixon got up from the ground, Tempest saw his father circle back and ride up to the somewhat stunned steer, who was still shaking his head, in order to drive him away from his son. The wily steer tossed his horns and refused to budge, but Bear's chestnut horse sideswiped him with a firm shoulder bump to divert his path, indicating he meant business. The steer gave in and began to trot lazily back toward the chute. Suddenly, he veered sharply away and began to charge with astonishing speed toward Dixon. Dixon spied him and bolted toward the fence as fast as his legs could carry. But before he could climb the rails, the steer knocked him down and thrust a horn into his chest.

Owen let out a scream while Tempest grabbed his face and forced him to turn away. Dixon's dad immediately roped the animal, yanking him from near his son and winding the rope tightly around his saddle horn to secure the steer in place. The old man's horse stood stock still as Bear dismounted and dashed over to his son.

"Mom! Lemme go!" Owen wriggled for all he was worth, sliding out of Tempest's grip like a slippery fish. He jumped down from the fence and ran as fast as he could toward Dixon, with his mother chasing after his heels. When they reached Dixon, he'd managed to rise to his feet with a blood stain on his chest seeping across his flannel shirt.

"Oh my God—you're hurt!" Tempest gasped, floored at the casual way Dixon had turned to his dad and began chatting like nothing unusual had happened. The two men even exchanged a hearty laugh.

"We've got to get you to emergency care!" she demanded.

Dixon's gaze flitted from Tempest to Owen, appearing puzzled. Then he glanced down at the red stain on his shirt. "Oh, that," he remarked, somewhat amused. "Thanks, Dad, for catching the bugger before he could do more damage."

"No problem," Bear smiled easily. He patted his son on the back and returned to his horse. Tempest winced when she saw Dixon unbutton his flannel shirt, revealing his toned chest covered in old scars. A puncture wound the size of a quarter near his heart was bleeding.

"No guts, no glory—my time was 4.8!" Dixon told Tempest proudly, wiping away the blood with the tail of his shirt. "We get tetanus shots around here, so as soon as I throw on some alcohol from the barn, I'll be fine." He tousled Owen's hair. "Heck, if you ain't getting hurt, you ain't in the game!"

Dixon's gaze settled on Tempest. For a moment, a surprising shadow crossed his face, one that had seen more than its fair share of rodeo accidents. "Kind of like....lending out your heart, huh?" he muttered with an arched brow. "Ain't that what you're always saying on the radio?"

"Um, not really," Tempest replied, a bit confused. "I tell people to guard themselves."

Tempest wasn't sure, but she thought she saw a flinch pass over Dixon's eyes. Maybe all those crash and burn relationships have gotten to him more than he lets on? she thought.

Or maybe he's wishing I'd brave up and take a gamble on him—

Startled by such a thought, Tempest shook her head, willing that wayward idea from her mind. When her gaze returned to Dixon, he'd lifted his palm to Owen's for a high five.

"Cowboys gotta be resilient, right?" he said. "Never know when you're gonna fall or," he glanced down at his wound, "get struck at the heart. That's why we call this place the Rambling Star Ranch." He tilted his head at the entrance gate. "'Cause us cowpunchers are just a bunch of rambling stars who chase through the sky, burning bright as we can. But you know what? As long as it makes you feel alive, you're doing something right. This ol' scratch will heal up in no time."

Dixon turned to head for the corral next to the arena.

"C'mon, Owen, let's go fetch Dumpling and take him back to the fairgrounds so we can get him dinner before nightfall."

Despite all of Dixon's bravado, Tempest couldn't help noticing that he winced as he began to walk toward the corral. Even so, he picked up Owen and hoisted him onto his shoulders, his legs swinging with long strides. Dixon gave his dad a wave in appreciation as he watched him on his horse leading the steer back to the chute. While Owen rode on top of Dixon's shoulders with his feet dangling, Tempest saw him break into a huge grin.

Like the happiest boy on earth.

And now, Tempest was the one doing the flinching.

15

That night, Tempest tossed and turned in her bed for what felt like hours. She squinted at her digital bedside clock, its glowing numbers displaying midnight. Releasing a long breath, she finally pulled her covers up to her chin, unable to deny the fact that she felt a bit...raw. And yes, maybe slightly fragile. All the while, she hated herself for it, because that's what Dixon had observed about her earlier that day.

But the one thing he hadn't mentioned is that she also felt...

Haunted.

It wasn't from the blood she'd seen on Dixon's chest, though that had certainly been a jolt.

And it wasn't even from the fact that he'd gotten hurt, doing what he clearly loved.

The truth was, it was from seeing Owen's face while he rode on Dixon's shoulders. As the sun was setting in the evening, a warm glow reflected over her son's cheeks, which were all scrunched up into a smile. Owen beamed like he was having the perfect day.

Tempest had never seen a look quite like that on her son before.

One of pride.

Joy.

And...stability.

Tempest bit her lip, her fingers clutching her bedspread too tight.

She couldn't deny the fact that Owen trusted that man. Looked up to him.

And felt *connected* to him.

Not once had her son displayed those emotions with his father. That man had been a stranger—to both of them. For more years than she wanted to admit. Than she should have *ever* allowed.

Tempest cringed. No matter how much she wanted to force the happy image of Owen and Dixon from her mind, that moment had shed light on a gaping hole in her heart. Bigger than the wound she'd seen on Dixon that evening.

It was the hollow cave she never admitted, but that she'd been carrying around for ages. Hitched to a man who hardly knew she existed, much less their son. Of course, she'd turned herself inside out trying to make it work—

For a woman who prided herself on being insightful, she knew she'd utterly failed.

And worst of all, failed Owen.

A boy who'd never gotten the opportunity to develop a positive relationship with a man.

And now, it was like they were being given a second chance—

Tempest's breath slowed at the thought. Then she swore she felt a silent presence in the room.

"Mom?" she heard Owen whisper. "Can I get in bed with you?"

"Of course, honey," she replied. "Did you have a bad dream?"

"No," he said with a slight yawn. "I just missed you."

Tempest was always a sucker for his affection, so she lifted up the covers and let him crawl into the bed, his soft cottony pajamas with bronco images sliding against her skin, still warm from sleep.

As Owen cuddled beside her, Tempest felt a lump rise in her throat. She gave him a peck on the forehead, drawing a deep breath to summon the courage to ask him the question. The *hard* question. She wanted to know if the sight of Dixon getting hurt had traumatized him—or perhaps brought back difficult memories.

"Sweetie, do you, um…miss Daddy, too?" She asked cautiously. "Since Dixon got hurt today, is that what disturbed your sleep—"

"No," Owen shook his head before she could finish. "I used to miss Dad's face sometimes, but he never did things with me. Not like Mister Dixon," he said flatly, releasing another yawn. "I really like him, Mommy. He makes me feel strong. Like I can do anything if I try hard enough."

A tear crawled down Tempest's cheek.

She swiftly brushed her face against her pillow, hoping Owen hadn't seen. After all her psycho-babble and pep talks with her son over the past year, nothing could compare to the confidence Dixon had been instilling in him.

Owen's breath felt warm and moist against her shoulder as he snuggled closer. "Can't wait to go back to his ranch tomorrow," he whispered in her ear. Then he paused for a moment, and Tempest could feel his little belly jiggling with laughter. "I saw him kiss you, you know."

Tempest's cheeks swelled with heat. "Oh, that was just to practice for the Cowboy Roundup, honey," she dismissed. "It doesn't mean he likes me—"

"Yeah, it does," Owen said with the kind of simple certainty that only eight-year-olds possess. Her son fell silent for a while, making Tempest feel uncomfortable. "Do you like him?" he asked.

Leave it to a third grader to get straight to the point, Tempest cringed. And I thought *I* was the therapist who asked all the penetrating questions.

Tempest stilled for a moment.

"Well, *do you*, Mommy?"

Swallowing at the dryness that suddenly parched her throat, Tempest remained silent for a while in the darkness.

"I...don't...know," she finally answered, feeling bewildered by everything that had happened lately. Dixon was cocky and kind—arrogant and caring—aggressive and sensitive. And sometimes he seemed to be completely dialed into her, like he'd read her mind. What on earth was she to think?

"Is he a good kisser?"

Tempest laughed a little.

"Yes," she sighed, unable to lie. "As a matter of fact, he is."

"Then why don't you know if you like him?"

"Because with adults, it's complicated——"

"No it's not."

"Are you going to start carrying a therapist card, honey? 'Cause you sure know how to get to the heart of things fast."

"You didn't answer."

Tempest rolled her eyes.

"To be honest, I do like him, Owen. I just don't know if Dixon is…safe…for us."

"Dixon says you never know until you take a chance on stuff."

"That's how people get hurt, honey. You saw the blood on his shirt today. He's a pretty big risk taker. Sometimes that can end badly."

Owen paused, thinking about what she'd said.

All at once, the silence in the bedroom felt thick to Tempest, the way the whole past year had felt thick to her. A heavy weight she'd had to bear, full of terrible mistakes, good and not so good intentions, what she did and didn't do. Thick with loss. Thick with fear. Thick with never knowing what the future was going to hold——

"Dixon smiled anyway," Owen said, cutting through her thoughts.

"What?" Tempest replied.

"He smiled. After he got hurt today. He said it was worth it, 'cause he'd finished in 4.8 seconds. I think he gets hurt a lot, Mom. He just deals with it."

Tempest's breath stalled.

She wanted to say love is far more complex than wrestling steers or being a cowboy, something that surely Owen couldn't grasp at his tender age. But the words wouldn't escape her mouth. Not after the image of Owen riding on Dixon's shoulders, looking so happy and secure, kept burrowing through her mind. All Tempest could think of to do in that moment was hug her son.

"Let's get back to sleep, honey," she whispered, her voice full of fatigue.

"Okay," Owen relented. "But Mom…"

As he trailed off, Tempested assumed he wanted her to get him a drink of water, or maybe a cookie, which was their usual bed time routine.

"Yes, honey?" she replied wearily.

"I think you should smile more, too."

Tempest could hear the sound of her own breathing in the dark as Owen's small voice evaporated into the night. She heard him yawn slowly as his small body surrendered to slumber. Relieved, she lifted her gaze to the ceiling.

Smiles, she thought, her eyelids beginning to feel heavier. She brushed Owen's soft hair across his forehead, envying his youthful confidence, the way he was prepared to dive headlong into life, like cowboys do. Rambling stars, Dixon had called them, burning bright.

All at once, Granny Tinker's words resurfaced in her mind, the strange thing she'd said when she'd first passed by her at the fairgrounds on the way to her booth.

"Why, look yonder," Granny had remarked, gazing at a star still twinkling in the early morning sky as if it were an omen. "You're just like that rambling star who needs to find rest."

Tingles skittered across Tempest's skin at the odd coincidence. She snuck a peek at the late hour on her bedside clock, then sank deeply beneath her covers, treasuring the warm feel of her son beside her. Finally, the two of them could get some much-needed sleep.

But when Tempest closed her eyes, all she could see in her mind was Dixon's and Owen's smiles.

16

"It's time to give it all you've got, Spencer. You're not getting any younger! What are you waiting for?"

The middle-aged man with salt and pepper hair and a plaid Wrangler shirt lifted his gaze to Tempest with traces of insecurity in his eyes. Ivy smiled at him from their booth and offered him a nod of encouragement.

"Look, Spencer," Tempest continued, her words picked up by her radio microphone, "you saw my roping performance for the Cowboy Roundup yesterday, right?"

"Yeah," he began to laugh. "You, um, fell on your face and got dragged."

"Exactly! I'm really bad at it, which just goes to show you how hard rodeoing is. But hey," she reached out and patted his arm, "life can get awfully boring if you never take any…chances."

Tempest chewed her lip, wondering who she was really

preaching to this time—Spencer or herself? She squared her shoulders and pressed on.

"Just remember, when you face plant in the dirt in life, you can always get back up," Tempest added. "So if you don't brave up and go get Opal, what makes you believe she's going to still be around for you?"

Spencer shifted his feet in the dirt, mulling it over. "You think I should hop in my truck and go get her right now?"

"You said you've been dreaming about her for months! Let me ask you this—if a bus hit you tomorrow, would you regret it if you didn't try?"

Spencer hung his head, his eyes following the criss-cross laces on his muleskinner boots. Then a man in overalls approached the booth, leading an ivory-colored alpaca in a pale lavender halter. When Spencer shifted his gaze to the animal, his eyes lit up.

Ivy gasped. "Lavender is the color of balance and harmony in love!" she said, bouncing on her heels. "This is a perfect match!"

Spencer and the man stared at her, befuddled.

"Well, Opal sure is pretty," Spencer mentioned to the man. "You're darn lucky, Tom."

"My luck just got better, too," Tom replied with a proud glint in his eyes. "This little lady won her division." He turned the alpaca's head so they could all see the large blue ribbon that hung from her halter. "And a local breeder gave me an offer of seven for her. You gonna beat that, Spencer? Or should I load her in that fella's trailer?"

"It's now or never," Tempest leaned forward and whispered into Spencer's ear. "Didn't you tell me a minute ago you've always wanted to be a top alpaca breeder?" Her hazel-green eyes bored into his. "Then go for it—with a smile on your face."

Spencer was taken aback by Tempest's moxie. He scanned the alpaca, her coat shining like new-fallen snow in the morning light. When she blinked her big, doe eyes, Ivy grinned, certain he was hooked.

"All right, I'll do it!" Spencer's chest swelled as he turned to Tom. "I'll give you eight for her. But only if you walk Opal over to my stock trailer and help me load her after lunch." He winked at Ivy. "With that lavender halter included."

"Deal! Eight-thousand it is," Tom agreed, shaking Spencer's hand. "I'll see you in the fairgrounds back parking lot after noon."

Tempest and Ivy shared wide-eyed glances. They'd thought the men were talking about hundreds, not *thousands*, of dollars. Tempest's cheeks warmed—clearly, what she knew about quality livestock could be held in a thimble.

"One more thing before I go," Spencer insisted, setting an elbow onto Tempest's booth with new-found confidence. "I'm feeling pretty lucky, so can I have a kiss? Like Dixon got yesterday?"

Tempest rolled her eyes. "Seriously?" She huffed out a breath. "That'll cost you an extra ten bucks. No—make it twenty, and only on the cheek. I'll donate the cash to 4-H."

Spencer grinned and gave her a peck as he slapped a bill onto the booth. "Thanks, Tempest!" he said, waving as he started to walk away. "Can't wait to see how you look in a swimsuit this afternoon!"

At that moment, Tempest caught the larger-than-life image

of herself on the huge scoreboard above the outdoor arena. It
was the deer-in-the-headlights photo taken during the roping
event yesterday. She squinted at the image and groaned—her
hair was a mess and the desperation in her eyes made her look
like she'd just been slapped. Beneath her picture were the
words, "Y'all come to see Tempest Wright in a swimsuit this
afternoon to compete in the Cowboy Roundup!"

Ivy spied the picture, flashing Tempest an impish smile.
"Well, that couldn't be more timely—look what I brought
you!" She reached down into her purse and held up a bright
orange maillot. "A swimsuit! Since the Dash and Splash is
today, I picked out tangerine because it exudes optimism and
success. I'm sure it will help you win!"

"Can't you see that winning is my nightmare?" Tempest
pointed to her nearly cross-eyed expression on the scoreboard
as proof. "If they broadcast photos that awful for the rural TV
station, imagine what will happen when I'm in a swimsuit. I'd
rather the lens be on somebody else."

Ivy stubbornly draped the one-piece from Tempest's
shoulders, biting her lip. Her eyes brightened. "But this color
will look fantastic on you!"

"For walking a plank? Over a big cattle pond?" Tempest
buried her head in her hands. "You realize everyone's hoping I'll
fall into the mud, right?" She peeked through her fingers at Ivy.
"Around here, that's called county fair humor to sell tickets."

"No, it's more than that," Ivy said quietly. "I'm being
serious—this tangerine swimsuit will make everybody fall in
love with you, mud or no mud." Ivy's eyes glistened at the
possibilities. "And that's such a beautiful thing."

Tempest paused, struck by the sincerity in Ivy's gaze. Sometimes she forgot how dedicated Ivy was to her color therapy ideas. Finding love and belonging for others meant as much to her as Tempest's desire to help people better their lives.

"Funny you should bring up *love*, darlin'," Tempest heard a gravelly voice behind her.

She jerked around—there was Granny Tinker, along with her pals Jubilee and Pearl, standing at the corner of her booth. They were wearing their dark period dresses, of course, making them look dour as if they were the head matriarchs of the town.

"E-Excuse me," Tempest said, trying to overcome their startling presence. There weren't many people who intimidated her in this world, but Granny Tinker's wolfish gray eyes with their peculiar rings of gold in the middle always did the trick. "Are you ladies here for…advice?"

"We're helping the Cowboy Roundup today by passing out the swimsuits you have to wear," stated Pearl, the most petite member of the Trinity. "This outfit was approved by the Fair Board, since it's a family-friendly event." She handed Tempest a sleeveless navy shift with nautical accents. The garment was so blousy it looked like something worn to the beach a century ago.

Tempest spread the outfit across her booth, her eyes widening as she examined the voluminous fabric with a white sash designed to anchor it in the middle. "This isn't a swimsuit," she observed, "it's a…dress!" Then she dared to peek beneath the navy material. "Oh my God, what are these?" She uncovered a pair of white knickers intended to cinch at the knees. "*Bloomers?*"

"Yes, ma'am!" confirmed Jubilee, Granny's stouter friend with curly gray hair pulled into a bun. "Since we're in the Historical Society, we brought these 1915 replicas straight here from the town museum."

"Don't worry, darlin'," Pearl assured her, patting Tempest's hand. "Did you know I competed in the Cowboy Roundup myself years ago, wearing this cute little thing? That's how I roped my Emmett! He was the handsomest cowboy in the county back then. And Lord, did he ever take a shine to me in this get-up. It may look old-fashioned, but it sure shows off your legs to admiring glances! Lemme see, do you have nice gams?"

Pearl boldly stepped into Tempest's booth and lifted her pants leg, inspecting the contours of her calf and ankle. "My, my—you're quite lovely! I betcha Dixon Ramsey will be heart stricken. I tell ya, this Dash and Splash snags a man every time."

"But I'm not trying to snag anybody!" Tempest replied, overcome by the rise of her own voice. She quickly drew a breath to moderate her volume. "I'm just at the fair to help my son and to keep my radio show going."

"Aw, it don't matter, hon," Granny Tinker said in a surprisingly soothing tone, the kind that felt oddly to Tempest like a warm blanket had been wrapped over her heart. Granny's lips inched up on one side. "No matter what you wear," she said like a promise, "it's a waste of time to fight fate. Might as well relax and enjoy yourself."

With that, Granny turned on her crimson boot heels and

headed off, followed by Jubilee and Pearl as she sauntered back to their booth. Tempest couldn't tell what bothered her more —Granny's typically cryptic words, or the fact that she always acted nonchalant afterwards, as if she were surely harboring secrets.

"Those ladies are up to something strange, I know it," Tempest mentioned to Ivy. "Why haven't you insisted that they give you back your ruby heart charm yet? Might save you trouble later."

Ivy folded her arms with a smile. "Because they could achieve with my charm what I've haven't with color. Hasn't it crossed your mind that I'm taking notes?" She tilted her head at their booth with a sparkle in her eye. "I've heard the Trinity *never* fail to make a match."

"But a match isn't the same thing as...love," Tempest replied softly with a crack in her voice. "Of all people, I ought to know, considering my late husband. Just because two people are together doesn't mean they...belong...with each other."

Ivy studied Tempest's face with a sweetness that pierced her heart. "Well," she offered thoughtfully, "maybe that's why you require outside help. You know as well as I do that most people can't be trusted not to rely on their old patterns." Her lips curled a little at the corners. "Unless you want to stick to your same old path and change your radio name to Tempest the Train Wreck," she teased.

Tempest was unable to stifle a smirk at her intern's brashness, let alone her habit for skewering the truth to the bull's-eye. "Oh Ivy, I hear you, I really do," she admitted, slinging her arm around her shoulders. "And I get it—we all should self-reflect more. But may I officially declare that sometimes you're *impossible?*" She let out a soft laugh. "And I bet there's a color for that—"

"As a matter of fact, there is!" Ivy replied. "Cochineal—it's made from squashed bugs. And you happen to be *wearing* it right now. Takes one to know one, right?"

Tempest smirked, holding out the hem of her shirt. "Wait, I thought this hue is called raspberry."

"Same difference!" Ivy shrugged. "It still means you're just as headstrong as I am—"

"Attention everyone!" the fair announcer called out. "The Dash and Splash for the Cowboy Roundup is due to begin at the cattle pond at the east side of the fairgrounds in thirty minutes. This is one of our most popular events, so you might want to grab a seat now before the bleachers fill up. Cowboy Roundup contestants, please have your swimsuits on and be ready at the cattle pond at the top of the hour."

Tempest sealed her eyes, mentally preparing herself to actually put on bloomers, along with that awful, blue sack of a swimsuit. When she opened her eyes, she spotted Blossom huddled beneath a nearby tree. Blossom sat with her arms cradled around her knees, appearing to be shaking.

"Ivy," Tempest pointed discreetly at the tree, "is Blossom *crying* over there? I realize these swimsuits aren't exactly glamorous, but—"

"Let's go see," Ivy said, tugging on Tempest to leave the booth with her. A few moments later, the two of them reached Blossom and they quietly kneeled beside her on the ground.

"What's wrong, honey?" Tempest asked, stroking Blossom's long, red hair as she sobbed. She noticed Blossom's navy swimsuit was bunched up in her fist like a rag. "Don't worry, we all have to wear the same crummy outfit. Just think of us as a team. Okay, a really badly dressed team."

"The color navy predicts confidence and courage," Ivy said hopefully. "So things ought to go pretty well."

"That's not it," Blossom sniffled, raising her face to the two women. "My mom just came by and told me I'm gonna look like a cow in this outfit. Perfect for the cattle pond, right?" Blossom stared at a wad of cotton candy in the dirt. "She caught me eating fair food again and threw it to the ground and lectured me for the millionth time. Like my whole job in life is to look pretty according to *her* standards."

"Cow, huh?" Tempest issued a breath through clenched teeth, her patience with Betty starting to wear thin. "Well," she mulled it over for a moment, "there's no need to let your mother have the last word on beauty. Especially since her ideas are so archaic."

She grasped Blossom's elbow and lifted her to her feet, then carefully scanned her full figure in her overalls. Tempest tapped her lip. "Maybe it's high time we show your mother how *good* cotton candy can really look on your curves."

"Ivy," Tempest instructed as her intern stood up. She motioned to the fair office. "Would you mind checking if there's an old Cowboy Roundup regulation manual in the fair library? And while you're at it, see if you can borrow a stapler."

Tempest stared at Blossom with calculated resolve. "We might not be allowed to break the rules with these godawful swimsuits," she assured her. "But we sure as hell can do our best to bend them."

17

Tempest rolled in the fabric of Blossom's vintage swimsuit at both sides of the waist on the flat surface of her booth. Then she pounded the stapler with her fist like mad. When she was finished, she held up the garment and admired its now hourglass shape with a devilish grin.

"There!" she proudly handed it to Blossom. "That ought to hug your curves better and give your mother the shock of her life. Let's go to the ladies changing room in the main building—we only have fifteen minutes left to get ready."

Blossom agreed, her eyes betraying a hint of dread as she watched Ivy take Owen by the hand and leave to secure a place on the bleachers. Tempest and Blossom headed over to the changing room, then ducked into the stalls and threw off their clothes to slip on the awkward swimsuits. They emerged looking like wild, adventurous women—

From 1915.

Tempest saw herself in the mirror and busted out laughing.

"Oh my God, I've never looked so frumpy in my whole life!" She scrutinized the fabric that billowed over her bust and hips, tied in the middle like a sack and sagging in all the wrong places. "It's like I gained thirty pounds in my sleep and haven't exercised since the last century."

Still laughing, she flitted a gaze at Blossom.

"Holy cow!" she gasped.

When she realized her gaffe, Tempest quickly backpedaled. "Oh my, pardon the pun, Blossom. I didn't mean to compare you to real cows at all. In fact, you look...*gorgeous.*"

Blossom's cheeks turned a cherry hue, her lips rising in a timid smile. Tempest had never seen her in anything but oversized overalls before. Who knew there was a such a va-va-voom figure underneath? She'd meant to staple the swimsuit in strategic places to accentuate Blossom's curves, but she had no idea the woman's measurements rivaled old Hollywood film stars. With her shiny, long red hair, buttermilk complexion, big blue eyes, and figure that approximated 40-28-40, Blossom was the kind of woman destined to make most men in the county faint.

"This is fantastic!" Tempest exclaimed in relief. "No one's going to even see me on that plank with a knockout like you around. Get ready for the fair photographers to buzz around you like bees!"

"Really, you think so?" Blossom replied, hardly recognizing herself in the mirror.

"Consider me your bodyguard from here on out!" Tempest linked her elbow around Blossom's. "Because there isn't a man under fifty who's not going to think you're the best looking woman ever to hit this fair. Come on, superstar," Tempest tugged on her arm, "wait till your mother sees this. She'll be choking on her words like we stuffed cotton candy down her throat."

"Wait," Blossom hesitated at the door. "I-I don't like making her mad. I mean, there's always hell to pay whenever my mom doesn't get her way."

Tempest's eyebrows pinched. "Honey," she sighed, "I hate to go all Tempest the Terminator on you, but you need to make a decision. Are you going to let your mother rule your life, one carefully-placed criticism at a time? Or are you going to take control now, and do you what *you* want? It's time to show your mother by example what healthy boundaries really mean. Because you're at the fork in the road between youth and true adulthood, and here's the kicker—nobody becomes a grown up unless they want to. As in, takes personal responsibility and respects other people. You're well on your way, but it sure looks like your mom never hit that milestone."

Blossom stared at the tile floor for a moment, shifting her boots. "Um, should I give you a dollar for that?" she asked. "Because I think you just handed me my fifteen minutes of therapy again. Unless that virtual slap in the face was a freebie."

Tempest laughed.

"Naw, just be yourself, sweetie," she said. "I mean your *real* self, not who your mother tells you to be. That's more than enough for me. Now let's get out there and knock 'em dead."

"I take it all back. I can't do this!" Blossom sputtered, digging her fingers hard into Tempest's forearm. She stood at the bottom of the ladder for the Dash and Splash plank that extended fifty feet across a cattle pound. The weathered plank was slightly bowed with one rickety support beam in the middle, and on either side were two sets of bleachers on the grass overlooking the pond, filled to the brim with eager faces.

Including Ivy and Owen.

Tempest gave them a wave, then carefully peeled Blossom's fingers from her skin, wincing at the dents she'd made. She gripped her by the shoulders and stared into her eyes.

"Look, I know you're nervous. So why don't you let Hedda and me go first while you work up your courage?" She rotated her to look at the bleachers. "See, everybody here is rooting for you! The event will do a world of good for 4-H, and I'm sure it will be over fast. Plus, the plank is six whole inches wide. I've heard it swings up and down a bit, but if you walk quick, you'll get to the other side in no time."

"But I feel so…exposed."

"Why, because you're drop-dead beautiful, even in this pathetic sack of a swimsuit? You look better in this get-up than anybody could have dreamed—"

"That's the point," Blossom confessed timidly, looping a strand of red hair behind her ear. "I-I'm not used to being… seen. It makes me feel like I'm going to become target practice! I guess all along I wore the big clothes to try and make myself invisible to my mom," she admitted, wringing her hands. "You can't criticize what you don't see, right? Now the whole county will be ogling me. God knows what they're going to say—"

"You're right about that, darlin'," Hedda confirmed, startling Tempest and Blossom. She marched up to the two of them like a woman ready for Buffalo Bill's Wild West Show, fully outfitted in her vintage swimsuit and pink cowgirl boots and hat, which looked rather dapper together. She squinted and gazed Blossom up and down. "Take it from me, every onlooker out there will have a stupid opinion." Then she pointed a pink, ruffled parasol into the young woman's face. "But you ain't gonna let it get to you. Know why?"

Blossom shook her head, a bit frightened of the sharp end of the parasol.

"Cause us cowgirls don't give a damn!" Hedda slapped her knee and began to laugh. She opened her parasol and flitted it over her head, looking like quite the eccentric showgirl. "Let me tell you, rodeoing and 4-H are loaded with competitive bitches who are always ready to take you down. And I heard your mother ain't no peach either! So the trick is to walk a straight line with your head up high like you ain't got a care in the world. Nothing makes bitches back down better than a woman who knows who she is and ain't afraid to show it. You're a downright beauty, Blossom." Hedda gave her an encouraging smile. "And the more you own it, the more folks are gonna tie themselves in knots wishing they had your looks. So follow after me and Tempest on the plank like the queen that you are. How do you think I won Miss Outlaw Days Rodeo? It wasn't by being a shrinking violet! If you don't get up there and show your stuff like you've committed to, you're gonna have to answer to *me*. And I ain't a bit afraid to use this parasol on your butt! So who are you more scared of—the audience out there, or *me?*"

"You!" Blossom replied without hesitation, struggling to hide her smirk. "Hands down!"

"I'll second that motion!" a familiar voiced added from behind Tempest. She and Blossom glanced over their shoulders, spying Dixon Ramsey with his shirt off.

The sight was enough to steal the breath right out of Tempest's throat—

She was so overcome by his raw, physical appearance that for a moment she feared she might drool.

Embarrassed, she tried in vain to lift her chin, requiring the heel of her hand for support. This man was *beyond* good looking in his torn, faded jeans without a shirt, his muscular, tan skin reflecting a smooth, caramel color in the afternoon light. Despite the small bandage over his sternum where he'd gotten gored the day before, he was utter perfection in Tempest's book. She felt her fingertips begin to tingle like they were too close to a fire, just dying to run up and down his ridiculously-toned muscles.

Dixon immediately caught the derailment in Tempest's eyes. He broke into the kind of easy grin that said he was used to it.

"Good afternoon, ladies!" he greeted them brightly, slinging his thumbs into his jeans pockets as if he enjoyed the swooning effect his bare chest had on women. Then his eyes narrowed as he scanned Blossom's figure. "Good Lord," he said in disbelief, "are you *really* the same gal who works at the feed store?"

Blossom nodded, biting her lip.

Dixon arched a brow. "Sweetheart, in that outfit, I gotta tell ya that ain't nobody ever gonna look at you the same again." He leaned in a little closer. "Are you ready for all that attention?"

Blossom shot a glance at Hedda, catching her imperious gaze with her parasol upraised, as if she weren't afraid to use it. Pulling in a nervous breath, Blossom didn't dare shake her head.

"Listen, it's well past the hour to start the event, and the announcer told me the crowds are getting antsy," Dixon informed them. "I headed over here because I had a hunch this all might be a bit much for you ladies. So how about if I stand in the middle of the pond, ready to catch you if you happen to drop?" he offered gallantly. "Just think of me as your fall guy—if anybody gets coated in mud, it'll be me."

He gazed down at his torn jeans, a curl sneaking onto his lip. "Frankly, I usually swim nude in the lake on my ranch, but since this is a family event, I'll give folks the courtesy of keeping on my jeans. Wouldn't want to make the ladies blush, now would I?"

Thank God! Tempest thought, grateful for divine favors. Because the moment he'd said nude, she couldn't stop her mind from drifting to the picture of him skinny dipping—*and* peeling her clothes off to join him. Her thoughts became a runaway train, riddled with images of the moonlight caressing every inch of Dixon's heavenly wet skin. Tempest's breath became ragged and she shook her head to reclaim her bearings.

"Earth to Tempest!" Hedda jabbed her with her parasol. Her mouth broke into a wicked grin. "You ain't the only one toying with the idea of Dixon wet. If I win the Cowboy Roundup trip to dinner, I might insist on a midnight swim with him for dessert!"

Tempest smirked at Hedda's audacity and glanced up, spotting her halfway up the ladder. Dixon had already begun to walk toward the pond, and when he reached the edge, he sloshed through the water to his waist. Then he stood with his thick arms folded, waiting expectantly. He was so focused that he didn't even notice the women in the bleachers who'd clutched their hands to their chests, gobsmacked by his good looks. Then they pulled out their cell phones and began snapping pictures of him in a frenzy. All at once, Dixon's chances for finally being able to find true love on the scoreboard above the outdoor arena began scaling so high they became a blur, with the numbers rising faster than Tempest's eyes could track.

"Don't get distracted!" Hedda scolded from on top of the ladder. "I'm ready to walk that plank right now. You'd better file behind me, ladies, so we can be done with this thing."

Tempest nodded, following up the ladder after Hedda as the announcer called out the start of the Dash and Splash. He encouraged the audience to write down their favorite choice for the winner of the day on their ticket stubs and to drop them in the milk pail ballots stationed around the fair. They could also go to the wagering booth to place bets, if they were of the gambling persuasion. The crowd erupted into applause as Hedda stood at one end of the plank. She headed across, carefully stepping flat-footed in her pink cowgirl boots and holding out her arms with her parasol in the air. When she reached the middle, she even did a small pirouette to astonished gasps from the crowd, like she was simply taking a walk in the park. Then she finished off the rest of the distance quickly, climbing down from the ladder on the other side and throwing her arms in the air like a champion.

"You saw it yourself, folks!" crooned the announcer. "They didn't crown Miss Hedda rodeo queen back in the day for nothing! She made it across the entire pond in under a minute. Next up is our hometown radio host, Tempest Wright. Let's give her a round of applause to urge her on."

The thundering sound from the audience only increased Tempest's adrenaline as she scaled to the top of the ladder, leaving Blossom at the bottom. When she reached the plank, she drew a heavy breath and set her sights on the other side, afraid that if she glanced down at Dixon in the water, that's where her feet might subconsciously carry her. For a second, she sought out Owen in the crowd, throwing him a friendly wave.

"Just pretend that school let out, and Owen's on the other end of this plank as if it were the playground," she whispered to herself in her best coaching tone. "You're simply dashing over to greet him because you can't wait to give him a hug."

Closing her eyes, Tempest reached out her foot to test the plank. It seemed sturdy enough, so she batted her lashes open and summoned the gumption to go for it.

The crowd fell into a hush as Tempest slowly scooted her feet across the cattle pond like an amateur ice skater, not daring to look down for a second. She knew she didn't have Hedda's finesse or parasol, but she didn't care—she kept her eyes glued to the end of the plank as if Owen were there, waiting for his big hug and an after-school snack.

"Way to go!" Dixon hollered from below, making Tempest lose her concentration. Flailing her arms, she teetered badly, then barely forced her body straight again. Balance yourself! she chastised. After all those damn years of yoga, you ought to be able to namaste your ass across here like it was nothing. With firm resolve, Tempest determined to make a bee line for the end, shuffling her feet as fast as she could muster with her arms outstretched in a warrior yoga position. As soon as she reached the other side, she saluted the crowd, exhaling a huge breath of relief.

"Miss Wright clocks in at one minute and thirty-two seconds!" exclaimed the announcer. "Not quite enough to beat Hedda Grimson, but she's not the least bit wet, either. Now it's our last contestant's turn—let's show some enthusiasm for Blossom Barnhart!"

As Tempest began to stride over to the bleachers to join Owen and Ivy, instead of hearing the audience cheer on Blossom, the crowd fell eerily quiet. Curious, she turned around in time to catch everyone in the bleachers with their mouths gaped. Shielding her eyes, Tempest gazed up at the plank. The early afternoon sun had cast a warm glow on Blossom's red hair, infusing it to a fiery sheen, and her vintage swimsuit hugged her extraordinary curves as though it had been custom made. Tempest couldn't help giggling when she saw audience members whip out their cell phones to capture the statuesque woman who'd alighted onto the plank.

Nevertheless, Blossom was in her own world as she concentrated on making her way across the cattle pond, and she didn't even notice the ogling of the crowd. Slowly, she inched her barn boots across the wood with her knees slightly bent and her arms out, as if she were surfing. By the time she slid her way to the middle, a man in the bleachers stood up and released a piercing wolf whistle.

A chorus of chuckles arose from the audience.

Startled, Blossom glanced up like a spell had been broken, causing her body to sway. Fighting for balance, she began to circle her arms like windmills, when her boot slipped from the plank.

Short, choked breaths erupted from the crowd as Blossom descended toward the water. Dixon merely grinned like he'd been waiting for this all afternoon. He positioned himself directly beneath her, holding out his muscular arms with work gloves on his hands, as though he were merely preparing to buck another bale of hay. Then he caught Blossom easily and held her tight against his chest, to a roar of applause from the bleachers.

"Will you look at that!" crowed the announcer. "Our hero Dixon Ramsey spared Blossom from the splash part of the dash! And his Cowboy Roundup numbers couldn't get any better."

Tempest peered at the scoreboard, watching as another category debuted for Dixon: "Chances for succeeding in reviving country-style chivalry: 80/1."

Good God, she thought, the folks in this county will place bets on anything! Then Tempest happened to see Dixon struggle with his footing near a boggy patch of cattails while he was carrying Blossom through the cattle pond. He stumbled slightly and easily righted himself, but it was enough to send Blossom into a fitful of panic. She flailed her arms and insisted on wriggling from his grasp to set her boots into the water, only to twist her ankle slightly in the mud and capsize with big splash. Dixon instantly dove in his hands and hoisted her to her feet, when the audience once again fell silent.

The sight of Blossom Barnhart, with her suit sopping wet and clinging to her every curve like spray paint made a host of men groan as if Venus were rising from the sea. Entire swaths of male spectators appeared slayed in the stands, and even the announcer became incapable of words, simply taking in the vision. Then the silence broke as the audience began clapping wildly, while Blossom's chances for winning on the scoreboard soared faster than the county had ever seen.

"Well folks, that's certainly a first!" cried the announcer. "We've never had somebody's scores rise *higher* after falling into the water during the Dash and Splash, but then, we've never seen the likes of Blossom Barnhart before!"

At the edge of the cattle pond, Blossom buried her head in her hands, her shoulders beginning to tremble. Tempest dashed over to grab one of the towels that had been left on the pond bank for the contestants. She swiftly wrapped it around Blossom and cupped her cheek.

"I'm so sorry you got drenched!" Tempest consoled her. "Are you okay? That must have been a quite a shock."

Blossom shook her head. "Didn't you hear her?" She glanced in the direction of her mother in the bleachers, who was standing erect with her hands balled into fists. "She shouted her disappointment at me, saying I looked like a cheap mud-wrestler."

"Really?" Tempest tilted her gaze to the scoreboard again. "Because I happened to notice the new stats they put up for betting. Did you see what they wrote next to your name this time?"

Blossom squinted at the scoreboard. "Blossom Barnhart: Chances for receiving a hundred marriage proposals within the next half hour: 100/1."

Blossom swept her palms to her mouth and began to giggle.

"C'mon," Tempest set a hand on her shoulder. "Let's go back to the changing room and get you into your dry overalls before you get whisked off to the nearest wedding chapel." She inclined her head at Dixon, who was toweling off his feet by the pond. "My son and I are going to Dixon's ranch later, so I might as well help you peel out of this swimsuit while I can."

"Oh, you're headed to the Ramsey's ranch tonight?" Blossom brushed a lock of drenched hair from her face. "So are we." She dropped her gaze to the wet grass on the pond bank. "It was my mom's pushy idea, of course. But Mr. Ramsey finally said it was okay."

"Really? Dixon invited you?" Tempest was a bit puzzled since she assumed he would be busy coaching Owen.

"No," Blossom replied. She pointed to the old man sitting beside her mother in the bleachers, flanked by Bonner with his big paws digging into a tub of popcorn and making a mess. "It was his dad, Bear."

Since Dumpling had been behaving remarkably well lately, Dixon thought it best to simply reinforce a few showmanship drills with him at the ranch and then reward the yearling with some sweet feed of corn and oats mixed with molasses. While Dumpling was eating, Dixon offered Owen a different activity to mix things up a little—a riding lesson on his horse Bullet.

Tempest freaked.

"That animal is the equivalent of a high-octane rocket!" she said, clutching at her chest. "How fast does he go anyway —warp factor ten?"

Dixon chuckled. "That speed's unsustainable for anybody, including the starship *Enterprise*. Bullet maxes out at fifty miles an hour for a quarter mile. Don't worry, we'll start with a plain walk and proceed to a trot, then maybe let Owen lope if he's doing well."

"Lope?"

"That's cowboy lingo for gentle canter."

"What's cowboy lingo for petrified?" she asked, tangling her hands. She knew she was inching perilously close to Betty's style of hovering again, but she couldn't stop.

"Hmm," Dixon thought it about it for a second. "Two words—Tempest Wright," he replied. "I figure that's synonymous with chronically afraid of large animals."

Tempest gave him a swat, which only made Dixon laugh as he watched Owen head toward them after releasing Dumpling to stretch his legs in a corral.

"I'm ready, Mister Dixon!" the boy called out with a spring in his step, barely able to keep his feet on the ground.

Dixon motioned for Owen to join him beside the beautiful, iron-gray horse that was tied to the arena fence rail and already tacked up with a championship western saddle.

"Okay, Owen," Dixon instructed, handing him a helmet, "how many times have you ridden a horse?"

Owen shrugged. "Whenever we go to the grocery store, my mom lets me get on Trigger and put a quarter in."

"You mean, the coin-operated kiddie ride?" Dixon stroked Bullet's neck. "Believe me, this fella has a *lot* more horse power. But riding him is essentially the same—all you gotta do is find your balance and stay on. Since Bullet is bred to be very intelligent, the trick is to communicate with him in a way that he's been taught to understand."

Dixon hoisted Owen into the saddle and adjusted the stirrups, then advised him to keep his back rod-straight and his heels down. He led the horse to a line of six, white upright poles mounted on heavy discs in the center of the arena. After showing Owen how to hold the reins and steer left, right, and then pull back to stop, he directed the boy to try weaving Bullet through the poles.

"This here is called pole bending," Dixon glared over his shoulder to make sure Tempest stayed planted by the fence so she wouldn't interfere. "It's a bonafide rodeo event done for the fastest time. Folks say it derived from dodging horses around trees and sagebrush to find cattle, where they like to hide during roundups."

Dixon shielded his eyes to scan his ranch. "As you can see, we've got a lot of pines and sagebrush around here. In order to train my remuda to be the best cow horses, I always start them out with pole bending. That way they'll stay agile enough to find even the peskiest cattle, especially in draws or ravines where cows like to linger because the grass is moist. You'd be amazed at how well a twelve-hundred pound Angus can hide behind tall sagebrush when it wants to."

Tempest watched her son steer the horse to make a slow serpentine through the poles without knocking over a single one. Despite her concern for her son around large livestock, her chest swelled at how well he managed to ride the horse. Okay, so maybe Bullet was so tame and well trained that he could have navigated the poles in his sleep. But Tempest still felt a sense of pride.

"You ready to try a trot?" Dixon asked after Owen had successfully maneuvered his passes at the poles several times. "All you gotta do is give Bullet a nudge with your heels. But not too big a kick, or he'll shoot you through those poles like his namesake, Bullet."

Tempest's breath snagged in her throat. Why don't these animals come with disc brakes to keep them from going from

five to fifty miles an hour in seconds flat? she wondered. She
squeezed her hands together when she spied Owen giving
Bullet a gentle prod with his heels. The horse promptly
hastened his four-step walk rhythm to a brisk, two-step trot.

Owen bounced up and down like a bag of rocks. He
desperately clutched to the saddle horn, only to receive a swift
scolding from Dixon.

"Ain't no *real* cowboys out there who grab the saddle
horn!" he called out. "That's only for wrapping the rope when
you're lassoing cattle. Bring Bullet to a stop for a minute."

Dixon jogged over to them and showed Owen how to
absorb the percussive movement of the horse's legs by relaxing
the small of his back. Then he patted Bullet on the rump and
directed Owen to continue through the poles, sitting the trot a
bit smoother this time.

"Can we gallop?" Owen asked once he'd finished a few
more trotting rounds.

Dixon turned to Tempest and waved her over.

Tempest couldn't even bear to make eye contact at this
point as she joined Dixon in the center of the arena. *Of course*
Owen wanted to go faster! Didn't all boys live for that kind of
thing? She rolled her eyes at Dixon.

"Don't you dare say it," she warned him, folding her arms.
"Worrying about my child riding a speeding train around a
bunch of poles is *not* hovering. It's called common sense."

"He's going to do it anyway. You realize that, right?"
Dixon pointed out. "Whether it's go carts, mountain bikes, or
motocross—he's going to want to break a land record some
time. That's what kids do! At least here he's got a helmet and
adult supervision."

Stubbornly, Tempest's lips pressed together into a thin line. "So this lope thing," she mentioned in a testy tone, "how many miles an hour are we actually talking about?"

Dixon cast a proud gaze at his horse. "Well, if Owen listens to my instructions and barely slides his right heel forward and his left heel back, then squeezes them at the same time, Bullet will break into the slowest lope you've ever seen. You and I could jog faster than that gait. It's what Bullet's been trained to do—a smooth canter that won't scare young calves or even break a sweat. Of course, he can race to the finish line as fast as the best of them. Whether it's first gear or top gear, he's still a Ferrari—"

"Stop!" Tempest covered her ears. "I don't want to hear that. Let's just stick to the slow lope, okay?"

"Good enough." Dixon headed over to Owen to fill him in on the correct riding cues. After giving him instruction, he cautioned, "Whatever you do, don't lean forward, gather up the reins, and dig in hard with your heels—that's the command to gallop. *Fast.* If you accidentally give Bullet the wrong cues, just loosen your legs and lean back with a tug of the reins, and he'll stop."

Owen nodded while Dixon moved the poles farther apart to give the inexperienced rider more room to navigate. Then Owen slid his legs into the correct position and gave the horse a gentle squeeze. Just like Dixon said, the horse broke into a three-beat lope that wasn't a bit faster than his trot, but a hell of a lot easier to ride. His smooth, rocking motion helped Owen to easily stay in the saddle this time as they first traveled along the distance of the rail in the arena for several rounds until Dixon gave Owen the cue to aim for the poles. Owen and

Bullet made a fairly-smooth serpentine in one direction through the poles, then moved in a small semi-circle to return back to Dixon.

"That's amazing!" Tempest said, relieved as she walked over to Dixon and Owen, after Dixon gave her the go-ahead. "How can an eight-year-old who's never ridden a real horse before guide this animal so easily through the poles? It's like you just press a button, and Bullet does what he's told."

Dixon's lips crinkled at the corners like he'd heard that compliment a hundred times. "That's why I can charge the big bucks," he replied. "What you see in Bullet took decades of breeding to perfect with the best blood lines, plus a kick-ass training regime. You could put a toddler on that horse and win tonight at barrel racing. But you'd have to strap the kid down, because Bullet is the fastest sprinter I've ever seen. Folks want the most powerful performance horses to give them an edge over competition, but they also want them to be people-friendly with good minds. Which is cowboy lingo for not crazy."

"Too bad you can't breed girlfriends," Tempest teased, unable to resist. "I mean, this ranch and your training operation are all perfectly designed for long-term success." She gazed across the well-maintained barns and corrals filled with glossy, athletic horses that could obviously fetch top price. Not a single fence in sight needed repair, and the expansive property was so beautiful it resembled an oil-painting of Rocky Mountain cowboy country. "Kind of ironic, isn't it? In spite of your erratic dating record, this fancy ranch is like your Rorschach test."

"My what?"

"That's therapy lingo for hidden motivation," Tempest replied with a smirk. "On the one hand, your ranch shows you're into long-term stability and legacy. But on the other hand, your wiggy girlfriends always go off the rails. Let's see," she tapped her lip, mulling it over, "could you be the type who's attracted to hot messes because then you get to be the hero who cleans everything up?"

"I dunno," Dixon replied in a low, sexy drawl. "Wanna find out?"

Tempest's eyes grew wide, startled by his swift comeback. "What do you mean?"

"Well, you *did* offer me an evening by the fire, remember?" He turned and pointed to a fire ring made out of a circle of blackened stones on a nearby hill. "How about for a treat, we go relax by the fire this evening and watch the sun go down? That's what you promised me yesterday."

"I didn't promise anything! All I said was that a fire sounds…nice. Besides, are you comparing me to your typical hot messes?"

"You're the only one who can make that clinical call," he remarked with a glint in his eye. "I'm just a plain ol' cowboy who's asking you to sit by a fire."

Tempest stilled at the warm sensation that spiraled through her.

To be honest, it *did* seem like a lovely way to cap off the evening. She glanced over at her son who'd returned Bullet to a leisurely walk along the arena rail. At that moment, he halted the horse to watch her and Dixon parry with each other with a big smile on his face.

A smile…

Would it really kill me to take a chance, she asked herself, like Owen had mentioned last night? To simply hang out at the end of the day with someone who's been good to my son? If things don't work out, it's not the end of the world. Maybe it wouldn't hurt to be resilient for the first time in, like, a whole *year*.

And smile—

Tempest waved at her son, grinning to show her support.

And to show him she could do this.

She could be more light hearted. Take risks. Just like she wanted *him* to do in life.

"Wow, has anyone ever told you what a knockout you are when you smile?" Dixon said, as if sensing her struggle. "You know, you looked amazing in that swimsuit this afternoon."

"I did not!" she replied. "I looked homely and ridiculous."

Dixon moved in closer. All at once, his whole being seemed to wrap around her without so much as a fleeting touch. Yet Tempest sensed a shift—as if Dixon were occupying her space like it was *their* space, a private place where ordinary particles mysteriously co-mingled, and maybe even created something new. Oddly enough, his presence made her feel protected at the same time, and most importantly, not alone.

Tempest had forgotten how much she missed that, perhaps never had it. Because God knows her late husband had a way of draining the life blood out of her, making her feel as lost and stranded as an orphan. With Dixon so close, it made Tempest feel full in a way that she'd never admit she'd been secretly longing for. She didn't need a man to feel whole—she knew that. She had her own career and ambitions, and she was proud of her achievements. But dammit, it sure was nice to enjoy sharing a moment with this man, while she watched the little boy she loved more than anything in the whole world ride his beautiful gray horse.

And smile.

"If you ask me," Dixon noted in a low tone, "what you call homely and ridiculous in that dowdy old swimsuit is everyone's else's *amazing*."

Tempest turned and dared to glance up into Dixon's face, a mere few inches from hers. Only this time, there wasn't a hint of arrogance in his eyes.

He *meant* it.

The conviction in his eyes made Tempest tremble. Her heart beat faster, knowing her attraction to him was every bit as strong. Good God, who wouldn't be drawn to Dixon? The broad shoulders, beefy biceps, and the kind of rugged face that could make Hollywood film stars jealous was enough to work over any woman's heart. But it was the way he sidled up to her so easily, and made her feel damn comfortable close to his skin that really clutched a hold of her emotions. Nervous, Tempest reverted back to what she always did when her anxiety spiked —she threw him a wisecrack.

"Can I ask, for once, what the men in the Cowboy Roundup do to prove themselves to the women? You never had to don a hokey swimsuit. So far I've been dragged by a cow, forced to wear crummy swim clothes, and risked falling into mud. What do you guys do to prove yourselves to us?"

"I don't have to prove myself," Dixon replied with a mischievous gleam in his eyes, enjoying her sass. "Last time I checked, *I'm* the prize."

Tempest swatted him again, secretly taking pleasure in the

way he could dish out a barb whiplash fast. At least we're well matched, she thought, which made her relax a bit now that the conversation had taken a lighter turn. "I guess I shouldn't worry about it," she shrugged, "because we both know that Blossom's going to win. Who can possibly beat 40-28-40? She's built like a goddess."

"I wouldn't count out Hedda too easily," Dixon observed. "She's got one hell of a competitive streak, and half the county are seniors, you know. She's still quite the catch. Don't be surprised if your gun has chewing gum stuck in the barrel for the next event."

"*Gun?*"

"Yeah, for cowgirl mounted shooting. Don't worry—the revolvers only fire blanks, not bullets."

"Mom! Watch me lope around the arena again!" Owen called out.

Tempest smiled—it was only a matter of time before her son wanted all the attention turned back on him, like every eight-year-old, ever. She shielded her eyes from the glare of the slowly dipping sun and marveled at how well Owen rode Bullet's incredibly smooth gait. However, after several strides around the arena, Owen had a hard time maintaining the flexibility in his back that Dixon had coached him to maintain. Tempest saw her son begin to clench more and more with his legs to keep his balance. Then he gripped the reins too tightly in an effort to steady himself. In that moment, the horse began to rip around the arena at top speed, making them look to Tempest like a blur.

She screamed.

Not just any scream—the kind of primal scream of a

mother who would do anything to protect her son. She dashed toward the speeding horse, when she felt Dixon grab her by the shoulders, forcing her to a stop.

"It's okay!" Dixon shouted to Owen, refusing to loosen his grip on Tempest despite her thrashing arms. "Just relax your legs and lean back with a tug!"

Suddenly, Tempest saw her child and the gray horse engulfed in a massive cloud of dust. Her heart nearly stopped. "What happened?" she cried, wriggling fiercely against Dixon's grip. "Did they tumble in the dirt—"

"Wait," Dixon ordered, wrapping his arms around her so she couldn't budge.

With her heart in her throat, Tempest saw the dust begin to clear. There was Bullet, standing with his legs square beneath him and his ears perked up, as if pausing for the slightest next command. Owen had a massive grin on his face

"That, my dear," Dixon whispered in her ear, clutching her tightly as though he enjoyed holding her close, "is what we call a sliding stop. When Owen leaned back and pulled on the reins, Bullet did what he's been trained to do—he locked his hind legs and sat down on his haunches so he could stop on a dime. It takes a lot of work to teach horses that, and it makes them unbeatable when cutting cattle."

Tempest dared to breathe again. To her surprise, Dixon gave her a soft kiss on the cheek.

"I'm proud of you," he said. "For not getting in the way of your son's triumph. The fact that he stayed balanced through all that and didn't fall off sure shows his grit. Now if you don't mind, I'm going to go praise the hell out of your son."

"Owen!" Dixon called out, releasing Tempest and trotting

toward the boy. "You did fantastic!" When he reached him, he helped the boy dismount from the horse and gave his shoulders a squeeze. The pride that beamed from Owen's face brought tears to Tempest's eyes.

Dixon collected the reins and began to lead his horse alongside Owen while they walked back toward Tempest. In spite of how well things turned out, Tempest was still shaking and making every effort to calm her breathing. Even so, she hugged her son and removed his helmet to give him a kiss on top of his dusty head. "You were amazing, honey," she said. Then she glanced up at Bullet, slightly less afraid of him now that she'd seen for herself how expertly trained he was. Recalling her naivety about the cost of alpacas, she couldn't help being curious about Bullet's price tag.

"So, how much do you charge for a horse like Bullet?" she asked Dixon as he unraveled the cinch from the animal's belly and began to pull of the saddle.

"Well, given that he's a descendent of Doc Bar, is still in his prime, and has already carried me to six steer wrestling titles, I'd say he'd fetch about a hundred grand." Dixon turned to Tempest. "But I'd never sell my best friend. When it's Bullet's time to go, he'll be buried over there." He pointed to a tall tree on another hill. "Next to my mom."

Dixon's loyalty pierced her heart.

Tempest allowed his words to hang between them for a moment. As Owen began to lead Bullet toward the barn for his evening grooming, she pushed some dirt around with her boot and cleared her throat. "What happened to her, Dixon? All you said was that she died when you were young."

"Riding accident," he replied, turning to amble slowly with her toward the barn. "When I was ten. The horse was my dad's prized sorrel. Fiery, powerful, and totally undisciplined. My dad was never the same after that. He blamed himself for not training the animal better, and to be honest, it's the reason he turned to drink. Still, he didn't have the heart to shoot that horse in the head. He sold him to an experienced old wrangler."

"So...you've made it your life mission to breed and train horses that even a child could ride?" Tempest gazed at Bullet a few yards ahead of them with a totally new perspective. "Horses that are strong, and..."

"Safe," Dixon finished her sentence.

Tempest nodded. "Sounds like something we both prize these days," she said quietly.

Dixon looked at her. There was a yearning in his eyes that she didn't expect. Yet it seemed like it was for more than mere stability. It was for...

A place...

Perhaps a heart—

That could mean...home.

She realized in that moment that despite his overwhelming charm and good looks, Dixon had been his own kind of alone his whole life. Forced to grow up way too fast, to take on a mountain of responsibility, to always make sure everything was okay.

Including for Owen.

"You know, I was really out of line earlier," she admitted, feeling a twist of remorse. "You've done more than your fair share to prove yourself to us. The smiles I've seen on Owen's face lately are...priceless. I mean, especially after the year we've had——"

"Sh," Dixon said, pausing to put a finger to her lips. He glanced in the direction of his mother's grave. "No more talk of hard times, all right? C'mon, let's help Owen finish grooming and feeding Bullet and take a walk with him to that fireside I mentioned. After all, we have reason to celebrate."

"We do?"

"Yeah, you succeeded in not hovering *or* killing my horse today."

A laugh fluttered from Tempest lips before she could hold it back.

"You're on," she replied.

19

After they'd brushed Bullet down and fed him a flake of alfalfa, Dixon led Tempest and Owen on a short trail to the nearby fire ring on a hill. There, he pulled out a few wads of paper from his back pocket, which hinted to Tempest he'd been planning this all along. She couldn't help feeling flattered, and she drew her arms against her stomach to try and damp down the butterflies weaving inside. Then she encouraged Owen to sit beside her on the grass and snuggle as they watched Dixon make a cone of kindling from a pile of sticks beside the blackened stones. He stuffed the wads of paper into the base.

Dixon grabbed a few larger pieces of wood and set them in a triangle around the cone, then pulled a lighter from his pocket to ignite the crumpled paper. At first, small flames began to lick around the edges, but soon the kindling was engulfed in fire. Tempest was amazed at how fast it took off,

and she tugged Owen to sit with her farther away from the
ring. Within a couple of minutes, they could feel the heat
warming their knees and calves.

"High altitude and low humidity make this wood as dry as
matchsticks," Dixon noted, watching the flames climb higher.
"It's the reason we have to watch our forests for old brush and
dead trees." He glanced at a thick grove of pines nearby, then
up at the sky to check for ominous clouds. "Otherwise, a single
bolt of lightning can be a nightmare."

"Hey," Owen said, peering up at the sky as well. He aimed
a finger high over the horizon to where the sky was slowly
darkening to dusk. "I see some stars. Are those the rambling
ones, like on your gate?"

Dixon gave him an easy smile. His gaze traveled over the
boy's plump cheeks and bright eyes, then shifted to Tempest.
In that moment, Dixon's face seemed softer, a little more...
content...than she'd noticed before, and it made her feel warm
inside. He stared at the few twinkling stars that had emerged in
the sky, barely visible as the sun sank in the west and cast hues
of gold along with scattered threads of orange and purple.

"No, I don't reckon those are rambling stars," Dixon
remarked thoughtfully. "The way I see it, they're the ones that
might have found their way...home."

His eyes met Tempest's.

For a second she couldn't move, her heart tripping a beat.
It wasn't just Dixon's words, which certainly made
goosebumps alight on her skin because he seemed to be
referring to her and Owen—and maybe himself along with
them. It was the way he looked at her, making her feel like she
could finally relax a little and somehow lean into the inviting

blue depths of his eyes. Tempest drew a cautious breath and cleared her throat.

"It's so peaceful out right now, and the view is lovely up here," she said, studying the hues of the sunset that had begun to infuse the sparse clouds above them with vivid shades. She was struck by Dixon's comfortable presence, the casual way he stretched out his long legs and reclined on his elbows on the grass, looking like he didn't have a care in the world. Or a single thought for somewhere more important he had to be, like her late husband always did. His face and body were open —to the sky and to them—appearing satisfied to simply be with her and Owen. It made her feel more settled than she had in ages. Even so, Tempest's heart inched up her throat. She wanted to express her gratitude for his hospitality, but she felt a catch, as though doing so might make her more vulnerable and exposed. Why, oh why, was it so intimidating for *her* to confide her feelings, when she insisted that her clients do that all the time? Even badgered them to open up? The irony wasn't lost on Tempest, and she swallowed hard, making an effort to summon the words.

"I'm really glad you invited us here," she mentioned in a sincere tone. "It's a nice ending for the day. *Thank you*, Dixon."

Tempest's cheeks warmed from more than the fire. Okay, so maybe her words weren't particularly artful, but at least she'd spoken them.

Dixon's lips crept into a hint of a smile, as though he'd detected that she wasn't exactly the over-sharing type when it came to her own deep emotions. He was wise enough not to say anything, to allow the moment to linger between them before crowding it with words. His gaze caressed Tempest's

face, her hazel-green eyes and softly curved cheeks, glinting
with an amber palette from the fire.

"Any time," he replied softly, regarding Owen with a warm
glance as well. He stoked the fire with another crinkled piece
of paper from his pocket, pushing it in with a stick. Satisfied at
the rise of flames, he turned and appeared distracted for a
second, like he'd heard a random noise. Dixon's eyes
narrowed at an area down the hill. Then his face stilled to
stone.

He slowly rose to his feet.

Tempest shifted on the grass to see what troubled him. In
the distance, she spied Bonner, lumbering up the hill and
huffing hard. As the old black bear grew closer, he made odd,
clacking sounds from the back of his jaw, appearing agitated.

"Something's wrong," Dixon muttered, turning to
Tempest. "Bonner's deathly afraid of fire. If he's hungry after
dinner, he'll just raid the barn bins for oats, not come near
flames. This isn't good."

The bear paused a few yards before reaching the fire ring,
eyeing the flames as if wary of a rival predator. Then he tossed
his head at Dixon and released a low, raspy sound from his
throat. He slumped on the grass and turned to gaze at the
ranch house, pawing angrily at the dirt.

Tempest grabbed Owen and pulled him back, keeping a
healthy distance from the bear no matter how old and tame he
was supposed to be. She darted a glance at Dixon, who was
studying the direction of Bonner's focus. He followed the
animal's line of sight and broke into a jog to another spot
down the hill, scanning the area below. Tempest took Owen by
the hand and stood up, then guided him to make a wide swath

around Bonner to join Dixon. From their vantage point, the ranch house came into full view.

"Oh my God," Dixon said, staring down at his father who was behind the wheel of a green tractor. The man was driving erratically near the house, making wild, zig-zag paths. Every time he spun in a circle, nearly knocking out a pump-house and a few garden beds, they heard Bonner issue a deep-throated moan. All the while, Bear Ramsey appeared to be gesturing angrily and shouting at no one there.

Without another word, Dixon sprinted down the hill to reach his dad, who by now had decided to speed toward one of the barns. It was obvious to Tempest that his father was stinking drunk, and Dixon was going to try to stop him before he smashed into the building. Swiftly, she took her son and ran back to the opposite side of the fire from Bonner, where she instructed Owen to help her dig and throw handfuls of dirt to put out the flames. As the fire receded into puffs of smoke, she stepped away and peered down the hill at the tractor again, watching in horror as Dixon raced alongside the vehicle before it could hit the barn. Boldly, Dixon took a flying leap onto the tractor and tried to shove his father aside to grab the wheel, but Bear wouldn't budge. He hollered at an imaginary enemy and kept his hands fixed until Dixon seized him by the shoulders. The two wrestled with Dixon nearly falling from the vehicle. When Dixon managed to regain his footing, his father drew his arm back to throw a punch. But Dixon beat him to it, landing a right hook that sent his father sailing from the tractor onto the grass.

Dixon quickly shifted the gears and braked, a mere foot from the side of the barn. He sat and stared at the red building, struggling to catch his breath as if he could hardly believe he hadn't crashed. Then he sank his forehead against the tractor wheel.

By this time, Tempest and Owen had dashed down the hill, with Tempest yanking her cell phone from her pocket in case she needed to call 911. As soon as they neared Bear Ramsey, Tempest yanked Owen by the hand to a stop. She told him to sit down and stay put on the grass while she checked on Dixon's father. Owen nodded with sparks of alarm in his eyes.

"It's okay, honey," Tempest promised. "We'll get Dixon's dad whatever help he needs right away." With that, she raced over to Bear Ramsey, who was lying flat on his back on the grass.

Tempest kneeled to check the man's pulse, which was beating fast but regularly. Then she pressed her fingers over his forehead and his skull to feel for any bumps or signs of concussion, but all the surfaces were smooth. "Mr. Ramsey," she asked urgently, "is your vision blurry? Are your ears ringing, or do you feel nauseous?"

Bear squinted up at the sky, pausing to gauge how he felt. He shook his head, and Tempest exhaled in relief. Then she asked him if anything felt sprained or broken, especially along his spine, and she ran her hands down each of his limbs until he wagged his head. He said everything was fine, except his butt might be bruised. Tempest smiled a little and carefully helped Bear to sit up while she brushed off the grass and debris from his shirt.

"Where are the rustlers?" Bear asked her pointedly, gazing around and noticing the yard was empty. "Who's gonna protect Dixon's horses?" He shook his head and teetered a little, clearly drunk out of his gourd. "I was running em' off and one of those no-goods hit me! They must have skedaddled in a hurry." Bear slapped his knee and chuckled, proud of himself. "Good thing, too, because Dixon pours his whole heart and soul into them animals. That's what dads are for, you know. To protect their sons——"

"I'll take it from here," Dixon barked, jarring Tempest from behind. He stepped up and crouched beside his father, throwing her a fierce look. His deep-blue eyes betrayed the kind of raw, inner shame that took a lifetime to develop and never wanted to be revealed—and certainly hadn't desired to be put on full display in front of Tempest and Owen. "Don't say it," he warned her, holding up his hand. "Not one word of psycho-babble right now. Us cowboys have our own way of fixing things."

"By throwing punches?" Tempest replied.

Dixon glared at her. "If we have to."

Before she knew it, Dixon had picked up his father in his arms—a man who surely weighed over two-hundred pounds. "He'll be fine," Dixon asserted with no emotion, as if this were a hardly a new occurrence, "once he sleeps it off." Then he turned and began to march in the direction of the ranch house.

When Tempest looked over to check on her son, there was Bonner, sitting beside him like a faithful old dog. He watched Dixon carrying his father and released a big "boof," then clamored to his feet and jogged to follow after them.

"Mom!" Owen cried, running up to her and pointing at the loyal bear. "Can we go with them? We've never been inside their house before. I bet they have tons of rodeo trophies—"

"I don't think that's a good idea, sweetie," Tempest said, her heart breaking that her son didn't appear to understand all the ramifications of what they'd just seen. How could she tell him that Bear Ramsey's behavior wasn't a lark, and this is what a dangerous alcoholic looks like? "Maybe some other time, okay?" she offered. "We'd better get Dumpling and be on our way home."

She wrapped her arm around her son's shoulder and headed toward Dumpling's corral.

"Tempest!" a shrill, familiar voice cried out. "You can't leave now! Get back here."

Tempest let go of Owen and swiveled. Of all people, there was Betty Barnhart, Blossom's mother, waving at her from a distance. "Come on in the house—I have chips and salsa and some homemade soup! We'll make it a party."

Tempest's mouth dropped, unable to believe her ears. Then she recalled that Blossom had told her they were coming to the Ramsey's place that evening. Couldn't Betty *see* what had just happened? Especially since the tractor was butted up against the side of the barn and Dixon was *carrying* his father? Speechless, she simply stared at Betty, watching Blossom walk up next to her and wave as well, giving Tempest a shrug as if this were just her mother's usual brand of crazy.

"Let's go, Mommy!" Owen tugged on her arm. "I love chips!" Despite Tempest's stiffness and attempt to hold him close, Owen managed to bust free and began to run toward Betty and Blossom.

"No, wait!" Tempest cried. "Owen—"

Tempest headed after him, forgetting she was no match for her son in the sprinting department. He'd already reached Betty and started following her to the front door of the house before Tempest finally caught up to Blossom.

"What's your mother up to *this* time?" Tempest asked, panting. "Is she trying to teach you to cook for a crowd to impress Dixon?"

"Guess you can't be a queen without subjects," Blossom sighed. "My mom *loves* being around groups to have a bigger audience. I swear, if she didn't have me to boss around, she'd be out on the streets recruiting strangers."

Blossom blew out a breath as if mentally preparing herself to deal with Betty. Then she implored Tempest with her china-blue eyes. "Um, would you mind helping me collect our stuff from the house so my mom will get the hint it's time to go? I don't think Dixon needs our company right now."

"Sure," Tempest agreed, quite certain her son had already dived into the chips. It was probably too late to keep him from spoiling his dinner, but she wanted to make the effort anyway. She and Blossom headed to the door, and as soon as they stepped inside the house, Tempest realized Dixon was nowhere to be seen. She assumed he was probably settling his father into bed. She glanced around, surprised at the modesty of the ranch home with its well-worn leather furniture, ragged rugs, a yellowed pair of longhorns on the wall, and an ordinary kitchen with old, dented appliances—not the typical domain of a man with Dixon's wealth. The place was rather spare and dusty, looking like it hadn't seen a woman's influence in decades. Yet there was Betty, seated at the head of the dining room table with bowls of chips and salsa in front of her like she was already holding court. Owen sat in a nearby chair, wolfing down handfuls of chips. Despite Betty's hospitable smile, Tempest felt a trail of goosebumps wriggle down her spine. She wondered if Betty had designs on Bear now, since her daughter hadn't exactly been flirting with Dixon. In the center of the table, Betty had placed a vase of her homegrown flowers, and her eyes glinted warmly at Tempest.

"Come on over!" Betty remarked happily with a big smile. "Sit down beside me and have some chips with your son."

"I don't think snacks are very appropriate right now," Tempest replied, "given Bear's condition." She noticed Betty had covered her salsa with saran anyway, probably to keep it from spoiling.

Betty clicked her tongue. "Oh, don't worry." She stroked one of the pink flowers she'd brought with petals that flared into a trumpet. "It just proves how much he needs a woman's touch, doesn't it? Bear went to all the trouble to invite us here, but then I guess he got nervous and hit the bottle before we came. Who can blame him? He must be awfully lonely. I've heard a good woman is better than any twelve-step program, with all of the nurturing men need. I mean, look at this shabby house—these poor fellows could use some glue to hold their lives together."

Betty leaned forward and gazed sympathetically at Tempest. "Besides, we wouldn't want you to monopolize all of Dixon's attention this week, right? I'm afraid folks have been gossiping that their favorite radio star is starting to look a little desperate. Maybe it's best to be more detached and visit the Ramsey men in a group setting?"

Blossom's face turned beet red. "I'm so sorry," she

whispered to Tempest. "I *told you* she needs bodies to boss around."

Blossom stretched out her hand to dive into the chips, as if wanting to feed her face to compensate for her overbearing mother. When she lifted the saran wrap to dunk a chip into the salsa, Betty shoved her fingers aside and covered both bowls with her hands.

"Now-now, sweetie," Betty scolded. "You already know you need to drop more pounds. I brought these for Bear. I'll just pour my homemade salsa back into the jar and put it in the fridge for later this evening."

"No, you won't. Because Bear's going to be indisposed for quite a while, ma'am," Dixon broke in bitterly, entering the dining room from a hallway. "I put him to bed for the night."

"Speaking of Bear," Tempest said tenderly to Dixon, "I checked him for signs of concussion earlier, and he seemed okay. Be sure to watch him over the next few days for headaches, memory problems, sensitivity to noise or light—"

"The only light he's going to see," Dixon replied, "is from the inside of his eyelids till tomorrow morning. He's completely out. So much for staying on the wagon. But I'll keep an eye on him," he promised.

He pulled out his cell phone and called one of his ranch hands to escort Tempest and Owen with Dumpling back to the fairgrounds, since it was getting dark.

"Does that mean Blossom and I can stay?" said Betty, her eyes twinkling. "I brought more food for you." She pointed to a crock pot that she'd set up on the counter. "See—tortilla soup! Nothing makes men feel better than a good meal."

"Not unless you're ready to prop up a grown man under a

cold shower if he tries to get out of that bed," Dixon growled. "Which means you'd best move along with my ranch hand once he gets here."

While he was speaking, Tempest and Blossom had already begun to collect the crockpot and soup bowls in the hopes that Betty would follow suit and get ready to leave. But Betty appeared rooted to her chair as if it were slathered in glue. After they stashed the items in Betty's car and returned to the house, Tempest flicked a glance at Blossom, searching her eyes to see if she might take some control over her overbearing mother. Blossom registered her challenge, appearing anxious as though the effort might prove daunting. Nevertheless, she gave her a nod.

Blossom walked over to Betty, glancing at Tempest once more for courage. She began to lift her mother from beneath her shoulders out of the chair.

"Wh-What are you doing?" Betty said, her face washed in surprise.

"We're *leaving*, Mother," Blossom stated without an ounce of flexibility in her tone.

"But we haven't had dinner!" Betty attempted to wriggle from her daughter's grip. "Bear *invited* us."

Blossom didn't flinch. She checked Tempest again for nerve, and it emboldened her to drag her mother, gasping like a fish out of water, over to the door. "Tempest," Blossom said, "can you please put the salsa back in the jar and bring it with the chips to our car?" Then she sent Dixon a drained look. "And next time," she implored, "go ahead and manhandle my mother to the door like one of your steers when she overstays her welcome. Sometimes, it's the only thing she understands."

Tempest bit back an overwhelming urge to laugh and high five Blossom right then and there. "You go, girl," she whispered as soon as she'd put the salsa in the jar and grabbed the chips to meet Blossom at the threshold. She swung the door open wide and gestured at Owen to follow after them. When Tempest dared to sneak a peek back at Dixon, she was startled to see that his body had doubled over.

And he was howling at them in laughter.

20

"If toxic people were redeemable, they'd come with coupons!" Tempest said, still angry at Blossom's mother for the catty remarks she'd made last night in the name of being "helpful." She'd lost all patience with Betty, despite the advice she'd given Blossom earlier to be a bit more tolerant. Inhaling a breath to calm down, she cupped the cheeks of the bone-thin woman who stood in front of her booth and gazed compassionately into her eyes.

"Kayla, can't you see that you starved yourself because of a nasty comment your boyfriend made about your weight? Now he's running around claiming you're too skinny and need to put on muscle?" Tempest sighed. "It's the old, lost-in-the-funhouse game. No matter how you try to please him, the floor keeps tilting and mirrors reflect distorted images of you. What's he going to criticize next? Your hair, your job, your friends? The point is he controls you by keeping you on the defensive, and people like that will make you tear your hair out."

Tempest let out a huff. "So my advice is to take the thousand bucks he claimed you need to spend at a fitness resort to add muscle and get on a luxury singles cruise that sails far, far away from him. Hopefully to somewhere wonderful!"

Kayla choked back a sob. "B-But all I wanted was someone to hold my hand in the darkness and tell me...I'm not ugly."

"I'll do you one better!" Tempest grasped her hand. "I'll tell you the truth in broad daylight for the whole world to hear on the radio. You're gorgeous, Kayla! You have a lovely face and personality, and even your struggles and mistakes—they're all a part of your big, beautiful heart."

Tempest stepped out of her booth and wrapped her arms around her. "Hug your heart, Kayla, and be the first to love every part of you. Then the right people will follow suit and love you, too."

In that moment, Tempest felt something warm and heavy against her back. She glanced over her shoulder and spied Bonner the bear, who'd placed his big paws on her to join in the hug. Once her breath snagged at the surprise, she burst out laughing.

"See?" Tempest said. "Even this old bear wants to join your love fest. Don't worry, I've been told he's practically toothless. I guess we bonded last night when we saw—"

Tempest cut her words short, not wanting to admit they'd witnessed a near tragedy at Dixon's ranch and end Kayla's session on a negative note. "An awkward *incident*," she backpedaled, offering Kayla a smile.

Bonner dropped his paws and returned to munching a stash of honey buns he'd dragged with him and left on the ground. When Tempest looked over at *Hedda's Happy Homebaked* food truck, she saw Hedda give her a wink. So the secret was out! Old softy Hedda was the one who'd been supplying him all along.

"I see what you're doing!" Tempest called to her in a mock scolding tone. "No wonder this bear doesn't have any teeth left with all the sweets you've been peddling."

Hedda shrugged, feigning innocence. "It's not my fault! He's been stealing the day-old ones from my trash."

"Yeah, right." Tempest dug into her pocket and turned to Kayla, handing her a five-dollar bill. "Here, it's high time you treated yourself to a honey bun from Hedda's food truck." She smiled at Bonner. "I have it on very good authority that they're terrific."

"Boof," Bonner muttered. When Kayla walked away, he shuffled slowly after her, making a bee-line back to the food truck

"That's a wrap, folks," Ivy sniffled into the microphone. "H-Have a tippity-top, triumphant day." The moment Tempest turned off the radio console, she caught Ivy wiping at her eyes.

"That was so heart warming! Whether it's encouraging Blossom when her mom pressures her to diet, or Kayla when she believes she's not perfect enough, you have such a gift for instilling self-worth into people."

"Well, guess I had to become an expert on how to raise

self-esteem," Tempest admitted, "after all the mistakes *I've* made—"

"Excuse me," a man broke in, tapping Tempest on the shoulder. He held out a wad of cash. "Here's my ten bucks, ma'am. Plus tip."

Tempest gazed past him, suddenly realizing that there was a line of eager cowboys waiting for their turns for kisses. She leaned her head back and groaned. "Oh Ivy, I think we've created a monster. We've got to stop the kissing booth offer or we'll be here all day."

"What's wrong with that?" Ivy said. "Think of all the money we can raise!"

The men in the line cheered, grinning expectantly.

"Because it's gone too far," Tempest whispered, tilting her head to assess the number of enthusiastic cowboys—there were ten and counting. "Besides, if you're feeling charitable, why don't *you* give them kisses?"

"Ooh, I never thought of that," Ivy replied. She spotted a cute cowboy with red hair in the line and held back a shy giggle. "Um," she hesitated, gazing down at her frumpy pink cardigan, "do you think any of those guys will want to kiss *me*?"

Tempest paused, scanning Ivy's heart-shaped face and valentine-colored outfit. For the first time, she realized the depths of Ivy's lack of self-confidence. With all of her boldness to create her color therapy app, she'd naturally assumed Ivy was more positive about herself. Tempest brushed a kinky lock of brown hair from her face. "Ivy," she looked deep into her eyes, "you're beautiful—don't you know that? I bet if *you're* the one they find out they get to kiss, the line will be twice as long as for some middle-aged chick like me. On top of that," she smiled, assessing Ivy's slim figure beneath her loose sweater, "you're wearing the perfect colors, right? Here, let me prove it."

"Hey fellas!" Tempest called out. "I have to help my son in the cow barn, so my assistant will be the one to lip-lock for the next hour. Everybody okay with that?"

Hoots and whistles filled the air while the men eagerly waved their cowboy hats at Ivy. Her cheeks became as bright as a candy heart.

"Hold on, boys!" Tempest warned. "Before you get too excited, I want you to know that Miss Ivy has the right to refuse *anyone*. So you'd better make sure your teeth are brushed, you're freshly shaved, and your hair is combed. Got that?" She narrowed her eyes. "And you *must* treat her like a lady, or I'll broadcast every name of the louses who break these rules on my radio show. Ready? You've got fifteen minutes to spiff up. Go!"

While the men dashed off, Ivy giggled, her cheeks still beaming red.

"By the way," Tempest whispered, "I want you to keep the money, okay? I'll double whatever you make today and give it as a donation to the 4-H club."

Ivy sucked in a breath and nodded, unable to keep from grinning.

"All right, I'm off to help Owen. Just remember, you can close down the booth whenever you want." Tempest gave her a smile and wiggled her fingers in a wave. "Have fun!"

Tempest headed leisurely to the cow barn, knowing full well that Owen didn't need her assistance—he'd become quite proficient at grooming Dumpling himself. She simply wanted to give Ivy some space. When she met her son in the building, she was delighted to see that Annie had encouraged the children to embellish each cow pen with cute photos, posters, and banners showing how much their livestock meant to them. Owen rushed to his mother to brag that he'd won third place in the decorating contest, and he pointed to a big yellow ribbon hanging from Dumpling's pen. Thrilled, Tempest hugged him close and offered take him to see the bulldogging event, which had already begun in the main arena. Dixon was slated to compete soon, and Owen was eager to watch—as long as he also got a hot dog and curly fries.

As soon as they swung through the concessions aisle and reached the stands with their food, the announcer informed the crowd that they had to squeeze in too many rodeo events that day, so the next Cowboy Roundup competition would be the following afternoon. Tempest heaved a relieved breath while Owen snuggled his hand into hers.

"I heard the fair's doing really great," Owen said. "Thanks for helping, Mom. Mister Horton told Miss Annie that tickets have been selling like crazy ever since they started the Cowboy Roundup."

Tempest stilled, cherishing the gentle warmth of her son's hand against hers. It was instances like this that made every second worth it, no matter how much she'd been humbled by the Cowboy Roundup. Tears wetted the edges of her eyes— her son was actually *proud* of her! And naturally, she was bursting at the seams at everything he'd accomplished with Dumpling. To Tempest, this tiny moment proved that, after the year of hell they'd lived through, they'd done more than survive.

They'd *thrived*.

Tempest's grip tightened on Owen, and she brought his pudgy hand to her lips for a kiss.

"You're amazing, honey," she whispered. Then she saw Dixon's name appear on the scoreboard to compete next. "Look," she nodded at the chutes, "Mister Dixon's turn is coming up."

The announcer confirmed the Ramsey team was on deck, and Tempest and Owen watched their excited horses prance at the chutes, ready to take off in a shot. After the stock handlers made sure everyone was in their correct positions, the gate flung open for the steer, and in a flash the horses tore after him. Tempest was struck by how alert Dixon's dad seemed as the hazer, regardless of how much he'd drunk last night. His reflexes were lightning fast, keeping the steer perfectly in line as Dixon descended and grabbed the animal's horns while he dug his boots into the dirt. Faster than she and Owen could say "bulldogger", Dixon had turned over the animal's horns and swung him until he landed with all four hooves in the air. He let go and threw up his hands in triumph.

"Hot diggity, folks!" the announcer crowed. "Dixon Ramsey wrestled that steer in only 4.6 seconds. I believe that's a county fair record!"

The audience clamored with applause, and Bear Ramsey deftly herded the steer back to the corral area where he belonged. His smile was as big as the nearby mountain range for his son's success. Yet once again, Tempest noticed that he didn't seem a bit hungover. Maybe he's accustomed to that much alcohol, she thought, wondering if he'd been nipping all along on the sly. The crowd's clapping had yet to die down, and she smiled when she spied Bonner a few rows down from them, slapping his paws together with another stack of honey buns at his side.

Half a dozen more teams competed in the event, and the announcer called Dixon's name when it came to trophy time. As the audience swelled with cheers, Dixon stood alongside his father and lifted his trophy high in the air. But when Bear Ramsey waved at the crowd, Tempest observed that he wasn't aiming at Betty.

He was focused on…Hedda!

"Well, I'll be darned," Tempest muttered under her breath, turning to confirm that Hedda's booth had been closed and she was in the stands a few rows above them. "No wonder she's been giving Bonner honey buns. Bear's eye is on *her* this afternoon, not Betty. Could he be playing the field?"

"Mommy, what's playing the field?"

Tempest's cheeks prickled—she hadn't realized she'd mumbled that aloud. "Oh, just having lots of friends. C'mon, let's go congratulate Mister Dixon."

Tempest and Owen slipped from the stands and headed toward the arena, meeting Dixon half way. He held up his trophy that was nearly as tall as Owen and grinned. Owen broke into a run, and the second he caught up to him, Dixon proudly lifted the boy and held him aloft on his shoulder.

Just like a *dad* would—

Tempest's heart nearly ceased beating.

The sight of the two of them together, so familiar with each other and casually smiling, was secretly all Tempest could ever hope for in that moment. Her son was *happy*, alongside a man who was sincerely delighted to see him.

The same man whose eyes glinted at Tempest, just as pleased to see her.

Could this be happening?

Could she really be witnessing a possible…future…with Dixon?

"You know," Dixon remarked in a cocky tone when he caught up to her, gently setting Owen to his feet, "I never did get that glass of wine you promised."

"Promised?" Tempest replied. "*Again?*"

"You bet. It was supposed to be part of that whole fireplace thing, remember? That got cut short last night. But that doesn't mean we can't still have wine this evening, right?"

Dixon handed his large trophy to Owen to hold, digging his thumbs into his pockets. "I-I'm sorry for my dad's behavior," he confessed to Tempest. "Guess he fell off the wagon—for the millionth time. Welcome to my world. Can I make it up to you? The Outlaw's Hideout Bar and Grill in town has a great happy hour."

"Ooh, I could look after Owen!" Ivy burst cheerfully beside Tempest, startling her. Tempest shifted her gaze to her booth, which clearly Ivy had closed once her hour was up.

Ivy stepped over to Owen and rifled his hair. "We're best buds, huh? And I've yet to beat you at gin rummy."

Owen nodded vigorously, excited about spending more game time with her.

"I'll only babysit," Ivy qualified for Tempest, "if you let me pick out the colors you're going to wear." Then she waved a thick wad of cash in front of her face. "Look, I topped two hundred bucks! I even gave out my number to one of the guys —with the dreamiest red hair!" She gazed down at her sweater. "Isn't pink a miracle?"

"No, *you're* the miracle—because you're wonderful inside and out," Tempest replied. "And if you look after Owen, I'll give you another hundred this evening. But only if you call that guy you mentioned, okay? Maybe next time, *you'll* be the one going to happy hour."

"Awesome!" Ivy grinned. Then she subtly pointed at the Trinity's booth. Blossom was there, surrounded by a gaggle of cowboys who were vying with each other to buy her pie. "Have you noticed Blossom today? Looks like she's not afraid of eating whatever she wants anymore after the Dash and Splash. Maybe you could, um…encourage her to wear pink and meet you tonight with one of those guys? You know, for some *adulting* time away from her mother?"

Tempest tilted her head, bemused. "You really *are* a natural matchmaker! Although I don't think she needs to wear pink to attract more men—her overalls seem to be doing just fine."

Dixon directed a glance at Blossom. "Just make sure she chooses a cowboy with the fastest truck. He might need a rifle too, considering her mother—I wouldn't put anything past Betty. And as for you," he switched his gaze to Tempest, "I'll pick you up at your place at five o'clock."

"Pick me up?"

"Yes, ma'am," he replied. "That's what cowboys do. We open doors for women, too. And we've been known to spread our jeans jackets over mud puddles—*and* rescue ladies from charging cattle. Call me old fashioned if you want, but you might learn to like it."

"Um...okay." Tempest tangled her fingers together, a bit taken aback by her own self-consciousness. It felt like a century since she'd gone on a *real* date.

"Don't forget a rose!" Owen insisted, smiling up at Dixon. "I know where the wild ones grow—they're really pretty. I bet my mom will love 'em." The earnest way he gazed into Dixon's eyes pierced Tempest's heart.

Dixon patted him on the shoulder. "I like the way you think, young man. You know, everything you've shown me lately proves that you've sure got what it takes."

He dipped down to Owen's eye level and gave him a proud smile.

"To make a mighty fine cowboy."

21

T empest was trembling in her boots. So much for the Queen of Tough Love! As a middle-aged chick, she had no idea anymore how she looked to the opposite sex. Was her hair style okay? Should she have put on a dress? While she was at home, she'd decided to go with a more casual, mountain-town outfit like what everyone else wore in Bandits Hollow: a pair of jeans and boots with a nice shirt for stepping out. And she'd allowed Ivy to choose the teal-colored blouse, which Ivy claimed lent a touch of serendipity to new adventures. But after Dixon had picked her up and then opened the door for her at the Outlaw's Hideout Bar & Grill, Tempest realized she was about to enter the official "on the market" zone.

With no slick defenses.

Nobody was going to listen to her usual snark about how she didn't need anybody, because the whole world could see she was on a date with Dixon. And they'd probably have small-town opinions about it.

Tempest knew she should be more relaxed as a mature adult. Okay, so she and Dixon were likely to cause a stir since the Cowboy Roundup was still going on, like Betty had insinuated. But since all of his relationships had gone up in flames before this, surely nobody would take them that seriously?

Except *her*—

Try as she might, Tempest couldn't lie to herself about her attraction to Dixon. While she'd been sitting in his truck on the way over, she couldn't help noticing the heady aroma of his skin, a mixture of fresh mountain air, alfalfa, and the slightly musky scent of a man who worked outdoors from dawn to dusk. Like usual, his hair was flecked with streaks of gold, and those hands—strong and thick from years of ranch labor. Not to mention Dixon's face, with the kind of features that could have illustrated adventure tales of cowboys from a century ago.

Dixon was drop-dead handsome—there was no doubt about it.

And more importantly…he was kind.

As well as doing his damndest to be a gentleman to her.

He'd even arrived with a handful of fresh-picked, wild roses for her, like her son had suggested. And he was right— she loved them.

Who *wouldn't* fall for this guy?

Yet unlike the nights when they'd been training Dumpling, and she'd had her son to worry about, now there were no distractions. It was simply her and this incredibly good-looking man in close proximity, heading to a place that sold alcohol.

And perhaps heading for *more* than that?

Tempest stood before the open door of the Outlaw's Hideout Bar and Grill, feeling like she was about to pass over a threshold—to a whole new life as a single woman. No more hiding behind Tempest the Terminator, or being a busy mom, or a professional therapist, or any other comfortable persona, except for the very vulnerable woman she felt like she was now.

"Ready?" Dixon asked, gesturing for her to enter the bar.

The second Tempest drummed up her courage and stepped inside, she was greeted by a chorus of hollers from the local cowboys who were bellied up to the bar.

"Apparently, everybody's impressed you're here," Dixon remarked lightly. He set a firm hand on the small of her back, as if sensing her misgivings.

Tempest's breath stilled—his warm hand felt so good, so protective in that moment. She'd forgotten what it felt like for a man to behave as if she *belonged* to him, and her muscles eased a little against his palm.

Yet to her dismay, she spied a TV monitor on the wall with her Cowboy Roundup stats lit up as bright as the Las Vegas strip. Then the screen launched into video footage of her and the other ladies walking the plank of the Dash and Splash in their dowdy swimsuits.

Another chorus of cheers erupted from the bar, along with the clinks of whiskey glasses.

"This is hardly an anonymous date, is it?" Tempest

mentioned to Dixon. "Hope you weren't gunning for privacy tonight."

"All I'm gunning for is wine," Dixon replied, his eyes glinting at the enthusiasm of the bar patrons. "What kind do you like?"

"Um, at this point, I'll take something harder," Tempest confessed. "Like a shot of tequila?"

"My kind of gal," Dixon said. "Hey Mike—how about a shot of Knob Hill for me and Roca Patron for the lady here?"

Mike gave him a nod. While he was preparing the drinks, Tempest swiveled, her eyes adjusting to the dim light of the bar. In the back of the room, she spotted Blossom—chatting with a cute cowboy! Tempest knew she had a tendency to hover, but she simply couldn't resist asking Blossom how she managed to slip away from her mother.

"Excuse me for a sec," she said to Dixon as soon as he handed her the drink. She waved at Blossom and walked up to her, nudging her with her elbow.

"I have to pose the million-dollar question," Tempest chided, her cheeks tugging into a smile. "How'd you ditch your mom this evening? I'm surprised she hasn't injected a chip under your skin to track your every move."

"Well," Blossom said with a proud sparkle in her eye, "I reminded her that Bear Ramsey was probably home alone tonight, since you mentioned you were coming here with Dixon. That made her take off like a hound dog after a single man's scent!" Blossom brought her fingers to her face and giggled. "Of course, I didn't tell her *I* was coming here, too—I insisted Annie needed my help at the cow barn. And I turned off my cell phone, which I'm sure will make her panic once she figures out she doesn't know where I am." Blossom sidled up to Tempest and lowered her voice. "Get ready for Hurricane Betty to blow through here any minute looking for me. The only thing on earth that will make her leave a single man's side is a broken leash."

"Wow, you sure have your momma's number," Tempest laughed. "And you're really starting to take control of your life, aren't you?" She glanced around. "Maybe you should consider going to another place to elude Hurricane Betty? Might make the evening last longer."

"They're having a bonfire at the Circle Bar K Ranch tonight," the cowboy at her side offered. "I hear they're gonna roast marshmallows and make S'mores."

"Oh my gosh, I *love* S'mores!" Blossom smiled, not a bit self-conscious anymore about what she ate. "What are we doing here? Let's go!"

Blossom linked her arm in the cowboy's, giving Tempest a wink. Tempest relished watching her new-found confidence as they headed across the bar, until she saw a man stop Blossom before she reached the door. He pointed to a side room with an inflatable pit that featured a mechanical bull.

"Hey ladies!" he called out, sending a pointed stare to Tempest. "Did you know you can earn a thousand bucks for riding our mechanical bull? The one with the best score gets the dough! Usually we have ten or so cowboys join in, but since *you* gals are the stars of the town lately, we'll make it just between you two. You on?"

Blossom's mouth hung open. She slowly turned and her gaze met Tempest's.

Tempest understood immediately what was going through

her head—that thousand dollars would be enough for her to make a deposit on her very own apartment. As luck would have it, this silly bar activity could mean Blossom's...freedom.

Dixon walked up to Tempest. "You don't have to do this if you don't want to," he whispered. "Since your son had never been on a real horse before Bullet, I figure you're not up to speed either."

Tempest shook her head, her pulse racing. "You don't understand. Blossom really *needs* that money. To break free, I mean."

"From...Betty?" Dixon guessed, searching her eyes.

"Exactly," Tempest replied. "I've got to do it."

Dixon smiled softly, cuffing her chin with his fist. "Then go get 'em, Tiger. If anybody's got the guts to do something they've never tried, it's you."

"Tempest the Tiger, eh?" she asked, lifting a cool brow to hide her growing panic. "Kinda suits me. Got any tips for riding a bull?"

"Just treat it like making love," Dixon replied with a cocky curl to his lip. "Relax and keep a nice, smooth rhythm, and you'll do just fine."

Tempest's cheeks spiked with heat. "That so?" She raised her chin to pretend he hadn't sent a line of sparks up her spine. "I'll keep that in mind."

Tempest gave the man a thumbs up to indicate she was game, and she watched as he guided Blossom first over to the mechanical bull. Blossom easily swung onto its back like a woman who'd been riding all her life. Then she listened as the man warned her to hold onto the stiff rope, not the horns, with her free hand in the air.

The man headed to a podium console and counted down from three to make sure Blossom was ready before he pressed the power button. He cranked several dials that sent the mechanical bull into a gentle rocking motion with a few swivels thrown in. Everyone's eyes in the bar were glued to Blossom. In her modest, faded overalls, she moved with the bull like it was easy, her ample breasts and hips swaying to the rhythm while her beautiful red hair tossed from side to side. Somehow, she managed to look like a country goddess astride the bull, her fluid gyrations making all of the cowboys gather around the inflatable landing pad with wistful looks in their eyes.

Tempest and Dixon headed over as well, and Blossom smiled like she was having the time of her life as the man toyed with a joystick on the console that increased the bull's bucking and spinning speed. Nothing appeared to faze Blossom—she remained in perfect balance, as if she were born to be the sweetheart of the rodeo, even when the man jiggled the joystick to make the bull move harder and crow hop. Every shimmy of her voluminous figure sent sighs through the crowd of cowboys until the console's buzzer finally signaled eight seconds.

The mechanical bull jolted to a halt. Blossom waved at the men, enjoying their whistles as the cowboys whipped out their wallets and threw dollars at her like she'd just descended from a stripping pole. Though their gestures made her blush, she eagerly scooped up the cash from the bull pit and stuffed it into the bib of her overalls before meeting up with Tempest.

"Your turn!" she giggled, glancing down at her bulging bib. "Make it good and you'll haul in a profit, too!"

Tempest blew out a breath, her eyes wide. In all honesty,

survival was her only goal, and she threw back what was left of the shot of tequila in her hand, giving the glass to Dixon and pounding her chest with a wheeze. She knew she didn't have half the voluptuous curves of Blossom, and the last time she checked, her balance was so bad she had to avoid high heels. But this moment wasn't about *her*—it was about giving Blossom the chance to escape her mother's mind games. Surely that was worth swallowing her pride and climbing onto a fake bull? Tempest steeled her resolve and headed into the inflatable pit with unsteady steps, stumbling a few times to laughter from the crowd. Then she hesitantly mounted the mechanical bull, her face washed pale as the men began to chant "Temp-est! Temp-est!". Their enthusiasm only made her cling to the stiff rope for dear life. Trembling, she dug in her heels and gave the man at the console a quick nod, and he set the mechanical bull into motion.

Tempest began to roll her hips to keep up with the rocking rhythm of the bull. As long as she didn't look down at the pit, she hoped she'd be okay, keeping her gaze glued over the fake animal's ears. Then she happened to spy the monitor across the bar that featured her Cowboy Roundup stats. A new category flitted across the screen: "Likelihood of riding her way into cowboys' hearts: Blossom Barnhart 100/1, Tempest Wright 70/1, Hedda Grimson—yet to be determined."

Tempest's mouth sank, wondering who in the bar was secretly videoing them and fueling those scores? Then she spied a cowboy with a wicked grin and his cell phone held high above the crowd. Part of her fantasized about getting even, maybe stringing him up by his boot from the fairgounds announcer's stand? Yet she had to admit that riding the bull wasn't so bad—kind of like sitting on a seesaw with Owen, which she'd done a hundred times. But then the man at the console fiddled with his joystick, and soon Tempest found herself whipping into tighter circles with jarring bucks thrown in. Petrified, she threw her arms around the bull's plastic neck, attempting to cling for all she was worth. After several more nasty bucks and a nearly vertical, upthrusting tilt, she let out a blood curdling scream as she found herself flinging high into the air.

And into the arms of Dixon Ramsey.

As the buzzer sounded, Dixon smiled, managing to remain standing in the inflatable pit and keep his hold firm on Tempest.

Bewildered, Tempest glanced around, realizing he must have jumped into the bull pit just as her body had been hurled in air.

"Whoa, Nelly!" Dixon laughed, gazing into her eyes. "Maybe you need someone to pick you up when you fall more often? You could have done quite the belly flop."

"Oh my gosh, thank you!" Tempest sputtered, desperately focused on regaining her breath as he walked her out of the pit in his arms. Her mind was still spinning, yet she felt so steady in his strong grip, and the hardness of his chest made her feel supported and safe. Dixon gently set her to her feet and grasped her shoulders to keep her from teetering.

"Congratulations—you survived!" He gave her shoulder a pat. "Just think, you'll have lots to talk about tomorrow on the radio."

Tempest peered into Dixon's eyes. "I'm just happy it's *over*. Thanks again for stepping in. It sure would have been embarrassing to face plant in that pit. And I have a feeling that image would have been broadcast all over Bandits Hollow."

"No doubt," Dixon replied, so close he could he kiss her. "But all kidding aside, I'm proud of you for giving it a shot," he whispered, allowing his lips to gently brush her ear. "For Blossom's sake."

Tempest felt the warmth of his breath linger against her skin as the man at the console stepped in front of the crowd. "That's a thousand-dollar payout for Blossom Barnhart tonight!" he cried, jolting her from her thoughts. He headed to the register at the bar to get the cash, then he walked over to hand it to Blossom, who waved the money in the air like she'd won the lottery. She trotted up to Tempest to give her a hug.

"Me and Levi are going to go celebrate with S'mores!" she grinned. "Thank you for being a good sport, Tempest—it's going to change my whole life!"

Tempest grasped Blossom's cheeks, though she still felt a bit woozy from the bull and the tequila. "You deserve it, sweetie," she assured her. "Now go have yourself a ball. With chocolate and melted marshmallows on top."

"Sounds perfect!" Blossom smiled, stuffing the money into her overalls before she tugged on Levi's arm to walk toward the door. When the two of them reached the threshold, she paused to give Tempest a wave before they stepped into to the night.

Tempest turned to Dixon. "Mind if I sport you for another shot of tequila?" she asked. "It's gonna take a bit more medicine for my nerves to settle."

"You're on," Dixon nodded, holding up two fingers to Mike for an additional round. "It's time to celebrate again."

"Celebrate?" Tempest said.

"Yeah. Because of you, Blossom's been emancipated tonight. I say that calls for one hell of a toast." He looped an arm around her shoulder and gave her a squeeze.

As soon as Mike brought over the drinks, Tempest clinked glasses with Dixon and threw back the tequila, feeling the silky liquid course down her throat in a warm stream. The second the alcohol hit her stomach, the room pivoted as if she were still on the bull, but she didn't care. At least the tequila made her feel more relaxed and glowy inside, and she was happy she'd managed to put a grand into her friend's pocket.

"I have an idea," she mentioned to Dixon, bolder than usual after getting a bit tipsy. "Since you're so good at catching me, maybe we could go outside for a while? Get some fresh air and look up at those rambling stars? If I wobble on the boardwalk, I'll count on you to catch me."

Dixon's gaze met hers, his midnight-blue eyes so arresting it made her startle. "There's nothing I'd *rather* do, Tempest," he moved in so close she could feel the warmth of his breath, "than hold you in my arms and stargaze with you. "

His words made shivers inch down her spine, but his touch was gentle and firm as he placed his hand again on the small of her back. As they moved toward the door, a thunderous boom suddenly echoed through the bar. Everyone fell silent at the sight of Betty Barnhart at the doorway of the Outlaw's Hideout Bar and Grill. She'd swung open the front door so hard that it made framed pictures drop to the floor.

In that moment, Betty glared at Tempest like a gunslinger from an old western movie, ready for a duel.

"Where is she?" Betty demanded, her eyes narrowing.

"Where the hell's my daughter! *You're* the one who put all those crazy ideas in her head, and now she's running all over town like a hussy. With the kind of men who don't deserve her!"

Tempest stared at the woman like she'd lost her mind. Is this what out-of-control helicopter moms really look like? Note to self, Tempest thought, don't *ever* let this be your future.

The cowboys who'd drifted back to their barstools filled the air with laughter. Nevertheless, Betty squinted at the nearby TV monitor. When she spied her daughter's name above Tempest's for a mechanical bull riding score, she stomped her foot and pointed at the screen.

"Goddammit, right there is proof she was here!" Betty marched up to Tempest, meeting her nose to nose. "Everyone in town knows you're washed up and will do anything for a man. Yet you have the gall to teach my daughter the same thing? Just because you couldn't keep your husband doesn't mean she has to lower herself for any old ranch hand."

Tempest sighed, her brows furrowing. This wasn't the first time she'd dealt with crazy in her therapy practice—people who preferred to scream into her face rather than deal with their issues. But it was certainly new to dole out professional guidance in a bar. She glanced at a clock on the wall and stared back at Betty.

"Shouldn't you be spending the evening with someone your *own age* right now?" Tempest suggested. "Leading your *own life* instead of spying on your adult daughter? By the way, if you take up any more of my time, I'll have to bill you—"

"How can I," Betty cut her off, "when Bear Ramsey wasn't home—he trotted off with Hedda! You soured him against me, too! Just like you brainwashed my daughter. But what goes around comes around, and I bet you won't be able to keep Dixon for fifteen minutes. I used to feel sorry for you after reading your book. But now I see there's a reason you can't hang onto a man, you meddling bitch!"

Tempest shook her head. "Well Betty, you're hardly the first person to call me that after I helped empower their family members. Now if you'll excuse us," she grasped Dixon by the hand to head toward the door, "we have to get going."

"Oh no you don't—not until you tell me where Blossom is!" Betty screeched.

To Tempest's astonishment, Betty pulled back her arm and took a swing—but not before Dixon yanked hard on Tempest's shoulders so she'd be out of reach. He immediately planted his palm on Betty's forehead to keep her at bay while she flailed her fists.

"Please leave," he threw a disarming smile at Tempest. "Before my arm gets tired and I decide to steer wrestle Betty to the floor. Like Blossom told me to."

The bar patrons began to chuckle, and Dixon shot a glance at a cowboy seated near the door.

"Do me a favor, okay?" he said. "When I slip outside after Tempest, lock the door and barricade it with your table. Use a gun if that's what it takes to keep Betty here."

Dixon dug in his pocket and tossed the man a fifty-dollar bill. "And for your trouble, buy this lady and yourself as many rounds as you can till she passes out. That way she won't bother us until the goddamned morning."

"**M**aybe I should have decked her," Tempest muttered, feeling twinges of regret that she'd *ever* encouraged Blossom to give her mother some slack. The woman was relentless! Tempest gazed out the front window of Dixon's truck as they drove down a moonlit back road that meandered through the mountains. "I realize Betty's entitled to her issues," she sighed, "but a good wallop might be the only therapy that will get through to her."

"Not unless you want to spend the night at the police station," Dixon replied.

"Why, what are you saying—wouldn't you post bail to get me out?"

"No," he shook his head with a smirk, "because I'd be in the cell right next to you. Especially after the way Betty's been slinking around my dad. Thank God he decided to focus on Hedda."

"Sounds like he's a good judge of character," she shrugged. "Even if he did fall off..."

Dixon stilled.

Tempest made no effort to finish her sentence. She knew this topic was raw for Dixon—an aching wound that had been festering since childhood, and she could tell he'd always been forced to be the adult in this situation. So when he ran a hand through his hair and paused to gather his breath, as if he might actually talk to her about it, she felt moved.

"My dad," Dixon began in an unsettled tone, "swore he didn't touch a drop of alcohol that night." He shook his head. "Not the first time he's lied. But when I carried him in the house, his breath didn't smell like Jim Beam, his usual poison. The next morning we got in a big fight, and he challenged me to find a bottle in the trash or anywhere. I was so mad I threatened to kick him out for good, but he was right—there wasn't a trace in the house or the barn, or even his truck."

Dixon turned to Tempest. "Then again, addicts are experts at hiding things."

Tempest nodded. "Well," she mulled it over, "it was a bit strange. He didn't act like he was hungover when he helped you win the steer wrestling trophy."

"Aw, that's second nature," Dixon said. "Drunks like my dad can do things they've practiced a hundred times from muscle memory, no matter how hungover they are. I have a hunch Betty's spicy salsa covered the alcohol smell on his breath. To be honest..."

Dixon's jaw began to work back and forth, as if his words were particularly painful.

"I didn't have the heart to totally kick him off the ranch.

His ranch. Just like he couldn't shoot the horse that killed my mom."

Dixon gripped the steering wheel tighter, his knuckles pressing white beneath the moonlight. "Before my mom died, my dad built up our entire ranch himself. He believed in his dream and worked his ass off to buy the land and livestock. Hewed logs from our property and built the house and barns with his own hands. Bear Ramsey was the kind of cowboy everybody looked up to."

Dixon shot a glance at Tempest, his eyes smoldering with determination and pain.

"Everything I have, everything I've *ever* achieved," he said with a brittle crack in his voice, "is just an extension of..."

Dixon drew a long breath.

"Him."

Tempest's heart broke for Dixon, and she scooted closer and set her hand gently on his knee.

"It's okay to love your dad," she said, "in spite of his flaws. People are complicated, and he can be your hero and a thorn in your side at the same time. That's not psycho-babble—it's the truth, Dixon. We all have our light and dark sides."

"Well, the dark side of me banished him to live in the barn until he sobers up for good," Dixon said with a tightness to his lips. "Us cowboys never turn our backs on our own. But I figure once winter sets in, he'll think twice about drinking and sleeping out there in the cold."

"Whoa, so you're a believer in tough love, too?" Tempest observed. "As I recall, you *did* already sock him in the face. Isn't that enough punishment—"

"If he's gonna hit the bottle and keep doing donuts in our

yard with a tractor," Dixon growled, "he's gonna get more punches from me. God knows, the rehabs I paid for didn't work, and maybe that's what it's gonna take for him to clean up. But what I won't ever do," he said, his jaw slicing back and forth again, "is abandon one of my own. Ranchers stick by family. Over the years, I've saved far too much livestock during heavy snows or birthing seasons that came from the top bloodlines *he* purchased to turn around and ditch him now. I don't care if I never see his face again and he dies in that barn. But dammit, until then he'll have meals and a bed."

"Yeah, you do," Tempest said softly, staring down at her lap.

"Do what?"

"Care. You care a *lot*. Or you would have sent him packing a long time ago."

Dixon fell silent, his gaze studying the way the moonlight limned the branches of the pines that lined the backcountry road.

"He's the only family you've got," Tempest said quietly. She cleared her throat, daring to broach the subject. "Is that, um, why you've always courted unstable women? So you had an excuse not to bring them home where they might see your dad?"

"*You* weren't supposed to see that either," Dixon seethed.

Tempest noticed he wasn't arguing her point, and she felt awful for the shame Dixon had endured.

"Well, your dad did say something interesting before you met us on the grass," she mentioned, hoping to console him a little. "In his delirium, he thought he was *protecting* you and your horses against rustlers. Because he wanted to be a good dad."

"Right. That's what he claimed when he got sober six months ago. He wanted us to be a family again. He even knocked himself out to apologize for his past. Now it's all gone to hell."

Tempest chewed her lip, aware that sobriety had its share of stops and starts. "If it makes you feel any better," she offered delicately, "I don't think Hedda will put up with Bear very long if he's drinking again." She lifted her gaze to the moonlit horizon. "For all we know, he might turn out to be Betty's next project to fix. Especially now that Blossom's got her wings."

"Nothing doing," Dixon snarled. "You've seen how Betty is —drunk or not, my dad would leave her ass, too. All those nasty things she said to you in the bar," he glared at Tempest for a moment, "they're the same remarks everyone in town whispers about *her*. After she came here about a year ago from Oklahoma with Blossom and her stepdad in tow, the guy up and split. They haven't heard a word from him since."

"Wow, guess her comments were classic projection, huh?" Tempest said. Despite her attempt to sound detached, heat began to crest on her cheeks. Dixon wasn't alone in experiencing shame, and Tempest found herself twisting her fingers at the similarities between her and Betty. Both of them were abandoned by men who had the gall to run around on them, and Tempest suddenly felt like a hypocrite for pointing out Betty's flaws.

"J-Just because there's gossip about Betty doesn't mean there wasn't any truth to her accusations," Tempest admitted to Dixon. "She's not the only one around here who was fooled by a man and got...ditched."

To Tempest's astonishment, Dixon suddenly veered his truck into a turn-out by the side of the road, creating a cloud of dust. He'd originally claimed they were going for a slow moonlit drive down a rarely-traveled backroad. But now he cut the engine and swiveled to face her. Boldly, he cupped her cheeks in his hands.

"Tempest," Dixon stated in dark voice, verging on fury, "any man would be a *fool* to cheat on you." He studied her eyes as if determined to reach her soul. "Quite frankly, if your husband hadn't died already, I would have shot him. Because he had to be an idiot not to see the gold in you."

Tempest's breath stalled, rendering her speechless.

"Listen to me—you're not one bit like Betty. You give and give to everyone who comes within a mile, and you really *care* about how they're doing, inside and out."

Gently, Dixon pressed his lips to her forehead for a soft kiss and peered into her eyes. "I heard you pray before your radio show this morning," he said. "It's pretty damn obvious how much it matters to you to say the right things. To help people, I mean."

"You *heard* that?" she said. "Don't tell me the Fair Commission had my booth bugged after all—"

Dixon chuckled. "I know, I know—they go a bit far, but not *that* far. I think Ivy must have turned on your radio console before you realized it."

Tempest sunk her head in her hands. "Oh God, I feel so transparent."

Dixon peeled her fingers away, curling her hands into his

and staring into her eyes. "What's wrong with that? The way you care, from the bottom of your heart, is incredible. I knew you were everything I wanted from the first second I saw you."

Tempest's breath seized at his confession, and she began to tingle all over. Then a memory floated past her thoughts. "Wait a minute," she paused, "didn't I run my hands all over your chest in the dark entryway to the covered arena?"

"Yep," Dixon replied with a rise to his lips. "My kinda woman! Then you insisted on leading Dumpling outside, even though you didn't have a clue how to deal with that yearling. Your beauty, your grit, and yeah, sometimes your stubborn temper—it all shows how passionate you are. Like maybe... well...you're strong enough to deal with us Ramseys and ranch life. Come hell or high water. I mean, without..."

His voice drifted off.

"Running away?" Tempest guessed. Her eyes darted back and forth over her lap, suddenly realizing why Dixon had been a perennial bachelor. He'd been *testing* those women. To see how tough they were. Whether they could survive the realities of a ranch, as well as the ghosts of the Ramsey's past.

Dixon hesitated, choosing his words carefully. "Tempest... you're the only woman I've brought anywhere near my ranch in years. Who I trusted to bring *home*. The Rambling Star Ranch that my dad built up, that I forged a new future with— it means everything to me."

Tempest's molars gripped the insides of her cheeks.

"Believe me, if people in town gossip that you must be crazy to date the likes of me," he said, "then you're definitely *my* kind of crazy. And I've been hoping that...I'm yours."

Tempest met Dixon's gaze. She scanned each feature of his

rugged face outlined by the moon's rays before searching his eyes. Then she studied them carefully as if she were weighing Dixon to see if he…

Measured up.

All at once, she leaned over and reached for the door handle to give it a hard jerk. Without warning, she bolted from Dixon's truck into the darkness.

"Wait, where are you going?" Dixon called out, unable to see where she'd darted to in the night. He jumped out of his truck and squinted to help his eyes adjust to the low light. Yet Tempest wasn't walking along the dusty berm. Or across the road, either.

In fact, she wasn't anywhere in sight—

"It was a joke!" he cried, spinning a three-sixty to look for her. "I didn't mean you're *really* crazy. I meant you're the right type of person for me. Tempest, where are you?"

Dixon paused, listening for any sounds, but the night fell silent. He cursed under his breath that the dome light inside his truck had burned out a month ago, and he hadn't gotten around to fixing it. He knew that starting up his truck and turning the headlights toward the forest would only blind him to the subtleties of her tracks. Instead, he dashed to the edge of the trees and began to search desperately, dropping to his knees to try and detect footprints, broken branches, a thin trail —any small trace of her.

But it was futile.

"Great, just great!" Dixon spit out angrily, trying to recall if he had a flashlight. "Way to go, Ramsey! You scared the crap out of her, so she bolted like all the rest. She'd rather get spooked by coyotes than be near you—"

Suddenly, Dixon was engulfed in a dark curtain of fabric, unable to see as his jacket and shirt were forcefully yanked over his head.

"What the hell?" he muttered, wondering if this was some kind of bizarre kidnapping and readying his fist to take a swing.

Yet once his jacket and shirt were ripped off and tossed aside, he saw Tempest standing before him with her hands on her hips. She had a very serious look on her face.

Then she abruptly ran her fingers up the warm, smooth skin of his deeply muscled chest in the dark, just like she did in the arena corridor on the first day they'd met. A light gasp escaped her lips, as if she'd been dying all along to do that again.

"I want a *real* kiss this time, cowboy," she demanded in a startling tone. "Not one that's stolen on the fly. A deliberate, I-want-to-keep-you-around-for-a-long-time kind of kiss."

Dixon's eyes were as wide as the moon as he scanned her face and figure, taking in the glints of silver that descended over her cheeks, breasts and hips. He couldn't hide the fact anymore that she took his breath away, and it required everything he had to try to respond in mere words. Dipping his forehead gently against hers, he hesitated to even sweep his fingers over her moonlit cheek because he knew he'd lose all control—for a whole lot more than a kiss.

"Let's see," Dixon gazed deeply into her eyes. "Are you telling me you want an I'm-falling-head-over-heels-for-you type of kiss? Over every single inch of your body? Because that's sure as hell what I'd like to do with you right now."

"Exactly!" Tempest replied without missing a beat.

"Everything you said to me in your truck—well, it made me want to make love to you. And quite frankly, my son's with Ivy for only another hour, so we gotta get moving. By the way, that's not crazy—that's totally common sense."

"Say no more," Dixon replied in a husky tone. He easily hoisted Tempest into his arms and held her close against his firm chest. Then he dipped his head to brush his lips against her cleavage and breathed in deep, as though he'd been wanting to do that all night. His hands gripped her tighter, cherishing her body in his embrace, and he pressed his lips to hers for a kiss.

Not a stolen one this time.

But an electric, claiming kind of kiss that told her he had every intention of keeping it up for as long as he could get away with.

When Dixon broke free, he swallowed several breaths and walked over to the back of his truck, where he noticed that Tempest had already spread out several of his blankets—that's where she'd gone when he couldn't find her. He placed her body gently on the blankets and climbed in.

Delicately, he began to remove her clothes, button by button, piece by piece, and slowly peeled away the fabrics from her skin as if he were revealing a rare treasure. When he got to her lingerie, he simply gazed at her for a moment, allowing his eyes to follow each curve and swell of her body, before slipping her bra and underwear from her skin. Then his breath hitched. He dipped down and kissed her breasts, a deep groan issuing from his chest as he drew in the smell of her at the same time, as if he hoped to inhale her within. Before Dixon could remove his jeans, Tempest reached up and did it for him, unzipping his fly and sliding his pants to his ankles while he kicked off his cowboy boots.

At the sight of his fully revealed body, Tempest paused for a long moment to take in the contours of his rippled physique that were highlighted by the moon's rays. The sculpted beauty of Dixon's tightly-muscled arms, chest and abs made her struggle to take in air.

When she finally managed to inhale, Tempest tilted up her lips to lightly kiss the puncture scar beside his heart that he'd gotten while bulldogging. Then she met his gaze and watched him steal a glance up at the stars that dotted the sky over their heads.

"Tempest," he whispered, his tone more grave than she expected, "I'm gonna give you a night of stargazing you'll never forget. But only if you promise me one thing."

"What's that?" she replied barely above a whisper.

"Don't ever run away again," he said, his eyes locking on hers. "You scared the bejabers out of me."

He was *serious*.

Tempest simply smiled, and the generous gleam in her eyes told him everything he needed to know—

She was here, now.

And quite possibly for the long haul.

"Sh," she said, slipping a finger over his lips. "Isn't it time to let your body do the talking, cowboy?"

Tempest ran her fingers through his thick, starlight-flecked hair and pulled his body closer to hers, relishing the warmth of him over every inch of her, the place between her legs that had caught on fire. When Dixon's thick arm circled beneath her on the blanket, she exhaled a breath like she'd found...

home. But then she felt something odd tremble beside her fingers on the blanket. It had a soft, velvety texture, and was rimmed by a silky strand. When she collected it in her hand and raised it to the moonlight, she smiled.

In her fingers was a small bouquet of wild roses, tied together with a satin ribbon.

23

At dawn the following morning, thin bands of light sifted through pine boughs to the forest floor, glinting off the moist blades of grass like stars. Granny Tinker sat on the steps of her wagon, wrapping a red ribbon around the stems of two, freshly-picked wild roses. When she finished crafting her bow, the flowers quivered in her hand.

Yet the air around her remained still.

A strand of brass bells that hung from the door knob to her wagon began to jingle.

Granny arched a brow and glanced up.

There, in the small clearing where her wagon was parked, stood a fox.

Holding her gaze, the fox skittered a few steps toward her and froze. It slowly hunched down, shifting its black paws in the grass and locking its amber eyes on her.

As if tracking her soul…

Granny drew a long breath, never letting go of the fox's line of sight for second.

The fox lifted its nose in the air and sniffed. It let out a sharp cry like someone was coming.

"Much obliged," Granny whispered, dipping her head in respect. She watched the fox get up and dart across the clearing, disappearing into the nearby brush.

Standing to her feet, Granny turned to walk up the steps into her wagon with her small bouquet. She closed the door quietly behind her and headed past a cast-iron stove toward her bed loft in the back that was covered by quilts and embroidered pillows. In front of her bed was a rustic table and chairs where she took a seat. Carefully, she placed the wild roses into a dainty vase on the table, fluffing up the petals and leaves to make them look spry.

Suddenly, a heavy knock rattled her door. Then a series of hard poundings began to rock her wagon as if the world were about to end.

"Come on in," Granny called out in a matter-of-fact tone. "Ain't like I haven't been expectin' you."

The wagon door slowly creaked open and Betty Barnhart poked her head inside.

"I-I have to talk to you!" She wheezed as if she'd been running through the forest since the first ray of sunrise. But when she tried to step inside the wagon, she felt a weight press against her chest that prevented her from budging. Panicked, Betty glanced down at the strange black hash marks that were painted on the wooden floor. Before her eyes, they appeared to vibrate like snakes, as if they held some invisible venom that kept her from pushing her way in.

Granny sighed, not the least surprised.

"You of all folks oughta know the power of foxglove ink," she said dryly, shooting a glance at her floor. "To keep away those with ill intentions. Works better than any guard dog."

Betty stared at her like she was crazy, yet her mind began to race. While studying an old flower book once, she'd stumbled across folklore that claimed the dye from foxglove leaves drawn in crossed lines kept evil from entering a home. But then, those flowers were supposed to call in fairies and foxes, too! This woman has to be unhinged, Betty thought, but she was desperate.

"I have good intentions, I promise!" Betty pleaded, studying the wiggly marks on the floor. "I'm here for my daughter!"

Granny nodded, turning to reach a row of small vials on a shelf behind her. She grasped a bottle and uncorked it, emptying a bit of yellow powder into her palm. It was as fine and delicate as pollen, and Betty startled when Granny tossed it over the wagon floor in a thin cloud. The particles slowly settled on the wood like a light rain.

The black hash marks stilled.

Granny glared at Betty with her wolven-gray eyes, rimmed at the pupils in gold.

"Well hurry up," she insisted. "I ain't got all day."

Betty sucked in a breath, noticing as she took tentative steps across the threshold that she no longer felt repelled by a barrier. She scurried over the hash marks on the floor like they were hot coals and collapsed into a chair across from Granny, nearly tipping it over.

Betty righted the chair and situated herself on the red

velvet cushion, then threw the large purse she'd been carrying onto Granny's table. When she happened to spy clouds beginning to form in a crystal ball near Granny, she leaned back as if the ball might bite her.

"You're the town fortune teller, right?" Betty pressed in a hushed tone, wringing her hands. "Who's supposed to have… special powers? That's what everybody says."

"You ain't gotta whisper," Granny scolded as if she were dim. "Ain't nobody in these parts at this hour." She tilted her head at her bouquet. "Except my wildflowers. As for fortunes, I got a habit of telling it like I see it, which makes some folks uneasy, that's all. Now why in Heaven's name have you knocked yourself out to see me at daybreak, Elizabeth Meyer-Goodwin-Barnhart-Smythe?"

"W-Wait," Betty stammered, her eyes flaring wide, "how do you know all of my married names? Except for the last one —I don't know a soul named Smythe."

"Oh, you will," Granny replied. "'Cause that's the one you're gonna use to write your pen pals from Cañon City. After your next move, of course."

Granny gazed at her crystal ball, watching the murky clouds separate to reveal a young, curvy woman in overalls with long, red hair.

Betty gasped and pointed at the ball, careful not to touch it. "There she is! There's my Blossom!" She stared at Granny with earnest eyes. "She's been running around all night with some ranch hand who's poor as a church mouse. She didn't even come home this morning. I haven't been able to find her anywhere! Here—"

Betty dove her hand into her purse and began to pull out

wads of cash. Then she turned her bag over and shook it vigorously, emptying out every bill and coin. She shoved the pile of money toward Granny.

"I'll give you any amount you want," she vowed, "for a spell or a charm. Anything to get my daughter back on track! I don't want her mixing with ne'er-do-wells who'll drag her down and spin her life out of control—"

"Control," Granny wagged her head, pushing the money away from her to Betty. She leaned back and crossed her arms. "Now that's where I reckon you and I differ. Seems to me life is more like my crazy quilts." She angled her head toward her bed loft. "You never can tell which direction the patterns will sway. But you got a hankering to steer things your way all the time, don't you, Betty? Even if you gotta cheat fate? As for me, I ain't in the business of making souls do a damn thing unless something inside 'em wants to. But you've never settled for those terms, have you?" Granny studied the cash on the table. "Where'd you get all this money, anyway?"

Betty winced as Granny glanced into her crystal ball, which had filled up again with a dark haze. As the mist began to clear, in the centre of the ball was a narrow creek running through a ravine, surrounded on both sides by tall sagebrush.

A thin cry escaped Betty's lips when she recognized the sight, and she slapped her palms to her mouth. Quickly, she grasped at the money on the table and clutched it to her chest.

Granny cackled at her, the sound ringing off the walls of her wagon. Then she narrowed her eyes, staring Betty down.

"I bet you already know the story about how fairies put foxglove blossoms on foxes' paws so they can't be heard when they steal chickens. My, my, you sure been a quiet little thing, huh Betty? Trouble is, so are the folks you like to control. Now listen to me—"

Granny turned and pulled another vial from her shelf. This one was larger and filled with delicate, white wildflowers. It had a faded label on the front with a script that said *Wand Lily*.

"You know, I've heard the nickname for these pretty things is Mountain Death. I'd sure watch my steps if I were you. After all, you ain't the only one around here who knows her flowers."

Betty recoiled from the table with the bills squeezed against her chest, unable to rip her gaze from Granny. "W-What are you implying?" she spit out, her arms trembling. "I'm just a concerned mother!"

"Who has quite the knack for gettin' what she damn well wants." Granny wiggled the vial in front of her. "Now you head on out before I lose my patience. And while you're at it, you can start letting Blossom lead her own life."

Granny glanced at the bouquet of wild roses she'd made that morning. She plucked the flowers from the vase and tucked them into Betty's purse.

"Here, give these to Blossom for me," she said, handing Betty her purse. "If she ever comes home again, that is." Her smile stretched wide, revealing her gold tooth. "Tell her Granny Tinker sends her blessing."

❧ 24 ❧

"Fess up, I wanna hear all about it!" Ivy said with a big grin, her hands gripping Tempest's shoulders. "You looked a bit messy when you got home last night. You even had hay stuck in your hair!"

Tempest's cheeks turned crimson. "Oh my God, was I *that* obvious?" she said, grateful that Owen had already gone to bed by then.

"The smile on your face sure was!" Ivy chided with a gleam in her eyes. "I bet the color teal I picked out for you worked like a charm."

"Um, I guess it did," Tempest conceded, trying to restrain her smirk. "Let's just say last night was everything I could have hoped for."

"I knew it!" Ivy jumped up and down. "More proof that my color therapy really works. Would you consider writing a review on my app?"

"Only if it's anonymous," Tempest replied, not wanting to invite the whole world into her dating life.

"No problem!" Ivy pulled her phone from her pocket to check the time. "So, what's the topic going to be for the radio show today?"

Tempest's chest swelled, and she was feeling rather proud of herself. "This morning is going to be all about taking chances, even if you've been hurt in the past. You know, living life boldly again. Sound good?"

Ivy pressed her hands to her heart. "Oh Tempest, that's perfect." She gave her a surprisingly hard hug. "I'm so proud of you. That you stepped out, I mean."

Tempest bit her lip. It was a little embarrassing to have your own intern rooting for you not to be a wallflower anymore. Yet she had to admit Ivy was right—she *did* feel more outgoing in that pretty teal shirt. The night had been so amazing, in fact—looking at the stars while tangled up in Dixon's body after heart-stopping sex—that she found herself still reeling by mid-morning the next day.

Tempest clutched Ivy's hand and gave it a squeeze. "Well sweetie, it's time to get back down to business." She flicked her gaze to the radio console, then closed her eyes for a moment of silent prayer, like she usually did before flipping on the power switch. But when she glanced up, she happened to spy Blossom dashing toward her booth. Tempest's eyes flew wide, hoping Blossom didn't have some kind of disaster with Levi last night that now required damage control.

"Tempest—Tempest!" Blossom called out, reaching the booth with a huff. "I got my first kiss last night! I mean, that wasn't from truth or dare at a sleepover in sixth grade."

"Wow," Tempest replied, hoping for the best. "And were you...*happy*...afterwards?"

"Ecstatic!" Blossom threw her arms in the air like wings. "It was the best night of my whole life." She stared earnestly into Tempest's eyes. "Levi gave me a *real* kiss. The kind you remember for a long time that might lead to...other things."

"That's great!" Tempest pressed her lips to hide her giggle at their kinship in that moment. She was quite certain that somewhere in Bandits Hollow, Betty must be in a heated rage. "I'm so happy for you!"

"Well, *you're* the one who gave me the courage to do it. Which I'm going to need today, too."

"You are?"

"Yeah, because the mounted shooting competition starts in an hour," Blossom reminded her. "Didn't you check the schedule? We have to fire guns for the next Cowboy Roundup event. If you head over to the covered arena with me now, you can practice with Hedda's help. I already saw her there this morning—she's a crack shot."

Tempest swung a panicked look at Ivy. She had no clue how to shoot a weapon, and she was pretty sure she'd end up looking like a fool.

Ivy smiled. "Don't worry," she assured her. "You can go over to the arena and let me do the broadcast from here. Just think, it could be my chance to bold, like you." She gave her a wink. "As long as you let me plug my *Rainbow of Love* app at the end?"

Tempest took a step back in amazement.

Ivy had grown so much since the shy, young intern she'd first met at the beginning of summer who always wore her heart on her sleeve. Now she was feeling self-assured enough to take on therapy questions for the radio show? Tempest braced herself while she gazed past Ivy at a couple of eager people who'd already lined up at the booth.

Why not? she thought. It would be great for Ivy's resume and boost her self-esteem by a mile. Besides, the show always ends with a qualifier that listeners should consult their own licensed professionals before heeding any advice. Of course, Tempest thought, Ivy can be a bit kooky at times with her color theories, but she oozes enough cheer to make anybody's day. What could it hurt?

Tempest mulled it over, feeling a twist in her stomach as her hovering tendencies kicked in. She'd worked so hard to build up the popularity of her radio show over the last six months. Yet Ivy had never missed a single day or even been late all summer, plus she was a fourth-year psychology student. Could she really find it in her heart to let go of her show for a mere fifteen-minute broadcast?

Get over yourself, she scolded her own ego in her best Tempest the Terminator voice. *Give the girl a chance, just like you did for Owen.*

"You're on!" Tempest agreed. She leaned over to turn on the radio console and offered Ivy a smile. "Go for it," she beamed as she handed her the microphone, feeling as proud as if Ivy were her own daughter. Then she blew her a sweet kiss for good luck. As Ivy launched into the usual radio show greeting with her eyes ablaze, Tempest quietly stepped out of the booth.

"All right, let's head to the arena for shooting practice," she whispered as she linked her arm in Blossom's. "It might come in handy to know how to handle a gun," she pointed out, "if your mom gets wind of you kissing Levi. I bet she'll be furious."

"No doubt," Blossom replied. "And you know what? That's okay. For the first time in my life, I'm fine with it. She can worry and criticize me all she wants, and I'll just smile anyway." A carefree giggle escaped Blossom's lips. "Especially *after* I get an apartment. And maybe my very own gun." She gave Tempest a wink. "To keep my nosy mother at bay, of course."

"Listen up, ladies!" the announcer addressed the Cowboy Roundup contestants standing in the indoor arena. "I want you to imagine that you're in an old western town in 1895."

He motioned to the colorful replicas of storefronts that lined the inside of the ring, which included a saloon, a bank, a town hall, a jail house, and a bordello. "All the men are out on a big cattle drive, when these nasty outlaws arrive to take over." He tipped his head at the wooden, life-size gunslingers with balloons tied to their chests that were standing in front of each building. "And *you're* the only ones left to defend the town! Are you ready? Fair assistants, bring these ladies their weapons and horses."

Tempest was surprised to see Owen and several of his 4-H pals trotting into the arena to hand her, Hedda and Blossom their own revolvers and stick horses. Naturally, Hedda's horse was painted pink, while Tempest's was pinto and Blossom's was black. Tempest cupped her son's cheek for a second, then grasped her horse and gun, giving him a smile before he scurried back to the bleachers beside one of the livestock pens.

"In normal mounted shooting events, contestants ride *real* horses," the announcer told the audience. "But since we all know Tempest Wright is a city slicker, we decided to go easy on her with the fake kind!" He paused as laughter rippled through the crowd. "Now, here are the rules, ladies—this is a timed event, so when you hear the buzzer, you need to gallop from the barrel race alley into the arena and do a big loop while firing at the balloons on the outlaw characters. Then you'll race as fast as you can back to the alley. But before you exit, you gotta give Dixon Ramsey a big kiss to welcome him back from the cattle drive and show him you cleaned up the town. That makes Dixon's part real easy, except for one thing —contestants will be judged not only on their time and number of balloons popped, but also for how well they kiss Dixon!"

The crowd broke into laughter as Tempest stared nervously at her single-action, .45 caliber revolver. During the last hour, Hedda had shown her and Blossom how to pull the hammer back and fire the black-powder blanks at balloons she'd set up for practice. But now Tempest faced charging forward on a stick horse while attempting to shoot in front of the whole town! Is it possible to look any sillier? she thought. Could blanks backfire?

Tempest understood their guns had no projectiles, and Hedda told her it was the heat and gas from firing the powder that broke the balloons. Yet the sound alone rattled her—even with ear plugs—and she wasn't sure if the powder could somehow blow up in her face. Then another thought struck her. What if they secretly had people at each station who might try to *fire back?* She scanned the outlaw characters with a serious look.

Hedda stepped up and squeezed her arm. "Aw honey, you'll take 'em out like a pro!" she encouraged. "Just pretend you're in a big ol' movie with your six-shooter where the good guys always win. And at the end you get to lock lips with Dixon!" She grinned at Dixon a few yards away, whose irresistible smile managed to make him look charming even on a brown stick horse. "That's a damn fine reward if I ever saw one!"

Tempest peeked at the stands where Ivy was sitting for a moment of support, not too far from Bear and Bonner. Levi was beside them and grinning eagerly down at Blossom. Of course, Betty sat strategically in the seat right above Dixon's father, jabbering non-stop and handing him popcorn in her lame effort to flirt. Bear seemed to ignore her, but Bonner wasted no time seizing the popcorn tub with his paws. Within seconds, he'd downed the whole thing.

"Hedda Grimson," the announcer called out, "you're up first! Let's give this fine lady a hand." The crowd applauded as Hedda stared with a badger's focus at the wood storefronts and outlaws in the arena. As soon as the buzzer sounded, she tore toward the saloon with surprising speed, galloping in her pink cowgirl boots that matched her hat and stick horse. Like a seasoned shootist, she aimed her revolver with precision at the first outlaw, nailing him in the chest. To the delight of the audience, the balloon burst open with a red spray that trickled down the outlaw's shirt, making the crowd clap wildly.

Hedda proceeded to the next building and blasted the outlaws' balloons with ease. Tempest was taken aback by the harsh noise and spurting blood packs, and she quickly wriggled her earplugs in tighter. Holy cow, she thought, this event's not only kind of lawless—it's marginally homicidal. Then she happened to notice a man sitting near Owen on the bleachers who wasn't clapping.

He wasn't cheering, either—

In fact, he appeared pale with a horror-stricken look on his face, even though it was obvious this was all a game. When Hedda circled farther in the arena and managed to bust every balloon at the next set of storefronts, the man's gaze remained glued to the blood splatter on one of the outlaw's chests. Finally, Hedda galloped her stick horse up to Dixon and threw her arms around him for a full-on kiss worthy of an old western movie. Afterwards, Dixon made his stick horse rear in delight and waved his hat with his swashbuckler grin at the crowd. But as the audience stood to their feet and erupted in hoots and cat calls, the man Tempest had spotted stayed frozen in his seat, grimacing as if he'd just witnessed a tragedy.

"Boy howdy, that Hedda Grimson has a dead aim and is a mighty fine kisser!" the announcer crooned after she dashed back into the alley to stand beside Blossom and Tempest. "With a time of only two minutes, she's certainly worth your votes today! Next up is our feed-store favorite, Blossom Barnhart!"

As soon as the 4-H kids ran out to replace the balloons on the wooden outlaws, they took their seats on the bleachers and the buzzer sounded. Blossom sprinted on her black stick horse toward the outlaws with a determined look in her eyes, and Tempest snuck a glance back at the man who sat near Owen.

Rather than watch Blossom, the man had stood to his feet and was staring at the first outlaw as the fresh balloon burst with blood, his eyes stretched wide like he was witnessing the death of a close friend. His hands clenched into fists, and his body began to shake so hard that Tempest feared he might fall down. When sweat broke out on his forehead in large beads and began to drip down his temples, her breath shuddered. It was then she realized what was happening.

The man appeared to be experiencing a flashback.

Tempest recognized the signs of PTSD from domestic abuse victims she'd counseled in the past. The nervousness, sweating, trembling, and most of all, the sensory immersion into a traumatic memory that made a person see and hear what others couldn't. The man's PTSD may have been created by abuse, crime, war—a host of different circumstances. But the one thing Tempest knew for certain was that if he was experiencing flashbacks, he needed help right now, and she felt duty bound to get over there to check on him.

While the crowd applauded in celebration of Blossom, Tempest hadn't even noticed that Blossom had already finished her round and kissed Dixon. She saw Owen leave the bleachers from his spot near the man to replace the balloons and heard the announcer tell her it was her turn to start. This time, Owen plopped down with one of his 4-H buddies on a different bleacher and yelled to his mother to go for it. Even so, Hedda had to give her a small shove to make her move forward.

Dutifully, Tempest did a cursory loop around the arena,

pointing at the balloons yet careful not to actually fire her gun so she wouldn't further traumatize the man in the stands. The audience moaned for her each time the balloons failed to burst and no blood dribbled out, but they were particularly disappointed when she reached Dixon and only gave him a peck on the cheek. Tempest yanked out her earplugs and gazed intently into Dixon's eyes, grabbing his arm.

"Help me," she whispered. She shot a glance at the man in the stands.

The man, who seemed to be in his thirties, still had an expression of shell-shock on his face. But now his hand was buried into his denim jacket pocket.

And he appeared to be pointing a gun—

"I think he's experiencing a flashback," Tempest said in a hoarse voice to Dixon, her heart speeding in her chest. "From PTSD. Let's move his way with very calm motions while people leave the building," she instructed, noticing in relief that Owen had already darted out with his 4-H friends. "Hopefully, we can talk this guy through it."

Dixon's eyes grew as big as the balloons when he spied the weapon that appeared to be pointing from the man's pocket.

"That's Matt White, the town farrier," he whispered back. "He returned from Afghanistan a while back. Folks say he saw his best friend killed in an ambush."

Dixon slid a glance at Tempest. "You're *not* going with me," he warned. He tipped his head toward the alley. "I'll sneak into the corridor from over there and come from behind him to take him down."

"And get *shot?*" Tempest replied. "He might think you're

the enemy, Dixon. *No* aggression. Do you hear me? Or this could go south in a hurry."

All at once, Ivy came up from behind them. "Hey!" she said kindly. "Sorry about your crummy score, Tempest. But look on the bright side, you did really great in the other events."

"Ivy," Dixon said in a low tone, "duck into the corridor and go as fast as possible to the Fair Steward over there by the exit." He motioned to Horton Brown near the door. "Tell him to get Matt White's brother Jack. *Now*," he said gravely. "Then find the 4-H kids and make sure Annie keeps them in the cow barn, understand?"

Ivy's mouth dropped and she checked Tempest's reaction, who swiftly gave her a nod.

"We'll meet you later back at the booth, okay?" Tempest promised, tilting her had at Horton for Ivy to get a move on.

The moment Ivy hastened to the exit and disappeared with Horton, Tempest exhaled a huge breath of relief that they were both safe now, despite the fact that her heart was still careening. She noticed that Matt continued to breathe rapidly, his chest heaving in and out as though he'd just seen a violent attack. When she and Dixon cautiously moved toward him and stepped onto the bleachers, he winced like the echo of their feet on metal was the sound of an enemy approaching. All the while, his hand was firm on something pointing from his pocket.

"Five senses—we need to help Matt notice everything around him," Tempest whispered to Dixon. "Grounding his emotions in the present can defuse his fear."

"Matt," she said tenderly while approaching him, "the

event's over for the day. You're safe now. See?" She motioned at the empty arena as the last few stragglers disappeared through the exit.

"Stop right there! Who are you?" Matt demanded, his eyes taking on a wild look.

Tempest saw his protruding pocket twitch harder. Instinctively, she held out her hand to keep Dixon from rushing forward, knowing his protective impulse.

"I'm Tempest, a 4-H mom," she replied, "and boy, I sure am hungry now. Everyone's gone to get fair food. Mmm, you can smell Brody's burger stand from here. What do you like best on burgers, Matt—ketchup or mustard?"

Matt's eyes darted back and forth, slowly beginning to focus on the lack of people in the arena. Though his face was still ashen white, he tilted up his head and took a sniff, appearing to register the scent of the burger stand nearby.

"B-Burgers?" Matt finally said. His lashes fluttered for a second while he appeared to come to grips with the environment around him. "I like both on burgers—ketchup and mustard. And cheese, too. Y-You said your name's Tempest?" he asked. "You're here for 4-H?"

"That's right," Tempest replied. "We're here for the fair. See?" She cautiously swept her hand to point out the empty arena again.

Matt shook his head and squinted at the bleachers across the arena from them, as if to confirm where he was, and that the crowds were really gone. Steadily, his breathing began to regulate.

Dixon took a few wary steps to his side. "Whoa, with all that talk about fair food you guys are making me hungry." He gave him a gentle smile. "Do you like onion rings too, Matt? I hear your brother Jack is around—maybe you can share a fresh batch of one of those big, fried baskets."

Relaxing a little, Matt pulled his hand from his jacket pocket to wipe the sweat off his brow. His eyes narrowed and he studied the moisture on his hand, as if reading his palm for some long ago memory. All the while, Dixon bravely inched next to him and subtly slipped the gun from his jacket pocket. Matt appeared too absorbed by the glistening sweat on his palm to notice.

Dixon stole a glance at the short-barreled revolver with a *KL* on the handle, a historic replica brand used for mounted shootings. He figured it meant Matt had been practicing the sport earlier that day, and the gun was loaded with blanks. But there was no way to be certain, so he quietly inserted the revolver into the opposite side of his jeans before Matt could detect him. Secretly, Dixon gave Tempest a thumbs up.

"So," Dixon mentioned to Matt, "are you a fan of the sport they had for the Cowboy Roundup today? I hear it's the fastest growing event in rodeo."

Matt nodded his head slowly as though a spell had been broken. "Yeah," he replied, studying the storefronts and wooden outlaws. "When I compete, they don't use fake blood in the balloons. Guess that was for effect." He gave Dixon a hesitant look.

"Well, thank God it's over," Dixon said cheerfully. "Because my kisser was getting worn out. Hey," he remarked with a casual air, "isn't that your brother Jack over there?"

Matt's brother came into view from an entrance gate, and Dixon gave him a slight wave. When their eyes met, it was clear that Dixon and Tempest didn't need to offer any explanation. Jack already knew his brother's issues.

"Yo, Matt!" Jack called out. "Time to get some chow, bro. You ready for one of those Brody burgers?" He offered his brother a friendly smile. "Maybe we can visit Dr. Simmons afterwards. We haven't been to the VA in a while—he might like a burger, too."

Dixon gently wrapped an arm around Matt's shoulders and helped escort him down from the stands. When they reached Jack, Dixon quietly slipped Matt's gun into his brother's jacket pocket. He released Matt as if nothing had happened.

"Nice to see you guys," Dixon said with a tip of his head. "Hope you enjoy those burgers. Don't forget the basket of onion rings. They're awesome."

As Matt and Jack headed off through an exit, Dixon waited until they were gone and immediately ran back to Tempest. He threw his arms around her and hugged her for all she was worth, lifting her from her feet. Then he set her down and kissed her on the forehead, burying his face into her hair.

"I could have lost you," he said hoarsely. He leaned back and studied her eyes with awe. "Tempest, that was the single *bravest* thing I've ever seen anyone do."

"You were no slouch either," she replied in a shaky tone, struggling to steady her heart from the whole incident. "I mean, you could have left. To save your own skin—"

"No I couldn't," Dixon stated in a firm tone. He stared at her with an intensity that threw her. "Not if my life depended on it."

"Why's that?" she asked, taken aback. "We won't know for

sure if that gun had blanks or bullets unless we talk to Jack. You could have been shot, Dixon."

Dixon studied her, puzzled. His eyes searched hers as though the answer should be clear.

"Because I told you already—we *stay*. You're in Bandits Hollow, remember? Where guys like me don't leave at the first speck of trouble. Ranchers can't control the weather, or what happens to cattle, or whose barn burns down. All we've got to hang onto is each other, Tempest. For as long as it takes to get through."

Tempest's eyes began to tear up, and her throat tightened. She knew it was partly from the intense adrenaline that hadn't stopped snapping through her veins. Yet it was also because those were the kinds of words she'd never heard from a man, not even her late husband. Until that moment, she hadn't realized that deep inside, she'd secretly been longing to hear such a promise her whole adult life. From a man who genuinely wanted to be by her side.

Through thick and thin.

She began to tremble, and Dixon wrapped her in his arms again.

"You know, we make a pretty good team," he whispered with a tinge of pride in his voice. He held her like he never intended to let go.

Tempest tilted her head back and looked up at him. "You think so? Are you telling me you want to become a therapist now? It can get pretty rocky sometimes."

"No," Dixon replied decisively. "What I'm telling you is, I like...*protecting*...you." He squeezed her tighter. "While you work miracles, of course."

In that moment, Tempest sank into his arms. Though they'd just been through a harrowing experience, she felt safe —and secure enough to allow her body to relax.

Dixon rocked her gently for a long time. Then he cupped her temples and gave her a kiss.

"That wasn't a stolen kiss, by the way," he whispered in her ear.

Tempest smiled. "Okay," she teased in a weary tone, hoping to lighten the mood a little, "what kind of kiss would you call it this time, cowboy?"

Dixon didn't take the bait for second. He studied her eyes with a serious expression. "That's the kiss of someone who stays, Tempest."

He ran his fingers through her curly, light-brown hair, his stare never wavering.

"For as long as you'll let me."

25

Tempest was relieved the following day when the first woman who came up to her booth wanted know how to make her cat come when he was called. At least this would be easier to navigate than the ordeal during the Cowboy Roundup. She smiled warmly, yet prepared to inform the woman in no uncertain terms that it was impossible.

"Missy," Tempest said to the short, bespectacled woman with dishwater blonde hair, "no one can train cats to show more affection. Or to obey rules, for that matter. They're cats! Aloof and self-serving—kind of like my late husband. About all you can do is encourage them to use a litter box."

Ivy grasped Tempest's arm. "Can I offer her some tips?" she asked softly, still aglow from taking over the radio show the previous day. Pleased with her self-confidence, Tempest nodded.

"Well, I've noticed that my cat Periwinkle only comes to

my lap when I wave her pink mouse toy," Ivy said, pointing at her sweater. "You see, pink is a *very* reliable color for relationships. Not too overbearing, just a nice, welcoming shade. The second Periwinkle sees me wiggling that stuffed mouse, she comes running!"

"Ivy," Tempest corrected gently, making sure she talked into the microphone so radio listeners could hear the biological truth, "cats can't see colors the same way we do. It's more like shades of gray with some muted hues."

"I know!" Ivy defended, sounding every bit the college student. "But animals can *feel* pigments." She turned to the woman. "Luckily, I've researched this science for my color therapy app. Did you know *every* color radiates its own distinct frequency due to its wavelengths? For example, red is very powerful, since it has a larger wavelength than, say, the color blue, which is much shorter. Because of that, colors have both physical *and* psychological effects on us—and on cats!"

Tempest squinted at her. "Okay," she remarked, still entertaining doubts, "then let me ask you this, did that toy happen to come stuffed with catnip inside?"

Ivy dipped her chin. "Hmm, now that I think of it," she tapped her lip, "when you squeeze the mouse, it does feel like there's something dry and leafy in there." Tempest could practically see the light bulb flicker on over her head. "Oh my gosh, how did you guess?"

"Just a hunch," Tempest smiled.

"That's a fantastic idea!" Missy gushed. "Pink catnip toys. Wow, you two work really well together." She grasped Tempest's hands. "I'm so glad you allow your assistant to help with radio questions. Between the both of you, there's nothing you can't handle. Thanks from all the cat lovers!"

Ivy grinned proudly as the woman walked away toward the elephant ear booth while Tempest signed off for the radio listeners.

"You know," Tempest flipped the power switch off on her console, "I got so many compliments on your advice yesterday that it made me think maybe you should start your *own* show someday. People said you opened up a whole new world of color for them. It might drive more traffic to your app."

Ivy pressed her hands to her cheeks. "D-Do you really think I could succeed? And people might listen?"

"Sure!" Tempest replied. "When the fair's over, we should practice more during the rest of the summer. Maybe add a color of the week to the broadcast schedule? But only if you *promise* to back up your color counseling with scientific facts. You know, to keep the advice well rounded."

"That would be the best!" Ivy squealed, throwing her arms around Tempest for a hug. "Who knows, maybe I could actually carve a career out of this?"

"I hope so." Tempest gazed into her brown eyes. "Because you have a really big heart for helping others, Ivy. You're gonna make a terrific therapist one day—"

"Hi Mom," Owen greeted, interrupting their chat. When Tempest glanced down, she spied an odd pout on her son's face, even though he'd just returned with a tower of freshly-fried potato chips alongside Dixon. Owen tilted up his gaze and frowned at his mother's less than stellar numbers flashing from the scoreboard above the outdoor arena. "Maybe you should sign up for a shooting class," he suggested, his tone mired in disappointment. "You missed every single balloon yesterday."

Tempest was lost for words. How could she explain to her son that she'd been distracted by an emergency of someone in need?

"Well, funny you should mention that," Dixon mentioned in a quick save. He finished swallowing a handful of chips. "I was thinking that after the fair's over, perhaps you two might consider coming to my place for shooting practice?"

He gazed with a hopeful expression at Tempest, sending a feeling of warmth all over her body.

"I have a shooting range set up with targets on a corner of my property," Dixon added. "Of course, you'd both need me to teach you all about gun safety before we got started. How does that sound?"

"Great!" Owen grinned, his feet nearly floating off the ground. He appeared to completely forget his mother's poor performance, much less the fact that he might need her permission to handle a gun.

Dixon stared at Tempest, and in his eyes was such pure anticipation that she was genuinely flattered. It quickly became clear that this was about more than developing a new skill. It was about keeping their *connection* going, for both her and Owen. In that moment, she noticed the muscles rippling in Dixon's face while his jaw worked back and forth, waiting expectantly for her answer.

Tempest didn't dare look at Ivy, since she'd put on a light green shirt that morning that Ivy called "chartreuse." Naturally, she claimed it invited longevity in relationships. Taking a deep breath, her gaze flicked from Dixon to Owen.

"We'd love that," she affirmed. "But you have to let us do something in return. Like…maybe cook you dinner some time?"

Dixon's eyes lit up. Ivy reached over and snuck a pinch on Tempest's elbow, gloating over the accuracy of her color analysis.

"That sounds great," Dixon replied. He felt a tug on his shirt and dropped his gaze.

"Mister Dixon," Owen nervously thrust his hands into his overalls pockets, "did you, um, remember that my show class is this afternoon?"

"Are you kidding?" Dixon said. "It's what we've been working hard for all this time! We'd better get some last minute practice in, young man." He nodded at Tempest with a glint in his eyes before he and Owen turned to head for the cattle barn.

"God, I hope that show goes well," Tempest whispered to Ivy. "Because Owen's been dreaming about it all summer long."

She twined her hands and closed her eyes for a quiet prayer.

Dear God, she begged from deep within her heart, please don't let Dumpling run over anyone today. Make a pile of angels sit on him if you have to. And protect all the kids and Annie in the arena.

Tempest's eyes fluttered open. She folded her arms, watching Dixon and Owen saunter together to the cattle barn, talking with each other and laughing.

"Amen," she whispered under her breath.

"As you can see from the program," the announcer broke in over the loudspeaker at the cattle barn, "it's four o'clock—time for the Late Summer Angus Yearling Bull class! This division is only for bulls that were birthed last July or August. We have some very hard-working 4-H kids here today who're hoping to win top prize, so let's line up those yearlings!"

Owen held tightly onto Dumpling's lead line. He shifted a nervous gaze to Annie, who stood by the rail watching him with an eagle eye. Tempest and Ivy began to cheer for him from the bleachers, bolstering his confidence.

"You're gonna do great," Dixon encouraged, giving Owen a pat on the back while they both stood beside the arena entrance gate. "You could win this in your sleep. Now step on out there and show them what Dumpling can do."

Owen hauled in a breath and nodded. He did a last-minute check of his buttoned-down western shirt and jeans for any signs of hay or dirt, and he made sure to straighten the number attached to his chest. Appearance was *very* important to the judges —and to Annie—and he wanted to put his best foot forward. When he led Dumpling into the arena, he did one more peek into the stands, watching his mother swell with pride. It was the first time all summer she'd seen him without a layer of dirt, and he could tell she was so impressed she could hardly contain herself.

Owen walked Dumpling to the center of the arena and lined him up alongside the other yearlings, facing the judge. He stood in front of Dumpling and used his show stick the way Dixon had taught him, lightly tapping the yearling's hooves to nudge him to stand square. When Dumpling set his legs correctly, Owen rubbed his belly with the stick for a reward.

The judge was a grizzled old man Owen didn't recognize. He started out by scanning the yearlings in line and dictated his first impressions to a teenage girl to mark down on a clipboard. Then he motioned for all the animals to circle the small arena, while he carefully inspected the way each one walked. After about fifteen minutes, he made the signal for them to line up in front of him again, and Owen's heart climbed into his throat. This was the part where the judge would scrutinize every aspect of the yearlings to determine how worthy of becoming sires they might become, based on their physical attributes.

One by one, the old judge examined each animal down the line, paying particular attention to its shoulders, chest, hindquarters, and the straightness of the legs. When he came to Dumpling at the end, he cocked a suspicious brow.

Owen's heart dropped to his feet.

Though Dumpling was incredibly well behaved after Owen had learned all of Dixon's training tips, the judge frowned while he looked over the yearling like he was some kind of fraud. Then he let out an impatient huff, as though Dumpling's conformation had come up short and his time had been wasted.

The judge headed to front of the line again and whispered his last comments to the girl, who wrote down his words at a furious pace. When she was finished, she handed the judge his notes, and an assistant trotted out to the arena to give him a microphone.

"We're all set for the results for the Late Summer Angus Yearling Bull class," the judge informed the crowd. "I'll be calling out the winners in descending order and highlighting the features of the yearlings who've earned top prize."

Owen peered at his mother again, who had her hands on her chest, clearly trying to calm her beating heart. Ivy's eyes were glued to him as well, and Dixon had joined them in the bleachers. He sat beside Tempest with a grave look that indicated he was just as invested as Owen's mother.

Yet despite the support of friends and family, the rest of the class became an exercise in panic for Owen. Time after time, the numbers the judge called out for ribbons weren't Dumpling's. Then he launched into detail to praise each winning animal, even commenting on the positive aspects of yearlings that hadn't earned awards. But by the time the judge got to Dumpling, it was another story.

"In last place, out of thirteen contestants, we have number 501," the judge said. "Owen Wright with his yearling Dumpling. Coming in at 1,025 pounds, this red Angus is unfortunately too tall, making his beef-to-bone ratio rather low. His legs are on the slim side and his rib cage is lacking in barrel width as well, so I'm afraid he doesn't carry the kind of genes that should be passed down for the breed. On a good note, however, Dumpling has been quite well behaved this afternoon, given the rumors of his violent tendencies that have circulated ever since the fair started."

The audience burst into laughter.

Owen's cheeks flamed as red as his western shirt, while his heart pumped out of control.

Everyone was *laughing* at him—

At his beloved pet and playmate for the last six months, the animal he'd poured everything into so that this day might go well. And now he and Dumpling had become a joke?

Owen heard half a dozen kids snickering. He sent them dirty looks, which only prodded them into louder chuckles.

"Not everyone can be a winner," the judge pointed out dryly as he handed back the clipboard to his assistant. "Which is why it's probably best to turn yearlings like this into market steers so at least they can be sold by the pound. Now let's give a big round of applause to all of our contestants with Bandits Hollow enthusiasm."

Family members and 4-H leaders clapped briskly as the line of yearlings turned to head out of the arena according to their place in the competition, with Owen and Dumpling following last.

As soon as Owen made it to the exit gate, Dixon and Tempest were at his side in a shot, trying to console him. Owen brushed them off with tears streaming down his cheeks. Even Annie came up to compliment him on how safely he'd shown Dumpling, and what a credit he'd been to their 4-H club, but it was no use. Owen jerked on Dumpling's lead line and walked with quick, determined strides to escape them, clearly wanting to spend some time alone with his animal back in the cattle pen area. After Tempest waited as long as she could stand, she bolted a few steps to try to catch up with him, when Dixon pulled her back.

"Let him be," he said in a soothing tone. "Losing is part of growing up. Let him sit with his feelings for a while before you invade his space."

"But he's sobbing!" Tempest countered.

"Yeah, I know—because it hurts." Dixon peered into Tempest's eyes. "In this part of the world, we don't give out participation ribbons. You gotta earn everything. Failing is the road to victory someday, *if* his mother will be big enough to let it happen. Don't take this moment away from him."

Tempest's shoulders sank.

"How long?" she muttered.

"What do you mean?"

"How long do you think I should I *wait?*"

Dixon chuckled a little and put his arm around her.

"Just give him half an hour, okay? To feed Dumpling and groom him and then cry into his fur. Believe me, Owen will feel a lot more settled after that."

Dixon checked his cell phone for the time and slipped it back into his pocket. "I gotta get the horses ready and fetch my dad—we promised to help round up steers for the roping event. Let me know when you might want to cook that dinner," he remarked with a delight he couldn't hide. "I'm looking forward to it."

As Dixon walked off, Tempest spied Blossom crossing the fairgrounds to head into the cattle barn. Secretly, she envied her, since she knew Annie usually invited her to help the kids put away their animals. Tempest glanced at the time on her phone and sighed after realizing she still ought to wait fifteen more minutes before talking to Owen. When Blossom spotted her, she began to veer her way.

"I'm sorry Owen didn't win anything," Blossom confided

after reaching Tempest. "I know how much it meant to him." She gave her a half-smile. "But Annie's thrilled with how he handled Dumpling. If it's any consolation, she asked me to help chaperone while she takes the kids to the ice cream booth once they're done with their chores. To congratulate them on all their hard work."

Tempest nodded, feeling raw inside about the way things turned out. She dropped her gaze to the ground. "Well, Dixon told me it's a good maturing experience for him," she admitted, trying to convince herself of that same wisdom. "Trouble is, it's hard for us moms to let our kids navigate their own way in life."

When Tempest looked up, she saw Betty making her way toward them with a big grin on her face. She had one of her floral arrangements in tow.

"Oh God, speaking of moms," Blossom sighed. "Got any earplugs? She already laid into me yesterday for staying out late, and now it looks like she's got a blue ribbon. Which will fuel her fire, of course."

"Blossom baby!" Betty hailed, picking up her pace before Blossom could make a quick exit. "I won the flower arrangement class—Grand Champion! See?" She flapped the huge blue ribbon that was pinned to her basket. "We Barnharts *always* win!"

Betty swiveled to Tempest. "Too bad about your son," she mentioned with a cynical air. "I heard things didn't go well for him today. Hope he's taking it in stride." She lifted her gaze to the scoreboard above the outdoor arena that featured Tempest's terrible stats. "Guess *both* of you have been bottoming out lately. But don't worry, Hedda may look like she's in the lead, but the Cowboy Roundup is ultimately a popularity contest." She turned and glowed at her daughter. "You *still* might get the most votes to date the best looking guy in town, honey!"

Betty's floral arrangement fluttered in her hands with her excitement.

"Mom," Blossom moaned, "I don't want to date someone almost old enough to be my father. I want to date Levi again. He's kind, considerate, and *my age*."

"Really?" Betty countered with a gleam in her eye. "Then how come I just saw Levi at the beer tent, flirting with a bunch of other girls? Oh, and he was so drunk he could barely stand up. You should hear the sleazy things he says about women when his lips are loose. Some gentleman."

Blossom's face fell. She looked toward the beer tent and spied two pretty girls supporting Levi's arms so he could manage to reach a nearby trash can to throw up. Slowly, Blossom pulled a crumpled rose bouquet from her overalls bib. "Levi gave me these flowers this morning," she muttered in disbelief. "He said he found them in his truck. He thought it was, you know, a sign he should keep seeing me." She shot a glance at the Historical Society pie booth. "Like maybe it was an omen from the...Trinity."

"Oh dearie," Betty shook her head. "It's called being a sweet-talking, poor ranch hand! He gave you some lousy bouquet that he didn't even bother to buy at a florist? I've told you a hundred times—that's how losers operate. They say all kinds of things and flit from one hussy to another because the truth is they have no class. I bet Dixon's starting to look a whole lot better to you now, isn't he?" She stroked her daughter's hair. "Gotta rack up those dates before you get old. And don't forget—no fair food! Nobody wants a gal who looks like Porky Pig."

Blossom folded her arms and sank into herself, appearing to lose all the confidence she'd worked so hard to develop lately. Furious, Tempest was about to slice and dice Betty's dark soul and serve it up to her on a plate, when Betty turned her back to both of them to look toward the beer tent again. There was Hedda, stumbling through the exit gate while doing her darndest to hold up Bear Ramsey to keep him from falling.

Tempest's mouth dropped—Bear was obviously as snockered as Levi. Within seconds, she saw Dixon dart across the fairgrounds toward his father to relieve Hedda. When he managed to bolster Bear from around the waist and direct his steps toward the parking lot, he glanced up and met Tempest's gaze.

Dixon's blue eyes were burning flames. He dipped is head in shame.

Betty clicked her tongue. "Oh my," she remarked, "I bet Hedda won't have much to do with that poor old man anymore, with all of his problems." She stared at Blossom. "I *told you* those Ramsey men need a woman's touch in their lives! Look at Dixon, handling that burden all alone. Now that my competition's over, I'm going to offer to help him with his dad. In fact," she shoved her flowers into Tempest's hands and shot a victorious glance at Blossom, "we can *both* help! It wouldn't hurt to extend neighborly charity to the Ramseys right now."

Blossom blinked, her eyes glistening with tears. She studied Levi, still throwing up, then scanned the awkward steps of Bear as he tried to make it to the parking lot with Dixon.

Tempest peered over the flower heads and arched a brow. She met Blossom's gaze and shook her head at Betty's intrusiveness, her eyes daring Blossom to do something about it. Blossom heaved a breath and turned to Betty.

"No, mother," she stated, even though her voice cracked a little. She flicked the tears from her eyes and thrust up her chin. Then she removed the flower basket from Tempest's grip. "I'll take your flowers to the Arts and Crafts building for you. But if all you want is to chase the Ramsey men during clearly a hard time, you're on your own."

Blossom began to march with the basket away from her mother, when she hesitated for moment and turned around.

"Oh, and by the way," she announced to Betty, her eyes narrowing to slits, "I'm moving out."

26

Tempest felt awful for both Blossom and Dixon.

She watched Dixon predictably shrug off Betty's help with Bear and walk away, dragging his father along with him while Bonner followed faithfully behind. When they reached the concession aisle to head toward the parking lot, Tempest turned to Ivy, who'd caught up to her with a slice of pizza in her hand.

Tempest was about to open her mouth, but she found no words. Sometimes, even for an experienced therapist like her, there weren't any easy clichés that were adequate to describe the problems of real life. Her silence said everything.

Ivy spotted Dixon with his inebriated father before they disappeared into the parking lot. She nodded at Tempest, seeming to understand.

"Wanna bite of pizza?" Ivy asked, trying to cheer her up. "It's really yummy. I can go get you and Owen a slice. They have this buy-one, get-the-other-half-off deal—"

"Tempest!" they both heard a raspy voice. "Tempest!"

When they spun in the direction of the sound, they saw Annie running toward them at full tilt.

"They're gone!"

The moment Annie reached them, she doubled over to catch her breath. "The kids were feeding their animals before ice cream, and somehow Dumpling broke out of his pen. It's near the back door and the bottom wires were snapped, like he'd rammed them. He must have wriggled out."

Panting, she seized Tempest's arm in desperation. "We can't find Owen! We looked everywhere in the building—he must be out searching for him. Pole fences surround the whole property to keep livestock in, so hopefully he's around here."

Annie grabbed Tempest by the shoulders and stared into her eyes.

"I'm not going to lie to you—Angus can be amazing jumpers once they hit the yearling phase. If Dumpling leaped over the fairgrounds fence, Owen's probably trying to follow his tracks."

Tempest's blood fell to her ankles, her face washing white. The strident voice of the announcer broke over the PA system.

"Attention all fairgoers: we are currently searching for a lost boy. Owen Wright is eight years old with blonde hair and wearing a red buttoned-down shirt and jeans. His Angus yearling got loose from the cattle building, and he may be trying to find him. We suspect wherever the yearling is, the boy is nearby."

Tempest wanted to run—here, there, everywhere at once —whatever it took to find her son. She'd gladly tip over booths or take apart buildings down to the joists if that's what was required to locate Owen—anything to hold her child close and safe. Her natural instinct was to scream his name over and over at the top of her lungs, which she did while rotating a three-sixty to scan the fairgrounds, until she felt like she might explode.

But Owen was nowhere in sight.

"We must make a plan," she determined to Annie and Ivy, her mind a swirl. Gathering her wits, she launched into full Tempest the Terminator mode and directed them to help her search outside the cattle barn, studying the ground for the yearling's hoof marks—hopefully followed by the tread marks of her son's tracks—Justin Roper boots, round toes, youth size 4. When they reached the barn, sure enough, there appeared to be several yards of hoof prints in the dirt that veered from the back doorway, along with impressions of the right type of child's boots trailing close behind. But then a few more feet ahead, there where too many prints from fairgoers criss-crossing their tracks to distinguish their direction anymore. Tempest threw back her shoulders and told the ladies to stop.

"It's time to broaden out," she insisted while surveying the breadth of the fairgrounds. "Annie, you go search the north end," she instructed, "and call me if you see anything—anything at all." She swiveled to Ivy. "You search the south end, and do the same." When Tempest spied Blossom dashing toward them with a world of concern on her face, she let out a relieved breath, knowing this trustworthy girl would do everything in her power to help. "Blossom, go search the east end of the fairgrounds for Owen," she directed without wasting a precious second. "I'm going to scour the west end, and recruit every security guard I can find to comb this place.

All of you, call me immediately if you see the smallest sign of their tracks, okay? There might be a trail of molasses corn and oats on the ground by his footprints, since he could be trying to tempt Dumpling with his favorite food to catch him."

Each of the women nodded and fanned out in different directions, their backs hunched as they carefully examined the ground, only rising to ask fairgoers if they'd seen any signs of the child. Tempest swiftly beat a path to the west end of the fairgrounds, her face determined as if she were readying for war.

If only Dixon were here—he knows exactly where cattle like to stray! she thought, her mind churning a mile a minute as she studied the ground. Didn't he hear the announcer say that everyone's looking for Owen before he drove off in his truck? Couldn't he have called a ranch hand to take Bear home?

Tempest had already dialed Dixon's phone several times while she was searching near the cattle barn, but no one answered. Despite her fierce resolve to locate her son, she clutched her head, her mind warring inside. She knew Dixon had his own problems right now, which certainly could have made him ignore calls. But the fact that he was totally unreachable sent a well-worn, knee-jerk reaction inside her like lightning through her veins.

This is just like after my husband died, she thought.

When the chips fall down, you're always on your own, honey! No man's ever stayed around to help you, let alone rescued you when you needed it. So you'd better buck up and face that fact, Dixon or no Dixon—and keep the hell moving.

Dropping to her hands and knees, Tempest crawled over

the dirt, scrutinizing every small depression in the soil and hunting for tiny grains of corn or oats—the slightest possible signs of her son. Despite her Queen of Tough Love mojo, tears begun to trickle down her cheeks and dampen the dirt with large circles. Tempest clenched her jaw, refusing to give in to them.

"To hell with not being a hover mom!" she sputtered under her breath through gritted teeth. "I'm going to hover and cover every inch of this whole damn earth, if that's what it takes. I *will* find my son—even if I have to kill myself doing it."

By nightfall, there was still no sign of Owen. Tempest had checked every fence, inspected every building, talked to each booth operator. For all intents and purposes, Owen had simply vanished. Yet all of the gates and parking lots were consistently monitored by staff to ensure that children only went home with their respective caregivers. Tempest's heart tore at the edges—of course, that had been Dixon's stringent policy as Safety Commissioner all along. A lot of good he did her now! She'd tried calling him more times, but there'd been no answer, and she remained at a total loss for where Owen could be. When it finally came near closing time for the fairgrounds, a security guard walked up to her with a flashlight in his hand.

"Ma'am, we've all been helping you look for three hours, and it's about time to shut the place down. The local police are on this—they'll keep investigating after the gates close."

"Do they have any search dogs?" Tempest pressed with a crack in her voice. "What about the Ramsey's bear Bonner, for Christ's sake! Don't they pick up scents a million times better than German Shepherds? I can go get Owen's jacket and let Bonner take a sniff—"

"I'm sure the police will do whatever they think is right, according to protocol," the security guard replied. "I've already give them your cell number. The best thing you can do right now is go home, in case the police need more information from you. To be honest, ma'am, you seem like you're ready to collapse and in no shape to drive." He glanced up and saw Blossom with her mother heading toward them. "Look, there are the Barnhart ladies—I'm sure they'll give you a ride."

Tempest squinted at the two women walking her way, looking as thoroughly exhausted as she was. She'd already sent Ivy home an hour ago, and Annie had to give several of the 4-H kids a lift back to their families.

"I have no idea what happened to Dixon!" Betty threw up her hands when she reached Tempest, enjoying the dig. "Surely he was done taking care of his dad and could have helped us search by now?" She shrugged, folding her arms. "Guess he's got *other* priorities. Blossom and I can take you home, honey, if you need a ride. You look totally beat—"

Tempest stiffened, holding up a hand to halt Betty's worthless chatter—that included her usual barbs, of course.

No, Tempest thought adamantly. I will *never* give up on searching for my son.

Though she'd been looking so hard that her whole body trembled, she swiveled to stare at the west gate a few yards away that was lit up by fair lights, the one that led past Dixon's ranch. He'd mentioned once that cattle often head toward draws and ravines, where the grass is moist and tasty, like near the meadows that lined that whole area beyond the fence. What if Dumpling had done that? she considered. Animals could smell water and fresh greenery for long distances—what if he'd jumped the fence there? And Owen had followed him?

Tempest studied the dark veil beyond the fence, swallowing hard at her parched throat from so much shouting for her son. Then she inhaled a big breath and turned to face the security guard.

"Thank you so much for all your help," she said sincerely. She dropped a quick glance at his flashlight before gazing up at Blossom and Betty, nodding her appreciation. "I'm deeply indebted to all of you."

Without warning, she ripped the flashlight right out of the security guard's hand.

Tempest raced like a bat out of hell, her legs burning and her lungs raw until she reached the fence. Summoning up her courage, she vaulted over the pole rails into the darkness.

"Owen!" Tempest called, her voice so raspy she could barely shout anymore. All she could see was the narrow beam of the flashlight in the dark, making it feel like the night was closing in on her. An owl hooted, and she startled, pausing for a moment to regain her breath. She pressed forward and scrutinized the overgrown grass in front of her for any sign of Owen. This meadow must look like heaven to a yearling, she thought, still unsure if the two of them had escaped here. Soon, she came across a patch of bent-over tufts with another path of lightly pressed grass beside it. Perhaps the tracks of Owen and Dumpling? She followed them toward a stand of trees, yet she still didn't spy any creeks or ravines that might attract a yearling—or the young boy who could have gone after him. As she headed warily forward, she saw the glow of a lantern.

Tempest pushed past draping pine boughs to discover that

the lantern hung beside the door of an old wagon, tucked into a small clearing shrouded by trees. All at once, an owl swooped beside her, its wings flapping silently in the darkness. Tempest let out a gasp, when she saw the owl land on the domed roof of the wagon. Hesitating, she narrowed her eyes at the clearing and dared to keep stepping forward. Could there be moist grass *here?* she wondered. She knew she wasn't far from Dixon's fence line, where the grass was heavy and lush. She trained her flashlight on the clearing when she heard a long hoot as the owl alighted into the air again. Tempest glanced up, spotting a tall silhouette a few feet ahead of her, crowned by a halo of gray hair that reflected the silver rays of the moon.

Granny Tinker—

"Good evening, my dear," she mentioned softly, without of lick of surprise.

Tempest swung her flashlight straight into Granny's face, the beam blindingly bright.

"Turn that damn thing off," she advised. "If you want to find your son."

"What?" Tempest burst. "W-What do you know about Owen?" She ran up to Granny and grabbed her black velvet dress by the collar. "Where is he?" she demanded, shaking her slightly. "Tell me!"

Granny arched a brow, returning her stare with remarkable patience. She slowly peeled Tempest's fingers from her dress.

"Don't give me any garbage about flowers or true love!" Tempest cried desperately. "Just tell me where my son is! Where's the nearest draw? Has Owen found Dumpling near water? Is that where they went?"

Granny Tinker collected both Tempest's hands in hers, and wrapped her long, warm fingers around them, holding them tight. Tempest couldn't understand it, but the effect was oddly settling. Yet it didn't stop her heart from racing.

"What most folks never reckon is that I ain't the most powerful person in these parts. Iron Feather is."

"H-Have you lost your mind?" Tempest stammered in a panic. "Iron Feather's been dead for a hundred years—"

"Suit yourself," Granny replied as the owl called from high on a ponderosa bough. "But he's always had quite the knack for finding children. Now if I were you, I'd keep that flashlight turned off and follow that owl by the light of the moon."

Granny glanced up at the nearly full moon above them that shone platinum hues all around the clearing. Tempest tilted her head, realizing she could actually see more nuances in the landscape now without the harsh beam of the flashlight.

"What are you saying," Tempest pressed, still overcome with worry. "Why would I follow a goddamned owl? Is this some kind of weird magic?"

"No, sweetheart," Granny sighed. "It's called love. The only real power there is."

To Tempest's surprise, Granny reached into the pocket of her black velvet dress and pulled out the ruby heart charm, watching the way its facets twinkled under the moonlight. She slipped it into Tempest's palm and folded her fingers over it. When they heard the owl again in the distance, its call reverberating through the trees, Granny turned with Tempest's hands in hers in the direction of the sound.

The ruby heart charm grew oddly warm.

"Oh my God," Tempest whispered, shivers running down

her body. She peered into Granny's gray-gold eyes, highlighted by glints of the moon.

"Is this for real?"

Granny clutched her hands tighter. "Only your heart can tell you that, darlin'."

At that moment, Tempest heard a soft moo echo in the distance, in the opposite direction of Dixon's ranch. She tore her hands away from Granny, her grip fixed on the charm like it was her lifeline. Her heart bolted in her chest—that was Dumpling's moo, she was certain of it. Just as surely as she knew the cry of her own child.

"Thank you!" Tempest said breathlessly, wrapping her arms around Granny to give her a hug. She was about to tear off in the direction of the cow's sound when Granny grabbed her arm.

"I happened to notice earlier that Dixon's horse is gone from yonder corral." She tipped her head in the direction of his ranch. "Now I wonder what the hell he'd be doing out riding at this hour? When he's the Safety Commissioner and that little boy went missing from the fair? Must be searching for wayward critters, if you ask me. Which you didn't, but I'm feeling particularly generous tonight."

Granny nodded in the direction of the cow's moo. "Slip Creek is a half a mile thataway. I hear cattle really like the grass over there. Now tuck that flashlight into your back pocket so you might have some hope of finding it."

Tempest thrust the flashlight into her khaki pants.

And ran—

She ran and ran until she thought her lungs would melt. All the while, an owl soared in front of her.

Guiding her steps under the moon.

Tempest held the ruby heart charm in front of her like a divining rod, turning each time it grew cold until it became warm again, then hastening in that direction. The owl traced her every move, flying a few feet ahead no matter which way she turned, as though it already knew where she'd go. Under normal circumstances she'd be spooked out of her skull, but right now she didn't care—as long as she might be heading toward her son. She heard the soft moo again, only closer this time, and her heart leaped.

"Owen?" she called out urgently. She felt like she'd been running for miles when her foot suddenly slipped on a spot of gravel. Within an instant, she found herself sliding down a steep incline. She couldn't tell if it was the side of a hill or a ravine, or even into a well. When her body skittered over a pile of rocks to a stop, she clutched her chest and attempted to catch her breath. Then she glanced up.

All she saw before her, beside a thin ribbon of water that reflected the moonlight, were dry, white bones.

The half a dozen scattered bones gleamed under the moon like a pack of predators had licked them clean, erasing the creature's identity.

Tempest screamed.

What is this, she thought, a never-ending nightmare?

Crawling backwards as fast as she could, she coughed dust from her lungs and tried to take her eyes off the gory sight. All at once, she backed into something tall and hard, like the trunk of a tree. Scrambling to her feet, she whipped around.

"Hi Mommy," Owen said softly.

Her son was in Dixon's arms. And he was smiling—

"My baby!" Tempest seized her child from Dixon's grip. "Oh my baby!" she sputtered, hugging him tightly. She brushed her hand over his forehead and stared into his eyes, shining in the moonlight, to make sure he was real.

"You dropped something." Dixon's eyes glinted, clearly pleased to see her. He kneeled down and picked up the heart charm that had landed by his feet in a spot of sand. Then he held it up, sparkling in the moonlight, and slipped it into her front pocket.

"Mom," Owen whined, "I'm *not* a baby. I'm eight, remember?" He pointed over Tempest's shoulder. "I found Dumpling all by myself!"

She turned and saw the yearling tied firmly to Bullet's saddle horn, a little farther down the creek bed. Dumpling didn't look a bit happy about it, and he let out a mournful moo.

"Oh honey," Tempest rocked Owen in her arms, "how did you find Dumpling this far from the fairgrounds?" She gazed at the crumbling, rocky bank that had obscured his tracks. "You've never even been here before."

"The old man showed me," Owen said. "I ran from the fairgrounds to look for Dumpling. When I got kinda lost, he took me by the hand."

"Wait—who did, sweetheart? Who are you talking about?"

"The Indian man. He led me here. He told me not to worry about the bones because nothing could harm me with him around." Owen shrugged and motioned down the creek bed. "Dumpling was right there, eating grass."

Dixon's eyes met Tempest's. His expression was just as bewildered as hers.

"An Indian man *led* you here?" Dixon clarified. "What did he look like?"

"He was tall with long hair. He looked like the guy on the wanted posters at the fair. He stayed until he saw Mister Dixon on his horse. He said Mister Dixon would take care of me. Then he smiled and went away."

The haunting cry of an owl rippled through the darkness, making Tempest tremble. She kissed Owen on the forehead. Tears glistened in her eyes, and she sealed them shut before she could cry, because she knew she'd be unable to stop.

"God bless that man," she whispered, pressing her cheek against Owen's. "Whoever he is."

"Can you put me down now, Mom?" Owen wiggled until she had no choice but to set him on his feet. "I wanna pet Dumpling."

Tempest's heart tripped in her chest. It took everything she had to allow her son to walk away from her to go see his yearling. When she saw him caressing Dumpling happily, she turned to Dixon, unable to keep the tears from flowing anymore.

"Thank you! Oh God—thank you so much for holding on to my Owen!" she said between sobs. "Where were you, anyway?" she whispered in a feeble attempt to hide her despair. "I tried calling, hoping you might be done with your dad. But you were…*here?*"

"Tempest," Dixon said gently. He wrapped her in his arms

like a warm blanket. "Of course I was out here. What on earth made you think I wouldn't search the backcountry to help find Owen?"

"Because you didn't answer! I even tried calling your office. They said they had no idea where you were——"

"I'm sorry in all the ruckus that I left my cell phone at home." Dixon shook his head. "I got distracted by my dad's condition. Please believe me—the second I heard Owen was missing, and there might a possibility he was searching for Dumpling, I saddled Bullet to comb the wilderness beyond the fairgrounds. I knew nobody at the fair or the police station would think of looking in the draws and ravines, but that's probably where Owen and Dumpling would be."

He cupped her face in his hands. Though his skin was rough, his palms felt strong and secure. "Turns out I was right. Now for God's sake, will you let me put you and your son on top of my horse so I can lead you home? And make sure you're *both* safe now?"

Tempest slipped the ruby heart charm from her pocket, holding it tightly in her palm like a compass. Tingles skipped down her spine when it began to feel warm in her hand.

Not only warm, she swore she could feel it throb—to the rhythm of a heartbeat. She thought about what Granny had said, how she had a hunch Dixon would be out here searching for wayward critters. And told her to listen to her heart.

"Yes," Tempest whispered, wiping the tears from her cheeks with her sleeve. Still shaking, she gazed up at the moon, then over at her son, who grinned broadly at the delight of being next to his yearling again. For a moment, she allowed her eyes to fall shut, trying to let the fact that her son was actually okay trickle down into her soul. Then she looked up at Dixon.

"Please," she said, her voice a low rasp and nearly spent. "Please take us home."

❧ 28 ❧

Tempest caressed Owen's hair and gave him a soft kiss on the forehead. She pulled his sheets and blanket up to his chin and tucked him into the bed.

"Good night, honey," she whispered, even though Owen had already fallen asleep by the time she'd set him down. Tempest paused to stare at her beautiful boy, safe and sound in his own bed, doing her best to etch this moment in her heart forever. She was about a million miles from being able to sleep with all of the chaos they'd been through, so she quietly backed away from the bed. Then she tip toed through her living room to the outside porch.

There was Dixon, sitting silently near the door on the wood bench. When she edged over and gently lowered herself to sit beside him, for a long time he said nothing. He simply slipped his arm around her shoulders and held her close.

Tempest began to sob into his chest, and he made no

attempt to stop her. He let her be, occasionally stroking her hair.

"I-I nearly lost everything," she confessed through choked breaths. "Everything." Her whole body started to shake, and he tightened his grip on her.

She let her grief flow freely for as long as she needed, until she reached a point where she couldn't summon more tears. Cautiously, Tempest raised her head and peered into Dixon's eyes.

"I-I don't know if I can do this," she stammered.

"Do what?" he replied gently.

"*Us.*"

She let a weighted minute pass, struggling for breath against her swollen throat.

"I-I can hardly process what just happened, no matter how much fancy training I have," she admitted. "I'm still too raw. From the passing of my husband a year ago, and now...*this.*"

She gulped another halting breath and shook her head. "God almighty, I thought the roller coaster had died down by now. You know, smoothed out a little and was heading toward home. Maybe I *am* fragile, Dixon, like you said. No matter how hard I've tried to fortify myself."

"So...what does that mean?" Dixon replied softly. "Are you telling me you're going to...run away?"

Tempest cringed.

She knew what he was thinking—that she was bolting from him, from any type of real relationship, just like all of the other crazy women he'd known.

"No," she hesitated, thinking it through. "I'm giving you the chance to...run away. From *me*. From hitching your ride to another derailed woman. Don't you see that, Dixon? You can't fix me. I'm like all of the other hot messes you dated. My heart's broken." Her head dipped in fatigue. "Regardless of what I've done to pull myself together, I'm still fractured inside."

"Or...more whole?"

Dixon lifted her chin with his finger and turned her to face him, staring unflinchingly into her eyes.

"Isn't *that* what you're really afraid of? That I might climb into your heart and refuse to leave till the day I die? So what if that gives you more to lose. Isn't tucking those you love inside your heart what life's all about?"

Tempest's throat crimped.

He'd said the word—

That word.

Love...

Dixon spied the edge of the ruby heart charm that she had in a white-knuckle grip in her hand. He carefully wedged it away from her palm.

"Believe it or not, I've got a tough love tip for you, Tempest the Terminator," he said, holding up the heart charm. His face eased into a generous smile. "You're *not* gonna fall apart this time. Because when somebody cares about you, and I mean *really* cares about you, it makes you stronger than you were before—forever. And forever is something I've been looking for my whole damn life. Somebody to count on for once. Somebody to face things with, no matter how hard things get."

"How do you know *I* won't be the one to leave?"

"Because you're not a quitter!" Dixon shook his head. "And neither am I. Yeah, love is a big risk, but that's what I mean by tough love—we're tough enough to take it. To take our time and see where this might eventually lead. To shoot for the stars."

Dixon stared up at the night sky, scanning the canopy of twinkling lights.

"I'd sure like to explore the great unknown with you." He grasped her hand. "I hear it's a beautiful vista."

Tempest gazed up at the stars. For a moment she pressed her hands hard against her chest, encouraging her heartbeat to slow down and relax. To try and experience the moment.

"I think that sounds like...an amazing adventure," she whispered, her fingers feeling the heavy throb of her heart. "As long as you stay by my side." Tempest leaned against him, fully surrendering to his embrace.

"It's okay," Dixon whispered. "You're safe now. Your son is safe, too. Whether you believe it or not, Tempest, you've found *home*. Here, with Owen and me in Bandits Hollow."

Dixon gave her tender kiss on the forehead and rocked her in his arms. He let the time pass slowly without a word, until they heard soft giggles behind them. When they turned around, they saw Owen beneath the glow of the porch light.

"Mom," he said with a mischievous grin, "I didn't get my bedtime cookie."

Owen stepped over to the bench and wriggled himself between them to sit down. Then he swung his legs back and forth, enjoying the closeness they had with each other. "I can't wait to go shooting at Mister Dixon's ranch," he said excitedly. "It'll be fun to learn something new."

Tempest nodded. "You're right, honey." She slipped her arm around his waist to give him a squeeze. Then she cupped his cheek to tilt his head against her shoulder. "It *will* be good. To learn a few things that maybe we haven't done before. Things that are…worth trying."

A tear inched down her face.

"Why are you crying, Mommy?" Owen asked.

He lifted his small hand to brush the dampness from her cheek. She gave him a warm smile, her lips pressed together to keep them from trembling. Tempest was beyond grateful that her son was alive. Grateful for the man who'd found him who was now sitting beside them. Grateful for the beautiful stars above.

"I'm just touched because the stars are really pretty tonight," she said.

"The rambling ones? The ones that have found home?"

Tempest's eyes met Dixon's. He laced his fingers through hers and held her hand tight.

"Yes," she replied. "Those ones."

Her lips curved into another smile, and she gave Owen a peck on the forehead.

"Now let's go inside, sweetie," Tempest said, feeling the heart charm that was in Dixon's hand grow warm against hers. "And get some cookies."

🏵 29 🏵

A few days later marked the final event to close out the fair—the Wranglers Waltz, where the winner of the Cowboy Roundup would be announced. Tempest had taken some much-needed time off to recuperate, and she gave Ivy a break too. Now they both stood beside Owen and gazed at the big spread of lawn that stretched before the fairgrounds bandstand. It seemed like the whole town had shown up to dance on this soft, dusky evening as musicians played country melodies in three-quarter time. Some people, like the Fair Treasurer Faye Simmons, wore square dancing outfits to look extra special beneath the strings of outdoor lights that criss-crossed over the grass. Others had simply put on their best jeans and boots, with colorful rodeo shirts to make the event more festive. As the fiddlers played a sweet rendition of "You Make The Moonlight", the fair announcer stepped up to the microphone on the bandstand and scanned the crowd.

"All right folks," his voice soared over the melody, "we're minutes away from broadcasting the winner of the Cowboy Roundup! It's anybody's guess after all the ballots are counted who'll ride in that golden wagon this evening with Dixon Ramsey. But for those of you who've been placing bets, don't believe any rumors until the winner is officially revealed right here! Our very own Fair Steward Horton Brown and Fair Board President Tripp Conway are busy tallying up the names as I speak."

The announcer gestured at the two men counting up ticket stubs at a card table in a corner of the bandstand. "While you're waiting," he said, "for a special treat we've invited the Historical Society to set up their wares on the other side of this lawn." He tipped his head at the Trinity women behind their booth, and they smiled and gave the crowd a wave. "They'll be handing out their renowned, rose-petal chocolate truffles to each couple who waltzes at least half an hour around the lawn this evening. So get on out there and dance! You know what everybody says about the Historical Society's homemade goodies. Wait, is that *love* I see floating in the air?"

The audience chuckled while Jubilee and Pearl each held up a chocolate truffle and clinked them together like wine glasses. Granny Tinker folded her arms and stared straight at Tempest with a knowing look.

Tempest's breath seized in her throat. She hadn't seen Granny since the night Owen went missing, and she found it impossible to wrest her eyes away.

Truth be told, she owed Granny *everything—*

Because of her, she'd found her son in the pitch black

night, out in an area of the backcountry that she'd never even seen, safe in Dixon's arms.

And for all she knew, Dixon might have been guided by that woman's mysterious forces, too.

Tempest grabbed Owen's hand and took several strides over the grass, as if a magnetic force were pulling her toward the beautiful woman with long gray hair across the lawn. She wanted to thank her from the bottom of her heart.

"Wait, where are you going?" Ivy burst through Tempest's thoughts, tugging on her sleeve. "You can't leave with that handsome young man! I gotta have someone to dance with to get those chocolates." Ivy gave Owen a sly smile. "Who knows, we might even find true love tonight."

Ivy bent down to peer eye level at Owen. "Those girls in 4-H are awfully cute," she remarked, "and I heard half of them have a crush on you. Maybe it's because you like to wear overalls that match your eyes. Denim blue is a shoe-in for inspiring affection."

Owen groaned. Tempest smirked at his reaction to the idea of ranch girls with their hearts on their sleeves. Since Ivy was so eager to snag some homemade chocolate, she couldn't see a reason for Owen not to give dancing a whirl.

"Come on, give it a try," she encouraged her son, knowing that Ivy had stayed late because she wanted to hear who'd won the Cowboy Roundup. "Just for a few rounds, okay?"

Owen rolled his eyes like the notion was silly.

Tempest chewed her lip, aware that it was poor form to bribe your child, but hell—she'd given up being mother of the year a long time ago. "I promise," she whispered in his ear, "if you waltz with Ivy, I'll get you ice cream afterwards. Deal?"

Crossing his arms, Owen paused before giving a response. Even as an eight-year-old, he knew he had his mother over a barrel, and he wasn't about to waste it.

"Two scoops," he whispered back. "With as much whipped cream as I want. And caramel syrup on top?"

"You're on," Tempest replied, admiring his bartering skills. "As long as it's *after* you eat dinner."

Owen's eyes twinkled in victory. He hesitantly put his hand into Ivy's so she could lead him toward the middle of the lawn. They managed to stumble through a few triple-time dance steps as the band continued to play, with Ivy directing their moves to show Owen how to waltz. Although there were several stumbles on the grass, and one unfortunate misstep into a patch of mud, Tempest beamed.

They looked utterly adorable.

"Mind if we join 'em?" Tempest heard a familiar, husky voice behind her. She drew a breath and slowly turned to see the handsome face of Dixon. He had an eager look in his eyes that made her heart flutter a beat.

"Funny seeing you here," she teased, just as delighted to see him. "I thought you might want to save your energy, since you're the star of the show tonight. Who do you think might win?"

Dixon gently grasped Tempest by the hand and swept her onto the lawn, as if his body were telling her the answer. He launched into flowing steps, which she found remarkably easy to follow, though she hadn't engaged in a waltz in over a decade.

"As long as I get to dance on this beautiful evening with

you," Dixon said in a soft tone, "as far as I'm concerned, I've already won."

Tempest blushed—only because she felt the same way. "But aren't *you* the prize tonight, Mister Ramsey?" Her lips turned up at the corners, loving the smooth way he directed her through the box steps and promenades of the country version of the waltz. He threw in a delightful spin every few yards that made her feel like they were floating.

"Depends on what you consider a prize," Dixon replied, his eyes never leaving hers. "I'm always happy to go out with a beautiful woman—and all of the women in the Cowboy Roundup fit that bill. But I was hoping," he cocked a brow, "that no matter what happens, we might keep on dancing like this on starlit evenings for a long time."

The musicians began to play a lovely rendition of "Dare to Dream". Dixon looked over Tempest's face like she was all he could ever hope for, and it made her reel in a sharp breath. He held her closer and leaned beside her ear. "A guy can dream, right?"

Tempest searched his eyes. "So can…a lady," she added, feeling for the first time since her husband had died that life had truly opened up for her again. And perhaps had become something altogether new. As well as—dare she think it—something wonderful? "Any time you want to dance beneath those rambling stars," she whispered back, stealing a glance at the sky, "I'll be ready."

"Pardon me," Dixon ribbed her, clearing his throat. "We can start by you cooking that dinner you promised. Even if it's by a campfire." He leaned beside her ear again. "You always look beautiful beneath a night sky."

Then he whisked a lock of hair from her forehead. His gaze caressed every contour of her face, and his eyes settled on hers as if they'd found what they'd long been looking for.

"Oh, that's right—dinner," Tempest nodded, feeling warmth rush up her spine at the way he took her in. His focus was intense, like there was nowhere else he could imagine being except dancing in a small town in the Rocky Mountains with this woman. "We should set a date—maybe soon on a clear night."

She glanced over at Blossom, who was dancing slowly with a tight grip on Levi's hands at the other side of the lawn. "Speaking of dates," she murmured, surprised to see the two of them together. "Blossom seems awfully forgiving of Levi all of a sudden. They're dancing with each other like he was never drunk. And they appear to be holding on for dear life."

"That's because they *are*," Dixon replied, his voice low and serious.

"What do you mean?" Tempest noticed that Hedda was dancing with Bear as well. She shook her head. "Did I not get the memo? Are women around here the most tolerant on earth? Both those guys were stinking drunk two days ago."

Dixon studied the way their feet moved over the blades of grass. "Well," he mentioned carefully, looking up at Tempest, "Levi didn't actually get drunk that afternoon. Neither did my dad."

Tempest did a double take.

"How can that be—we saw them with our own eyes."

Dixon's jaw worked back and forth, the way it always did when he was trying to formulate the right words. He pulled a long breath and met her gaze.

"The police got an anonymous tip a couple of days ago to inspect Betty's home for signs of Dead Men's Bells. That's folk lingo for foxglove. If consumed, it can create a toxic reaction. They were able to get a search warrant, and they found evidence that Betty was using poison to control people."

Tempest's jaw dropped.

"Control people? What the hell?"

Dixon sighed as though nothing he was about to tell her was going to get any easier.

"Betty could make people seem drunk, since small amounts of foxglove mimic inebriation. Apparently, she could also provoke…death. I mean, after they confirmed that it was her former husband who was in the ravine that night when Owen went missing."

Tempest dug her heels into the grass, bringing their waltz to an abrupt halt.

"Th-They found his *body?*" she stammered.

"Yeah. Those bones we saw…that's what was left of her last husband. I called the police after I got you and Owen home safe that evening and led them to that spot. They have reason to believe he had poison in his system that made him delirious and become lost in the backcountry. The police found his skull in the sagebrush with some hair left on it, and parts of his clothing and wallet nearby. Hair analysis will determine how much foxglove he was given over time."

Tempest felt like she was about to hyperventilate, and she forced her lungs to slow down to try and regulate air.

"I-I don't understand," she sputtered. "What did they find in Betty's house that made them think *she* did this? More flowers? How can that make her a suspect—"

"After they got the anonymous tip, they discovered contaminated food and beer in her fridge," Dixon replied. "Along with her toxic recipe wedged into an old flower book. Foxglove is a spicy ingredient you can hide in, well…salsa…for example."

Tempest plastered her hand over her mouth, her stomach doing flip flops. Then she leaned down to clench her knees and gulped several breaths until the sensation passed. When she straightened up, Dixon gripped her elbow and led her to a nearby bench to sit down.

Dixon took her hand and folded his large fingers over hers, gently stroking her skin with his thumb. "Looks like Betty had a habit of going through husbands to collect life insurance," he informed her. "I guess her crazy goal this time was to make my dad seem pitiful and in need of her charms. Remember when I told you he didn't smell like liquor the last time he was tipsy? That's because he never had any."

"Oh God," Tempest whispered in shock. She scanned the lawn until she found Bear Ramsey with Hedda again. "Was your dad *really* her next mark?"

"Seemed to be her M.O. Nobody knew it in Bandits Hollow, but the police said her nickname in Oklahoma was Black Widow Betty. She'd been sucking men dry and doing away with them for years, but there wasn't enough evidence to catch her before."

Dixon inclined his head toward Blossom, still dancing with Levi on the lawn. "Her daughter cooperated with the search. She was really brave."

"Did Blossom suspect something all this time?" Tempest gasped. "How do you know all this?"

"Since I led the police to the bones, and mentioned the salsa incident with my dad, Officer Iron Feather asked me to go to the station to identify the salsa from her fridge. It was still in the same jar. The police had my dad tested for traces of poisoning, and the results were positive." He lifted his gaze to Blossom again. Although she was dancing with Levi using a rather stiff gait, she tilted her head high like a woman refusing to drown.

"Blossom's in shock, of course," Dixon pointed out. "But she didn't seem entirely surprised. When she mentioned to the police that her mother had helped her lose twenty pounds recently," he let out a slow breath, "the police had her tested, too. I think you already know what the results were."

Blossom and Levi stopped dancing for a moment and swiveled to glance at the Historical Society's booth. While the three women were setting out chocolates, they returned her gaze with oddly stoic expressions, like a storm was brewing.

"Oh my God, is Blossom okay? We need to check on her—"

Tempest lurched forward from the bench to dash toward Blossom. Before she could gain more than a yard, Dixon caught up and slipped his arm around her elbow to hold her back.

"Don't you see what's happening?" he said.

Confused, Tempest followed the aim of his attention. Under the strings of outdoor lights, she spotted Betty, dressed to the nines like always, marching over to the Historical Society booth. She had a stern look on her face with her eyebrows scrunched, as if she were about to demand more than her fair share of chocolates. At that moment, two police officers got out of a squad car that had been parked beyond the lights in the nearby shadows. As soon as they reached the booth, the policemen began to talk to Betty in an official manner. It was no surprise to Tempest when Betty threw up her hands and started arguing with them. But her eyes grew twice their size when one of the officers locked Betty's wrists behind her back in hand cuffs. Betty hung her head, apparently realizing they meant business. Her shoulders slumped a little as they briskly escorted her to their squad car. Tempest swept her gaze around the lawn—with all of the commotion of brisk dancing and loud band music, no one else appeared to notice.

Except Blossom.

"We've gotta talk to her." Tempest's eyes implored Dixon's. "See if there's anything she needs."

Dixon gave her a nod and headed with her toward the other side of the lawn. As they neared Blossom, they slowed their pace and walked cautiously up to her. Tempest gently tapped her on the shoulder.

When Blossom faced her, she had tears running down her cheeks. Yet she appeared oddly calm beside Levi, despite her reddened eyes, like she'd been expecting this to happen. Tempest wrapped an arm around her.

"I can take you to the station, if you want," she said softly. "So you can be with your mom. I'll stay there for as long as you need."

Blossom stole a glance at Levi and shook her head.

"I...I have a ride," she replied.

In spite of her effort to appear strong, Blossom began to wither in Tempest's arm.

"Y-You said once that it's okay to love your mom," she managed to utter with a crack in her voice. "I don't even know how to anymore. What will that mean, visiting her in prison? She'll probably end up in Cañon City."

Tempest lightly brushed the tears from her cheeks with her sleeve. "The most important thing is to be kind to *you* right now, honey. You can trust your heart to do what feels right, when you're ready. Till then, it's up to you to decide what love looks like in this situation. Do you understand?"

Blossom nodded, her body beginning to shake with sobs. She dug her hand into her overalls pocket, her fingers trembling as she held up Tempest's crumpled business card.

"C-Can I still call you some time?" she said. "I mean, to talk?" She kept her eyes focused on the card till she dared to check Tempest's reaction.

"Of course, *any* time," Tempest promised. Without another word, she hugged Blossom, holding on extra tight. She knew there were no comments that could truly console her. There was only the warmth and strength of a true friend. One who'd stand by her, which Tempest fully intended to be.

Blossom pulled back slightly, registering the kindness in Tempest's eyes. She gripped both of Tempest's hands for a moment as a wordless thank you. Then she nodded at Levi and joined him to head toward the parking lot on the other side of the lawn. When they reached Levi's truck and he opened the passenger door, Blossom paused and turned toward Tempest one last time. She lifted her hand in a wave and then slowly dipped inside. Tempest watched as the two of them drove off and veered toward a county road.

"Hey, where's Blossom going?" Ivy asked as she walked up

to Tempest and Dixon with Owen alongside her. "Doesn't she wanna hear who won the Cowboy Roundup? I can't wait!"

"She had, um...some pressing matters to attend to," Tempest replied, biting her molars to steel against tears. Pausing, she took in a slow breath. "It's probably time to get your chocolates, right?" she remarked, hoping to distract Owen and Ivy from the sad turn of events. The last thing Tempest wanted was candy right now, but she knew she'd promised her son. "Let's take a little walk and check out the Trinity's booth."

"Can I have two?" Owen pleaded, though he didn't look any worse for the wear from dancing.

"It's not my call to make," Tempest replied, wrapping her hand around his. "That's up to the ladies in the Historical Society. But you can have mine if you only get one."

"Mine, too," Dixon added, tousling Owen's hair as they made strides toward the booth.

Drawing closer, goosebumps began to skitter over Tempest's skin at the thought of facing Granny Tinker. Her eyes locked on Granny's, but the woman swiftly held up a hand to prevent her from speaking. While Pearl and Jubilee finished setting out enough chocolate truffles on a tray to feed a small army, Granny cleared her throat.

"There's only one thing I gotta say to you," she blurted before Tempest could mention a word. Granny leveled a gaze at her with those strange, gray eyes that always seemed to peer through souls. "Ain't there somethin' you're forgettin'?"

Tempest traded glances with Dixon and Ivy, confused.

Granny dropped her focus to the khaki pants Tempest was

wearing. All of a sudden, the heart charm inside Tempest's pocket began to grow warm.

"Oh my gosh!" Tempest said. She dug the charm out of her khakis and gave it to Ivy. Then she clasped her hands over hers. "I-I can hardly convey how much this has meant to me," she told her. "Please keep it safe—forever. It's *really* special." She shot a brave glance at Granny, holding onto their secret.

"Thanks!" Ivy replied happily. She held the charm up to the hanging lights, watching its facets sparkle with a smile tickling at her lips. Then she slipped it into her jeans.

"Now hurry up and take some chocolates," Granny ordered them, lifting up the tray of truffles. She squinted and plucked out two to hand to Tempest. "Here's a couple of nice ones you can give to Hedda and Bear. With my congratulations, of course."

"Congratulations?" Tempest asked.

Granny cackled—that infamous laugh that could rattle dishes in cupboards and quite possibly unnerve the dead. She handed Tempest a small bag with the Historical Society's logo on it to carry the chocolates.

"You'll see," she nodded.

"Attention everyone," the announcer broke over the microphone as the band stopped playing. "*Now* is the moment you've all been waiting for! Hold on to your hats, because the official winner of the Cowboy Roundup is…"

He waited for the band to do a brisk drum roll accentuated by the clang of a guitar.

"Miss Hedda Grimson!"

Tempest whipped around, only to see Granny Tinker in the booth release another one of her jarring bursts of laughter.

"Ain't done by a long shot," Granny remarked mysteriously with a half-smile, rocking back and forth on her heels.

Jubilee and Pearl elbowed each other with smug looks, as if they'd placed bets on the winner. They both popped chocolates into their mouths, rolling them against their bottom lips like tobacco chew. Tempest began to wonder if there was more in those truffles than chocolate and rose petals, and she made a mental note to test one before giving it to Owen.

Jubilee arched a brow at Granny. "You've got quite the gleam in your eye all of a sudden. What have you been up to *this* time?"

"Aw, she ain't doing nothin'," Pearl butt in. "Everybody knows Evangeline just understands things…ahead of time. It's in her blood."

Granny remained silent while the two women parried, allowing them to think whatever they liked. A bit baffled, Tempest turned to look at the stage, where she saw Hedda ascending the steps of the bandstand. Two teenage 4-H girls squealed and rushed over to set a glittering tiara on her head, then wrapped her body in a pink satin sash.

Hedda grinned at the crowd like she was born for this.

She gave the audience a skilled, pageant-style wave while a golden frontier wagon drawn by palomino horses pulled onto the lawn. A TV film crew raced up the steps of the bandstand to push their cameras into her face. Hedda gave them a winning smile as the 4-H girls threw gold confetti at her that sparkled under the lights.

"What would you like to say to everyone," the announcer asked, "miss former rodeo queen and now winner of the Cowboy Roundup?"

Hedda graciously accepted the microphone from him and paused to gaze at the crowd.

"I'm so honored to be selected by y'all," she stated in a sincere tone. "And I'd like to thank everyone who voted. It will certainly be a thrill for me to ride in the golden wagon this evening. My gratitude also goes out to Dixon for going above and beyond the call of duty to support our fair. But since the contest rules only say I have to go on a date with a Mister Ramsey, I've decided to choose...Bear!"

Gasps erupted across the lawn, followed by a roll of murmurs.

"Damn!" Jubilee expelled a huff from the booth. "Bear Ramsey? I didn't see that coming, but I guess a woman has a right to change her mind."

"Kinda makes sense if you think about it," Pearl noted. "Those two have been eyeing each other throughout the whole fair."

"Ain't no surprise, really," added Granny, nodding at the results. "Hedda's always had a knack for shootin' the bull's-eye, and she never settles for second best. Sorry about your luck, Dixon—I didn't mean to imply you ain't worthy."

Dixon began to chuckle. "Fine by me." He sounded rather relieved by the change of fortune. "Hedda deserves the very best this town has to offer—and if that's my dad in her estimation, then so be it."

"Oh my gosh," Ivy muttered, pressing her hands to her chest. "This budding romance was under my nose all along, and I didn't see it!" She shot a glance at Tempest. "Hedda's even wearing *pink!* I can't wait to tell my fans how well that color works, even for seniors. Isn't this spectacular?"

"It's pretty darn awesome," Tempest agreed as Hedda waved once more for the crowd.

The audience launched into wild applause for Hedda while she stepped down from the bandstand to meet Bear Ramsey beside the golden wagon. The two of them pleased the crowd with a light kiss and smiled like newly-crowned royalty. But when they opened the wagon door, a bounding blockade of black fur crossed their path and jumped inside before they could take another step. Surprised, they soon saw Bonner poke out his head and release a loud "boof". Hedda and Bear burst into laughter. Then they joined Bonner in the wagon while the audience roared their approval and threw their hats in the air.

Ivy sighed at the sight as if all of her fairy tale dreams had been validated. Owen, on the other hand stomped his foot to get his mother's attention.

"Mom," he said, "can we go now? I'm starving. You haven't let me have a single chocolate yet, and you *promised* me ice cream, remember?"

Tempest hoisted him in her arms. She didn't feel particularly hungry at that moment, but her little boy didn't have a stomach big enough to wait.

"Okay, honey. We'll go get some dinner now. *Then* you can have ice cream," she replied sternly.

Tempest slid a glance at Dixon. "I can't believe after all your hard work," she said, still a bit dumbstruck, "it turns out you aren't getting the date tonight."

"Well, my carriage might not be golden," Dixon replied with one of his disarming smiles. "In fact, it's a rusty old green. But if you and Owen are up for it, I'd love to give you both a ride to the Golden Wagon Restaurant for dinner. You'd make this ol' cowboy feel pretty damn lucky."

"Really? In your big truck?" Owen bounced excitedly in his mother's arms. "Let's go, Mom!"

"He's right, we'd better go soon," Dixon added, clearly on Owen's side.

"Why's that?" Tempest asked.

"Because," Dixon shuffled his boots in the grass with a sly grin, "if we wait too long, my truck might turn into a pumpkin. God knows how many mice might start scurrying around."

Tempest laughed. "Okay," she said, turning to Ivy. "Will you consider going too, and let me buy you dinner tonight? After all you've done this week, it's the least I can do."

"Um, to be honest," Ivy hedged, twisting her palms together as her lips slid into a smirk. She inclined her gaze to a cowboy with red hair who was leaning against the bandstand. He smiled shyly and gave her a wave. "Somebody already beat you to it."

"Oh my," Tempest said, intrigued. "Does this fine fellow have a name?"

Ivy's cheeks swelled with pink. "As a matter of fact, he does—it's Rusty."

"Of course your date tonight has the name of a color!" Tempest giggled. "It must be fate." She leveled a more serious gaze at Ivy. "*Please* promise me you won't over-analyze what the color of his name means, or the red shade of his hair. All right? Now you go and have a great time. I'll buy you that dinner another evening."

Ivy grinned and turned to trot across the lawn toward Rusty.

Tempest heard chuckles behind her. She looked over her shoulder just in time to catch the three women of the Trinity high-fiving each other. Pearl snatched a wild rose that had been sitting on the booth and hid it behind her back, as if it might betray some kind of culpability. She and the other women pressed their lips together for as long as they could muster to try and appear more prim and upstanding.

But then their laughter burst forth and rang across the lawn.

After Dixon sat down on the other side of Tempest and Owen in a red booth at the Golden Wagon Restaurant, they decided to keep things simple and choose the night's special: steaks and bacon-cheese mashed potatoes with fresh green beans. The entree was renowned for being mouthwatering in the county, yet Dixon grew oddly quiet after they placed their orders. As soon as the waitress left, he shot a glance outside the window at Bonner, who was moping for treats near the restaurant door, since Hedda and Bear had been given their own private dining room for their date where dogs—and bears—were definitely not allowed. Dixon smiled a little at the moody and tenacious bear, then pulled a crumpled envelope from his jacket pocket and set it on the table.

"I gotta be honest." He drew a hesitant breath and flicked his gaze from Tempest to Owen. "There's actually another reason I wanted to see you two this evening. Guess you could say I have an ulterior motive, like Bonner, but it's for more than getting a meal." He pushed the envelope toward Owen. "Would you mind opening that up and giving it a read?"

Owen glanced at his mother. He cautiously grasped the envelope and pulled out a document from inside, then spread it on the table with his small palms. It looked like a typical cattle registration certificate, the kind he had to show the Fair

Steward before he entered Dumpling in the Angus yearling class. Owen squinted at the words.

"American Milking Devon," he read aloud, carefully enunciating the breed title in an effort to impress Dixon. He lowered his gaze to the next line. "Name: Sweet Drop Dumpling. Date of Birth: July 15—"

"Hey," he glanced up, "that's the same month Dumpling was born!"

"You're right about that," Dixon said. "I ran across the rancher you got Dumpling from yesterday at the feed store. When I mentioned you'd shown your yearling at the fair, he told me he'd just discovered that he'd accidentally gotten the registration papers mixed up in the glove compartment of his truck when he sold Dumpling." Dixon paused and leaned his elbows on the table. "He gave me the right certificate and asked me to pass it on to you. Dumpling's *not* an Angus, Owen. He's a Devon."

Owen's face sank. "He's not a *real* Angus?" he whimpered, as if that somehow made his beloved yearling defective.

"No. That's why his legs are a little long and his chest is not as deep. It's also why his horns were cut off at three months old," Dixon pointed out. "The rancher said he'd gotten Dumpling at an estate auction of some eccentric farmer who had rare livestock, and he didn't even know what a Devon was. Owen," Dixon said, grasping his little hands, "I looked it up. Devons are early American heritage cattle that are extremely valuable. People will pay a *lot* of money to use Dumpling as a sire."

Owen's breath stalled, his eyes stretching wide. "Does that

mean we get to keep him, Mommy?" He swiveled to his mother.

"Of course, honey," she said, beaming at Dixon. "Even if he wasn't worth a lot, because he's your *friend*." She examined the certificate on the table. "We'll have to mail the wrong registration we got back to that rancher. But can I make a request, sweetie?"

Owen nodded.

"Will you let me hold this for you in a safe place when we get home? So it doesn't get lost?"

Owen slipped the document back into the envelope and handed it to his mother. She tucked into her purse for safekeeping.

Then Dixon took that moment to pull something else from his pocket. It was a small, blue velvet box that looked rather worn at the edges, like it was quite old. To Tempest's surprise, Dixon stared at his lap and shifted in his seat. She'd never seen him so nervous before.

"I, um, bought this from a lady I happen to know," he explained, his eyes glinting with anticipation. He set the box on the table and slid it toward Tempest. "Go ahead—open it. It's to congratulate you on surviving the Cowboy Roundup." Dixon's mouth creased into a half-smile. "Guess neither of us won this time around. But hey, we lived to tell the tale."

Tempest studied the box, her heart quickening. She cautiously lifted the lid. Inside was a beautiful owl pendant on a thin strand of leather. The owl appeared to be intricately carved from some kind of antler or bone, with delicate etchings all over to show its feathers. She gently wedged the pendant out of the box and studied its ivory-colored contours in her palm.

"Oh my," she said, faltering for words.

"The lady I got it from promised it would mean something to you," Dixon added proudly.

Shivers skipped down Tempest's spine.

"What lady—who did you get this from?"

Dixon sent a glance across the room to Granny Tinker, who was sitting with Pearl and Jubilee in another booth. The three women looked at him with glints in their eyes. Then they held up their whiskey glasses and tapped them together for a toast.

"Oh, just a nice travelling sort of gal who likes to sell things from her wagon," Dixon replied. "Do you like it? She said it was carved over a hundred years ago. By a dear friend," he shrugged at the anachronism, "whatever that means."

Tempest examined the sparkling, faceted eyes on the owl that looked like they might be Colorado topaz, the kind she and Owen had seen in the local mining museum. She smiled a little, recalling what Ivy had told her once when she'd asked what no color at all means, like glass or transparent gems. Naturally, Ivy had said those were the best indications of all— they meant her path to true love was clear.

"It's-it's beautiful," Tempest voiced softly, touched by Dixon's kind gesture.

"Mommy, when are you gonna marry him?" Owen cut in, wriggling impatiently in his seat.

Tempest blushed at the eagerness in his eyes. "Sorry," she remarked shyly to Dixon. "He can be a bit blunt sometimes. Gee, wonder where he got *that* from?"

"You didn't answer," Owen pressed, nudging her with his shoulder.

"Some things don't have easy answers, sweetie," she explained, her cheeks getting redder by the second.

"Yeah they do." Dixon reached out and gently grasped her hand. "If you let 'em. Life doesn't always have to be complicated. Sometimes the best things are…simple."

The way he looked into her eyes, like they *belonged* together, sent trickles of warmth and elation coursing through her veins. The feeling was so fresh and new, yet embracing, that she found herself gripping Dixon's hand tighter to keep it from slipping away.

"Does that mean *soon?*" Owen piped up. He huffed and met his mother's eyes with a penetrating look. "I wanna keep going to Dixon's ranch."

"You know, I'm kinda partial to the word *soon*," Dixon echoed. His eyes glinted at Owen's in camaraderie. "It has a nice ring, don't you think?"

All at once, a lightning bolt struck outside. The flash illuminated a great horned owl that was perched on the limb of a tree across the street from the restaurant. Rather than be startled, Tempest felt a peculiar bloom of softness arise in her chest. Gazing out the window, she watched as the owl turned its head and lifted its wings to take to the air. It soared toward the next lightning bolt that struck in the distance. A full moon peeked just above the treeline on the horizon, casting shades of silver over the bird's wings.

"Guess that's why they call it the Thunder Moon," Dixon said at the flash of the next lightning bolt, followed by a deep rumble. His lips turned up at the corners. "But Owen's right—

you never did answer the question." His eyes glinted with as much hope as her son's. "What's your take on the word...soon?"

Dixon and Owen peered at her expectantly.

Tempest smiled, feeling a distinct warmth begin to center on her heart, pooling more with each heartbeat. In that moment, she felt full, like her whole world was quite possibly sitting in that booth.

Everything she wanted.

Everything she...loved.

Another lightning bolt flashed.

"It's funny how quick lightning is...and how powerful," she said. She stroked the owl pendant in her palm and lifted it up to peek at the back. She was surprised to see a faded inscription etched there that looked like it was once filled with ink.

> Sooner than later,
> Love comes home to rest,
> When the heart opens as wide
> As an owl's wings.
>
> — *V.H.*

Tempest couldn't help smiling, her body tingling all over.

"Something tells me," she nodded at Owen, "that we'll be spending a lot of time at Dixon's ranch."

"Starting soon?" Owen said.

Tempest glanced at Dixon, feeling like she could fall into the welcoming gaze of his midnight-blue eyes. She leaned forward and gave him a soft kiss, enjoying the sound of Owen's inevitable giggles.

"Yes, honey," she replied to Owen as she sat back down. In that moment, she wanted to memorize the dear looks on both their faces for all time. She reached across the booth and gathered Dixon's hand in hers, then Owen's, holding them firm and bringing them up to her heart.

"Starting…real soon," she said.

Tears collected at the corners of Tempest's eyes. She gave them both a nod.

"It's that simple," she smiled.

EPILOGUE: THE THUNDER MOON

As the full moon shone through the pine boughs, Granny Tinker walked arm in arm through the forest with Jubilee and Pearl back toward her wagon. The three women were a bit tipsy from their shots of whiskey at the restaurant, but they knew this trail like the backs of their hands.

"I do believe you've outdone yourself this time with love matches, Evangeline," Jubilee mused when they spied Granny's wagon in a nearby clearing. "Let's see, Tempest and Dixon, Hedda and Bear, and then…what's that girl's name? The one who's always wearing pink?"

"Ivy," Pearl answered. "Ivy and Rusty have definitely become an item—I saw them holding hands and walking into the restaurant tonight just before we got our meals. Three couples brought together in one month? That might be a land record for you, Evangeline."

"Aw, I can't take all the credit," Granny replied, her face and hair illuminated with a silver sheen as they reached the clearing. She peeked up at the sky. "Blame it on the Thunder Moon," she said, her lips inching into a smile.

"Well, as far as I'm concerned, it's time to celebrate some more," Jubilee insisted, squeezing Granny's elbow. "I have some pie leftover at my house. And I never told you, but I still have some of that thimbleberry wine we made last year. It should be really good by now."

Pearl gasped. "Why, Jubilee!" She peered through the pine boughs at the Lazy C Ranch in the distance. "Are you admitting that you *hid* bottles of our wine for an entire year?"

"Had to!" Jubilee chuckled. "Or else you two would never have let it age! Believe me, it's heavenly now. My cellar does wonders."

"Sounds like you've been nipping quite a bit," Granny noted with a cocked brow.

"Only a little," Jubilee remarked swiftly. "But don't worry, I saved most of it. You of all people oughta know that the best things in life are worth waiting for."

In that moment, the three women heard a horse's whinny travel across the clearing, resounding through the pines. Granny Tinker halted in her tracks, forcing Jubilee and Pearl to stop as well.

"Did you hear that?" Granny said. "A horse?"

"For Heaven's sake, we're surrounded by ranches," Jubilee replied, a bit impatient.

"No, I mean...*that* horse," Granny said.

Pearl and Jubilee gazed at her curiously. Then they squinted at Granny's wagon up ahead in the clearing and shrugged, unsure what she meant.

"*His* horse," Granny emphasized.

Pearl's breath hitched. She looked up at the full moon and across the sky for a moment, then over at Jubilee. "Could it be?" she said in a hopeful tone, as if perhaps the right stars had aligned. "Jubilee," she jiggled her friend's arm, "let's head on over to your house and check out some of that wine and pie." She smiled. "You know, give our Evangeline some space."

Pearl hugged Granny around the waist and planted a kiss on her cheek. "True love knows how to outwait time," she whispered. She gave Jubilee a tug on the elbow. "Come on, ol' friend. Let's go inspect your cellar."

Granny watched the two women walk beyond the clearing into the pines, disappearing past the dark boughs in the direction of Jubilee's ranch.

Then she heard a whinny again.

"Spook?" she muttered, inching closer to her wagon.

A dappled gray mare's head peered from behind her wagon. The horse nodded like it recognized her.

"I-Is that you?" Granny's mouth dropped a little. She took a couple of steps forward, narrowing her eyes at the murky darkness beyond the horse.

"Virgil?" she whispered, her voice strained with hope. "Are you...here?"

A tall, rugged man in a long duster emerged from the black velvet night. Under the bright moonlight, his eyes were the same piercing, turquoise blue she'd always remembered. She scanned his chiseled features, toughened by years of frontier living and framed by wayward silver hair. He was the handsomest highwayman she'd ever seen, then or now. There weren't many things on this earth that could make

Evangeline's heart race, but the sight of Virgil Hollow was one of them.

Virgil walked up and grabbed her face for a fierce kiss. He wrapped his large arms around her and held her close, swaying as if to make sure she was real. Then he gave her another kiss, engulfing her with his whole body—the kind of kiss that defied all time.

"How can you be here?" she said when they broke free. Still in shock, her heart pounded a mile a minute.

"It's the Thunder Moon." Virgil gave her his crooked, bandit smile—the one she could never forget. The one that remained in her blood and bones and heart for as long as she would take breath. "Iron Feather's grateful to you," he said. "You gave the boy a home. An evermore, mountain home. Because his mother's heart now has a place to rest."

He clutched her face again and peered into her gold-gray eyes, watching the way they flashed under the moonlight.

"He prayed for you, you know. To come help him," he said.

"Who did? The boy, or Iron Feather?" she replied.

Virgil smiled again—he was so handsome it nearly made her heart stop.

"Both," he said. "Some ol' owls can't refuse a little boy's prayer."

Her eyes glistened in the moonlight. Virgil knew his beautiful Evangeline wasn't the crying sort, but even she couldn't resist the charms of a child.

"Will it be like this now?" she asked, searching his face. "Will you be coming in July? Not just the Cold Moon in December, but the Thunder Moon, too?"

An owl's call echoed through the pines like a formidable sentry who'd been watching them all along.

Virgil scanned her features again, licked with platinum hues as if she were so beautiful that even the moon was jealous of him and trying to claim her by painting her silver.

"All I know is that the more you stitch hearts together," Virgil nodded, "the more ours are bound beyond time, too." He handed her a wild rose from his pocket. "Dance with me?"

"But there's no music—"

Virgil patted her chest. "Yes there is."

He slipped his arm around her waist and grasped her hand. Then he pressed his chest against hers, unable to steal his gaze from her face under the moonlight. His boots began to shift in a three-beat motion.

They swayed as one, and a light wind picked up, its tones coursing up and down through the pines.

And damned if Evangeline Tinker didn't start to hear music.

A light melody soared over their heads on the soft breeze, as if the wildflowers and ponderosas had lifted their bountiful boughs in song.

ALSO BY DIANE J. REED

THE IRON FEATHER BROTHERS SERIES...

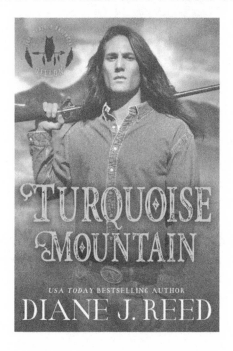

He's a fierce protector of his land and sacred heritage—
and only a strong woman can capture his wild heart.

Available at your favorite retailer, and at dianejreed.com

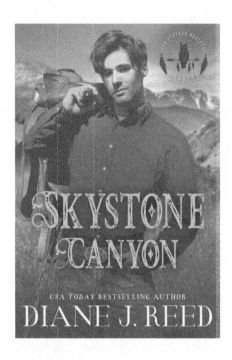

He's the toughest cowboy on patrol fighting darkness—
until a rare woman reminds him of the light in his
heart...

Available at your favorite retailer, and at dianejreed.com

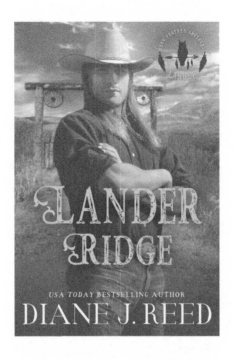

For the cowboy who wins at everything, losing his heart to
the only woman who can reach his soul is the greatest risk
of all...

Available at at your favorite retailer, and at
dianejreed.com

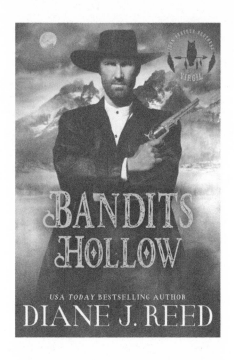

On a clear winter night, the Cold Moon shines a light that illuminates the past...

Available at your favorite retailer, and at dianejreed.com

ABOUT THE AUTHOR

USA TODAY bestselling author Diane J. Reed writes happily ever afters with a touch of magic that make you believe in the power of love. Her stories feed the soul with outlaws, mavericks, and dreamers who have big hearts under big skies and dare to risk all for those they cherish. Because love is more than a feeling—it's the magic that changes everything.

To get the latest on new releases, sign up for Diane J. Reed's newsletter at dianejreed.com.

Made in the USA
Las Vegas, NV
15 April 2022